I wrapped my arms around her and held her, rocking back and forth.

"Make them stop, Markie," she pleaded. "The wolves are howling again. Please make them stop."

There was the business about the wolves again. I didn't have the faintest idea what it meant.

"Blood!" she wailed in a voice filled with horror. "It's all over me! I'm covered with blood!"

She began to tremble violently. "Cold!" she said. "The water's so terribly cold!"

Then she suddenly started whispering, her lips very close to my ear—and she wasn't whispering in any language I could understand. . . .

By David Eddings
Published by Del Rey Books

REGINA'S SONG

DAVID & LEIGH
EDDINGS

BALLANTINE BOOKS • NEW YORK

Published by The Ballantine Publishing Group
Copyright © 2002 by David Eddings and Leigh Eddings

www.ballantinebooks.com

ISBN 0-345-44899-5

Manufactured in the United States of America

First Hardcover Edition: July 2002
First Mass Market Edition: January 2003

OPM 10 9 8 7 6 5 4 3 2 1

For Angela and Pat—
for providing theological and political advice
before they went back to Ireland.

PRELUDE

Andante

Les Greenleaf and my dad, Ben Austin, had served in the same outfit during the Vietnam War, and twenty-five years later they could spend whole afternoons swapping war stories. They both grew up in Everett, a town thirty miles north of Seattle. And they both worked at the same place, since my dad was a sawyer at Greenleaf Sash and Door, Inc.

Aside from that, they couldn't have been much more opposite. Les Greenleaf was a Catholic, a Republican, and a member of the National Association of Manufacturers. My dad was a Methodist, a Democrat, and a member of the AFL-CIO. Les Greenleaf had investments, and Ben Austin lived from paycheck to paycheck. They were on opposite sides of just about any fence you could think of.

"Buddyship," though, tends to jump over all kinds of fences. I guess that when people are shooting at you, you get attached to the guy who's covering your butt.

Back during the late sixties, staying out of the army and the war in 'Nam had been every young man's major goal in life. Rich kids could get a student deferment if they were smart enough to get into college, but working-class kids had to take their chances.

Les and my dad both graduated from high school in 1967. My dad promptly married pretty Pauline Baker, his high-school sweetheart and went to work at Greenleaf Sash and Door.

Les Greenleaf enrolled in the University of Washington, joined a fraternity, and majored in parties. He flunked out at the end of his sophomore year.

My dad had evidently had a little spat with mom, and just to show her how independent he was, he enlisted in the army—something he might not have done if he'd been completely sober. He *was*, however, sober enough to sign on for only *two* years rather than the customary six.

As it turned out, Les Greenleaf was inducted on the same day, so they started out together. My mom had been pregnant—with me—during her little argument with dad, which might have explained why she'd been so grouchy.

Anyway, Ben and Les went off to war, and mom stayed home and sulked.

I was about a year and a half old when they got out of the army, and I was among the guests at the wedding of Mr. Lester Greenleaf and Miss Inga Wurzberger. I was the one who slept through the whole ceremony. Inga was obviously of German extraction—Bavarian, I think—and she'd been a sorority girl at U.W. while Les was concentrating on cutting classes. The wedding had taken place in a Catholic church, and I guess my dad had been a little uncomfortable about that—but buddyship prevailed.

Inga and my mom got along well together, and starting back when I was still a toddler, we often visited the Greenleafs in their fancy home in a posh district of Everett. Since I was absolutely adorable in those days, I was always the center of attention during those visits, and I thought that was sort of nice.

My time in the limelight came to an abrupt halt in 1977 when Inga blossomed and bore fruit—a pair of twin girls, Regina and Renata, who definitely outclassed me on the adorability front. As I remember, I was fairly sullen about the whole thing.

Regina and Renata were identical twins—so identical that not even Inga could tell them apart—and when they first started talking, it wasn't English they were speaking. I'm told it's not uncommon for twins to have a private language, but "twin-speak" is supposed to fade out before the pair get into kindergarten. Regina and Renata kept their private dialect fully operational all the way into high school.

There was a whacko social theory at that time to the effect that twins would grow up psychotic if they were dressed alike. Inga blithely ignored it and followed the ancient custom of putting the girls in identical dresses every morning, the sole difference being a red hair ribbon for Regina and a blue one for Renata. She carefully checked their little gold name bracelets every morning to be certain she wasn't getting them mixed up. I think it was those hair ribbons that set the girls off on what the Greenleafs called the twin-game. Regina and Renata swapped ribbons three or four times a day, and as soon as they learned how to undo the clasps on their name bracelets, all hope of certainty went out the window.

Those two had all sorts of fun with that twin-game, but now when I think back, maybe they were trying to tell us something. The pretty little blond girls had no real sense of individual identity. I don't think either one ever used the word "I." It was always "we" with Regina and Renata. They'd even answer to either name.

That bugged their parents, but it didn't particularly bother me. *My* solution to the "identification crisis" was to simply address them indiscriminately as Twinkie and to refer to them collectively as the Twinkie Twins. That made the girls a little grumpy right at first, but after a while it seemed to fit into their conception of themselves, and they stopped using their given names and began to address each other as either Twinkie or Twink—even when they were using their private language.

In a peculiar way, that got me included in their private group. Our families were close to begin with, and because I was seven years older than they were, the chubby, golden-haired twins looked upon me as a big brother. I had to tie their shoes, wipe their noses, and put the wheels back on their tricycles when they came off. Every time they broke something they'd assure each other that "Markie can fix it." Every now and then, one of them would slip and say something to me in twin-speak, and they always seemed a little disappointed and even sad when I didn't understand what they were saying.

As their official surrogate brother, I spent a lot of my childhood and early adolescence in the company of the Twinkie Twins, and I learned to ignore their cutesy-poo habit of whispering to each other, casting sly looks at me, and giggling. By the time I moved up into high school—an event most adolescents view as something akin to a religious experience—I was more or less immune to their antics.

In May of my sophomore year, I turned sixteen and got my driver's license. My dad firmly advised me that the family car was *not* available, but he promised to check at the union hall for job opportunities for young fellows in need of a summer job. I wasn't too hopeful, but he came home with an evil sort of grin on his face. "You've got a job at a sawmill, Mark," he told me.

"No kidding?" I was a little startled.

"Nope. You go to work on the Monday after school lets out."

"What am I going to be doing?"

"Pulling chain."

"What's 'pulling chain'?"

"You don't really want to know."

I found out why I wouldn't after I'd joined the union and reported to work. I also found out why there were *always* job openings in sawmills when the job involves the green chain. Sawmills convert logs from the woods into planks. After a green hemlock log has spent six or eight weeks in the millpond soaking up salt water, it gets *very* heavy, and it's so waterlogged that it sends out a spray when it goes through the saw. The planks come slithering out of the mill on a wide bed of rollers called the green chain. They're rough, covered with splinters, and almost as heavy as iron. "Pulling chain" involves hauling those rough-sawed planks off the rollers and stacking them in piles. It's a moderately un-fun job. More-modern sawmills have machines that do the sorting, pulling, and stacking, but the sawmill where I worked that summer hadn't changed very much since the 1920s, so we did things the old-fashioned way. I didn't like the job very much, but I really, *really* wanted my own car, so I stuck it out.

I'd been an indifferent student at best up until then, but after the summer of '86, my attitude changed. There might just be a doctoral dissertation in psychology there—*The Motivational Impact of the Green Chain* maybe. I became a much more serious student after that summer, let me tell you.

Pulling chain *did* earn me enough money to buy my own car, of course, and that's very important to red-blooded sixteen-year-olds, since it's widely known in that group that "You ain't nothin' if you ain't got wheels." The Twinkie Twins weren't very impressed by my not-very-shiny black '74 Dodge, but I didn't buy it to impress *them*. They were only third graders and by definition unworthy of my attention. They were blond, still chubby with the remnants of baby fat, and they were at the tomboy stage of development.

Time rushed on in the endless noon of my adolescence, and it seemed that before I'd turned around twice, graduation day was staring me in the face. The gloomy prospect of pulling chain loomed in front of me, but good old Les Greenleaf stepped in at that point. I'm sure there was a certain amount of collusion involved when right after my high-school graduation an opening "just happened" to show up at the door factory, and my dad presented me with my reactivated union card. The Monday after graduation I went to work at Greenleaf Sash and Door. I was now a worker. I even went to union meetings.

I think the highlight of my first year at the door factory

came on the day when all the kids in Everett had to go back to school, but I didn't. My delight lasted for almost a whole week. Then it gradually dawned on me that I actually missed going to school. That green-chain scare in the summer of my sophomore year had turned me into a semiserious student during my last two years at school, and now I didn't know what to do with myself. The door factory only filled forty hours a week, and my dad had our television set permanently locked on the sports channels. I've always been fairly certain that the world won't come to an end if the Seattle Seahawks don't make it into the Super Bowl. I took to reading to fill up the empty hours, and by the summer of 1990, I'd plowed my way through a sizable chunk of the Everett Public Library.

Just for kicks, I took an evening course at the local community college in the autumn quarter of that year, and I aced it. I was a little surprised at how easy it'd been.

I took another course during the winter quarter, and that one was even easier.

I latched on to a steady girlfriend at the community college that winter, and we both skipped the spring quarter. We broke up that summer, though, and I started taking courses as a sort of hobby. I didn't really have any kind of academic goal; you might just say I was majoring in everything.

Wouldn't Everything 101 be an interesting course title?

That went on for a couple years, and by then I'd racked up a fairly impressive number of credit hours. My dad didn't say anything about my snooping around the edges of the world of learning, but he *was* keeping track of my progress.

There was another strong odor of collusion about what happened in late November of 1992. We'd been invited to the Greenleafs' for Thanksgiving dinner, and after we'd all eaten too much, my dad and the boss got involved in a probably well-rehearsed discussion of an ongoing problem at the door factory. There were only four saws, and orders were starting to back up because each saw could only cut so much door stock in eight hours. This meant that the boss had to pay a lot of overtime, which was great for the sawyers right at first, but after it got to be a habit, there was a lot of grumbling about ten- or twelve-hour days. The solution was fairly simple. It's called swing shift. One sawyer would have to work from four in the afternoon until half past midnight. There'd now be five sawyers instead of four, and the boss wouldn't have to buy a new saw or pay overtime.

Guess who got elected for swing shift. And guess who'd now have all kinds of free time during the normal daytime hours at Everett Community College. And guess who was coerced into taking a full course load. And guess who was the only one in the room who didn't know this was coming.

You guessed 'er, Chester.

I think the Twinkie Twins got more entertainment out of this elaborate scam than anybody else did. They were high-school freshmen now, but they'd reverted to whispering in twin-speak, giving me those sickeningly cute smirks, and giggling.

I carried a full course load in both the winter and spring quarters in 1993, and that satisfied the requirements for graduation. It'd taken me four years to reach the point that a full-time student achieves in two, but I was now an Associate in Arts and Sciences—with honors, no less. And I had a major in English, but with a lot of those "everything" courses that didn't apply.

I went through the cap and gown ceremony with the Austins and Greenleafs in the audience, and after the ceremony we all went back to Greenleaf Manor for another of those "let's steer Mark in the right direction" sessions at which I was usually outnumbered six to one.

Inga Greenleaf led the assault. "What in the world were you thinking of, Mark?" she demanded, waving a copy of my transcript at me. "Your grades are very good, but half the courses you took weren't even remotely connected to your major."

"I didn't *have* a major when I started, Inga," I explained. "I was just browsing. It was only after a year or so that I finally settled on English."

"There are some definite holes in this," she told me, still brandishing my transcript. "I've checked with the University of Washington, and you'll have to take a couple of courses this summer to fill in the gaps. Les has contacts with some local banks, and your grades are good enough to qualify you for a student loan."

I threw a quick look at my dad. We'd already discussed *that* at some length. He shook his head slightly.

"I'm sorry, Inga," I said flatly. "Let's just forget that student loan business. Sooner or later, I'm going to have a mortgage on a house biting chunks out of my paychecks, and probably car payments as well—that ol' Dodge can't run forever. I'm not going to add a student loan on top of that. I *won't* hand three-quarters of my paycheck to the Last National Bank to pay interest. I'll look for a part-time job, but no jobbee, no schoolie, and that's final."

"Oh, goodie!" one of the twins said, clapping her hands together. "We get to keep him!"

"Shush, Twink," her mother snapped. I don't think she even realized that my Twinkie invention had crept into her vocabulary.

The boss was squinting at the far wall. "When you get right down to it, Mark, you've already *got* a part-time job."

"It's *full*-time, isn't it?" I replied.

"Of *course* it is," he replied sardonically. "A guy who works by the hour paces himself to make the job fit the time. If you bear down, I'll bet you could finish up in four or five hours a night, and if it starts to pile up, you could clear away the leftovers on Saturday."

"And if you're really serious about getting an education, you can live at home and commute to the university," my mom added. "Your dad and I can't send you to Harvard, but we *can* give you a place to live and regular meals. That way, you won't have to rent an apartment or buy groceries."

"Our big brother's going to get away from us after all," one of the twins lamented in mock sorrow.

"Nothing lasts forever, Twink," I told her.

"Who's going to tie our little shoes?" the other twin said.

"Or glove our little hands?" the first girl added.

"You'll both survive," I told them. "Be brave and strong and true, and you'll get by."

They stuck their tongues out at me in perfect unison.

"This *is* going to crowd you, Mark," Les warned me. "You won't have very much free time. Don't make the same mistake *I* made when I went there. I managed to party my way onto the flunk-out list in just two years."

"I'm not big on parties, boss," I assured him. "Listening to a bunch of half-drunk guys ranting about who's going to make it to the Rose Bowl doesn't thrill me. We can give the university a try, I guess, and if it doesn't work out—ah, well."

I filled in the gaps on my transcript that summer, and on a bright September morning, I drove down to the University of Washington to register. After I'd plodded through all the bureaucratic nonsense, I wandered the beaten paths to knowledge for a while—*long* beaten paths, I might add, since the campus measures about a mile in every direction. I finally found Padelford Hall, home of the English Department. After I'd located my classrooms, I drove back to Everett to get to work.

I took a stab at the "full-bore" business the boss had mentioned, and I found that he was right. I cleared everything away in just under five hours. That made me feel better.

Classes began the following Monday, and my first class, American Literature, started at eight-thirty. There was a kind of stricken silence in the classroom when the instructor entered. "It's Conrad!" I heard a strangled whisper just behind me.

"Good morning, ladies and gentlemen," the white-haired professor said crisply. "Your regularly scheduled instructor has recently undergone coronary bypass surgery, so I'll be filling in for him this quarter. For those of you who don't recognize me, I'm Dr. Ralph Conrad." He looked round the classroom. "We will now pause to give the more timid time to beat an orderly retreat."

Now, *that's* an unusual way to start a class. I thought he was just kidding around, so I laughed.

"Was it something I said?" he asked me with one raised eyebrow.

"You startled me a bit, sir," I replied. "Sorry."

"Perfectly all right, young man," he said benignly. "Laughter's good for the soul. Enjoy it while you can."

I glanced around and saw that fully half the students were grabbing up their books and darting for the door.

Professor Conrad looked at those of us who'd remained. "Brave souls," he murmured. Then he looked directly at me. "Still with us, young man?" he asked mildly.

His superior attitude was starting to irritate me. "I'm here to learn, Dr. Conrad," I told him. "I didn't come here to party or chase girls. You throw, and I'll catch, and I'll still be here when the dust settles."

What a dumb thing *that* was to say! I soon discovered just how tough he really was. He crowded me, I'll admit that, but I stuck it out. He was obviously an old-timer who believed in the aristocracy of talent. He despised the term "postmodern," and he viewed computers as instruments of the devil.

He had his mellower moments, though—fond reminiscences about "the good old days" when the English Department resided in the hallowed, though rickety, Parrington Hall and he was taking graduate courses from legendary professors such as Ebey, Sophus Winther, and E. E. Bostetter.

I maintained my "you throw it and I'll catch it" pose, and that seemed to earn me a certain grudging respect from the terror of the department. I wouldn't go so far as to say that I aced the course, but I did manage to squeeze an A out of Dr. Conrad.

I was a bit startled at the beginning of winter quarter when I discovered that I'd been assigned to a new faculty advisor—at his request.

Guess who *that* was.

"You've managed to arouse my curiosity, Mr. Austin," Dr. Conrad explained, after I rather bluntly asked him why he'd taken the trouble. "Students who work their way through college tend to take career-oriented classes. What possessed you to major in English?"

I shrugged. "I like to read, and if I can get paid for it, so much the better."

"You plan to teach, then?"

"Probably so—unless I decide to write the Great American Novel."

"I've read your papers, Mr. Austin," he said dryly. "You've got a long way to go if that's your goal."

"It beats the hell out of pulling chain, Dr. Conrad."

"Pulling chain?"

I explained it, and he seemed just a bit awed. "Are you saying that people still *do* that sort of thing?"

"It's called 'working for a living.' I came here because I don't wanna do that no more."

He winced at my double negative.

"Just kidding, boss," I told him. And I don't think anybody'd ever called him "boss" before, because he didn't seem to know how to handle it.

By the end of winter quarter that year I'd pretty well settled into the routine of being a working student. There were times when I ran a little short on sleep, but I could usually catch up on weekends.

I finished up the spring quarter of '94 and spent the summer working at the door factory to build up a backlog of cash. Things had been a little tight a few times that year.

The Twinkie Twins were high-school juniors now, and they'd definitely blossomed. Their hair had grown blonder, it seemed—chemically modified, no doubt—and their eyes were an intense blue. They'd also developed some other attributes that attracted *lots* of attention from their male classmates.

Looking back, I'm sometimes puzzled by my lack of "those kinds of thoughts" about the twins. They *were* moderately gorgeous, after all—tall, blond, well built, and with strangely compelling eyes. It was probably their plurality that put me off. In my mind they were never individuals. I thought of them as "they," but never "she."

From what I heard, though, the young fellows at their high school didn't have that problem, and the twins were very popular. The only complaint seemed to be that nobody could ever get one of them off by herself.

It was during my senior year at U.W. that I finally came face to face with *Moby Dick*. The opening line, "Call me Ishmael" and the climactic, "I only am escaped to tell thee" set off all sorts of bells in my head. Captain Ahab awed me. You don't want to mess around with a guy who could say, "I'd smite the sun if it offended me." And his obsessive need to avenge himself on the white whale put him in the same class with Hamlet and Othello.

Moby Dick has been plowed and planted over and over by generations of scholars much better than I, though, and I didn't really feel like chewing old soup for my paper in the course. Dr. Conrad was our instructor, naturally, and I was fairly certain that he'd take a rehash of previous examinations of the book as a personal insult.

Then I came across an interesting bit of information. It seems that when Melville was writing *Billy Budd*, he kept borrowing Milton's *Paradise Regained* from the New York Public Library, and I began to see certain parallels.

Dr. Conrad found that kind of interesting. "I wouldn't hang your doctoral dissertation on it, Mr. Austin," he advised, "but you might squeeze an MA thesis out of it."

"Am I going for an MA, boss?" I asked him.

"You bet your bippie you are," he told me bluntly.

"Bippie?"

"Isn't it time for you to get back to Everett and make more doors?" he asked irritably.

I considered the notion of graduate school while I was trimming door stock that evening. It was more or less inevitable—an English major without an advanced degree was still only about two steps away from the green chain. With an MA, I could probably get a teaching job at a community college—a distinct advantage, since the idea of teaching high school didn't wind my watch very tight.

I had a sometime girlfriend back then, and she went ballistic when I told her about my decision to stay in school. I guess she'd been listening to the ghostly sound of wedding bells in her mind, which proves that she didn't understand certain ugly truths. *Her* father was a businessman in Seattle, and mine was a working stiff in Everett. I don't want to sound Marxist here, but old Karl was right about *one* thing. There *are* real differences between the classes. A rich kid doesn't have to take his education too seriously, because there are all kinds of other options open for him. A working-class kid usually only has one shot at education, and he doesn't dare let *anything* get in his way, and that includes girlfriends and marriage. The birth of the first child almost always means that he'll spend the rest of his life pulling chain. Reality can be very ugly, sometimes.

This is very painful for me, so I'll keep it short. In the spring of 1995, the twins attended one of those "kegger parties" on a beach near Mukilteo, just south of Everett. I'm not sure who bought the kegs of beer for them, but that's not really important. The kids built the customary bonfire on the beach and proceeded to get red-eyed and rowdy. There were probably forty or fifty of them, and they were celebrating their upcoming graduation for all they were worth. Along toward midnight, things started to get physical. There were a few drunken fights, and a fair number of boys and girls were slipping off into the darkness for assorted boy-girl entertainments.

At that point Regina and Renata decided that it was time to leave. They slipped away from the party, hopped into their new Pontiac—a graduation present from their folks—and started back to Everett.

Regina, the dominant twin, probably drove. Renata had her driver's license, but she almost never took the wheel. They took the usual shortcut that winds up through Forest Park. It was in the vicinity of the petting zoo where they had a flat tire.

As best the authorities were able to reconstruct what happened, Regina left the car and walked to the zoo to find a phone. Renata stayed with the Pontiac for a while, then went looking for her sister.

The next morning the twins were discovered near the zoo. One was dead, raped and then hacked to death with something that wasn't very sharp. The other twin was sitting beside the body with a look of total incomprehension on her face. When the authorities tried to question her, she replied in a language that nobody could understand.

The authorities—assorted cops, detectives, the coroner, and so on—questioned Mr. and Mrs. Greenleaf extensively, but they didn't learn much: the boss and the missus were shattered and even in the best of times, they couldn't translate the girls' private language—they couldn't even tell the girls apart. So after the cops discovered that Regina was the dominant twin, they *assumed* that it'd been Regina who'd been murdered and Renata who'd gone bonkers.

But nobody could prove it. The footprints routinely taken of all newborns turned out to be missing from the records at Everett General Hospital, and identical twins have identical DNA. Logic said that the dead girl was most likely Regina, but logic wasn't good enough for filling out forms.

Les Greenleaf nearly flipped when he saw his daughter listed as an "unidentified female" in official reports.

The surviving twin continued to answer all questions in

twin-speak, and so the Greenleafs had no choice but to put her in a private sanitarium in the hope that the headshrinkers could wake up her mind. They had to fill out papers, of course, and they arbitrarily listed their surviving daughter as Renata—but *they* couldn't prove it either.

The murder remained unsolved.

My folks and I attended the funeral, of course, but there was no sense of that "closure" social workers babble about, because we couldn't be certain *which* girl we were burying.

We didn't see very much of the boss at the door factory that summer. Before he'd lost his daughters, he'd usually come strolling through the yard a couple of times a day. After the funeral, he stayed pretty much holed up in his office.

In August of that year that I had an even more personal tragedy. My folks had visited the Greenleafs one Friday evening, and as they were on their way home, they encountered what the cops refer to as a "high-speed chase." A local drunk who'd had his driver's license revoked after repeated arrests for "driving while intoxicated" got himself all liquored up in a downtown bar, and the cops spotted his car wandering around on both sides of Colby Avenue, one of the main streets in Everett. When the lush heard the siren and saw the red light flashing behind him, he evidently remembered the judge's warning when his license had been lifted. The prospect of twenty years in the slammer evidently scared the hell out of him, so he stomped on his gas pedal. The cops gave chase, of course, and it was estimated that the drunk was going about ninety when he ran a red light and plowed into my folks. All three of them died in the crash.

I was completely out of it for a week or so, and Les Greenleaf took over making the funeral arrangements, attending to legal matters, and dealing with a couple of insurance companies.

I'd already enrolled for my first quarter of grad school that fall, but I called Dr. Conrad and asked him to put me on hold until winter quarter. My dad had been shrewd enough to buy mortgage insurance, so our modest home in north Everett was now mine, free and clear, and the life insurance policies covering both of my parents gave me a chunk of cash. Les Greenleaf suggested some investments, and I suddenly became a capitalist. I don't imagine that I made Bill Gates very nervous, but at least I'd be able to get through graduate school without working for a living at the same time.

I'd have really preferred different circumstances, though.

I kept my job at the door factory—not so much for the wages as for something to keep me busy. Sitting at home wallowing in grief wouldn't have been a very good idea. I've noticed that guys who do that are liable to start hitting the bottle. After what'd happened in August, I wasn't *too* fond of drunks, or eager to join the ranks of the perpetually sauced-up.

I made fairly frequent trips to Seattle that fall. I didn't want the university to slip into past tense in my mind, so I kept it right in front of me. As long as I was there anyway, I did a bit of preliminary work on my Melville-Milton theory. The more I dug into *Paradise Regained*, the more convinced I became that *Billy Budd was* derivative.

It was in late November, I think, when Mr. and Mrs. Greenleaf and I actually got some *good* news for a change. Renata— we had agreed among ourselves by then that it almost certainly *was* Renata in that private sanitarium—woke up. She stopped talking exclusively in twin-speak and began answering questions in English.

Our frequent contacts with Dr. Fallon, the chief of staff at the institution, had made us aware that twin-speak was common—so common, in fact, that it had a scientific name— "cryptolalia." Dr. Fallon told us that it shows up in almost all cases of multiple births. The secret language of twins isn't all that complicated, but a set of quintuplets can invent a language so complex that its grammar book would run to three volumes.

When Renata stopped speaking in cryptolalia, though, her first question suggested that she wasn't out of the woods yet. When a patient wakes up and says, "Who am I?" it usually gets the psychiatrist's immediate attention.

The private sanitarium where she was being treated was up at Lake Stevens, and I rode up with Les and Inga on a rainy Sunday afternoon to visit her.

The rest home was several cuts above a state-supported mental hospital, which is usually built to resemble various other state institutions where people are confined. This one was back among the trees on about five acres near the lakeshore, and there was a long, curving drive leading to a large, enclosed interior court, complete with a gate and a guard. It was obviously an institution of some kind, but a polite one. It was a place where wealthy people could stash relatives whose continued appearance in public had become embarrassing.

Dr. Wallace Fallon had an imposing office, and he was a slightly balding man in his midfifties. He cautioned us not to push Renata.

"Sometimes all it takes to restore an amnesiac's memory is a familiar face or a familiar turn of phrase. That's why I've asked you three to stop by, but let's be very, very careful. I'm fairly sure that Renata's amnesia is a way to hide from the death of her sister. That's something she's not ready to face yet."

"She *will* recover, won't she?" Inga demanded.

"That's impossible to say right now. I'm hoping that your visit will help her start regaining her memory—bits and pieces of it, anyway. I'm certain that she won't remember what happened to her sister. That's been totally blotted out. Let's keep this visit fairly short, and we'll want it light and general. I have her mildly sedated, and I'll watch her very closely. If she starts getting agitated, we'll have to cut the visit short."

"Would hypnotism bring her out of it?" I asked him.

"Possibly, but I don't think it'd be a good idea right now.

Her amnesia's a hiding place, and she needs that for the time being. There's no way to know how long she'll need it. There *have* been cases where an amnesiac never recovers his memory. He lives a normal life—except that he has no memory of his childhood. Sometimes, his memory's selective. He remembers this, but doesn't remember that. We'll have to play it by ear and see just how far she's ready to go."

"Let's go see her," Inga said abruptly.

Dr. Fallon nodded and led us out of his office and down a hallway.

Renata's room was quite large and comfortable-looking. Everything about it was obviously designed to suggest a calm stateliness. The carpeting was deep and lush, the furniture was traditional, and the window drapes were a neutral blue. A hotel room in that class would probably cost a hundred dollars a night. Renata was sitting in a comfortable reclining chair by the window, placidly looking out at the rain writhing down to sweep the lake.

"Renata," Dr. Fallon said gently, "Your parents have come to visit you, and they've brought a friend."

She smiled rather vaguely. "That's nice," she replied in a fuzzy sort of voice. Dr. Fallon's definition of "mildly sedated" might have differed from mine by quite a bit. It looked to me as if Renata was tranked to the eyeballs. She looked rather blankly at her parents with no sign of recognition.

Then she saw me. "Markie!" she squealed. She scrambled to her feet and came running across the room to hurl herself into my arms, laughing and crying at the same time. "Where have you *been*?" she demanded, clinging to me desperately. "I've been lost here without you." I held her while she cried, and I stared at her parents and Dr. Fallon in absolute bafflement. It was obvious from their expressions that they had no more idea of what was going on than I did.

First Movement

ADAGIO

CHAPTER ONE

"What's happening here?" Les Greenleaf demanded, after Renata had been sedated into a peaceful slumber and we'd returned to Fallon's office. "I thought you told us that she has total amnesia."

"Evidently, it's not quite as total as we thought," Fallon replied, grinning broadly. "I think this might be a major breakthrough."

"Why does she recognize Mark and not us?" Inga sounded offended.

"I haven't got the faintest idea," Fallon confessed, "but the fact that she recognizes *somebody* is very significant. It means that her past isn't a total blank."

"Then she'll get her memory back?" Inga asked.

"Some of it, at least. It's too early to tell how much." Fallon looked at me then. "Would it be possible for you to stay here for the next few days, Mark?" he asked. "For some reason, you seem to be the key to Renata's memory, so I'd like to have you available."

"No problem, Doc," I replied. "If the boss can drop me off at my place, I'll grab a few things and come right back up the hill."

"Good. I'll want you right there when Renata wakes up. We've made a connection, and we don't want to lose it."

Les and Inga took me back to my place when we left the sanitarium. I tossed some clothes and stuff into a suitcase, grabbed some books, and drove my old Dodge back to Lake

Stevens. I was as baffled as everybody else had been by Renata's recognition of me, and it'd caught me completely off guard. There'd been a kind of desperation about the way she'd clung to me—almost like somebody hanging on to a life raft.

"We don't necessarily have to mention this to her parents, Mark," Fallon told me when I reported in, "but I think you'd better be right there in the room when Renata wakes up. Let's not take any chances and lose this. All the rooms here have surveillance cameras, so I'll be watching and listening. Don't push her or say anything about why she's here. Just be there."

"I think I see where you're going, Doc," I told him.

The shot Dr. Fallon had given her kept Twink totally out of it until the next morning, and that gave me time to think my way through the situation. I was still working through my grief at losing my parents, but it was time to put my problems aside and concentrate, here and now, on Twink. If she needed me, I sure as hell wasn't going to let her down.

I pushed the reclining chair over beside her bed, pulled the blanket up around my ears, and tapped out.

When I woke the next morning, Renata was still sound asleep, but she *was* holding my hand. Either she'd come about halfway out of her drug-induced slumber and found something to hold on to, or she'd just groped around for it in her sleep. Then again, it might have been *me* who'd been looking. It was sort of hard to say.

One of the orderlies brought our breakfast about seven, and I tugged on Twink's hand a couple of times. "Hey, sack-rat," I said, "rise and shine. It's daylight in the swamp."

She woke up *smiling*, for God's sake! That's sick! *Nobody* smiles that early in the morning!

"I need a hug," she said.

"Not 'til you get up."

"Grouch," she accused me, her face still radiant.

*   *   *

That first day was a little strange. Twink watched me all the time, and she had a vapid look on her face every minute. I tried to read, but it's awfully hard to concentrate when you can feel somebody watching you.

There was also a fair amount of spontaneous hugging.

I checked in with Dr. Fallon late that afternoon, and he suggested that I should probably let Twink know that I wasn't going to be a permanent fixture. "Tell her that you'll have to go back to work before too much longer. Let her know that you'll visit her often, but you have to earn a living."

"That's not entirely true, Doc," I told him. "I've got a few bucks stashed away."

"You don't need to mention that, Mark. We don't want her to become totally dependent on your presence here. I think the best course might be to gradually wean her away. Stay here for a few more days, and then find some reason to run back to Everett for an afternoon. We'll play it by ear and see how she reacts. Sooner or later, she's going to have to learn how to stand alone."

"You're the expert, Doc. I *won't* do anything to hurt her, though."

"I think she might surprise you, Mark."

There was another bout of hugging when I got back to Twink's room. That seemed just a bit odd. There hadn't been much physical contact between the twins and me in the past, but now it seemed that every time I turned around, she had her arms wrapped around me. "Renata," I said finally, "you *do* know that we aren't alone, don't you?" I pointed at the surveillance camera.

"These aren't those kinds of hugs, Markie." She shrugged it off. "There are hugs and then there are hugs. We don't do the other kinds of hugs, do we? And I wish you wouldn't call me 'Renata.' I don't like that name."

"Oh?"

"I'm Twinkie, remember? Only people who don't know

me call me 'Renata.' I knew that I was Twinkie the moment I saw you. It was such a relief to find out who I *really* am. All the 'Ren-blah-blah' stuff made me want to throw up."

"We don't get to pick our names, kid. That's in the mommy and daddy department."

"Tough cookies. I'm Twinkie, and I'm so cute and sweet that nobody can stand me."

"Steady on, Twink," I told her.

"Don't you think I'm cute and sweet, Markie?" she said with obviously put-on childishness, fluttering her eyelashes at me.

I laughed. I couldn't help myself.

"Gotcha!" she crowed with delight. Then she threw a sly glance at the surveillance camera. "And I got you too, didn't I, Dockie-poo?" she said, obviously addressing Dr. Fallon, who was almost certainly watching.

"Dockie-poo?" I asked mildly.

"All of us cute and sweet nutcases make up pet names for the people and things around us. I have long conversations with Moppie and Broomie all the time. They aren't *too* interesting, but a girl needs *somebody* to talk to, doesn't she?"

"I think your load's shifting, Twink."

"I know. That's why I'm in the nuthouse. This is the walnut ward. They keep the filberts and pecans in the other wing. We aren't supposed to talk with them, because their shells are awfully brittle, and they crack up if you look at them too hard. I was kind of brittle when I first got here, but now that I know who I *really* am, everything's all right again."

She was sharp; she was clever; and she could be absolutely adorable when she wanted to be. I *definitely* hoped that Doc Fallon was watching. I was certain that her distaste for her name was very significant. Now she had "Twinkie" to hold on to, so she could push "Renata"—and "Regina"—into the background. Maybe "Twinkie" was going to be her passport back to the world of people who call themselves "normal."

* * *

I stayed for a couple more days, and then I used the "gotta go to work" ploy Fallon had suggested to ease my way out—well, sort of. I didn't really stay away very much. As soon as I got off work at the door factory, I'd bag it on up to Lake Stevens to spend the evening with Twink.

Once she'd made the name-change and put "Renata" on the back burner, Twink's recovery to at least partial sanity seemed to surprise even Dr. Fallon. Evidently, her switchover to "Twink" was something on the order of an escape hatch. She left "Regina" behind, along with "Renata," and she seemed to grow more stable with each passing day.

Dr. Fallon decided that she was doing well enough that it'd probably be all right if she took a short furlough for Christmas.

It was a subdued sort of holiday—1995 hadn't been a very good year for any of us. Twink's aunt Mary, her dad's sister, was about the only bright spot during the whole long holiday weekend, which might seem a bit strange, in view of the fact that Mary was a Seattle police officer. But she'd always been fond of the twins, and now she refused to treat Twink as if she were damaged merchandise—the way Les and Inga did. She smoothly stepped over the blank spots in Twink's memory and more or less ignored her niece's status as a mental patient on furlough. That seemed to help Twink, and the two of them grew very close during that long weekend. That in turn helped *me* raise a subject that had worried me more than a little.

It was on Christmas Day that I braced myself and finally broke the news to Twink that our schedule was about to change. "I'll still be living at home, Twink," I reassured her, "but I'll be going to classes at the university instead of working at the door factory. I'll have to study quite a bit, though, so my visits might be a little shorter."

"I'll be fine, Markie," she said. Then she gave me one of those wide-eyed, vapid looks. "Have you heard the news?

Some terribly clever fellow named Bell came up with the niftiest idea you ever heard of. He calls it the telephone. Isn't that neat? You can visit me without even driving up the hill to the bughouse."

Mary suddenly exploded with laughter.

"All right, Twink." I felt a little foolish. "Would it bother you if I gave you a phone call instead of coming up there?"

"As long as I know that you care, I'll be fine. I'm a tough little cookie—or hadn't you noticed?"

"Maybe you two should clear that with Dr. Fallon," Inga suggested, sounding worried.

"I'll be fine, Inga," Renata assured her. For some reason, Twink had trouble with "Mom" and "Dad," so she called her parents by their names instead. I decided to have a talk with Fallon about that.

After the holidays, I returned to the university and started taking seminars, beginning with Graduate English Studies. That's when I discovered just how far down into the bowels of the earth the main library building extended. I think there was more of it underground than above the surface. Graduate English Studies concentrated on "how to find stuff in the Lye-berry." *That* deliberate mispronunciation used to make Dr. Conrad crazy, so I'd drop it on him every now and then just for laughs.

I was still commuting to Everett, even though the two hours of driving back and forth cut into my study time quite a bit. I had a long talk with Twink, and we sort of worked out a schedule. I'd visit her on weekends, but our weekday conversations were held on the phone. Dr. Fallon wasn't *too* happy about that, but headshrinkers sometimes lose contact with the real world—occupational hazard, I suppose.

Renata's amnesia remained more or less total—except for occasional flashes that didn't really make much sense to her. Her furloughs from the hospital grew more frequent and lasted for longer periods of time. Dr. Fallon didn't come right out and say it, but it seemed to me that he'd finally concluded that Twinkie would never regain her memory.

Inga Greenleaf, with characteristic German efficiency, went through Castle Greenleaf and removed everything even remotely connected to Regina.

When the fall quarter of 1996 rolled around, Dr. Conrad decided that it was time for me to get my feet wet on the front side of the classroom, so he bullied me into applying for a graduate teaching assistantship, the academic equivalent of slavery. We didn't pick cotton; we taught freshman English instead. It was called Expository Writing, and it definitely exposed the nearly universal incompetence of college freshmen. I soon reached the point where I was absolutely certain that if I saw, ". . . in my opinion, I think that . . ." one more time, I'd be joining Twinkie in the bughouse.

I endured two quarters of Expository Writing. But when the spring quarter of 1997 rolled around, I tackled my thesis and I demonstrated—to my own satisfaction, at least—that *Billy Budd* was a seagoing variation of *Paradise Regained*, with Billy and the evil master-at-arms, Mr. Claggart, contending with each other for the soul of Captain Vere. Since Billy was the hands-down winner, Melville's little parable was *not* the tragedy it's commonly believed to be. My thesis ruffled a few feathers in the department, and that was enough to get my doctoral candidacy approved and my MA signed, sealed, and delivered.

When Twink heard that I was now a Master of Arts, she launched into an overdone imitation of Renfield in the original *Dracula* movie. I got a little tired of that "Yes, Master! Yes, Master!" business, but Twinkie had a lot of fun with it, so what the hell?

I took the summer of '97 off. I *could* have taken a couple of courses during summer quarter, but I needed a break, and now that Renata was an outpatient at Dr. Fallon's private nuthouse, I wanted to be available in case her load started to shift again. Of course, Fallon wasn't about to let her stray *too* far. Twink had a standing appointment to visit him every Friday afternoon for an hour of what psychiatrists choose to call "counseling"—at 150 bucks an hour. Twink wasn't too happy about that, but, since it was one of the conditions of her release, she grudgingly went along.

It was probably my connection with the university that nudged Twink into deciding to enroll there. That made her parents nervous, but Twink was way ahead of them. "I can probably stay with Aunt Mary, Les," she told her father. "She *is* a relative after all. Imposing on relatives is one of those inalienable rights, isn't it?"

The boss looked dubious. His sister had violated one of the more important rules of the Catholic Church when she'd divorced an abusive husband, and her frequent comments about "the Polack in Rome" had offended Les more than a little. "Maybe," he said evasively. "Let's find out what Dr. Fallon has to say." It was fairly obvious that old Les was trying to pass the buck. I had a few doubts about the idea myself, so I tagged along when the boss went to lay the idea in front of Dr. Fallon.

"It's an interesting idea," Fallon mused. "Your daughter's been a bit reclusive since she left here, and the college experience might help her get past that. The only problem I can see is the pressure that goes with attending classes regularly, writing papers, and taking tests. I don't know if she's ready for that yet."

"She could audit a few courses for a couple of quarters," I suggested.

"Audit?" Les sounded startled.

"It's not like an audit by Internal Revenue, boss," I assured him. "All it means in a college is that the student sits in and listens. Twink wouldn't have to do any course work, or write any papers, or take any tests, because she wouldn't be graded. Wouldn't that take the pressure off her, Doc?" I asked Fallon.

"I'd forgotten about that," he admitted.

"It isn't too common," I told him. "You don't come across very many who take classes for fun, but we've got a special situation here. I'll check it out and see what's involved."

"That'd put it in an entirely different light," Fallon said. "Renata gets the chance to broaden her social experience without any pressure. What kind of work does your sister do, Les?"

"She's a cop."

"A police officer? Really?"

"She's not out on the street with gun and nightstick," Les told him. "Actually, she's a dispatcher in the precinct station in north Seattle. She works the graveyard shift, so her days and nights are turned around a bit, but otherwise she's fairly normal."

"How does she get along with Renata?"

"Quite well—at least during the few times she visited us when Renata was on furloughs from your sanitarium. Mary was always fond of the twins."

"Why don't you have a talk with her? Explain the situation, and tell her that this is something in the nature of an experiment. If Renata's able to deal with the situation, well and good. If it causes too much stress, we might have to reconsider the whole idea. Mark here can keep an eye on her and let us know if this isn't working. Renata trusts him, so she'll probably tell him if the arrangement gets to be more than she can handle."

"That still baffles me," Les admitted. "They didn't seem all that close before—" He broke off, obviously not wanting to mention Regina's murder.

"It's like the buddyship you and Dad picked up in 'Nam, boss," I told him. "The Twinkie Twins grew up believing that 'Markie can fix anything.' Maybe that's why Renata recognized me and couldn't recognize anybody else. I'm Mr. Fixit, and she knew that *something* had to be fixed."

"It's a bit more complicated than that," Fallon observed,

"but I think it comes fairly close to explaining Renata's recognition of Mark. As long as it's there, let's use it. I think we should give this a try, gentlemen. Renata's environment can be reasonably controlled, there won't be any pressure, and she can expand her social contacts and come out of her shell. Let's ease her into it gradually, and see how she copes. Just be sure she doesn't start missing her Friday counseling sessions. I'll definitely want to keep a close eye on her myself."

I'd known Mary Greenleaf since before the twins had been born, because she'd been a frequent visitor at her brother's house in Everett when I'd been the center of attention there. We'd always gotten along, and when the twins had come along, she'd been nice enough to keep on paying a little bit of attention to *me*, instead of dropping me like a hot rock, the way everybody else seemed to do.

She was about ten years younger than her brother was, and she lived in the Wallingford district in Seattle, about two miles from the university campus. I think her proximity to the campus might have played some part in Twink's decision to take a run at the university rather than the local community college.

Mary'd married young, and it hadn't taken her very long to discover that her marriage had been a terrible mistake. Her husband turned out to be one of those "Let's all get drunk and then go home and beat up our wives" sorts of guys.

She got to know a fair number of Seattle policemen during those years, since they routinely picked up her husband for domestic violence and hauled him off to jail.

Then there'd been counseling, which didn't work; and eventually restraining orders, which didn't work either, since Mary's husband viewed them as a violation of his right to slap his wife around anytime he felt like it.

Then Mary had filed for a divorce, which upset her priest and sent her husband right straight up the wall. He nosed around in several seedy taverns until he found some jerk willing to sell him a gun. Then he'd declared an open season on wives who object to being kicked around.

Fortunately, he was a rotten shot, and the gun he'd bought was a piece of junk that jammed up after the third round. He *did* manage to hit Mary in the shoulder before the cops arrived, and that got him a free ride to the state penitentiary for attempted murder.

Mary sort of approved of that.

She knew that he'd get out eventually, though, and that was probably what led her to take up a career in law enforcement. A cop is *required* to carry a gun all the time, and Mary was almost positive that sooner or later she was going to need one. A more timid lady would probably have changed her name and moved to Minneapolis or Boston, but Mary wasn't the timid type.

Right at first, she'd spent a lot of her spare time at the pistol range practicing for her own personal version of the gunfight at the OK Corral. Her church didn't approve of her divorce, but Mary had come up with an alternative—instant widowhood. As it turned out, though, her husband irritated the wrong people in the state pen, and he suddenly came down with a bad case of dead after somebody stabbed him about forty-seven times.

Mary didn't go into deep mourning when she heard the news.

I liked her: She was one heck of a gal.

Les Greenleaf wasn't happy about Twink's decision to move to Seattle. I think he hoped his sister would reject the idea of having her niece move in with her. But Mary shot him right out of the saddle on that one when he and I drove to Seattle in August of '97 to talk it over with her.

"No problem," Mary said. "I've got plenty of room here, and Ren and I get along just fine."

"You *do* understand that she's just a little—" Les groped for a suitable word.

"Screwball, you mean?" Mary asked bluntly. "Yes, I know all about it. I'm used to screwballs, Les. Half the people I work with aren't playing with a full deck. Renata's going to be fine here with me."

"Well," he said dubiously, "I guess we can try it for one quarter to see how she does. But if it starts giving her problems . . ." He left it hanging.

"I'll be here, too, boss," I told him. "I'll get a room nearby and, between us, Mary and I can keep Twink on an even keel."

"You're going to have to let go, Les," Mary told him. "If you try to protect her for the rest of her life, you'll turn her into a basket case. I love her, too, and I won't let you do that to her. She comes here; and that's that." Mary wasn't the sort for shilly-shallying around when it came to making decisions.

The chore of moving Twink to Seattle fell into my lap. Her father had a business to run, and I wasn't doing anything important anyway. There was a lot of driving back and forth between Everett and Seattle involved in easing Twink into her new situation, and the whole procedure took the better part of two weeks. There are people who can move halfway across the country in less time, but we all wanted to take it a little slow with this move. Stress was the last thing Renata needed.

"Why's everybody so uptight about this?" she asked me while I was driving her back to Everett to pick up some more of her clothes. "I'm a big girl now."

"We just want to make sure you're not going to come unraveled again, Twink," I told her.

"My seams are all still pretty tight," she said. "Actually, I'm looking forward to this. Les and Inga keep tiptoeing around me like I was made out of eggshells. I wish they'd learn how to relax. Mary's a lot easier to be around."

"Good. Let's keep it that way." I hesitated slightly, but then I sort of blurted it out. "Your dad's got a real bad case of protective-itis, Twink. He's not happy about this whole project, but Doc Fallon overruled him. Fallon believes it'll be good for you—as long as we can keep the pressure off. Your dad would much rather wrap you in cotton batting and keep you in a little jewel box."

"I know," she agreed. "That was my main reason for suggesting the university instead of the community college. I've *got* to get out from under his thumb, Markie. That house in Everett is almost as bad as Fallon's bughouse. I need to have *you* somewhere nearby, but Les and Inga are starting to give me the heebie-jeebies. Whether they like it or not, Twinkie *is* going to grow up."

That caught me a little off guard. Twink had been kind of passive since she'd come out of Fallon's sanitarium, but now she sounded anything *but* passive. This was a new Twinkie, and I wasn't sure where she was going.

It was a dreary Sunday in early September when I went cruising around the Wallingford district to find a place for *me* to live. I stuck mostly to the back streets, where there were older houses that had seen better days. Almost all displayed that discreet ROOMS TO LET sign in a front window. Generations of university students had fanned out from the campus in search of cheap lodgings, and property owners all over north Seattle obligingly offered rooms, many of which took "cheap" all the way down to the flophouse level.

The thing that attracted me to one particular house was an addition to the standard ROOMS TO LET placard. It read FOR SERIOUS STUDENTS ONLY with "SERIOUS" underlined in bright red ink.

I pulled to the curb and sat looking at the self-proclaimed home for the elite. On the plus side, it was no more than five blocks from Mary's house, and that was fairly important. It wasn't in very good condition, but that didn't bother me all that much. I was looking for a place where I could sleep and study, not some showplace to impress visitors.

Then a bulky-shouldered black man came around the side of the house carrying a large cardboard box filled with what appeared to be scraps from some sort of building project. The black man had arms as thick as fence posts, silvery hair, and a distinguished-looking beard.

I got out of my car when he reached the curb. "Excuse me, neighbor," I said politely. "Do you happen to know why the owner of this house is making such an issue of 'serious'?"

A faint smile touched his lips. "Trish has some fairly strong antiparty prejudices," he replied in a voice so deep that it seemed to be coming up out of his shoes.

"Trish?"

"Patricia Erdlund," he explained. "Swedish girl, obviously. The house belongs to her aunt, but Auntie Grace had a stroke last year. Trish's sister, Erika, was living here at the time, and she put in an emergency call to her big sister. Trish is in law school, and Erika just finished premed, so they weren't *too* happy to be living in the middle of a twelve-week-long beer bust. I've lived here for six years, so I've more or less learned to turn my ears off, but the Erdlund girls aren't that adaptable. They announced a no-drinking policy, and that emptied the place out almost immediately. Now they're looking for suitable recruits to fill the place back up."

"I don't want to be offensive," I said carefully, "but aren't you a bit old to be a student? You *are* a student, aren't you?"

"Oh, yes," he replied. "I'm a late bloomer—I was thirty-five before I got started. My name's James Forester," he introduced himself, holding out his hand.

"Mark Austin," I responded, shaking hands with him.

"What's your field, Mark?"

"English."

"Grad student?"

I nodded. "Ph.D. candidate. What's your area?"

"Philosophy and comparative religion."

"How many people do the Erdlund girls plan to cram into the house?"

"We've got two empty rooms on the second floor. There are a couple of cubicles in the attic and several more in the basement, but they're hardly fit for human habitation. Auntie Grace used to rent them out—el cheapo—to assorted indigents who always had trouble paying the rent, maybe because they routinely spent the rent money on booze or dope. That's where most of the noise was coming from, so Trish and Erika decided to leave them empty and concentrate on finding quiet, useful people to live in the regular rooms."

"Useful?"

"There are some domestic chores involved in the arrangement. I've got a fair degree of familiarity with plumbing, and I can usually hook wires together without blowing *too* many fuses. The house has been seriously neglected for the past dozen or so years, so it falls into the 'fixer-upper' category. Have you had any experience in any of the building trades?"

"I know a little bit about carpentry," I replied. "I've spent a few years working in a door factory up in Everett. Let's say I know enough to back off when I'm out of my depth."

"That should be enough, really. The girls aren't planning any major remodeling. Replacing wallboard that's had holes kicked in it is probably about as far as it'll go."

"No problem, then."

"I think you and I could get along, Mark, and I'm definitely outnumbered right now. It's very trying to be the only man in the house with three ladies."

"Who's the third girl?"

"Our Sylvia. She's in abnormal psych—which is either her field of study or a clinical description of Sylvia herself. She's an Italian girl, cute as a button, but very excitable."

"You're all alone here with two Swedes and an Italian? You definitely need help, brother."

"Amen to that." He paused. "Do you happen to know anything about auto mechanics?" he asked me then.

"Not so's you'd notice it. I can change a flat or replace spark plugs if I have to, but that's about as far as it goes. My solution to any other mechanical problem is to reach for a bigger hammer. Does somebody have a sick car?"

"All three girls do—or think they do. Auto mechanics seem to turn into rip-off artists when a girl drives into their shop. That's why these three want to have an in-house mechanic. Last winter, Sylvia was ready to sue General Motors because her car wasn't getting the kind of mileage GM promised. I tried to explain that warming the car up for an hour every morning *might* have had something to do with it, but she kept insisting that as long as the car wasn't moving, it shouldn't make any difference."

"You're not serious!"

"Oh, yes. Sylvia has absolutely no idea at all about what's going on under the hood of her car. She seems to think that warming the car up to get the heater running has no connection at all with putting it in gear and driving it down the block. Every time I tried to explain it, I ran into a solid wall of invincible ignorance." He shook his head sadly. "Now that you're aware of some of our peculiarities, are you at all interested in our arrangement?"

"I wasn't really thinking about a room and board kind of situation," I replied dubiously. "I keep irregular hours, and I've been living on Big Macs for the past few years."

"Erika's likely to tell you that a steady diet of Big Macs is the highway to heart surgery, Mark. The girls tend to over-mother everybody in the vicinity. And they scold—a lot. You get used to that after a while. Nobody here is really rolling in money, so the room and board's quite reasonable. The food's good, and the girls take care of the laundry. To get the benefits, though, you lose your Saturdays. Saturday is national fix-up day around here. If you're interested, I can show you around the place."

"Aren't the ladies here?"

"No. They're all off visiting before classes begin."

"I might as well have a look," I agreed.

"Come along, then," he said, starting toward the antique front door with its small, ornate glass inserts.

"Are there any other house rules I should know about?" I asked when we reached the porch.

"They aren't too restrictive. No dope sort of fits in with the no booze policy, and the no loud music stipulation doesn't really bother me."

"I can definitely agree with *that* one. Any others?"

"No in-house hanky-panky is the only other restriction. The girls aren't particularly prudish, but they've encountered problems in that area in the past."

"That's been going around lately," I agreed, as we went on into the entryway.

"The rule runs both ways," he continued. "The girls are off-limits, but the boys are, too. We're not supposed to make passes at them, and they're not supposed to make passes at us. No physical stuff on the premises."

"It makes sense," I agreed. "Emotional involvement can get noisy." I looked around. The entryway had a pre–World War II feel about it. A wide staircase of dark wood led up to the second floor, and an archway opened into a living room that was quite a bit larger than the ones in more contemporary houses.

"The downstairs is girl territory," James told me. "Boy country's upstairs." He led me on into the living room. The ceilings were high, the windows all seemed tall and narrow, and the woodwork was dark. "Elegant," I noted.

"Shabbily elegant," James corrected. "It's a bit run-down, but it's got a homey feel. The dining room's through those sliding doors, and the kitchen's at the back. It's got a breakfast nook, where the girls and I've been taking most of our meals. Let's go upstairs, and I'll show you the bedrooms."

We went up the wide staircase to the second floor. "My place is at the end of the hall," he told me, "and the bathroom's right next to it. The two at this end are vacant." He opened the door on the right.

The room had the sloped ceiling you encounter on the second floor of older houses, and it'd obviously seen some

hard use over the years. It was quite a bit larger than I'd expected, and the contemporary furniture looked dwarfed by
the generous size of the room.

"The fellow who lived here before prohibition came into
effect was a drunken slob," James told me, "and he was hard
on furniture. He wanted to get physical when Trish kicked
him out after the third time she caught him sneaking whiskey
in here, but I reasoned with him and persuaded him not to."

"Persuaded?"

"I threw him down the stairs, then tossed all his stuff out
the window."

"That gets right to the point, doesn't it?"

"I've had a fair amount of success with it—one of the ad-
vantages of being bigger than a freight truck. The rest of the
party boys who lived here got the point, and they were all
very polite to Trish after that. What do you think about the
place, Mark? Would you like to take a stab at it?"

"I think I might give it a try. A quiet place to study sort of
lights my fire. When are the girls likely to come home?"

"Tomorrow—or so they told me. I'll give you the phone
number, and you can check before you come by. I'll put in a
good word for you with the ladies. I don't think you'll have
any trouble getting admitted."

"Thanks, James. I'll keep in touch." We shook hands, and
then I went out to my car. James had a "Big Daddy" quality
that I liked. I was sure he and I could get along. The girls, of
course, might sour the deal, but I decided to keep an open
mind until I met them. The overall arrangement seemed almost too good to be true, but I wasn't about to buy into some
kind of absolute dictatorship where I'd be low man on the
totem pole. I was going to have to wait until tomorrow to find
out exactly which way the wind blew.

CHAPTER TWO

Mary Greenleaf met me at the front door when I got there, touching a finger to her lips. "She's sleeping," she said softly. "All this scampering around has her worn down to a frazzle." She stepped out onto the porch, quietly closing the door behind her.

"She *is* all right, isn't she?"

"Sure, it's just the moving and settling in."

"I've got some things to take care of here tomorrow," I told her, "so I'll grab a motel room for a couple of nights. If Twink's feeling unsettled, I'd better stay close."

She nodded. "I wonder why it is that you were the only one she could recognize when she finally came to her senses."

"I got this here dazzlin' personality," I kidded her. "Hadn't you noticed that?"

"Sure, kid," she said dryly. "You want a beer?"

"Not right now, thanks all the same."

"Did you find a room?"

"I think so. The landladies are away today, but I'll talk with them tomorrow. I think it's going to work out. The house rules should keep things quiet."

"Sounds good, Mark," she noted.

"The place is sort of shabby," I told her, "but quiet's a rare commodity in student housing."

"We've noticed that at the cop shop. The riot squad's on permanent standby alert at the north precinct. When the parties start spilling out into the street, we get *lots* of nine-one-one calls."

"I can imagine. Oh, there's something I've been meaning to ask you—you're a dispatcher, right?"

"That's what they tell me."

"Do you have to wear a gun to work?" I already knew the answer, of course, but I wanted to pinpoint the location of that gun. Twink *was* a recent graduate of Fallon's sanitarium, after all, and you don't really want a gun lying around unattended in a situation like that.

Mary smiled faintly and pushed up the bottom of her sweater to show me the neat little holster on her left side. "She has to be with me all the time," she told me. "I thought everybody knew that. If you're a cop, you wear a gun—whether you're on duty or off."

"That could be a pain in the neck sometimes."

"You bet it is." Then she frowned slightly. "Do you happen to know if Ren ever took driving lessons?" she asked.

"Of course she did. Why?"

"It must be one of the things she blotted out, then. I suggested to her that maybe her dad should buy her a car—it's a good two miles to the campus from here. But she told me that she doesn't drive."

"She didn't, not very often. Regina usually took the wheel when the twins wanted to go someplace."

"Maybe that explains it. Anyway, she told me that she's got a ten-speed bicycle at home. Next time you go up to Everett, she'd like to have you pick it up for her."

"Hell, Mary, if she wants to go anyplace, I'll pick her up and drive her there. This is rain country, and I've never seen a bike with windshield wipers."

"You're missing the point, Mark. Ren *doesn't* want a chauffeur; she wants independence. If you volunteer to become her own private taxi driver, it'll just be an extension of that cotton batting my idiot brother wants to wrap her in. She may not actually *use* the bike very often, but just knowing that it's here should give her a sense of self-reliance. That's really what this is all about, isn't it?"

"You're one shrewd cookie, Mary. It would have taken me months to work my way through *that* one."

"Oh, there's something else, too. Ren forgot a box of tapes and CDs. She brought the player, but she left all her music at home."

"Count your blessings," I told her. "Kid music hasn't got much going for it but loud."

"I think Ren might surprise you, Mark. She's into Bach fugues and Mozart string quartets."

"I didn't know that."

"I think it might have been Regina's idea in the first place. Maybe Renata's picking up a few echoes from the past. Stranger things have happened, I guess."

"You've got that right. The human mind is the native home of strange. I'd better go rent a motel room before everything gets filled up. Tell Twink that I'll stop back later—or give her a call."

"I'll let her know."

I found a vacancy in a motel just off Forty-fifth Street and spent the rest of that gloomy Sunday reading Faulkner. Southern writers can take some getting used to.

I called Twink along about suppertime. She seemed OK, so I kept it short.

Monday was drizzly. What else is new? It's almost always drizzly in Seattle. I called James about ten o'clock, and he told me that the ladies were home. "Tell them I'll be right over," I said, pulling on my coat as I grabbed my keys.

James met me at the front door. "I put in a good word for you, Mark," he told me. "I think you're in."

"You're a buddy," I told him.

"You can hold off on those thanks until *after* you've met the ladies," he cautioned. "Trish takes 'serious' out to the far end, Erika takes it in the other direction, and you never know *where* Sylvia's coming from. They're in the kitchen."

"Let's go see if I can pass muster," I said.

Like all the other rooms in the house, the kitchen was fairly large, and it had the breakfast nook James had mentioned to the right of the arched doorway.

The three ladies in the kitchen were obviously waiting for me, and it occurred to me that James might have overstated my qualifications. There was a certain deferential quality hanging in the air as I entered.

One of the Erdlund sisters was a classic Swede, tall, blond, and busty. The other one was more svelte, and she had dark auburn hair. The third girl was, as James had told me, cute as a button, tiny, olive-skinned, and with huge, liquid eyes and short brunette hair.

"Here's our recruit, Trish," James told the blond girl. "His name's Mark Austin. He's a graduate student in English and a member of the carpenter's union. Mark, this is Trish, our glorious leader."

"I wish you wouldn't do that, James," she scolded, standing up and looking at me speculatively. Trish was nearly as tall as I am, but that's not unusual in Seattle, where six-foot-tall blond girls roam the sidewalks in platoons.

"Sorry, Trish," James apologized. "Not *too* sorry. More like medium sorry."

"He teases us all the time," she told me, smiling. "I'm pleased to meet you, Mr. Austin." She held her hand out and when we shook, I noticed that she had a fairly firm grip.

"Did James fill you in on our house rules?" she asked.

"No booze, no dope, no loud music, and no hanky-panky," I recited. "I understand that you've got some renovations in mind as well."

"They're part of the arrangement, Mr. Austin. I think you'll find our room and board rate very reasonable, but that's because Erika and I expect a certain amount of physical labor as well. Our aunt's going to be in a nursing home from here on out, and my sister and I want to fix the house up so that we can put it on the market and sell it. We'll try to confine the work to Saturdays so that the rest of the week's quiet. James deals with electricity and plumbing, and you'd be our resident carpenter. Would that cause you any problems?"

I shrugged. "Probably not. I'm a fairly good knock-around carpenter. As long as we stay clear of the building code, I can probably handle things. I gather you want to avoid building permits and inspections, right?"

"Definitely. If we get into building permits, we come face-to-face with union-scale carpenters, and we don't have that kind of money."

"We could always take up begging, Trish," the auburn-haired girl suggested. "Sell pencils on street corners with a little tin cup."

"My sister Erika," Trish said sourly. "She's the smart-mouth in the family."

"How can you say that, Trish?" Erika asked with wide-eyed innocence.

"As long as we're introducing ourselves," the small, cute brunette at the table said, "I'm Sylvia Cardinale."

"We refer to her as the Godmother, Donna Sylvia," James told me, grinning at her.

"Would you like to have me make you one of those offers which you can't refuse, James?" she asked in an ominous tone.

"Oops," he replied casually.

"We're obviously clowning around, Mr. Austin," Trish apologized. "We'll get around to being serious after classes start—at least I *hope* so. Would you like to look at the vacant rooms?"

"James showed them to me yesterday," I replied. "I'd like to have another look at the one on the right side of the stairs, though. I've got an idea that we might want to talk about."

"Of course," she said, and led us all upstairs. A battered bed stood against the wall I was interested in, so I pushed it out of the way and pulled out the tape measure I'd brought. "I think this might actually work," I muttered, half to myself.

"What have you got in mind, Mr. Austin?" Trish asked.

"Permanent bookshelves," I told her, thumping the heel of my hand against the wall in search of the studs. "Fourteen inches," I mused. "This baby's well built." Then I turned. "Here's the idea," I told the group. "Most students use the standard brick-and-board arrangement for bookshelves, but that's wobbly, and occasionally the whole makeshift thing collapses. It occurred to me that permanent bookshelves wouldn't wobble, and they'd provide a lot more shelf space. I need *lots* of shelf space, because I've got books by the yard."

"Won't that be sort of expensive?" Trish asked me.

"Not really," I told her. "Unless you start getting into exotic woods, lumber's fairly cheap around here. Oh, one other thing. James tells me that there are some empty rooms in the basement. If it's okay, I'd like to put this furniture downstairs and bring in my own."

"You have your own furniture?" Erika asked. "That's unusual. Most students travel light."

"I've got a house up in Everett," I told her briefly, not really wanting to go into too much detail. "I'll be renting it out, I guess, so I'll have to put most of the furniture in storage."

Trish looked around at the room. "If we're going to empty the room out anyway, we might as well paint it before you move in."

"I gather that we've all sort of agreed that I'll be living here?" I said, looking at the others.

"I think we'll be able to get along with you, Mark," Erika said, "and the house rules should protect you from any predatory instincts that crop up in the downstairs part of the house."

"Erika!" Trish said in a shocked tone.

"Just kidding, Trish. Don't get worked up."

"There *is* something you might want to consider, Trish," James said. "This place will probably always be student housing, and permanent bookshelves in every room would definitely up the market value, don't you think?"

"It would, wouldn't it?" she agreed. "How long do you think it'll take to build *your* bookshelves, Mark?"

I shrugged. "Two or three days is about all, and once I get the process down pat, the shelves in the other rooms won't take nearly that long."

"All that sawing and pounding is likely to disrupt things," Sylvia protested.

"Not if I take good measurements," I disagreed. "The guys at the lumberyard can cut the boards to my numbers, so there won't be very much sawing, and I'm not going to use nails. Books are heavy, and nails tend to work loose. I'll use wood screws instead. I want this puppy bolted to the wall."

"You *are* going to paint it, aren't you?" Trish asked me.

"No, a couple coats of dark stain would be cheaper, and stain dries faster."

"We *want* you," Erika said with ominous intensity.

"Steady, toots," Sylvia told her.

"When would you like to move in, Mark?" Trish asked.

"Today's what—the eighth?"

She nodded.

"Classes start on the twenty-ninth, but I'd like to get settled in a couple of weeks before that. Moving my furniture and building the bookshelves won't take too long, so why don't we zero in on the fourteenth for move-in day?"

"Sounds good to me," she agreed.

I checked out of the motel and drove to Everett with my windshield wipers slapping back and forth in a sort of counterpoint to Ravel's *Bolero* coming from the car's cassette player.

When I got to my house in north Everett, I turned up the thermostat and started sorting through my stuff, moving nonessential items to another room. All I was going to need in the boardinghouse would be my bed, desk, dresser, and books.

I called Twink that evening. She seemed to be pretty much OK, so I kept it short. Then I went back to sorting and boxing.

By midafternoon on Tuesday, I had things fairly well organized, so I went by the office of the rental agency that was going to take care of the house for me and gave them a spare set of keys. "I'm a little pushed for time right now," I told the agent. "Could you make arrangements with a moving and storage company for me and have them pick up the furniture?"

"We'll take care of it for you, Mark," the agent told me. "That's one of the things you're paying us for."

"I guess," I said. "Oh, another thing. The place needs a good cleaning. Could you get hold of some professional housecleaners to go in and make things presentable?"

"We'd do that anyway. We've had a lot of experience with this sort of thing."

"Good. I'm a bit out of my depth. I've chalked a big red 'X' on the door of my room. My books, clothes, and the furniture I'll be taking are in there. Tell the movers and cleaners to leave that room alone. I'll pick that stuff up this coming weekend."

"Right," he agreed. "Don't worry about a thing, Mark. We'll take care of everything for you."

Yeah, he would—for a hefty chunk of the monthly rent.

Then I went over to the door factory to check in with Les Greenleaf.

"How's Renata doing, Mark?" he asked me with a worried look.

"She seems to be settling in, boss. It took her a few days to get used to your sister's work schedule, but she seems pretty much OK now."

"I still think we're rushing into this." Then he sighed. "Did you find a place to live?"

"Yeah. It's only a few blocks from Mary's house, so if Twink starts coming unglued, I can be there in a flat minute."

"I appreciate that, Mark. Inga and I worry a lot about Renata, but you're the one she seems to turn to."

I shrugged. "Listen, I think I've come up with something that might ease her into things at U.W. It might not be a bad idea if the first class Twink audits is mine. That'll put a familiar face at the front of the room on her first time out, so she won't get wound up quite so tight. After she gets her feet wet, she'll be able to move on, but let's not throw her into deep water right from the git-go."

"That might be the best idea I've heard all day, Mark. Just knowing that you'll be around if she needs you is taking a lot of the pressure off me."

"That's what friends are for, boss." I stood up. "I'll stay in touch. If Twink starts having any serious problems, I'll pass the word, and we can jerk her out of Seattle and bring her home again. Meanwhile, I'm going to talk with Dr. Fallon and find out exactly what I should be watching for. I'm sure there'll be a few warning signals, and I ought to hear what they're likely to be."

"You're taking a lot of time and trouble with this, Mark."

"It's that big-brother thing, boss. Oh, I almost forgot—Twink wants me to pick up her ten-speed and a box of tapes and CDs she left behind. If it's OK, I'll swing by your place this evening to pick them up." Then I remembered something. "Would it be OK if I tapped the mill scrap heap a few times?" I asked him.

"Are you building a house?" He looked amused.

"I've already got a house, boss. It's in the wrong town, but it's mine. No, the place where I'll be staying needs a few modifications—bookshelves, mostly. If I can rummage through the junk lumber in the scrap heap, I might save the landladies a few bucks."

"Help yourself," he said.

"Thanks, boss. I'd better bag on up to Lake Stevens and have that talk with Fallon."

*   *   *

But the doctor was a little vague when I asked him about warning signals. He made a fairly big issue of "compulsive behavior."

"Define 'compulsive,' Doc," I suggested.

"Anything she takes to extremes—washing her hands every five minutes, ignoring her appearance, radical changes in her eating habits. You know her well enough to spot anything unusual. If something *seems* abnormal to you, give me a call. You might want to have her aunt keep an eye on her as well."

"If you were going to bet on her recovery, what would you say the odds are, Doc?" I asked bluntly.

"Right now I'd say fifty-fifty. This first term at the university is crucial. If we can get her past this one, the odds should get better."

"We're still in the ifsy-andsy stage, then?"

"That comes close, I'd say."

"If she goes bonkers again, she'll have to come back here, won't she?"

He winced at my use of the word "bonkers," but he didn't make an issue of it. "She'll probably have to come back here a few times anyway, Mark. Recovering from a mental illness is a long, slow process, and there are almost always setbacks. That's why those Friday sessions are so important. I'll need to reevaluate her on a weekly basis just to stay on the safe side."

"You're a gloomy sort of guy, Doc, did you know that?"

"I'm in a gloomy profession. Just watch Renata very closely for the first few weeks and report any peculiar behavior to me."

"I'll do what I can," I promised.

I drove back to Everett, where I stopped by the Greenleaf house for Twinkie's bike and music. The trunk of my car was fairly full of all the usual junk that winds up in car trunks, so I lashed her bike to the roof of my Dodge and drove back to Seattle. I hauled into a motel, rolled Twinkie's bike into the room, and crashed. I'd put in a couple of busy days, and I was pooped.

Mary was still asleep when I went by the next morning, but Twink was up and moving. "You actually remembered," she said when I carried her box into the kitchen. "Did you bring my bike, too?"

"Naturally. It's tied to the top of my car. Where do you want it?"

"Put it on the back porch for now."

"You've got quite a collection here," I said, tapping the box.

"I can't remember much of it," she admitted. "After I went home from the nuthouse, I spent a lot of time listening, but none of it stirred up any memories. What were you doing up in Everett?"

"I had to pick up a few things and arrange to have the furniture put into storage. I'm not going to be living there, so I'm going to rent the place out."

"Nothing ever stays the same, does it, Markie?" she said sadly.

"In theory, it's supposed to be getting better, Twink."

"Oh, sure."

"Cheer up, baby sister. In my infinite wisdom, I've decided to let you sit in during a class conducted by Super Teacher."

"Super Teacher?"

"Me. I'll teach your socks off, kid. I'm so good that sometimes I can barely stand myself."

"Be serious, Markie."

"I am. I teach a section of English 131, and Dr. Fallon wants us to ease you into things here—familiar faces and all that stuff. It seems to me that the two things sort of click together. You get exposed to the world of education by somebody you know, and I get to keep an eye on you at the same time I show you how unspeakably brilliant I am. Isn't that neat?"

"You just want to show off."

I shrugged. "If you got it, flaunt it, kid. What time does Mary usually get up?"

"About two—or so. She doesn't get off work until seven."

"Are you going to be all right, Twink?" I asked her. "I've got a bunch of stuff I should take care of."

"I'll be fine, Markie." She patted the box I'd just delivered. "I've got my music now."

"Keep the volume down, Twink. If you wake Mary up, she might get grouchy, and she packs heat."

"Heat?"

"She wears a gun. She *is* a cop, you know."

"I've got earphones. She won't hear a thing."

"I'll call you this evening, Twink. Stay out of trouble."

"I'll be good," she promised.

I drove over to the boardinghouse to take some measurements for my bookshelves. My room was empty now, and I'd decided to get the carpentry and painting out of the way before I rented a truck to pick up my furniture.

Trish stood in the doorway watching. "Why do you keep taking the same measurement over and over, Mark?" she asked.

"It's one of the rules, Trish—measure three times, because you can only cut once. It's real hard to un-saw a board."

"I can imagine. I definitely think permanent bookshelves in every room is an excellent idea. Students always need places to keep their books." She came in and sat down on the single chair I'd left in the room. "What's a carpenter doing majoring in English?" she asked curiously.

"I came in through the back door, Trish. I like to read, and if I major in English, I can get paid for it."

"Our dad works in a sawmill up in Everett," she told me.

"Do you and Erika come from Everett, too?"

"No, we're from Marysville—not that you can tell anymore where Everett leaves off and Marysville starts."

"You've got that right, Trish. Give it a few more years, and everything from Vancouver, B.C., to Portland's going to be just one big city—a long, skinny city. What got you interested in law school, Trish? Working stiffs like your dad and mine don't usually have much use for lawyers."

"Our dad sort of pushed Erika and me into what he called 'the professions,' " she replied. "He didn't want us to grow up to be waitresses or store clerks. Erika's at least twice as smart as I am, so she was a shoo-in for a scholarship here, but after I graduated from high school, Dad finagled a job for me in a local law office. It was the senior partner there who pulled enough strings to get me a scholarship in the pre-law here."

"Boy, does *that* sound familiar," I noted. "My dad worked at Greenleaf Sash and Door up in Everett, and after I'd taken a few courses at the community college up there, I had whole bunches of people herding me in the direction of the university. It's almost like a slogan sometimes—'Workers of the world unite! Send your kids to college!' "

"Upward mobility," she said. "It's all right, I suppose, but we tend to grow away from our parents, don't we? Erika and I don't have too much in common with our folks anymore. Erika sprinkles her conversation with medical terms, and I'm starting to talk fluent legalese. Half the time I don't think Mom and Dad understand what we're saying. It's sort of sad."

"At least they're still there, Trish," I told her. "I lost my parents in a car wreck a couple years ago."

"Oh, Mark!" she exclaimed. "I'm so sorry."

"Things like that happen, Trish. We grow up thinking that everything in the world is permanent. It isn't, though. Things change all the time." Then I smiled faintly. "Aren't we starting to poach on James's territory? I'm supposed to talk about split infinitives, and you're supposed to talk about tarts."

"That's 'torts,' Mark," she corrected me.

"Ah," I said. "What's your preference, Trish? Do you like strawberry torts or raspberry torts?"

She burst out laughing. "You're a funny person, Mark."

"It's probably a fault. Sometimes I think we take ourselves

too seriously. A little laughter now and then's probably good for us."

"We don't laugh much in law school," she said, "or in the law firm where I work either, for the matter."

"You're still working for a living, then?"

"I'm a law clerk in a big firm downtown—more finagling by my old boss in Marysville. My scholarship covers tuition and books, and my downtown job puts groceries on the table."

"Been there," I said, taking another measurement. "Done that."

"I'm sure you have."

"Has Erika got an outside job, too?"

"Oh, yes. She puts in a lot of hours at a medical lab—blood tests and all that. Erika's so good with a needle that she can pull a quart or two out of you before you even know what she's up to. It's none of my business, but how do you make ends meet? Are you building houses on the sly, maybe?"

I sighed. "No, Trish," I told her. "The insurance on my folks gave me plenty of money. I can probably get by for quite a while before I have to go looking for honest work again."

"How many shelves do you think you'll be able to put along that wall?" she asked, quickly changing the subject.

"Quite a few, actually. These ten-foot ceilings give me a lot of room to play with. Of course, books come in all sizes, so there might be variations. I'll probably have to play it by ear in each room. Your law books are fairly uniform, so your shelves should be nice and even. Mine could end up pretty higgledy-piggledy."

She stood up. "I'd better go get started on supper," she said.

"Have fun," I told her, going back to my measurements.

CHAPTER THREE

As luck had it, the rain let up—briefly—on Thursday morning, so I made a quick trip to the nearest lumberyard. Working with wet boards is a real pain, so I took advantage of the break in the weather. A pickup truck would have made things a lot easier, but I didn't have one, so I lashed the boards to the top of my car instead. It's not the best way to transport lumber, but if you pad the top of the car, it'll work—and it wasn't as if the house was all that far from the lumberyard.

When I pulled up in front of the house, there was a scruffy-looking young fellow standing on the porch ringing the bell.

"They're not home right now," I called to him when I got out of my car.

"Any idea of when they're likely to be back?" he called.

"It shouldn't be too long. They were going to hit the grocery store this morning. The pantry's running low."

"You live here?" he asked me, coming down off the porch.

"Not yet, but I will be by next week. Are you looking for a room?"

"Yeah. It'd be a long commute from Enumclaw. What's this 'serious' business?" He gestured at the sign in the front window.

"The landladies have opinions," I told him, struggling with the knots that held the boards to the top of my car.

"Let me give you a hand," he offered.

"Gladly. We'll have to lug these boards around to the side. I'd like to get them into the basement before it starts raining again."

"You said something about opinions," he said, while we were untying all my knots.

I outlined the basic setup while he helped me off-load the lumber, ending with the no-no list: "No booze, no dope, no loud music, and no fooling around on the premises. The term they use is 'hanky-panky.' Their main objective is to keep the noise level down so that everybody can concentrate on study."

"I could probably live with that," he told me as we carried the boards around to the outside basement door.

"You're a student, I take it?"

"It wasn't entirely my idea," he said glumly. "I work for Boeing, and they leaned on me to go to grad school. It was too good a deal to pass up, so I'm stuck with it. They cover the tuition and pay me my regular salary to hit the books. In theory, my major's aeronautical engineering, but I'm not supposed to talk about what I'm really working on."

"Top-secret stuff?"

"Sort of, yeah—Star Wars kind of crap."

"I'm Mark Austin, by the way."

"Charlie West," he introduced himself, and we shook hands. "Are the Erdlund girls thinking about total prohibition?" he asked then. "I usually have a few beers after work, so I probably couldn't always pass a breathalyzer test."

"They don't take it quite *that* far, Charlie," I assured him. "They just don't want us getting all lushed-up on the premises. Far as I know, we're not talking about blue-nosed puritan morality here, just peace and quiet."

"I can go along with that. Do they get worked up about cooking in the rooms?"

"It's a room and board setup. The girls do the cooking and the laundry."

"What do the guys do?"

"The heavier stuff—plumbing, carpentry, that kind of thing. That's why we're lugging all these boards inside: I'm building bookshelves. Right now they're on the lookout for somebody who knows a little bit about fixing cars. They've been burned a few times by mechanics who specialize in making out the bills. Do you know anything about auto mechanics?"

"I could probably build a car from the ground up, if I really wanted to. That's my pickup out front. It doesn't look too sharp on the outside, since I haven't gotten around to the paint job yet, but you should see the engine. You don't hardly ever come across a Mach-3 pickup."

"You're kidding, of course."

"I wouldn't swear to it. I've never punched it all the way out. The speedometer only goes up to 120, and I can bend the needle in about two blocks."

"That sort of makes you a serious candidate, Charlie. Would living in the same house with a black man give you any problems?"

"No. A green one might make me nervous—they tell you to watch out for them. They've got all kinds of bad habits— mating with spruce trees, eating public buildings, worshiping sewage treatment plants, all the weird crap. What's your major, Mark?"

"English. Do you think Boeing might want to pay me to sit around reading Chaucer?"

"I wouldn't bet on it, but with Boeing, you can never be sure. Who's the black guy?"

"James—he's in philosophy."

"Heavy," Charlie said admiringly.

"You wouldn't want to mess with him," I cautioned. "He's got a George Foreman build, and he backs up the Erdlund girls by looking mean and flexing his muscles. When Trish says 'jump,' James tells you how high. He handled most of the evictions when the no-booze policy went into effect. You usually only have to throw a guy downstairs once to get your point across."

"This sounds like a real fun place to live."

"The girls should be back before long. I'm not sure exactly *where* Sylvia is—possibly over in the psych lab trying to drive all the white mice crazy."

"Is she another one of the Erdlund girls?"

"No, they're Swedes. Sylvia's Italian—in abnormal psych."

"Fun group."

"Are you interested?"

"You sound like a recruiting sergeant."

"We've just got one empty room left, and I'd like to get somebody in there before classes start. If it stays empty, Trish might send the rest of us out trolling for prospects. I'm a little busy for that, what with putting up all these bookshelves. Trish likes the idea so much that I'll probably be building bookshelves in bathrooms and closets before the end of the school year. I just hope that wood screws are going to be beefy enough to hold the weight."

"Use lock screws," he suggested. "They expand when you tighten them, so they're locked in place. If you put your shelves up with *those* babies, they'll outlast the house itself."

"I'll give it a try."

We were coming back around the house when the Erdlund girls pulled up out front. Trish was driving, and her car was stuttering and popping as she drove up.

"Little problem with the timing," Charlie noted.

"Can you fix it?" I asked him.

"Piece of cake."

The girls got out of the car and started hauling out bags of groceries.

"Hey, babe," I called to Trish, "this is Mr. Goodwrench, and he's thinking about signing on."

"Why does everybody think he's a comedian?" she said, rolling her eyes upward.

"Sorry," I apologized. "This is Charlie West. Boeing's paying him to go to graduate school, and he tinkers with cars in his spare time."

"Really?"

Charlie was looking at the tall Erdlund girls with an awed expression. "Swedish girls come by the yard, don't they?" he muttered to me. "I bet those two could play a wicked game of basketball."

We went over to the car, and I introduced the girls to Charlie.

"How did you get Boeing to pay your way?" Erika asked him.

"It was their idea, not mine," Charlie replied. "Boeing's always interested in guys who might come up with ideas they can steal and patent. I'm involved in a program I'm not supposed to talk about, and if I happen to stumble across some whiz-bang new technology, Boeing's going to own it, and they won't even have to pay me any royalties for it."

"I thought the cold war was over."

"The old one is," Charlie replied. "The new one's just getting under way. The aerospace industry absolutely *hates* peacetime, because it cuts down the money-tree. Of course, if Boeing goes belly-up, Seattle turns into a ghost town. So everybody talks about peace, but they're not particularly serious about it. Peace is bad for the economy. Did you want to talk of graves, of worms, of epitaphs?"

"I didn't quite follow that," Erika admitted.

"Shakespeare," I supplied. "*Richard II.* Charlie here seems to be a Renaissance man."

"But I don't do ceilings," Charlie added.

I think his reference to the Sistine Chapel missed the girls.

"Did Mark fill you in on the house rules?" Trish asked him.

"I can live with them," Charlie replied with an indifferent sort of shrug. "I take a beer once in a while, but it's not my life work. Mark tells me you've got an empty room. Could I take a look at it?"

"Of course," Trish told him. "Let's get the groceries inside first, though, Erika."

"I'll give Mark a hand with the rest of his lumber," Charlie said. "Then you can show me where to flop."

"Don't let him get away, Mark," Erika told me with a peculiar fierceness.

"Those are a couple of spooky ladies," Charlie said, while we carried the rest of my boards around to the side.

"Swedish girls lean toward intensity," I agreed.

After we'd finished, Trish gave Charlie the tour. He only glanced briefly into the room across the hall from mine. "It'll do," he said almost indifferently. "I'll go back to Enumclaw and pick up my junk. Would it be OK if I put my tools in that basement room where Mark's got his lumber? I don't want to leave them in my truck. Good tools fetch fancy prices in pawnshops, so I don't want to take chances on having somebody swipe them. If it's OK, I'll move in on Monday."

"That's fine with me, Charlie," Trish told him.

"Would you mind if I painted the room?" he asked then. "Pink walls aren't my scene."

"It's your room," Trish told him. "Pick any color you like."

I spent the morning in the basement staining the boards, then I went to a hardware store and bought those lock screws Charlie had mentioned, came back, and started installing the shelves. It went quite a bit faster than I'd thought it would, and I was better than halfway through the job when I knocked off for the day.

I called Miss Mary's house when I got back to the motel, and Twink answered the phone. "Where have been, Markie?" she demanded. "I tried to call you four times today."

"I was building bookshelves. Are you all right?"

"I was just lonesome, that's all. I thought that maybe we could go to a movie or something."

"Is there anything showing that you'd like to see?"

"Not really. I'd just like to get out for a while."

"Have you eaten yet?"

"I was going to pop a TV dinner into the microwave."

"Why don't I take you out to dinner instead?"

"That'd be nice."

"I'll take a shower and change clothes. I'll be there in about forty-five minutes, OK?"

"Anything you say, Markie."

I realized that I'd been neglecting Twink for the past few days. I'd been busy, of course, but that was no real excuse.

I took her to a Chinese restaurant, and we pigged out on sweet-and-sour pork. Then we sat over tea and talked until the restaurant closed. Twinkie seemed relaxed and even quite confident. She was coming right along.

I was certain that I'd finish up the shelves and the painting on Friday, so I'd only have one more night in the motel before I'd be able to settle into my own room.

I got up fairly early and started painting as soon as I got to the Erdlund house. I wanted the paint to be good and dry before I moved in my furniture.

James stuck his head in through the doorway about noon. "Baby blue," he noted.

"I'm just a growing boy," I replied.

"Sure, kid. Who's this Charlie guy the girls are all up in the air about?"

"He's an aerospace engineer who works for Boeing. His hobby is cars, and that made the Erdlund girls wiggle like puppies."

"Is Boeing *really* paying him to go to school? Or is he just blowing smoke in everybody's ears?"

"I think he's giving us the straight scoop. He's a sort of slob who quotes obscure passages from Shakespeare and knows more about the Italian Renaissance than you'd expect from an engineer. He's a sharp one, that's for sure. He'll be moving in on Monday, and then you can judge for yourself."

"Nobody ever offered to buy *me* an education."

"We're in the wrong fields, James."

"It looks like you're almost finished," he observed.

"Three more shelves on top, then it's all done."

"Do you really have *that* many books?"

"Not quite, but I'm giving myself room for expansion.

When you major in English, your library grows like a well-watered weed. I'll get those last few shelves installed as soon as I finish painting. I want to polish it all off before the local U-Haul place closes. I'll rent a truck this afternoon and bag on up to Everett first thing tomorrow morning."

"I'll go along," he rumbled. "Loading furniture into a truck is a two-man job."

"I was sort of hoping you might make that offer," I said, grinning at him.

"Have you got everything up there all packed?"

"It's ready to roll." Then I went back to painting.

I finished up by midafternoon, and then I went to the U-Haul place and rented a truck.

James and I got an early start the next morning. It was Saturday, and of course it was raining. It *always* rains on weekends, or had you noticed? Monday through Friday can be sunny and bright, but come Saturday, you get rain. James and I talked a bit on the way north, and James told me that he'd started at the university after his wife had died of cancer. "I needed something to distract me," he said rather shortly. He clearly didn't want to go into any greater detail.

There was an awkward silence for a while as we drove past Lynnwood through the steady drizzle.

"What got you into English, Mark?" he asked finally.

"Dumb luck, probably." I launched into a description of my years at the community college and my early major in "everything."

"You sound like a throwback to the Renaissance—Mark da Vinci, maybe, or possibly Mark Borgia."

"It was an interesting time, that's for sure. Isn't that an old Chinese curse? 'May you live in interesting times'?"

"I seem to have heard that."

"I was just dabbling, James," I explained. "I wasn't even working toward a degree—I took courses in anything that sounded interesting. What got *you* into philosophy?"

He shrugged. "The usual stuff—'The meaning of life,' or the lack thereof." He seemed to hesitate a moment. "It's none of my business, but how is it that a young fellow who works for a living came to own a house? That usually doesn't come along until quite a bit later."

"It's an inheritance," I told him. "My folks were killed in a car accident, and there was some mortgage insurance involved in the estate."

"Ah," he said and let the matter drop.

We reached my house in north Everett, and I backed the truck up to the front porch. Then we hauled out my furniture and box after box of my books. Books aren't *quite* as heavy as salt, but they come close. James and I were both sweating heavily by the time we finished up. "Now I see why you needed so much shelf space," he observed.

"Tools of the trade," I said. "I guess I'm one of the last pre-computer scholars, so my books take up lots of room—which is fine with me. When I read something, it's on a real page, not a monitor. No hysteria about rolling blackouts."

I had to shift my emotions into neutral as I made a quick survey of the now-empty house—I didn't want to start blubbering.

"Tough, isn't it?" James said sympathetically.

"More than a little. I grew up here, so there are all sorts of memories lurking in the corners. There's a big cherry tree in the backyard, and the Twinkie Twins used to spend hours up in that tree eating cherries and squirting the pits at me."

"Squirting?"

"You put a fresh cherry pit between your thumb and fore-finger and squeeze. If you do it right, the pit zips right out. The twins thought that was lots of fun. It was a summer ver-sion of throwing snowballs."

"You have twin sisters?"

"Not exactly. They were the daughters of my dad's best buddy."

"Were?"

I hesitated for a moment. The story was almost certain to come out eventually anyway, so there wasn't much point in trying to hide it. "One of them was murdered a few years ago. The other one went a little crazy after that and spent some time in a private sanitarium. Now she's starting to come out of it—sort of. She's staying with her aunt down in Wallingford—about five blocks from our place. Her head-shrinker thinks that going to college might help her."

"I'm not sure that U.W.'s the best place to go looking for mental stability," James noted, as I locked the front door.

"Her aunt and I will be keeping a fairly tight grip on her," I told him. Then we closed and latched the back door of the U-Haul van and climbed into the cab.

"You seem to be quite involved with this surviving twin," James said rather carefully.

"There's none of that kind of thing going on, James," I told him, starting the engine. "The Twinkie Twins were like baby sisters to me, and once you've seen a girl in messy diapers, you're not likely to have romantic thoughts about her. I've just always looked out for them."

"Twinkie Twins?"

"In-house joke," I admitted. "Nobody could tell them apart, so I got everybody started indiscriminately calling them both 'Twink.' They pretty much stopped being Regina and Renata and started being Twink and Twink."

"I'll bet you could send Sylvia straight up the wall with that one," James said, chuckling. "The concept of group aware-ness might damage her soul just a bit."

"Bees do it, and so do ants. In a different sort of way, so do horses and wolves—and lions and elephants, if you get right down to it. If animals do it, why not people?" I carefully drove the truck off the front lawn and pulled out into the street.

"Did the cops ever catch the murderer?"

"No, and even if they do, I'm not sure they could convict him."

"I don't quite follow you."

"Nobody can be positive which twin was murdered."

"What?" He sounded incredulous.

"Well, nobody could ever tell them apart, and the hospital lost the footprints they took as newborns."

"Why not just ask the surviving twin?"

"She doesn't know who she is. She doesn't remember anything."

"Amnesia?"

"Almost total."

"What about DNA?"

"Identical twins have the same DNA. So if they ever catch the guy, they might be able to prove that he killed *somebody*, but I don't think they'll ever be able to prove *who*. A good lawyer might get him off scot-free—which'd be OK with me."

"What? You lost me again."

"Hunting season opens up along about then. If Twink's aunt doesn't bag the sumbitch, I might take a crack at him myself. I'm sure I could come up with something interesting to do to send him on his way. If I happen to get caught, I'll hire Trish to defend me."

"I still think the courts would send him away, Mark. Murder is murder, and if Jane Doe is the best the cops can come up with, he'll go down for the murder of Jane Doe."

"You live in a world of philosophical perfection, James. The real world's a lot more 'catch as catch can.' That's why we have lawyers." Then I remembered something and laughed.

"What's so funny?" he asked.

"Chaucer got arrested once—back in the fourteenth century."

"Oh?"

"He beat up on a lawyer."

"Some things never change, do they?" he said, as we pulled out onto the freeway heading south.

When we got to the boardinghouse, James and I carried all my stuff upstairs and stacked it in my room. All in all it'd taken longer than I'd thought it would, so I decided to motel it for one more night. I'd already put in a full day, and I was feeling too worn down to start setting things up. I took the truck back to U-Haul, paid them, and retrieved my Dodge. Then I went by Mary's place to check on Twinkie—I still felt guilty about the way I'd ignored her for the past week.

Mary was nice enough to invite me to dinner, and the three of us sort of lingered over coffee afterward.

"That sanitarium is pretty fancy, isn't it?" Mary said.

"I didn't quite catch that," I said.

"My weekly visit to Dockie-poo," Twink explained. "You forgot about that, didn't you, Markie?"

"I guess I spaced it out," I admitted. "How did it go?"

"Nothing new or unusual," Twink replied. "Fallon asked all those tedious questions and scribbled down my answers in that stupid notebook of his. I told him enough lies to make him happy, and then Mary and I dropped by the house and had supper with Les and Inga."

"Doesn't all that scampering around crowd you?" I asked Mary.

She shrugged. "Not really," she said. "Ren and I took off from here about three, so we missed the five o'clock rush."

"If it gets to be too much, I could run Twink on up there on Fridays. That's a light day for me most of the time."

"We can pass it back and forth, if we have to. I don't think it'll give me any problems, though."

"Did Fallon make any suggestions?" I asked Twink.

"Nothing I haven't heard from him before," she replied. "I'm supposed to avoid stress. Isn't that an astonishing suggestion? I mean, wow!"

"Be nice," I told her.

She made an indelicate sound and changed the subject.

About nine o'clock, I went back to the motel and fell into bed. Moving really takes a lot out of you.

*   *   *

By noon on Sunday, I had my bed and desk set up and most of my clothes hung in the closet. Then I started putting books on the shelves. After an hour or so of unloading boxes and randomly shelving, I stopped and stood in the center of the room, glowering at my bookshelves. They were an absolute masterpiece of confusion. Hemingway and Faulkner were jammed in cheek by jowl with Chaucer and Spenser, and Shakespeare was surrounded by Mark Twain, Longfellow, and Walt Whitman. "Bummer," I muttered. I knew that if I didn't organize the silly thing right from the start, it'd probably stay confused in perpetuity. Owning a book is very nice, but you have to be able to put your hands on it.

I sighed and started stacking books on the floor, separating English literature from American and throwing the miscellaneous stuff on the bed. I came across books I'd forgotten I owned.

By evening, I'd finally put things into some kind of coherent order, and that gave me a sense of accomplishment. Fortress Austin was now complete and ready to hold off the forces of ignorance, absurd clothing, and bad music. With my help, God could defend the right—or the left, depending on His current political position.

After dinner that evening—my first Erdlund Epicurean Delight—I called Twink to make sure she was still on the upside. She was all bubbly, so things seemed to be pretty much OK.

"You might want to start thinking about going to class, Twink," I told her. "The quarter starts two weeks from tomorrow. The class I'll be teaching starts at one-thirty in the afternoon, so you won't have to do that cracky-dawn stuff. I can stop by and pick you up, if you'd like."

"That's why they invented buses, Markie. I'm a big girl now, remember?"

"We've still got a while to kick it around, Twink. I'll be a little busy for the next two weeks, though. I've got a lot of things to take care of on campus."

"Quit worrying so much, Markie. It'll give you wrinkles. Sleep good."

The next morning, I drove to the campus to check in with Dr. Conrad.

"And how did you spend your summer vacation, Mr. Austin?" he asked me with a faint smile.

"Did you want that in five hundred words, Doc?"

"I think a summary should be enough—I probably won't be grading you on it."

"Actually, I spent quite a bit of time conferring with a headshrinker."

"Has our load been shifting?"

"I don't think so, but I'd probably be the last to know. Actually, the daughter of a family friend just graduated from a private mental hospital, and she'll be taking some classes here. First, I had to get her moved in with her aunt up in Wallingford, and then I had to relocate myself as well: I got a place not far from her aunt's. It's a boardinghouse with a few grad students from departments scattered all across campus—but don't worry, I'll try to hold up our reputation."

"I'm sure that if I'm patient, you *will* start to make some sense here."

"I wouldn't count on it, Doc. It's been a pretty scrambled summer. I think I'll go hide in the library for a couple of weeks to get my head on straight again."

"That sounds like a plan," he said sarcastically.

I spent the rest of the day in the library, and I didn't get home until about eight that evening. Trish got on my case for missing supper, but after some extensive apologies, she relented and fed me anyway. The mother instinct seemed to run strong and deep in our Trish.

After I'd eaten, I went into the living room to use the community telephone. I dialed Mary's number, but it was Twink who answered. I heard some weird noises in the background, and at first I thought we might have a bad connection.

"No, Markie," Renata said. "It's not the telephone. I'm listening to some music, that's all."

"It doesn't sound all that musical to me, Twink. What's it called?"

"I haven't got a clue. Somebody—maybe even me—taped something and forgot to label it."

"It sounds like a bunch of hound dogs that just treed a possum," I told her.

"I think they're wolves, Markie—at least on this part of the tape. Later on, the wolf howls gradually change over and become a woman's voice."

"You've got a strange taste in music, Twink."

"Would you prefer some golden oldies by the Bee-doles? Or maybe 'You ain't nothin' but a Clown-dawg' by Olvis Ghastly?"

"Try the Brandenburg Concertos, Twink," I suggested. "Avoid teenie-bopper music whenever you can. It's hazardous to your hearing, if not your health. Did your aunt go to work already?"

"She's taking a bath. I've got an awful headache for some reason."

"Take two aspirin and call me in the morning."

"Fun-*nee*, Markie. Funny, funny, funny. Go away now. My wolves want to sing to me." Her voice sounded sort of vague, but there was a peculiar throaty vibrance to it that I'd never heard before.

Then she abruptly hung up on me, and I sat there staring at the phone and wondering just what was going on.

CHAPTER FOUR

James woke me at quarter after seven on Tuesday morning. "Breakfast," he announced. "Oh, right," I said, coming up a little bleary-eyed. It was obviously going to take me a while to get used to regular hours. For the past couple of years, I'd eaten whenever it'd been convenient, but now I was living in a place where the meals came at specific times and were served in specific places—breakfast in the kitchen and dinner in the dining room. Lunch was sort of "grab it and growl," largely because our schedules wouldn't match once classes started.

I got dressed and staggered to the bathroom to shave and brush my teeth. Then I followed my nose to the kitchen. I really needed some coffee to get my engine started.

The girls, still in their bathrobes, were bustling around preparing breakfast, and they looked terribly efficient. Evidently, when the Erdlund aunt had been running the house, it'd been one of those "kitchen privileges" places where the boarders were permitted to cook their own meals, since there were still two refrigerators and a pantry. You almost never see pantries in contemporary housing. Like sitting rooms and parlors, they seem to have fallen by the wayside in the twentieth century's rush toward minimal housing made of ticky-tacky.

The cupboard doors, I noticed, were a little beat-up, and the linoleum on the floor was so ancient that the pattern had been worn off in places where there'd been heavy traffic. The worn places looked almost like game trails out in the woods.

"Mark!" Trish snapped at me, "Will you *please* get out from underfoot?"

"Sorry," I apologized. "I think that after the bookshelves, we might want to take a look at this kitchen. It's seen a lot of hard use."

"Later, Mark," Erika told me, grabbing me by the arm and hustling me out of the work zone. She pointed at a chair off in one corner. "There!" she told me, snapping her fingers. "Sit! Stay!"

"Yes, ma'am," I replied obediently.

Then she brought me a cup of coffee and patted me on the head. "Good boy," she said. Erika tended to be more abrupt than her sister. If she was going to practice medicine, she'd probably have to work on her bedside manner. She was going to take some getting used to, that much was certain.

So was her coffee. Erika obviously believed that the only substitute for strong coffee was stronger coffee. It was good, mind you, but it was strong enough to peel paint.

Sylvia set the table, and Trish was flipping pancakes with a certain flair. It was all sort of homey and pleasant, and things smelled good. I was sure I could learn to like this.

Then James and Charlie came down and we all took our places at the table and attacked Trish's pancakes.

"These are great, Trish," Charlie said. "I haven't had pancakes like these since the summer when I worked in a logging camp."

"I thought you were a Boeing boy, Charlie," James said.

"That came later on," Charlie replied. "I've worked lots of jobs—some good, some bad."

"You ever pull chain?" I asked him.

"Oh, gosh yes," he replied. "That one goes in the bad column."

"Amen to that," I agreed. "All the way down at the bottom."

"Anyway," Charlie continued, "you wouldn't *believe* the breakfasts they used to feed us in that logging camp—and an ordinary, run-of-the-mill dinner in a logging camp is pretty much like Thanksgiving. A logger can put away a lot of food. You aren't going to swing an eight-foot chain saw very long on a steady diet of Rice Krispies. That's why the kitchen's the most important building in a logging camp. If the boss is dumb enough to hire a bad cook, the whole crew's likely to quit after about a week—and the word gets around fast. By the end of May, that boss won't be able to find anybody who'll work for him." Charlie leaned back in his chair. "You get some strange people in logging camps. The hiring hall's a tavern on Skid Road here in Seattle, so there are a lot of drunks out there in the brush. We had a powder-monkey who showed up in camp the summer I worked there who had the shakes so bad that he'd set the bunkhouse to trembling as soon as he came through the door—and this was a guy who worked with *dynamite*, for God's sake! He drank up all the shaving lotion and hair tonic in camp by Wednesday, and then he caught the train back to Seattle. The camp was *way* back in the woods, so the train only came by three times a week— Sunday, Wednesday, and Friday—and that was the only way to get there."

"No roads?" James asked.

"Hell, no. We were forty miles back in the timber. The train hauled our logs out, so we didn't really need a road. The bull-cook was a dried-up old boy, and it was part of his job to build fires in the bunkhouse stoves in the morning. That was our alarm clock when we were moonlighting. He used gasoline to start the fire in the stove, and that can be noisy."

"Moonlighting?" Sylvia asked curiously.

"That's when you have to get up at three in the morning," Charlie explained. "When the fire danger gets up to a certain point, the Forest Service tells the loggers they have to be out of the woods by ten o'clock in the morning. Working in the dark with an eight-foot chain saw can get sort of exciting."

"I imagine so," James said. "Oh, by the way, Trish, Mark has a legal question he'd like to ask you."

"Are you in trouble with the law, Mark?" Trish asked me.

"Not that I know of," I assured her. Then I told them all about the twins, and about Regina's rape and murder, much as I had told James. "Assuming they ever *do* catch the guy," I asked, "would they have to prove the identity of the victim before they could get a conviction?"

"Haven't they ever heard of DNA?" Sylvia asked.

"No good," Erika told her. "Identical twins have the same DNA. I gather that the baby footprints are missing?"

I nodded. "I guess somebody at Everett General Hospital misfiled them. Well, Trish, what's the word? Can they convict if they can't identify the victim?"

"I'm sure they can." She didn't really sound all that positive, though. "I'll bounce it off one of my professors just to make sure."

"Did the surviving girl ever recover?" Sylvia asked. "I'd sure like to meet her."

"I could probably arrange that—she lives just few blocks away. But I don't want you to start crowding her."

"My," Trish said, "aren't *we* possessive?"

"Our families were close, so I was sort of a big brother to the twins. I told James, if the cops get lucky and turn up the sumbitch who killed Regina, I almost hope he *does* get off. I can come up with some very interesting things to do to him—things that go *way* past the tepid sort of stuff allowed by the criminal justice system. Fire and white-hot steel hooks—that kind of thing."

"Whoo!" Erika said. "This one's a real savage, isn't he?"

"Who was the surviving twin's psychiatrist?" Sylvia asked me then.

"Fallon. He runs that private sanitarium where she was staying."

"I've heard of him. He's supposed to be very good."

"Maybe so, but could we talk about something else?"

"Of course, Mark," Trish said quickly, and she adroitly changed the subject to resurfacing the kitchen floor instead.

After breakfast, I drove down to the campus; I'd encountered something I wanted to examine. It appeared that there'd been some fairly extensive contacts between Walt Whitman and an English group known as the pre-Raphaelites.

We tend to get compartmentalized in our thinking. It's almost as if British literature and American literature evolved on two different planets. The mail *did* get through, though, and we *do* speak approximately the same language the Brits speak. The possibility of transoceanic influence could be of genuine academic interest, so I headed to the library to pursue it a bit further.

I stopped by Mary's place on my way home.

"Where have you been?" Renata's aunt demanded when she opened the door. "I tried to call you, but nobody answered."

"I was facedown in the library," I explained. "I guess the rest of the gang at the boardinghouse had things to attend to on campus as well. Is something wrong?"

"Renata had a bad night. She was still awake when I got home from work."

"Did she tell you what was bothering her?"

"It was some kind of nightmare, and whatever it was, it must have been pretty awful. Evidently she was flailing around while she was dreaming, because she's got a lot of bruises on her arms."

"Maybe I'd better stay here tonight," I suggested.

"That won't be necessary," she told me. "I've got tonight off, so I'll be here to keep an eye on her." Then she gave me a speculative look. "Can you keep something to yourself, Mark?" she asked me bluntly.

"If you want me to, yes."

"I gave her a sleeping pill, and I'd rather that her psychiatrist didn't find out about it."

"Over-the-counter stuff?"

"No, a little heavier than that. Just about everybody who works graveyard shift has an open-ended prescription for sleeping pills. I won't make a regular practice of it, but any-time Ren starts getting all wired-up, I can put her down. Sometimes we have to bend a few rules."

"I don't have any problem with that. I'll give you a buzz later on this evening to find out how she's doing."

"*If* she wakes up. If she was as wrung-out as she seemed to be, she might sleep all the way through until tomorrow morning."

"It would probably be good for her. I've got a hunch that this back-to-school business might have her wound a little tight. We were hoping that auditing classes instead of taking them for credit might keep the pressure off her, but maybe we're still rushing things a bit."

"I'll watch her. If it gets to be too much for her, she can either drop the classes for a few weeks—or let it all slide until next quarter."

"I don't know about that, Mary," I said dubiously. "If the boss gets wind of anything like that, he might insist that she come back home."

"Then we'll just have to make sure that he doesn't find out, won't we?"

"We can try." I glanced at my watch. "I'd better get moving. If last night was any indication, the ladies get all torqued out when I'm late for meals."

When I got back to the boardinghouse, Charlie had his door open, and he was going at his walls with a paint roller. I stared into his room. "Boy, are *you* going to get yelled at!" I told him.

"Trish said I could paint the room any color I wanted," he said defensively.

"I don't think she's going to like it much," I predicted. "You don't come across very many rooms painted black."

"It's a neutral color. Nobody flips out when he sees a room painted white—or gray."

"Black's different. What made you decide on black?"

"It's sort of outer-spacey, don't you think?"

"It's definitely spacey. Are you thinking about adding stars later?"

He squinted at the dull black ceiling. "I don't think so. I think I'd like to keep the infinity effect. The ceiling's as close or as far away as I want it to be, and it moves kind of in and out when I look at it. The whole idea is to make it indefinite. I'll be working with some equations later on that won't have spatial limitations, and I'll need to be able to visualize them. I think those black walls and ceiling are going to help."

"I still think it'll make Trish flip out."

"She'll get over it. Did you happen to catch the news today?"

I shook my head. "I was down in the bowels of the main library. Is something going on I should know about?"

"We might have to start wearing flak jackets to class," he replied. "Some guy got knifed on campus—down by the crew dorm."

"Crew?"

"The rowing team—the guys who row those long, skinny boats in races. Their dorm's down by the edge of Lake Washington. The last word I picked up on TV was that the cops thought it was a gang-related killing."

"Whoopee," I said flatly. "As far as the cops are concerned, jaywalking's gang-related."

"They *do* sort of lean on it now and then, don't they?"

"They might be pushing this one a little. Gangs normally use guns, not knives." I shrugged. "I doubt that we'll get *too* much in the way of details from TV. The cops clam up when they're investigating something."

"Hello, up there," Trish called from downstairs. "We're home. Is everybody decent?"

"We're dressed, if that's what you mean," I told her.

"I'm coming up."

"Feel free," I called, then looked at Charlie. "You might want to close your door," I suggested.

"She'll see the paint job sooner or later, anyway," he replied. "Let's get the yelling and screaming over with."

Trish surprised the both of us, though. When she reached the top of the stairs, she glanced through Charlie's doorway and shrugged. "Interesting notion," she observed.

"You're taking the fun out of this, Trish," Charlie complained.

"It's your room, Charlie," she replied. "You have to live with it. Have you gentlemen heard anything about that murder on campus last night?"

"Just what came over the idiot box," Charlie told her. "Is the campus coming down with nervous?"

"The girls in the dormitories are a little worked up, and Erika and I *do* spend quite a few evenings in on-campus libraries. If some screwball's running around on campus, we might have to start taking a few precautions."

"From what I hear, the cops think it was one of those gang things," Charlie told her. "Those aren't usually dangerous for innocent bystanders—particularly when the guy who's doing the killing uses a knife. It's when they start shooting at each other that you have to take cover. City kids are rotten shots. What's for dinner tonight, babe? I skipped lunch today, and I'm starving."

The ladies fixed pork chops that evening, and they were way out in front of anything you'd get in any local restaurant. James arrived a little late for supper, and the girls scolded him at some length. I mentally confirmed "don't be late for supper" under my list of house rules.

"Are you guys up for a jaunt over to the Green Lantern Tavern this evening?" Charlie asked James and me.

"Here we go again." Erika sighed, rolling her eyes upward.

"We're not going to get all bent out of shape, toots," Charlie promised. "I want to have a talk with my older brother about that guy who got killed on campus last night. My brother's a cop, and he'll know a lot more details than we got from the news reports. He hits the Green Lantern just about every night on his way home from work. I can probably wheedle the story out of him. Then we'll know whether it's something we need to worry about."

James shrugged. "I don't really have anything better to do," he replied. "I'll come along. I can count the number of beers you drink and rat you off to Trish when we get home."

"You wouldn't!" Charlie said.

"Only kidding, Charlie. Relax. I never fink on a buddy."

"Male bonding in action," Sylvia said sardonically.

"And Budweiser's the glue in most cases," Erika added. "Take ten guys and a keg of beer, mix well, and they're stuck together for life."

"It's one of those guy things, Erika," I told her. "It crops up during hunting season—or just before the Super Bowl. I don't watch football on TV, so I'm sort of an outcast. Well, gentlemen, shall we tiptoe off to the Green Lantern and abuse our livers?"

Sgt. Robert West was a plainclothes detective with the Seattle Police Department, and he and his younger brother seemed to be fairly close, despite a pretty good number of differences between them. Charlie had bounced from job to job for a number of years, but Bob had taken aim at the Seattle Police Department when he'd been about fourteen, and he'd never even considered an alternate profession. He was a solid citizen with a wife, two kids, and a mortgage. He lived in the Wallingford district, and he customarily stopped by the Green Lantern after work for two beers—three on Friday, I learned later—then went on home. Charlie'd told James and me that you could set your watch by his brother. They looked quite a bit alike, but I doubt that Charlie even knew how to tie a necktie, while Bob wore one to work every day.

After Charlie had introduced James and me to his brother, he got down to cases. "I don't want you to bend any rules, big brother," he said, "but we'd like to know if we ought to start wearing bulletproof vests to class. If the gangs are moving onto the campus, it could turn into a war zone. What's the scoop on the guy who got knifed last night?"

Bob looked at James and me. "This won't go any further, right?" he asked us in a low voice.

"It stops right here," James assured him.

"All right, then. The victim was a fairly high-ranking member of a Chicano gang, and somebody obviously wanted to pass a message on to his pals. What happened down by the lakeshore last night wasn't your average, run-of-the-mill stab in the back. Somebody went to a lot of trouble to make it *very* messy."

"Who was the dead guy?" Charlie asked.

"His name was Julio Muñoz, and his gang's recently moved out this way to try to attract customers from the student body for various feel-good products. U.W. students have been doing dope for years, but they usually had to go to other neighborhoods to buy it. Julio and his buddies decided to set up a branch office in the university district. Evidently, another gang had the same idea, and they weren't too happy about the notion of a price war."

"Any ideas about *which* gang decided to carve up Julio?"

"Nothing very specific. Lieutenant Burpee thinks it might have been Cheetah, but Burpee's sort of obsessed with Cheetah. He's been trying to nail *that* one for about the last three years."

"Burpee?" James asked mildly.

Bob smiled faintly. "We don't call him that to his face. His real name's Belcher."

"It *does* kind of fit, I guess," James agreed.

"Who's this Cheetah?" I asked.

"A downtown drug lord. He's a mixed breed psychotic—part black, part Mexican, part oriental, part rabid bird dog. That's one guy we'd *really* like to get off the streets. He swings big-time drug deals and amuses himself with random murders. We haven't been able to pin him down because he hasn't got a fixed address. He never sleeps in the same bed

twice, and he's got two or three hundred aliases. Muñoz had
a rap sheet as long as your arm, but Cheetah's never been
busted, so we don't even know what his real name is. We've
got a rough description of him, and that's about all. I sort of
hate to admit it, but old Burpee might be right this time.
Cheetah tends to be exotic, and the cutting last night was *at
least* exotic. I've seen a few guys that were fairly well cut up,
but whoever went after Julio scattered pieces of him all over
the grass down by the lake. There's no way an undertaker's
going to be able to put him back together again, so we're
probably looking at one of those closed casket funerals."

"You saw the body, then?" Charlie asked his brother.

"I sure did. I got to the scene right after the uniforms did.
That one's going to give the coroner a real headache. Whoever took Muñoz out didn't stab him the way most knife
killers do. It was a carving, not a stabbing, and I'd guess that
it took Muñoz a long time to die. It wasn't for money, that's
certain. His wallet was still in his back pocket, and it was
loaded."

"It was strictly a drug business thing, then?" James asked.

"That's our current thinking. Most of Julio's arrests were
drug-related. He's been busted for that a half dozen times.
He's been a suspect in several shootings and a couple of
rapes, but we could never pin him to the mat on those. We
haven't nailed him on a dope deal for over a year now, though.
Evidently, he graduated from street dealing and moved up to
being a supplier. There's more money in that, I guess, but last
night it looks like he came up against one of the occupational
hazards of going big-time."

"The rubout?" Charlie guessed.

"The slice-out in this case. I don't think there was much
rubbing involved. Whoever took him out might have had
some experience as a meat cutter, since it sort of looked like
he was trying to bone out the carcass even after Muñoz died."

"Homicidal maniac stuff?" Charlie asked.

"Pretty much. It looked to me as if the cutter was pretty

well worked up. We'll probably have to wait for the autopsy to find out what kind of knife was involved. There didn't seem to be any stab wounds. It was all slices. What's surprising about it is that nobody in the vicinity heard anything. I'm sure it took Muñoz a long time to die, and nobody I've talked to heard any screaming. The only thing anybody heard was a dog howling."

"Then you don't think anybody on campus had any kind of connection with the killing?" Charlie asked him.

"Probably not. It's more likely that Muñoz was doing a drug deal down by the lake, and the opposition—whoever it was—caught up with him there. I don't think you're going to need a police escort to take you to and from class, Charlie, if that's what's got you so worried."

"Up yours," Charlie told him.

"Always nice talking with you, little brother," Bob said with a faint smile. Then he glanced at his watch. "Oops," he said. "Running late." He stood up.

"Say hi to Eleanor and the kids for me," Charlie said.

"Right. Stop by once in a while, huh?"

"I'll make a point of it," Charlie promised.

CHAPTER FIVE

I volunteered to drive Twink to Lake Stevens on Friday of that week, since I was free. All my scurrying around to get settled in for fall quarter might have been too efficient. Everything was in place, and I didn't really have anything important left up in the air.

Oddly enough, Friday was all bright and sunny, and I didn't even have to turn on my windshield wipers as Twink and I went north on Interstate 5.

Dr. Fallon spent the customary hour with Twink, and he seemed to be fairly satisfied with her progress. At least he didn't put her in a padded cell.

After the session, Twink and I went back to Everett for dinner with Les and Inga. It seemed to me that those weekly visits might not be a bad idea, and since Twink had to go north every Friday anyway, it fit together smoothly.

The following week *really* dragged on. *I* was ready to start classes, but the university wasn't quite up to it yet. I did a lot of puttering around with my bookshelf project and hit the library several times, but I didn't accomplish much.

The fall quarter began on Monday, September 29th, and I finally had to come face-to-face with John Milton. You don't walk into the Ph.D. exams in English unless you've got graduate seminars in Chaucer, Shakespeare, and Milton under your belt. Shakespeare and I get along fairly well, and Chaucer's a good buddy, but Milton seems a little silly to me. "How soon hath time, the subtle thief of youth, stol'n away my three and twentieth year," seems ridiculous coming from a guy who didn't shave regularly yet. Besides, Milton was wall-to-wall puritan, and puritans set my teeth on edge.

The Milton seminar was one of those early-morning things—seven-thirty to nine-thirty—and the first session was largely taken up with bookkeeping. Full professors generally prefer to ease themselves into harness. After class I drove back to Wallingford to have a word with Twink.

I didn't want to wake Mary, so I went around to the back door and tapped on the window. Renata opened the door, touching one finger to her lips. "She's still asleep, Markie," she whispered.

"No kidding? Gee, the day's half-over."

"Quit trying to be funny. Do you want some coffee?"

"Thanks, Twink, but I've had four cups of Erika's already, and that'll probably keep me wired until about midnight."

"Is her coffee that strong?"

"Industrial-strength. I just came by to tell you that I'll pick you up about twelve-thirty. Our class starts at one-thirty, and that'll give us plenty of time to get there."

"You don't have to do that, Markie. I've got my bike."

"Yes, Twink, I know all about the bike. This is the first day of class, though, and I want to show you exactly where Padelford Hall's located, where my office is, and how to find the classroom. After you've got the lay of the land, you can pedal around in the rain all you want."

"Oh, all right." She sounded peevish about it.

"What *is* your problem, Twink?"

"Everybody's treating me like a baby. I'm a big girl now."

"Save the declaration of independence, Twinkie-poo. I just want to make sure you've got the lay of the land before I turn you loose to roam around campus by yourself."

"Twinkie-poo?" she said. "Are we going back to baby talk?"

"Just kidding, Twink. I know most of the trees on campus by their first names, so I can save you a lot of time by showing you shortcuts and places where the traffic piles up at certain times of day. Let's just call this 'show Twinkie the ropes day.' I'm not trying to insult you or infringe on your constitutional right to get hopelessly lost down in the hard-science zone. Just humor me today, OK?"

"Yes, Master," she said with a vapid expression. "Yes, Master."

"I thought we'd gotten past that stuff, Twink."

"The old ones are the best, aren't they? If you want to baby me, I suppose I can put up with it for a day or so. But don't make a habit of it."

"Oh," I said then, "as long as I'm offending you today anyway, let's get something else off the table. Don't get too carried away with how you dress. The kids here are pretty laid-back when they go to class. Blue jeans and sweatshirts are just about the uniform of the day—every day. You probably wouldn't want to wear fancy clothes in the rain anyway, and it's always raining here in muck and mire city."

"Aww," she said in mock disappointment. "I was going to make a fashion statement."

"Save it for a sunny day, Twink. A lot of freshman girls try that on their first day of class, and they get pretty embarrassed when they find out that they're overdressed."

"What books am I going to need?"

"I'll give you some of mine. I've got lots of spares."

"I can afford to buy my own books, Markie. I've even got my very own checkbook. Les made a big point of that. There's oodles of money in there, and someday I might even be able to make it balance."

"Never turn down freebies, Twink—particularly when you're talking about books. I'll see you about twelve-thirty, then. I'm going back to the boardinghouse now to start rummaging around in *Paradise Lost*, and I'm not looking forward to it very much. I don't think Milton and I are going to get along well at all."

"Aw," she said, patting my cheek, "poor baby."

"Oh, quit," I told her. Then I left and drove back to the boardinghouse to dig into Milton. John-boy irritated me right from the git-go. He was such a show-off. All right, he was gifted, he was intelligent, and he'd been a member of Cromwell's government. Did he have to keep rubbing my face in it? Writing sonnets in Latin is probably the height of exhibitionism, wouldn't you say?

I hung it up about eleven o'clock and went downstairs to slap a sandwich together. Erika was there, brewing another pot of coffee. "Hi, Mark," she greeted me. "Coffee's almost ready."

"Thanks all the same, Erika, but I'm still trying to shake off the four cups I had at breakfast."

"Suit yourself." She was wearing a heavy-looking pair of horn-rimmed glasses that made her look older and more mature. They seemed to complete her. That deep auburn hair and golden skin had made her seem somehow almost unreal to me.

"Are the glasses something new?" I asked her.

"No, they've been around for years. I'm just giving my eyes a rest from the contact lenses."

"Trish says you've got an outside job," I said, rummaging in the refrigerator.

"At a medical lab," she told me. "It's not challenging, but it pays the bills. What *are* you looking for, Mark?"

"Sandwich makings. I've got the munchies."

"Go sit down. I'll fix you something."

"I can take care of it, Erika."

"Sit!" she commanded. "I hate it when people tear up the kitchen. Aunt Grace was too timid to scold the party boys, and the mess they made used to drive me right up the wall."

"James told me that you were living here before your aunt got sick," I said, moving out of her way and sitting down in the breakfast nook.

"I was strapped for cash," she replied. "I'd been working at a lab over near Swedish Hospital, and the headman there was a groper who couldn't keep his hands to himself. I cured him of that, and he fired me."

"Cured?"

"I threw a cup of scalding coffee in his face."

"Ouch," I said.

"He felt pretty much the same way about it," she said with an evil little grin. "Anyway, Aunt Grace had an empty room, and she let me stay here until I got back on my feet." She started putting some sandwiches together. "That's what set off our 'serious student' program. You wouldn't *believe* how noisy it used to be around here. After Aunt Grace had her stroke, I yelled for help, Trish came running, and we clamped down."

"James told me about that when I first found the place," I told her. "He said he backed your decision all the way."

"Oh, yes. And nobody in his right mind crosses James. Truth is, I had to nudge *Trish* to persuade her to put that 'no drinking on the premises' policy into effect. She was a little timid about it."

"Timid? Trish?"

"She was worried about the rent money. That was all that we had to pay Aunt Grace's medical expenses. I told her not to be such a worrywart. I knew that sooner or later we'd get the right kind of people here, and things would turn out OK."

"You're putting a whole new light on things around here, Erika," I said. "I assumed Trish was running the show, but you're the one calling the shots, aren't you?"

"That's been going on since we were kids, Mark. Trish wants people to notice her. I don't need that, so I let *her* stand around giving orders. As long as she gives the orders I want her to give, I don't interfere." She came over and handed me a plate with two fairly bulky sandwiches on it. "Here," she said. "Eat."

"Yes, boss," I said obediently.

She let that pass. "I'll bring you a glass of milk."

"I've sort of outgrown milk, Erika."

"It's good for you," she said. She poured me a glass of milk and brought it to the table.

This girl was going to take some getting used to, that much was certain.

After I'd finished eating, I went back to Mary's place to pick up Twink. I was fairly sure that Mary was still asleep, so I went around to the back door again to avoid waking her.

Twink was waiting for me, and she had one of those black plastic raincoats that always seem to make a lot of noise. They keep the rain off well enough, I guess, but they crackle with every move.

"Did you bring my books?" she asked.

"We'll pick them up at my office," I told her. "I don't keep my spares on my own bookshelves. They take up too much room. Let's hit the bricks, Twink. I want to get in and out of my little clothes-closet office before the suck-ups get there and go into the usual feeding frenzy."

"Suck-ups?" she asked.

"The ingratiators. The second-rate students who swindled their way through high school by laughing at the tired jokes of third-rate teachers, and the personality kids who'd *really* like to be my friend so that they can smile the C-minus they'll earn up to a B-plus."

"You're in a foul humor," she accused, as we went out to my car.

"It'll pass, Twink," I told her. "I always come down with the grouchies on the first day of classes. I know for an absolute fact that I'm going to come up against a solid wall of ineptitude, and it depresses the hell out of me."

"Poor, poor Markie. You can cry on my shoulder, if you want. Maybe if I mommy all over you, it'll make you feel better."

I laughed—I don't think I'd ever heard "mommy" used as a verb before. "When did you get mommified, Twink?" I took it one step further.

"Probably while I was in the bughouse," she replied. "Dockie-poo Fallon always prescribed mommification—or daddyfication—when one of the bugsies went brain-dead. He'd either mommify us or embalm us with Prozac. And believe me, if you really wanted to, you could probably calm a volcano down with Prozac."

We clowned around all the way to the campus, and I realized as I pulled into the Padelford parking garage that Twink had banished my grumpies. I was supposed to be taking care of *her*, but she'd neatly turned the tables.

"Where do you want me to sit when I go into your classroom, Markie?" she asked me when we climbed out of the Dodge. "Since I'm not a real student yet, am I supposed to hide under a desk or something?"

"Pick anyplace you want, Twink. The other people in the class won't know that you're only auditing, and I wouldn't make an issue of it. Just blend in."

"What am I supposed to call you?"

"Mr. Austin, probably. That's what the others are going to call me. Let's keep the fact that we know each other more or less under wraps—the other kids don't need to know. Doc Fallon says that you're here to get to know more people— 'broaden your acquaintanceship,' he calls it. I may not altogether agree, but let's play it his way for now. I'll give you some time for the after-class chatter before we go back home. Try to keep it down to about a half hour. Oh, don't get all bent out of shape about some of the things I'll say today, OK? It's a little canned speech I picked up from Dr. Conrad. It's called 'thinning the herd.' My life's a lot easier if I can scare the incompetents enough to make them go pester somebody else."

"You're a mean person, Markie."

"God knows I try."

Inside the building, I showed Twink where my office was, gave her the books she'd need, and led the way to the classroom. "Hang around out here in the hallway until the place starts to fill up," I advised. "Then drift in with the rest. Don't sit up front, but don't try to hide at the back of the room, either—that's where the hopeless cases usually are. Try to blend in as much as possible."

"You sound like a bad spy novel," she accused. "Next you'll be talking about code words, disguises, and invisible ink."

"Maybe I *am* being a little obvious," I admitted.

"*Real* obvious. I'm a big girl, and I know all about blending into the scenery."

"OK. Today's class won't be too long. We'll do the book-keeping, I'll deliver my speech, and then I'll split before anybody can pin me to the wall. You mingle a bit, then go back out to the garage. I'll be in the car."

"Why not wait in your office?"

"Because I don't want to spend the rest of the day here. The suck-ups will home in on that place like a pack of wolves. Are you going to be OK here?"

"I'm fine, Markie. Quit worrying."

"OK, I'll see you after class, then."

I went back to the garage to gather up the official-looking junk I had in the backseat, then I ran over my canned speech to make sure I'd hit all the high points. The first class session sets the tone for the rest of the quarter, so I wanted to be sure I had it right.

I kept a close eye on my watch and hit the classroom door at precisely one-thirty. I went directly to the desk, opened my briefcase, and took out the stack of papers I kept in there. Then I faced this year's crop of freshmen. "Good afternoon, ladies and gentlemen," I said briskly. "This is section BR of English 131, Expository Writing. My name is Austin, and I'll be your instructor. Please pass your enrollment cards to the left, and I'll distribute the course syllabus when I pick them up."

There was the usual stirring around while they tried to find the enrollment cards among all the other papers they'd been given on sign-up day.

"Quickly, quickly," I nudged them. "We've only got an hour, and we've got other fish to fry."

It didn't do any good; it never does. It still took them the usual ten minutes or so to get the cards to the end of each row. Then I gathered the cards and distributed the course descriptions.

"All right, then," I said after that was finished, "Let's begin. For most of you, this is your first day of college. You'll find that things here are quite a bit different from what you've been accustomed to. You're adults now, and we expect more from you. You're here to study and to learn. You're not here to occupy space; you're here to work. If you don't work, you'll fail, and then you'll get to do it all over again. This is a required course, and you won't get your degree until you've managed to get a passing grade from me or from one of my colleagues. Our goal is to teach you how to write papers that your professors can understand. Writing was invented several thousand years ago as a way to pass information back and forth between humans. Since most of you are human, it's a fairly important skill." I paused and looked around. "Non-humans, naturally, aren't required to take this course, so all nonhumans are excused."

It got the same laugh it always got. It was a silly thing to say, but a few laughs never hurt.

"Would you define 'human' for us, Mr. Austin?" a young fellow near the front of the room asked.

"You'll have to take that up with the folks in anthropology," I told him. "I operate on the theory that anybody whose knuckles don't drag on the ground when he walks is probably human. But we digress. As students, you'll need to communicate with your professors in a way slightly more advanced than grunts and whistles. That's why you're here. I'm supposed to teach you how to write, so we're going to write—at least *you* are—and you're going to start now. Your first assignment is a five-hundred-word essay, and just for old times' sake, why don't you take a run at the ever-popular 'How I Spent My Summer Vacation'? Since you've all probably been working on *that* old turkey since about the fifth grade, you should have a head start on it. You'll be graded on grammar, spelling, punctuation, and thought content. It's due on Wednesday, so you'd better buckle down."

There were sounds of serious discontent.

"Hey, gang," I said, "if that makes you unhappy, the door's right over there. You can walk out anytime you want."

There was the customary shocked silence when I dropped *that* on them. Teachers at the high-school level almost never invite their students to leave.

"I'm not your friend, people," I told them bluntly. "I'm not here to make you happy. If your papers aren't up to standard, you'll get to do them over again—and again—and again. You'll keep doing them over until you get them right, and that won't alter the fact that you'll be writing other papers as well, and you'll probably be rewriting those also. Things will definitely start to back up on you after a while if you keep turning in tripe."

"How much credit for class participation, Mr. Austin?" the young fellow who'd asked for a definition of *human* asked in a slightly worried tone. I get that question every quarter—usually from speech majors who'd sooner die than actually put something down on paper.

I shrugged. "None. You're here to write, not to talk. If you want to say something to me, write it down. Then type it, because I won't accept handwritten papers. Use pica type and standard margins. You might want to pick up a copy of the MLA style sheet. That's the final word on academic style."

I saw the usual look of blank incomprehension. "The Modern Language Association," I translated. "Try to write complete sentences; incomplete ones irritate me. Oh, one other thing. You'll encounter people out there who'll try to sell you papers. Don't waste your money. I've already seen most of them, so I'll recognize them. If you try to foist a secondhand paper off on me, you'll be taking this course over again, because I'll flunk you right on the spot. You should probably know that my flunk rate doesn't even come close to the bell curve. If I happen to get an entire class of incompetents, I'll flunk the whole bunch. Now, then, if you want to drop the course or change instructors, go to the Registrar's Office. Don't pester me with your problems."

I let that soak in just a bit. "Any questions?" I asked.

There was a sullen silence, and I was fairly sure that my deliberate mention of the registrar was ringing a few bells.

I looked around. "Not a word?" I asked mildly. "Not even a few whimpers? Aw, shucky-darn."

There was a nervous laugh. Evidently I'd gotten through to most of them. "You seem to have grasped my basic point, then," I told them. "The policy here is 'my house; my rules.' As long as you remember that, we'll get along fine. Class dismissed." I scooped up the enrollment cards, stowed them in my briefcase, and was out the door before any of the suck-up crowd could get in my way. A strategy of abruptitude works quite well when you want to make a clean getaway during those early sessions. Shock and run cuts the sniveling short; linger-longering just encourages it.

I went out to the garage, unlocked my car, and leafed through the enrollment cards to take a body count. There were too many, of course. There always are. My unfriendly speech in the classroom had been designed to correct that. Academic terrorism does have its uses, I guess.

I read some more of *Paradise Lost* while I waited for Twink, and after about a half hour she showed up. "You weren't really serious about all that grumpy stuff, were you, Markie?" she asked as she climbed in.

"Pretty much, yes. Did it hurt their feelings?"

"They were awfully pouty about it. They all agreed that a writing assignment on the first day of class was a violation of their constitutional rights or something."

"Gee, what a shame."

"You're terrible, Markie," she said with a wicked little giggle. "When we were coming down here you were saying something about a canned speech. Do you unload like that o~ every class you teach?"

I nodded as I started the car. "Yep—and it works. I've even made the P.E. Department's blacklist."

"That went by a little fast."

"Physical education involves the big, strong, dumb kids who make up the assorted teams that wear purple uniforms and try to whup the teams from California. The coaches of those teams have a list of names they hand out to their tame dummies. It's the 'Don't take no classes from these guys' list. It's an honor to have your name on that document."

"I'm so proud of you," she gushed, as we pulled out of the parking garage.

"Steady on, Twink."

"Some of the names your students were calling you were naughty."

"Good. I got their attention, then."

"The smart-mouth who asked you to define 'human' was even trying to put a petition together to lodge a protest with the administration about how mean you were. Not too many people were interested in signing it, though. Quite a few of them said they were just going to drop your class."

"Good. That's the whole idea. What you saw today was part of an academic game, Twink. The university administration tries to get a lot of mileage out of the teaching assistants by cramming as many freshmen as possible into those class-rooms. Some teaching assistants are softies who yearn for the approval of their students. I'm tough, and I don't make any secret of it. After the first week or so, I've usually weeded out the dum-dums, so *I've* got the cream of the crop, and my warm, fuzzy associates get the garbage. *My* students probably don't even need me, since they can already write papers that'll cut glass from a mile away. The warm-fuzzies get the semiliter-ates who couldn't find their way from one end of a sentence to the other if their lives depended on it. I picked up the business of academic terrorism from Dr. Conrad. Just the mention of his name scares people into convulsions." While we talked, I hooked into Forty-fifth Street to get us back to Wallingford.

"I think you're going to *love* my paper, Markie," Twink bubbled at me.

"You're just auditing the course, Twink, remember? Why write a paper if you don't have to?"

"I *want* to write one, Markie. I'm going to blow your socks off."

"Why? You won't get a grade out of it."

"I'm going to prove something, big brother. Don't start throwing challenges around unless you're ready to back them up. I can whup you any day in the week." She paused briefly. "It's your own fault, Markie. Sometimes I get competitive— particularly when somebody challenges me. You said you wanted a good paper. Well, you're going to get one, and you won't even have to grade it. Isn't that neat?"

That took me completely by surprise. Renata hadn't been quite that aggressive before—neither of the twins had. I'd known that they were clever, certainly, but they'd never flaunted it. Of course, Renata was older now, and the time she'd spent in Dr. Fallon's institution had probably matured her quite a ways past her contemporaries. The average college freshman comes to us carrying a lot of baggage from high school. High-schoolies are herd animals for the most part, and they're usually deathly afraid of standing out from the crowd. Once they move up to college, the brighter ones tend to separate themselves from the herd and strike out on their own. It usually takes them a year or so, though. Renata, it appeared, had jumped over that transition, and she'd come down running.

I definitely approved of this new Renata, and I was fairly sure Dr. Fallon would as well. This was turning out better than either of us had expected.

After I'd dropped Twink at Mary's place, I went back to campus to continue my examination of the connection between Whitman and the Brits. I hung it up just before five o'clock and actually got home in time for dinner.

"I'm supposed to tell you that Charlie's going to be late, Trish," James rumbled, as we gathered in the dining room. "I guess that something came up at Boeing, and the head of the program Charlie's involved with called an emergency meeting."

"That sounds ominous," Erika said. "When Boeing starts calling emergency meetings, it suggests that we might all need to go find bomb shelters."

"He wasn't too specific," James added, "but I got the impression that something fell apart because some resident genius at Boeing neglected to convert inches to centimeters on a set of fairly significant specifications. Charlie was using some *very* colorful language when he left."

"That *might* just make it difficult to hit what you're shooting at," I noted. "A millimeter here and a millimeter there would add up after a while."

"Particularly if you're taking potshots at something in the asteroid belt," James agreed.

"Have you got anything serious on the fire this evening, Sylvia?" I asked our resident psychologist.

"Is your head starting to come unraveled, Mark?"

"I hope not. I'd like to get your reading on something that happened today, is all."

"Whip it on me," she replied.

I let that pass. "The Twinkie twin I was talking about did something a little out of character today. Evidently, she's not quite as fragile as we all thought she was. She seems to be breaking out in a rash of independence. She even gets offended if I offer to drive her anyplace because she's got that ten-speed bicycle. Rain or shine, she wants to bike it."

"That's probably a reaction to the time she spent in the sanitarium, Mark. People in institutions usually aren't allowed to make many decisions."

"Rebellion, then?"

"Self-assertion might come a little closer," Sylvia replied. "In a general way, we approve of that—as long as it doesn't go *too* far. Could you be more specific? Exactly what did she do today that seemed unusual?"

"Well, she's auditing a course I teach—freshman English—basically pretending to be a student to get the feel of the place."

"Interesting notion," Erika said. "All you're really doing is moving her from one institution to a different one."

"Approximately, yes," I agreed. "Well, I assigned a paper today. She knows she doesn't have to write one, but she says she's going to do one anyway, and then she promised me that it'd be so good that it'll blow me away."

"You assign a paper on the first day of class?" Trish demanded incredulously. "You're a monster!"

"Just weeding out the garden, Trish," I told her. "It's the best way I know of to scare off the party people. Evidently, Renata took the assignment as a challenge, and now she's going to jump on it with both feet."

"She's making a pass at you, Mark," Erika said bluntly. "She wants to write her way into your heart."

"Get real," I said. "There's none of that going on."

"I wouldn't be so sure, Mark," Sylvia said thoughtfully. "It's not uncommon for a psychiatric patient to have those kinds of feelings for the therapist."

"I'm *not* Twink's therapist, Sylvia," I objected.

"Oh, really? You worry about her all the time, you do everything you possibly can to make her life easier, and you get all nervous if she does anything the least bit out of the ordinary. You're trying everything you can think of to make her get well. In my book, that makes you her therapist."

"I think you might be missing something, Sylvia," James said thoughtfully.

"Oh?"

"Mark's been a brother figure for Renata since she was a baby, and he's the only person she recognized when her mind woke up. Isn't it possible that this 'I'll write a paper that'll blow you away' announcement is an effort to gain Mark's approval?"

"He's a father figure, you mean?"

"Something along those lines, I suppose," he rumbled.

"Thanks a bunch, gang," I said sarcastically. "Now we've got a toss-up. Is she aggressively showing off, or is she just yearning for approval?"

"It amounts to the same thing, doesn't it?" Erika suggested.

"I've *got* to meet this girl, Mark," Sylvia said. "For right now, though, maybe you'd better talk with Dr. Fallon about it. He knows her, so he'll probably have some idea of what's *really* going on. It might not be anything very significant, but on the other hand . . ." She left it hanging.

I began to wish I'd kept my mouth shut. Twink was *my* problem, but now I'd opened a door that maybe I should have left closed. My housemates all seemed very interested in Renata's behavior, and I wasn't sure I wanted them to start muddying things up.

On the other hand, I didn't really have any idea of what was going on in Twink's mind, and maybe one of the inmates here could come up with a clue. At this point, I'd take all the help I could get.

CHAPTER SIX

I didn't sleep very well that night, and when I finally drifted off, I had some peculiar dreams involving Milton, Whitman, and Twinkie. For some reason, they were all ganging up on me, and the green chain kept turning up to complicate things all the more.

Anyway, I was a little foggy when I stumbled downstairs the next morning. James, Charlie, and the bathrobe brigade were clustered around the small television set on the kitchen counter, watching and listening intently.

"What's up?" I asked, homing in on the coffeemaker.

"A small-time hood got himself wasted last night," Charlie replied. "The TV reporters say it's a rerun of the Muñoz killing a couple weeks ago."

"Another one of those carve-up jobs?" I asked, pouring myself a cup of Erika's coffee.

"Was it ever," Charlie said. "Some of the reporters looked green around the gills. I guess there were body parts and guts all over the place."

Trish made a gagging sound. "Do you *mind*?" she snapped at Charlie.

"Sorry, babe," he apologized. "Anyway, this one was even closer to home than the Muñoz killing. They found the carcass along the shore of Green Lake in Woodland Park, only about a mile from here."

"Evidently the killing was close enough to the zoo to upset the animals," James added. "A couple of reporters mentioned that earlier. I guess everybody who lives in the vicinity heard lions roaring, elephants trumpeting, and the wolves howling up a storm. Somebody put in an emergency call to the zookeepers, and it was one of them who found the body and called the police."

"Anyway," Charlie continued, "the cops and the reporters are all sagely stroking their beards and announcing that there might just possibly be some connection between this murder and that one two weeks ago down on campus. Isn't that astounding? Two guys get gutted out in the same part of town within a couple of weeks, and the cops suggest that there *might* be a connection? Well, goll-*lee* gee!"

"Quit trying to be such a clown, Charlie," Sylvia scolded.

"People who announce the obvious with a straight face always bring out the worst in me," Charlie replied. "These reporters are all trying to look grim and serious while they go on and on about a 'serial killer,' but there's nothing like a few messy murders to fill up the blanks in the day's news."

"They've already come up with a name that I'm sure we'll have to listen to over and over for the next month or two," Trish told me. "They're talking about 'the Seattle Slasher' as if it's something of international significance instead of a turf war between a couple of rival gangs. You know how reporters can be."

"Oh, yes," I agreed. "I'm waiting for the day when one of the weather guys has a grand mal seizure—on camera—because there's a fifty percent chance of rain tomorrow. Was this latest dead guy another Chicano dope dealer?"

"Not with a name like Lloyd Andrews, he wasn't," she replied. "He seems to have had a fairly extensive police record, though, and drugs were involved in a few of his arrests—along with the usual low crimes and misdemeanors."

"He was a small-timer," Charlie added. "He might have sold a bag of crack once in a while, but he bought more than he sold. It looks to me as if he was one of those poor bastards who never did anything right. If he tried to steal a car, the tires would all go flat. If he thought some chickie had the hots for him, he'd get busted for attempted rape. If he planned a burglary, he'd pick the one house on the block with an alarm system. He was the sort of guy who gives crime a bad name. He definitely wasn't in the same class with Muñoz—which pretty much shoots old Lieutenant Burpee's theory full of holes. Cheetah doesn't dirty his hands on small-timers. He goes after the big boys."

Trish glanced over at the kitchen clock. "Oops," she said, "we're starting to run behind, girls. We'd better whip up some breakfast, or our boys will start wasting away."

The three of them bustled around, getting things ready. "Go watch the set in the living room," Erika commanded, pointing toward the front of the house. "Get out from underfoot while we're working."

"Yes, ma'am," James rumbled. "Shall we adjourn to the parlor, gentlemen?"

The three of us went through the dining room to the silent front of the house. James turned on the smeary old television set, and we all sat down to watch.

"—murders are only the latest in a long string of serial killings here in the Northwest," a reporter was sententiously reminding us. "The authorities are still searching for clues to the identity of the Green River killer, and this region was Ted Bundy's starting place. The Seattle Slasher, however, appears to be seeking male victims—at least so far."

"We might want to keep waving that in front of the ladies," James suggested. "They're a little nervous about murders in our own backyard—understandably, since there's somebody out there with a sharp knife."

"We might want to give some thought to the convoy principle," I added. "Maybe tack on a new house rule: 'Nobody goes out alone after dark,' or something along those lines—at least until this quiets down, or the Slasher wastes somebody in Olympia or Bellingham."

"Makes sense," Charlie agreed. "I don't think they're in

any real danger—those two killings seem to be gang stuff—
but maybe we ought to get real protective until the TV guys
find something else to babble about. Maybe they can go
back to blubbering over Princess Diana. 'Pavane for a Dead
Princess' is a nice piece of music, but it gets old after you've
heard it forty or fifty times. The funny thing about that story
is that the 'media' keeps trying to gloss over its own responsibility for that car crash. If they hadn't declared open season
on Princess Di, the vultures with cheap cameras wouldn't
have been chasing her."

"How did your emergency meeting turn out last night,
Charlie?" I asked him. "James told us some half-wit got inches
and centimeters mixed up?"

"He sure did. Engineering's in the clear, though. The draw-
ings clearly specified centimeters. It was a buyer who dropped
the ball, not us. Dear old Boing-Boing just spent a million
bucks of taxpayer money on a component that won't fit because some lamebrain in purchasing never heard of the
metric system. We'll hand it off to accounting, and they'll
juggle the books for us and smooth it over. Their jaws were a
little tight about it, though. The balanced budget crowd's
tightening the screws on the Defense Department, so we
don't have the keys to Fort Knox the way we used to."

"Aw," I said in mock sympathy, "poor babies."

"Come on, Mark. Look at all the wonderful things the defense industry's given us—the H-bomb, the neutron bomb,
nerve gas, smart bombs, laser sights, and all those cute little
bacteria that give people diseases nobody's ever heard of
before—'bubonic leprosy,' 'tuberculanthrax,' and 'the seven-
century itch.' How could we possibly get along without stuff
like that?"

"I don't know," I replied. "It might be nice to try it and find
out, though."

After breakfast, we scattered to the winds again. We hadn't
yet encountered each other down on the campus, since the

various disciplines were pretty well segregated. I don't think an antisegregation policy would ever float on a university campus. The races and sexes may be desegregated, but the disciplines? Never happen.

I fought with Milton all morning, concentrating on his "Areopagitica." Milton was a Puritan down to his toenails, and censorship lies at the soul of the Puritan ethic. So why does Johnny Milton tell us to print any damn thing we want to, and let it stand or fall all by itself?

Then Twink didn't show up for my one-thirty class, and I got concerned. Maybe she was having second thoughts about all her blustering and show-offery following the Monday class. That promise to blow me away *had* been a bit on the arrogant side; maybe now she was too embarrassed to look me in the face.

That option wasn't really open to her, though. Whether she liked it or not, Twink and I *were* going to spend this quarter in lockstep. I'd made promises, and I was going to keep them. When it became obvious that she wasn't just late for class, I decided that I'd thrash this out with her. If she didn't like it, well, tough noogies.

My class of freshmen was seriously diminished now. My canned speech on opening day had significantly thinned out the herd. Now it was time for the second canned speech, which had to do with reading critically, rather than accepting everything that shows up in print as if Moses had handed it down from Mount Sinai. I dove into my variation of "It ain't necessarily so," which might have gone over a little better if anybody in the class had ever heard of *Porgy and Bess*. Then I opened the door to formal logic. They got a bit wild-eyed when I mentioned the *"Post hoc, ergo propter hoc"* fallacy. There *were* a couple in the class who showed a few faint glimmers of grasping my point, and that's always encouraging. Trying to teach a classroom of wall-to-wall dum-dums can be terribly depressing.

Before we adjourned, I pointedly reminded them that their

"How I Spent My Summer Vacation" papers were due the next day. I was fairly sure *that* would clear away the rest of the goof-offs and only leave the good ones. That was the whole idea behind my "Professor Grouchy" act.

Mary was still in her bathrobe when she answered my knock, and she was looking a little frazzled.

"Where's Renata?" I asked. "She didn't make it to class today."

"She had another bad night, Mark," Mary replied. "These nightmares of hers are starting to worry me. She was shaking like a leaf in a windstorm when I came home from work. If this doesn't clear up, she might have to go back to Lake Stevens for a bit."

"It can't be *that* bad!"

"It's not good. I zonked her out with another sleeping pill, but I don't want to make a habit of that."

"Maybe I'd better call Doc Fallon," I said. "I've been trying to keep the pressure off Twink, but I might be doing something wrong. If nothing else, maybe he can prescribe a tranquilizer to unwind her spring a little."

"Tranks are only about one step away from heroin, Mark," she cautioned. "Let's not go down *that* road if we don't have to."

"Let's see what Fallon has to say. We can *hope* that this is just something temporary that'll pass once Twink gets used to the university. Guess I'd better stay here tonight when you go to work at the cop shop."

"That won't be necessary, Mark," she told me. "This is my day off, remember?"

"That's right, isn't it? I must have spaced it out." I looked at her a little more carefully. "You look awful, Mary," I told her bluntly.

"Up yours!" she flared at me.

"What I meant was that you're looking almost dead on your feet. You haven't been to bed yet, have you?"

"I dozed on the couch a bit. It's a good thing that I don't have to go to work tonight. Sleeping on the job's an official no-no."

"Was Twink doing anything unusual before you went to work last night?"

"She said she was writing a paper for your class—though I don't know how she could concentrate. She had the volume on her tape player turned way up."

"Kiddie music?"

"Not unless the kids have changed a lot here lately. It sounded like some woman singing to a pack of wolves."

"Oh, *that* tape. She's hooked on that one. It was mixed in with that box of tapes and discs I brought down from Everett."

"What's it called?"

"Who knows? One of the twins taped it off another tape— or maybe a CD—and forgot to label it. Twink gets kind of spacey when she listens to it." Then I snapped my fingers. "Now that I think back, she was listening to it on the evening before her *last* visit to nightmare alley."

"Maybe we ought to root around and find it—and then accidentally lose it or something. If that's what's causing these nightmares of hers, she doesn't need to have it floating around where she can get her hands on it."

"I'll take it up with Fallon when I talk with him. There are all sorts of possibilities kicking around. Both times happened on a Monday, so maybe it's Monday that sends her up the wall—or something else. Let's see what Fallon has to say before we lock anything in cement."

"That might be best," she agreed.

"Try to get some sleep, huh?"

"Sure, kid."

When I got home I dug out Dr. Fallon's phone number and punched it into the phone in the living room.

"Hey, Doc," I said when he came on the line, "this is Mark

Austin. Renata's been having some problems with nightmares. They must be moderately awful, because they've pretty much put her out of action."

"It's not uncommon, Mark. Outpatients are frequently troubled with nightmares."

"Could you write her a prescription for some kind of tranquilizer? Her aunt's been zonking her with sleeping pills, but I wanted to check with you before it went much further."

"What kind of sleeping pills?" His voice was a bit sharp.

"Hell, I don't know, Doc."

"Over-the-counter, or prescription?"

"Prescription, I think."

He started to swear.

"I take it you don't care for the idea."

"Sleeping pills are the *last* thing Renata needs right now, Mark. The basic ingredient in prescription sleeping pills is a barbiturate, and nightmares are one of the symptoms of a withdrawal from barbiturates."

"They're addictive?"

"Obviously. We have to use them on inpatients here sometimes, but we control the dosage, and we always bring the patient down very slowly. A short siege of withdrawal from barbiturates can throw years of therapy out the window. You're not supposed to be passing the damn things around like popcorn."

A cold certainty suddenly came over me. "You had Twink all spaced out on sleeping pills as soon as she arrived there, didn't you, Doc?"

"It's routine. A psychotic patient has to be stabilized before we can start any kind of therapy. *We* control the dosage, though, and we keep barbiturates locked up as tightly as opiates. If Renata's aunt leaves them lying around the house, God knows how many Renata's been popping on the sly."

"She wouldn't do that, Doc."

"Don't kid yourself. Does the term 'junkie' ring any bells for you, Mark?"

"They're *that* bad?"

"At least that bad—particularly when you're dealing with a psychotic."

"Psychotic? Come on, Doc. Renata's a little spacey sometimes, but she's hardly a raving lunatic."

"Oh, really? She comes through the door speaking a language only she can understand, and when she finally becomes coherent, she doesn't even know her own name. If that's not psychotic, it'll do until the real thing comes along. You tell her aunt to lock those damned pills away somewhere Renata doesn't know about. Let's not leave temptation lying around in the open. How's she doing otherwise?"

"It's a little early to tell. This is only the first week of class."

"Maybe that's what's bringing on these nightmares."

"Hell, Doc, she's taking to this like a duck takes to water. She's only auditing my class, but she's already writing papers that she doesn't have to. That's one of the things I wanted to talk to you about. Plus she gets belligerent every time I offer to give her a lift. She wants to ride that ten-speed of hers no matter what the weather's doing. I was talking it over with my housemates last night, and one of them's majoring in abnormal psychology. She thought this sudden outbreak of independence has to do with the time Renata spent at your place. Since a mental patient's life is pretty tightly controlled, Sylvia thinks that Renata might be going through a little spell of self-assertion to get the taste of that out of her mouth."

"That might come very close. Your friend there at the house might be useful. Has she met Renata yet?"

"Not so far, but she wants to, and the others are interested as well. We're all grad students, though, so we sort of outrank Twinkie. I don't want to intimidate her."

"Is your group aware of Renata's situation?"

"In a general way. I gave them a bare-bones synopsis of what Twink's been through."

"Maybe I'd better have a talk with the one in abnormal psych—Sylvia, did you say? You're personally involved with

Renata, and this Sylvia can probably be more objective, notice things that you'll miss. Why don't you have her call me?" He seemed to hesitate. "Are there any relationships floating around in your group that I should know about?"

"That's against the rules, Doc. I'm fond of Sylvia, but there's none of that involved. She's an Italian girl and sort of excitable, but she *is* sharp."

"Ask her to call me," he said again.

"Will do. She knows your reputation, so she might be a little gushy right at first, but she'll settle down. Meanwhile, I've got to hit the books, Doc."

"Learn lots," he told me in an amused sort of way.

After supper that evening, Charlie suggested that the guys might want to visit the Green Lantern to get the real story on the Woodland Park incident from his brother. James begged off, though. He was digging into Hegel's "thesis, antithesis, and synthesis" theory, and it was making him a little grumpy.

Charlie's brother was sitting at the bar nursing a beer and sourly watching the local TV reporter desperately trying to ride the "Seattle Slasher" story into the big leagues.

"Don't you get enough of that crap at work?" Charlie asked him.

"It's the bartender's set, Charlie," Bob replied, "and he's the one who runs the controls. The whole town's going wild about this 'Slasher' business. Do you want to call Mom? She's been trying to get hold of you for the past week."

"She's OK, isn't she?"

"She worries, Charlie. Mothers are like that—particularly when one of the puppies forgets to touch base every now and then."

"I've been pretty busy, Bob."

"Don't blow smoke in my nose, kid. It'll only take you five minutes. Do it. Get her off my case."

"All right, don't tie your tail in a knot, I'll call her. What's the skinny on this latest rubout?"

"Are you changing your major? Are we yearning to become a TV personality now?"

"Get real, Bob. You couldn't pay me to take a job like that. Everybody makes a jackass of himself once in a while, but those people do it on camera. No, we've got three ladies at the boardinghouse, and all this 'Seattle Slasher' stuff's starting to make them jumpy. If Mark and I can get the straight scoop on what's going on, maybe we can calm 'em down."

Bob looked around. "Let's grab a booth," he suggested. "We're not supposed to talk about these things in public."

We adjourned to one of the back booths, and Charlie and I each ordered a beer.

"If the ladies in your boardinghouse are really spooked about this 'Slasher' crap, your best bet would be to arm them with some of those little spray cans of Mace—or maybe pepper-spray," Bob told us. "If you squirt a guy in the face with one of those, it puts him out of action immediately."

"We hadn't thought of that," I admitted. "Where could we pick up stuff like that?"

"Any gun store should have it," he said. "I could swipe some for you, but our cans are bulky. The ones they make for ladies are usually attached to a key ring."

"Convenient. I'll look into it."

"They'll probably never have to use them, but just having them handy should give them a sense of security."

"So, what's really happening out there, Bob?" Charlie asked. "All we're getting from TV is a bunch of dog doo-doo."

"You didn't really expect the truth from a TV set, did you, Charlie? Television's entertainment, not truth. OK, about all we've got to go on so far are the similarities between this murder and the one on campus two weeks ago. We've got two semiprofessional criminals who got themselves cut to pieces in a parklike area late at night. Muñoz was a real pro, but this Andrews guy was more of a wanna-be. Andrews *did* have some gang connections here in north Seattle, but I don't think he actually qualified as a member. Lieutenant Burpee's trying to persuade himself that Andrews was more important than his record seems to indicate, but it won't float. I busted Andrews myself last year, and he didn't even come close to Muñoz. He had a day job pumping gas at a filling station, so it's obvious that his criminal activities weren't paying the rent. He was a small-time hanger-on who just happened to be in the wrong place at the wrong time."

"Are we saying that this 'Seattle Slasher' stuff doesn't float?" Charlie demanded.

"I'm not convinced yet," Bob replied. "It's possible we're looking at 'trademark' killings."

"I don't follow you," I admitted.

"It comes along every so often," Bob explained. "If you've got a gang out there that wants to put up 'no trespassing' signs on its own personal, private turf, chopping assorted rival gang members into mincemeat would probably get the point across in a hurry. These two killings *might* be the work of a single hit man, or it *could* be a new standard operating procedure. There's no *real* reason to keep on carving on the carcass after the guy's dead, is there?"

"Then you think it might just be some sort of advertising gimmick?" Charlie suggested. "Like 'look what's going to happen if we catch you poaching'? Is that what you're saying?"

"It's a possibility. There's no other connection between Andrews and Muñoz that we've been able to find."

"Then Burpee's theory about Cheetah might hold water after all," Charlie suggested.

Bob shook his head. "This isn't Cheetah's part of town. He's strictly a downtown boy. Far as he's concerned, north Seattle's a foreign country. I doubt he even knows how to get to Woodland Park, and if he went there, the trees and grass would spook hell out of him. He comes from a world of cement and telephone poles. What it boils down to is that we don't have enough to work with yet. Maybe after three or four more of these murders, we'll have a better idea of who we're dealing with, but for right now, everything's still up in the air."

"You're expecting more, then?" I asked.

"Isn't everybody? The whole damn town's holding its breath in anticipation." Bob looked at his watch. "I've got to run," he told us. "Call Mom, Charlie. Do it tonight, before you forget."

"I'll get right on it, Bob," Charlie promised.

"*Sure* you will," Bob said sarcastically. Then he turned and left the tavern.

"What do you think, Mark?" Charlie said. "Should we sound the all clear for the girls?"

"I don't think so. We don't know enough to start taking chances now. Let's stay close to the ladies until this guy moves on."

"*If* he moves on."

"If he doesn't, we'll just have to rearrange some things. Meanwhile, I'll hit a gun store and pick up some of those pepper spray key rings."

"Good idea." Then he shrugged. "It's all part of the fun of civilization, I guess."

"Did you want to take a run at 'solitary, poor, nasty, brutish and short,' sport?"

" 'Nasty' and 'brutish' maybe." He drained off his beer. "Let's hit the bricks, Mark. I've got work piling up back home."

CHAPTER SEVEN

I was a little foggy during my Milton seminar on Wednesday morning. I don't function too well that early anyway, and our lecture focused on the religious turmoil during the seventeenth century. Religious squabbles seem to send people off the deep end, and the announcement by some enthusiast that "my God's better than your God," almost inevitably sets off yet another war.

I stopped by a gun store after class and bought three of those pepper spray key rings Bob West had recommended. The little cartridge didn't look very big, but it probably carried enough to disable a single attacker. Our ladies weren't likely to need something for crowd control.

Then I went back to Wallingford to consider my options on my end-of-term Milton paper. I discarded the notion of a comparison of the early books of *Paradise Lost* to Dante's *Inferno* almost immediately. The geography and politics of Hell didn't thrill me very much. Maybe my best course would be to steer completely clear of *Paradise Lost* and concentrate on Milton's prose works.

Just after noon, I made myself a couple of sandwiches to tide me over until suppertime. Sometimes I think lunch is more a habit than a necessity. We don't really *need* to eat three meals a day—particularly when we aren't involved in physical labor. Eating when you don't really need to eat tends to make you roly-poly, and it's rapidly reaching the point where it's easier to jump over the average American than it is to walk around him. Dieting is now a major American industry, but a universal "let's skip lunch" attitude would put Weight Watchers out of business.

But I make a mighty fine sandwich, if I do say so myself.

I finished eating and glanced at my watch. It was almost twelve-thirty, and I decided to call Mary. It was raining again, and I thought I'd better find out if Twink was up and moving. If she was coming to class today, she'd need a ride.

"She left about ten minutes ago," Mary told me. "She said she wanted to bike it."

"It's raining, for Chrissake!"

"She's got a raincoat, Mark. Don't get all worked up."

"Did she get over whatever it was that knocked her out yesterday?"

"She's fine—all bright and bubbly. Everybody gets the blues now and then, but Renata bounces right back. I think it's a good sign, don't you?"

"We can hope so. Oh, I talked with Fallon about those sleeping pills. He sort of flipped out about it. I guess Twinkie was pretty well hooked on them in the sanitarium. They brought her down easy, but you might want to hide the ones you've got from her. Fallon thinks she might be a secret sleeping-pill junkie or something like that."

"That's ridiculous!"

"I'm just passing on what he said."

"Tell him to get stuffed. I know exactly what I'm doing. The only time I hit her with one of those pills is when she starts going around the bend, and that doesn't happen often enough for her to get hooked."

"Glad to hear it. Listen, I'd better get going," I told her. "It's time to teach up the young again."

"She'll be in your class today. Quit worrying so much."

"Yes, ma'am."

*   *   *

Once I got to Padelford, I checked my mailbox. As I'd expected, there were quite a few dropout cards. I went to my little clothes-closet office and quickly revised my class list. It was definitely getting closer to target. About one more heavy belt would bring it down to a reasonable size.

I hit the classroom door at exactly one-thirty. Since I was going to make a big issue of doing things on time, I thought it might be best to set a good example.

Twink was sitting near the center of the room, and she had a smug smile on her face. I took the roll and called in their papers.

"Now then, ladies and gentlemen," I began, "it's time to raise the issue of documentation. We refer to these friendly little messages to the reader as 'footnotes,' probably because they're at the bottom of the page. Documentation is the academic way to justify random pilferage. You can steal any idea you want—if you document in the traditional way. Don't just come right out and admit that you swiped this idea from Aristotle or Tom Paine. Your professor's going to *know* that you're swiping stuff, so you don't have to rub his nose in it. Follow all the conventional rules, and you won't disturb him while he's sleeping his way through your paper. If you get to be good enough at it, you can coast your way to a bachelor's degree without ever coming close to having an original thought. That's why we're here, isn't it? Immerse yourselves in mediocrity, and you're home free. Originality makes people think, and most of them would rather not."

I still don't know what set me off on *that* tack. Maybe it was Milton's fault. That particular Wednesday was definitely a downer.

I chalked out various footnote formats on the blackboard and generally piddled away the rest of the period. To be perfectly honest about it, I didn't feel much like teaching that day.

I wanted to have a word with Twink to make sure that she was OK, but she was a little too fast for me, and a couple of

suck-ups short-stopped me before I could get to the door.
They babbled on and on about how "absolutely fascinating"
they'd found my discussion of footnotes, and I had a hell of a
time getting away from them.

I stopped by my cubicle to check off the papers I'd collected against my current class list, and about midway through
the stack I came across the paper Renata had threatened to
drop on me. I knew it was hers because she'd used Twinkie as
her byline.

I set the other papers aside and took up hers . . .

HOW I SPENT MY VACATION
By Twinkie

*I spent my vacation in the bughouse, listening to the other
buggies screaming and laughing just to pass the time
away. Normal people can't seem to understand how nice it
is to be nuts sometimes, and that's very sad. People out
there in the world of normal have to face reality every day,
and reality is usually flat and grey and ugly, and time only
runs in one direction, and doorknobs can't talk. A true
nutso doesn't have to put up with that. We can make our
world as beautiful as we want it to be, since it has to do
what we tell it to do.*

Isn't that neat?

*In the world of nuts, nothing is real, so we can change
anything we don't like. If a day is beautiful, we can make it
last for a thousand years; if it's ugly, we can just throw it
away. If the sun is too bright, we can send it to its room,
and if the stars are too dim, we can tell them to burn more
brightly, and they will, just to make us happy.*

*That's what makes the world of nuts so much nicer than
the world of normies. Our truth wags its tail and licks our
fingers; their truth snarls, and it bites.*

Sometimes, sometimes, those of us in the world of nuts

think about the world of the normies, and we've pretty much decided that it might be sort of fun to visit it once in a while, but we certainly wouldn't want to live there. It's just too desperate and ugly, and the normies never seem to get the things they want, no matter how hard they try, and that's very sad.

People from the world of the normies used to visit us in the bughouse now and then, but they weren't really very much fun. They always looked so serious and worried, and they almost never laughed. Normies just can't seem to see the world the way we buggies see it, so they can't even begin to see how funny it is. They couldn't seem to relax, and their eyes got all wild when the nutso down the hall started to practice screaming. Don't they know that screaming is a fine art? In the Olympic games of the world of nuts, a perfect ten scream wins the gold medal every time.

I've moved back to the world of the normies now, and I know that I'm supposed to be serious and never laugh, but sometimes—sometimes—I scream a little bit, just for old times' sake. I make it a point to scream politely, though. It's not nice to wake the neighbors in the grey world of the normies. A few quiet little screams aren't really all that disturbing, though, and I always seem to sleep better after I scream.

And when I sleep, I sometimes dream of the world of nuts, and my doorknob sings to me, and my walls hold me tight, and I drift above the sky and look down at the desperate, grubby, ugly world of the normies where everybody is serious and worried, and never, never, ever smiles.

And I laugh.

"Jesus!" I said, gently putting the paper down. Damn! This girl could really write!

I had to find out if the paper was as good as I thought, so I went looking for Dr. Conrad. As luck had it, he was in.

"Are you busy, boss?" I asked him.

"Do we have a problem, Mr. Austin?"

"Not really. I think I just struck gold, is all. If you've got a few minutes, I'd like your opinion about this." I handed him Twink's paper.

He glanced at the title. "You didn't!" he said, almost laughing. " 'How I Spent My Vacation'?"

"It's a freshman class, boss. Most of the students are still at the 'Run, Spot, run' stage. This one's a cut or two above average, though. Tell me what you think."

He read through Twink's paper. "Dear God!" he said when he finished.

"I felt the same way, boss," I said smugly.

"Don't let this one get away, kid," he told me.

"Not much chance of that. She's the one I was telling you about a few weeks ago."

"Then she really *was* in an asylum?"

"Oh, yes. Her twin sister was murdered, and she went completely bonkers for a while. Now she's auditing my class. She didn't have to write that paper, but she did it anyway. Every so often she likes to show off. She *is* a sharpie, though."

"You've got that part right. If she stays even the least bit sane, do the department a favor and steer her in our direction. Somebody like this only comes along once or twice in a generation." He swiveled his chair around and turned on his copy machine. "You don't mind, do you?" he asked.

"Not a bit, boss. I may run off a few dozen copies myself."

It hadn't quit raining when I headed back to the boardinghouse, and Milton still hung over me like a dark cloud, but I was suddenly all bright and happy. Twink's paper had erased the gloom that'd been perched on my shoulder all day.

Not even grading that stack of papers could sour my day.

I went down to the kitchen while the girls were fixing supper. "I've got presents for you ladies," I told them.

"Oh?" Trish said. "What's the occasion?"

"Charlie and I had a chat with his brother last night, and big Bob suggested something that made a lot of sense. I picked up these neat little key rings for you—which I want you to have with you every time you leave the house." I laid the three rings on the kitchen counter.

Erika picked one up. "What's this little doohickey attached to the ring?" she asked me.

"Pepper spray," I told her. "Don't play with it, because it's loaded. You flip that little knob over, and it's ready to go. If you happen to encounter the world-famous Seattle Slasher, a quick squirt of that stuff will absolutely ruin his day. He'll be totally out of action for at least an hour—or so the clerk at the gun store tells me."

"Don't we need permits to carry those?" Trish asked me dubiously.

"Bob West didn't say anything about permits, Trish, and he's a cop, so he knows the rules."

"I don't know, Mark," she said. "I think having that thing in my purse might make me a little nervous."

"Nervous is better than dead," Erika told her. "Those spray things make sense, so do as you're told."

Trish grumbled a bit, but she did what her younger sister commanded. There was something about Erika that made Trish automatically snap to attention.

"What's got your clock all wound up, Mark?" James asked me at the supper table that evening. "You're acting like you just won the lottery."

"That comes fairly close," I admitted. "I ran head-on into talent today—in a freshman English class, of all places."

"Flowers *do* grow in the weed patches sometimes," he conceded. "Some snappy little *bon mot*, perhaps?"

"Beyond that, old buddy," I said smugly.

"You *are* going to share this with us, aren't you?" Sylvia asked pointedly.

"I thought you'd never ask. I just happen to have a copy with me."

"What a coincidence," Erika observed dryly.

"Be nice," I scolded. "My class turned in a paper today, and I found this tucked in amongst all the usual junk." I handed Twink's paper to James. "Here you go, partner," I said. "Wash the sour taste of Hegel out of your mouth with this."

James took the paper. "How I Spent My Vacation," he read aloud in that deep voice of his, "by Twinkie."

"Isn't that the girl you've been baby-sitting, Mark?" Erika asked me.

"That's her. Go ahead, James. Whip it on 'em."

He read Twink's paper to us, and there was a stunned silence when he finished.

"Wow!" Charlie murmured after a moment.

"Yeah, wow," Sylvia agreed. "I've *got* to meet this girl, Mark."

"Did they actually turn this young lady loose?" James demanded. "It doesn't seem to me that she was ready yet."

"She's just showing off," I told him. "She didn't even have to write the paper. She's only auditing the course."

"You don't come across too many people who write papers just for fun," Charlie said. "Was that why they locked her up in the bughouse?"

"Not really," I told him. "She had a few other problems as well. And don't joke about it—her headshrinker thinks she might have to go back inside a few times. I guess that's sort of standard—like kicking the cigarette habit."

"Psychosis is addictive?" Charlie asked.

"You heard her paper, Charlie," I replied. "The world of nuts is nicer than the world of normies. Your doorknob won't say things to you that might hurt your feelings, and it's only in the bughouse that you can try out for the Olympic Screaming Team. I showed Twink's paper to my faculty advisor, and he ordered me not to let her get away. Even if she's only playing with half a deck, she can still write circles around just about everybody else on campus."

"Does she behave at all normally?" Trish asked.

"Define 'normal,' " I suggested. "She doesn't walk on the ceiling or believe that she's Napoleon, but she *does* get a little strange now and then. She has good days and bad days, but I guess that's part of the process of recovery."

"She's got a crush on you, Mark," Erika told me. "You *did* know that, didn't you?"

"Get real," I scoffed. "She thinks of me as her big brother, that's all. Both Twinkie Twins felt that way when they were little."

"Where's she staying?" Sylvia asked me.

"She's living with her aunt—about five blocks from here. Why?"

"Because we want to meet her, of course," Trish said bluntly.

"Do you think her aunt might let her out for an evening?" Sylvia chimed in. "Maybe she could come for dinner—like tomorrow evening."

Then I remembered something. "I think I goofed," I apologized to Sylvia. "I was talking with Doc Fallon yesterday, and he wants you to give him a call."

"Me?" she asked. "What for?"

"We were talking about a problem Twinkie's having, and I mentioned your major. The notion of having a trained observer on-site appealed to him, since he's fairly sure that I'm missing things. So if everybody here's just dying to meet her anyway, we might as well get some mileage out of it."

James burst out laughing.

"What's so funny?" Trish demanded.

"Mark's suggestion fits right into this place, doesn't it?" he noted. "We *are* something on the order of an institution here, aren't we? We all have rules to obey and duties to perform. The sudden appearance of Mark's friend even defines what kind of institution we are, wouldn't you say?"

"I don't think that's funny at all," Trish told him disapprovingly.

"I wouldn't push it, James," Charlie advised. "Don't offend the ladies who run the kitchen. That's a good way to get a boiled two-by-four for breakfast—with built-in toothpicks."

We played around with that for a while, and then we all went back to our studies.

As luck had it, Twink made it to class on Thursday, and I even managed to catch her before she could get away.

"What?" she said irritably when I took hold of her arm.

"Don't be such a grouch," I told her. "Are you busy this evening?"

"I was going to save the world, but I suppose that can wait. What did you have in mind?"

"I'm supposed to invite you to dinner at the boardinghouse."

"All right," she replied almost indifferently.

"I'll pick you up about five."

"No. I'll bike it. It's not that far from Aunt Mary's."

"How did you know that? I don't remember that I've ever given you the address."

"You can't hide from me, Markie, you should know that by now. I'll be there about five." Then she disengaged her arm from my grasp. "See ya," she said, as she went off down the hall.

If she was trying to irritate me, she was doing a good job of it.

I retreated to the boardinghouse and spent the rest of the afternoon grading papers. If you want to ruin your day, spend an hour or two with freshman English papers. It was four-thirty when I finally set the papers aside and went down to see how the ladies were coming along with the cooking. This was the first time I knew of that we'd ever invited anybody to dinner, and it seemed to me that we were all a little jumpy about it.

"Are you going to go pick her up now?" Trish asked me.

"I offered, but she said she'd ride her bike instead."

"But it's raining," Sylvia protested.

"What else is new? It's only four or five blocks, and she's got a raincoat. She *says* she knows where the house is, but I'm going out to the front porch to flag her down, just to be on the safe side."

"Independence is all well and good," Sylvia said, "but she'll catch pneumonia if she keeps this up."

"Probably not," Erika disagreed.

I glanced at my watch. "I'd better get out there," I said. "I don't want her to zip on past."

I saw that it was raining harder when I went out onto the porch. Twink's stubborn attachment to that bike was going to keep her fairly soggy if she didn't get over it.

It was almost exactly five when she came pedaling around the corner with that silly plastic raincoat sticking out behind her like the tail assembly of a 747. As she pulled up in front of the house, she popped a wheelie by way of greeting.

"Show-off," I called to her.

"If you got it, flaunt it," she threw my own smart aleck remark back in my teeth.

We chained her bike to the banister around the porch, then she pulled off her raincoat and shook off the water. "Am I presentable?" she asked, holding out her arms and turning around for inspection.

"You'll do," I replied. "Oh, before we go in I should probably tell you that my roomies here have all heard your paper."

She shrugged. "The price of fame, I suppose," she said with an exaggerated sigh. "Did they like it?"

"It blew them away. That's what this invitation's all about. You might want to keep your guard up when Sylvia starts asking questions. She's majoring in nutsos, so she might try to probe around and find the *real* you."

"Fat chance," Twink replied. "I lost track of the real me a long time ago. How did *you* like my paper, Markie?"

"It loosened my socks, Twink. It definitely gave me something to brag about. How are you feeling? Mary told me you were out of it on Tuesday."

She shrugged. "It was just one of those bad days, that's all. I'm fine now—all cutesy and sweetsie again."

"Let's go on in and get the introductions out of the way. They're a pretty nice bunch, so don't get uptight because they're strangers. Your paper impressed the hell out of them, so they're all geared up to like you."

"That's nice. Quit worrying so much, Markie. It'll give you ulcers."

We went inside and down the hall to the kitchen. James and Charlie had joined the ladies, and everybody had that expectant look. "Guess who's coming to dinner," I announced. It was a goofy thing to say, but it seemed appropriate.

"Has he always been like this?" Trish spoke directly to Renata.

"Usually, yes," Twink replied. "Sometimes he's worse; sometimes not quite so bad. It might have to do with the phases of the moon, or something."

"I thought so," Trish said. "Maybe it's one of those guy things. I'm Patricia Erdlund, by the way. I usually go by 'Trish,' maybe because the inmates here have trouble pronouncing three-syllable words."

"Be nice," Erika murmured.

"My sister, Erika," Trish advised Twink, "the terror of the medical school. The cute teenie-weenie is Sylvia of Abnormality; the shaggy young fellow with greasy fingernails is Top Secret Charlie, who's not allowed to tell anybody what his major is, and the distinguished gentleman with the silvery beard is James, who thinks all the time—when he's not busy being the in-house bouncer."

Twinkie suddenly giggled.

"Was it something I said?" Trish asked.

"This is almost like coming home," Twink explained. "I just got out of one bughouse, and here I am in another one."

"Normal's out of fashion these days," Charlie suggested, "maybe because normal's boring."

"I've noticed that," Twink agreed. "Old blabbermouth Mark here tells me that he blew my cover yesterday and started running up and down the halls waving my paper around, so there's not much point in trying to hide my shady background, is there? I'm moderately crazy, but I don't eat the furniture or insist that everybody should worship me—even though I *am* God. That shows up fairly often in the nuthouse. *All* the nuts there knew that they were God—which is probably why they were there. You'd think that gods would know enough not to brag about it, but a nuthouse *might* be nothing but a home for dumb gods who aren't smart enough to keep their mouths shut."

"There's a doctoral dissertation for you, Sylvia," Erika said with a perfectly straight face. "If you present *The Divinity of the Insane*, you'd get a chance to study one of the local asylums from the inside."

"Go set the table, Erika," Trish said. "Dinner's almost ready."

We had ham for dinner that evening, and the ladies had gone all out with it, probably in deference to our guest.

Twink had turned the volume all the way up on her cutesy-pootishness, and she almost sparkled.

Sylvia, for obvious reasons, dominated the discussion at the dinner table. She had questions for Twink—lots of questions. Sylvia's major had exposed her to textbooks and learned theorists in her field, but she'd seldom had a chance to talk with a coherent subject. What her somewhat convoluted approach really boiled down to was the single question, "What's it *really* like?"

"Not very nice," Twink told her. "The keepers always seem to want to treat us like bad people—as if we were doing bad things on purpose. That's why we cheat a lot. We say things to the keepers that aren't really true, because it's fun to watch their eyes bug out, and there isn't much else to do for entertainment. Mostly, though, we're able to slip around them.

They ask us questions that we don't want to answer, and there are dozens of ways to avoid them. After a few months in the nuthouse you get good at that. The other nuts give lessons, and you can learn a lot by watching during the little group therapy sessions. The keepers think that talking can cure anything. All you have to do is say what they want to hear, and they'll wiggle like puppies and leave you alone. If they get *too* pushy, you can abolish them by putting on a blank face and pretending that they aren't there at all."

"They're only trying to help," Sylvia protested.

"Of *course* they are," Twink replied in a voice dripping with sarcasm. "They take lots of notes and wave them around during the keeper meetings to impress the boss. That's all they're interested in, isn't it? If they can't stay on the good side of the boss, they might have to go out and get an honest job and do real work. That was our advantage. They were afraid, and we weren't. The worst thing that could ever happen to us had already happened. We all *knew* that something awful had happened to us; we just weren't exactly sure what it was."

A slightly stricken look came over Sylvia's face.

"I'm sorry," Twink apologized. "I shouldn't have said that, should I?" She impulsively took Sylvia's hand. "You're cute and sweet and awfully sincere. The nuts won't pick on you when you go to work in the loony bin. They'll say things that you'll want to hear, and that'll make you feel good. The things they'll tell you won't be the truth, but who really cares? Nutsos take care of the people they like. We're a lot more generous than normies."

"It's all a scam then, isn't it?" Charlie suggested.

"Of course it is. I thought everybody knew that by now. If somebody really wants to get out of the bughouse, all he has to do is say things the keepers want to hear."

"Is that how *you* got out?" Charlie pressed.

"I thought I just said that. I'm probably still as wacky as I was when they locked me up, but once they stopped pumping me full of pills, I saw right away what I had to do. The only real problem I had was that I couldn't remember very much of what had gone on before I woke up. I can remember Markie here, but I didn't even recognize my parents. I guess I used to have a sister, but you couldn't prove it by me. Every so often I have little flashes about the past, but they don't make very much sense. I've learned not to worry about them. There's no point in worrying about the past, because it isn't going to come back. As soon as I realized that, I was ready to leave the bughouse. It took a while to persuade Dockie-poo, but I kept snowing him until he finally gave up and let me go." She looked fondly at Sylvia again. "That's the way things *really* are in the bughouse, small person. We say what we have to say to get the things we want and need."

"And just exactly what is it that you need?" Sylvia asked.

"What I need more than anything else is to have people stop asking me that question. The past—whatever it might have been—is all over now. Something happened back then that made me go bonkers. If I go back and look at it the way everybody seems to want me to, I'll probably turn right around and go bonkers all over again. I need to bury it and never try to dig it up. The nut-keepers can't stand that, so I made up some interesting lies to make them happy, and that's all it took to get me out of the bughouse."

"You *do* know that the awful-awful's likely to come sneaking back, don't you?" Sylvia suggested.

"No, it won't. I've closed that door and bricked it shut. From here on, my past began in the nuthouse when I was twenty years old. Nothing that happened before that—except for Markie—has any real importance. I'm going to pretend that I'm a normie, and I'll keep on doing that until I get it right. Now why don't we talk about the weather or something else that might mean something? The past is dead, and I'm going to make sure it stays that way."

Sylvia's face took on a stricken look. Renata had just effectively slammed a door in her face, and Sylvia wasn't the least bit happy about that.

To be honest about it, Twink's declaration of independence from the past caused me some problems as well. It *seemed* sensible, but once I dipped below that surface I got into a bucketful of worms. Those periodic nightmares of hers strongly suggested that the door to her past wasn't quite as tightly closed as she wanted to believe it was, and something kept sneaking through to claw at her mind while she was asleep. She could pretend to be a normie when she was awake, but I knew in my bones that she wasn't out of the woods yet.

CHAPTER EIGHT

Saturday being national fix-up day at the boardinghouse, I persuaded Charlie that we should take a run on up to Everett in his pickup truck so that we could plunder the scrap heap at Greenleaf Sash and Door for bookshelf material. Then I put in a call to Les Greenleaf to let him know that we were coming and to ask him to alert the watchman.

"I really got a kick out of that screwball friend of yours the other night," Charlie said as we went north on Interstate 5. "She sure cut the ground out from under Sylvia, didn't she?"

"Twink's good at that," I told him. "She'll only let snoopy people go so far, and then she jerks them up short. It was probably good for Sylvia, though. A quick dose of humility might tone down that know-it-all attitude of hers."

"Fat chance," Charlie snorted. "That whole department's stuck on that 'do you want to talk about it' routine. The Twinkie girl probably ruined the whole quarter for Sylvia when she said that the nutsos make up fairy tales to tell the keepers."

"What a dirty, rotten shame," I said. "Have you talked with Bob lately? If the cops have come up with something new on the local cut-up artist, we probably ought to know about it."

"About all they're sure of is that it's gang stuff," Charlie replied. "Burpee's still frothing at the mouth about Cheetah, but the rest of the cops aren't buying it. The north end cops are fairly sure that there's a new gang moving into the area, and they're using this butcher-shop approach to scare off the other gangs."

"Doing autopsies on guys who are still alive and kicking probably gets the message across. 'Get out of town or I'll gut you' is nice and simple."

There was a grizzled old watchman at the gate of the door factory, and he waved us through when he saw me. I recognized him, but I couldn't remember his name. "Hook a right at the far end of the yard," I told Charlie. "The scrap heap's on the other side of that long shed."

"Got it," he replied.

It was still drizzling, naturally, and pawing through wet lumber brought back not-so-fond memories of the green chain. It took Charlie and me about an hour to rummage through and pick out the boards that might work for us. There was quite a bit of good lumber in that scrap heap, but that's par for the course. Doors are right out where people can see them, so boards with visible flaws are usually discarded. My general plan was to use good lumber for the eye-level shelves and junk lumber near the bottom where all anybody could see would be the outside edge.

There are lots of ways to cut corners if you know how.

When we got back to Wallingford, we unloaded Charlie's pickup and stacked the boards in my basement lumber room. After lunch, I started taking measurements in James's room while Charlie worked on Trish's car.

"That Greenleaf girl's kind of evasive, isn't she?" James observed while I was writing down measurements. "She sidestepped just about every one of Sylvia's questions. And that paper she wrote opened some doors I didn't even know existed."

"It *was* a doozie, wasn't it?" I agreed.

Just then, Trish yelled up the stairs. "You've got a phone call, Mark."

"Be right there," I called back. I went down the stairs two

at a time and picked up the phone in the living room. "Yeah?" I said.

"It's me, Mark," Mary's voice came over the phone. "Ren and I went up to Lake Stevens yesterday, and when we were on our way back, she told me that she'd like to go to church tomorrow. I have to work tonight, so I'll be pretty tired, come morning. I was wondering if you could take her? It'll only be about an hour."

"Sure," I told her.

"Good. I'll take her to confession this afternoon, and she'll be all set to go."

"What's she got to confess? Even if she did something wrong way back when, she won't remember it."

"It's tradition, Mark. You go to confession before you take the sacraments."

"Even if you don't have anything to confess? That doesn't make sense."

"Religion doesn't *have* to make sense, Mark. When you get right down to it, I don't think it's supposed to. Do you know where St. Benedict's Church is?"

"Up by Woodland Park, isn't it?"

"Right. It's on Fiftieth Street. The priest there is Father O'Donnell."

"Swedish guy?"

"Quit clowning around, Mark. Ren wants to go to the nine o'clock Mass, so be here at eight tomorrow morning. Wear a necktie."

"Yes, ma'am."

After I hung up the phone, I went looking for Sylvia. The only time I'd ever been inside a Catholic church had been at Regina's funeral, so I wasn't all that familiar with the procedures during a regular service. I was fairly sure Sylvia could fill me in. You don't come across very many Italian Presbyterians.

"Nobody's going to get too excited if you miss a few things,

Mark," she assured me. "They'll know you're not Catholic as soon as you walk in."

"Oh?"

"There are things we do automatically, right from when we enter a church. Even if you tried to fake it, they'd spot you. Don't worry, nobody's going to scold you."

"Good. Churches make me a little nervous. I go to weddings and funerals, and that's about the extent of my involvement. Did you happen to call Dr. Fallon and fill him in on Twink's performance Thursday?"

She nodded. "He told me that we shouldn't take her too seriously when she goes running off through the weeds like that. I guess she's turned evasion into an art form. We've got a fairly unique situation here, Mark. Usually the patient's the one who has the deep, dark secret, and the therapist has to go digging for it. This time, *we* all know exactly what's troubling Renata, and *she* doesn't. We have the answer, but Renata doesn't want any part of it."

"Well, the ball's in your court now, Sylvia. I'd better get back to work. If Trish catches me goofing off, I'll get yelled at."

At dinner that evening, though, Trish came up with something that had nothing to do with bookshelves. She'd caught her foot on the edge of one of those worn places in the linoleum while the girls had been preparing supper. She hadn't fallen, but I gather that some dinner rolls made a break for freedom. "How big a project would it be to resurface the kitchen floor, Mark?" she asked me.

"It's nothing too major, Trish," I told her. "That linoleum in there probably dates back to the fifties. In those days, linoleum was pretty much like carpeting. You'd buy it in big rolls—along with a couple gallons of glue and a linoleum knife. Then you got to spend a week or so on your knees inventing new swear words. Now it comes in boxes. They refer to them as tiles, which isn't very accurate, but people know what it means. The tiles are a foot square, they're made of no-wax vinyl, and they're peel and stick. You peel the paper off the back, put the tile in place, and then stomp on it. It goes fairly fast, and the great part is that you can stop whenever you feel like it—you don't have that cumbersome roll of linoleum stretching across the middle of the floor. The only tricky part is cutting the tiles to fit around doorframes and along the edge."

"Is it very expensive?"

"Not really—twenty, maybe twenty-five dollars for a box of thirty. They've got sample books they'll lend you, so you can pick the one you like."

"Let's look into it—that floor's starting to get dangerous."

"I'll check it out on Monday," I promised her.

It wasn't raining on Sunday morning, and I thought that might be a good sign—if there really *are* such things as signs. I shaved carefully and put on my best dress-up jacket and pants. It took me a while to get the knot right in my necktie, but I finally got it even. I made a mental note to pick up one of those clip-on ties. I don't dress up often enough to be very good at tying my own.

Mary was just pulling into her driveway when I got to her place. I'd never seen her in uniform before, and she looked very official. The gun on her hip may have had something to do with that. She gave me a quick inspection before we went inside. "Don't you have a suit?" she demanded.

"I never got around to buying one. I don't run with the suit-and-tie crowd all that often."

"Well, it'll have to do, I guess," she said. "Let's see how Ren's holding up. She was a little nervous about this before I went to work last night. She hasn't been to church for several years now, and she seems to be afraid that she might forget a few things."

"I'll be surprised if she remembers *any* of the things she's supposed to do. Isn't that what the word 'amnesia' means?"

"You obviously haven't been around very many Catholics, Mark. The rituals are ingrained in early childhood. You *never* forget them, no matter *what's* happened to you."

"If you say so," I said, holding the door for her.

We found Twink in the kitchen, obviously agitated. "Where have you *been*?" she demanded, glaring at me.

"It's only quarter after eight, Twink, and it's no more than a mile to the church. We'll get there in plenty of time."

"Everything's going just fine, Ren," Mary assured her. "Don't get all worked up."

"Could we go now?" Twink asked me. She seemed on edge.

"Scoot," Mary commanded, "and don't make too much noise when you come home. I'm going to take a hot bath and crash."

"Sleep lots," I told her. "I'll take Twink out to brunch after church."

Twink shot me a nervous grin. "Isn't he just the nicest boy?" she said to her aunt.

"He'll do," Mary said with a yawn. "Go. Now."

Twink and I went back out to my car. "I wish she wouldn't worry so much about me," Twink said. "She hasn't been sleeping very well lately."

"We'll putter around this afternoon," I told her, as we pulled away from the curb. "If we stay away, maybe she can catch up on her sleep."

"That'd be nice," she said.

St. Benedict's Church sits on Fiftieth Street at the southern end of Woodland Park and, as I understand it, the building has a fairly conventional Catholic church layout. "New" is nice, I suppose, but "old" still has a lot going for it.

I assumed that I'd just stay at the back of the church during the Mass, but Twink wasn't having any of that. She got a death grip on my arm as we went inside and hauled me forward. I don't know which of us felt more awkward as we took our seats near the front, but when the organ began playing, Twink relaxed, and gave me a gentle smile.

There were several rituals that I didn't understand, but Renata moved effortlessly through the ceremony. I heard some people sitting nearby refer to the priest as "Father O," and I wasn't quite sure how to take that. Maybe it was a variation of "Daddy-O." They used it affectionately—sort of like a pet name. Maybe it had something to do with the lilting Irish brogue in which he spoke. I'd heard people fake a brogue before—usually on St. Patrick's Day, when *everybody* pretends to be Irish—but the real thing has a flow to it that you can't really imitate.

I also didn't understand much about the ceremony involved in taking the sacraments. I'm sure there was a lot more going on than there appeared to be on the surface, but Twink seemed peaceful, even serene when she rejoined me afterward. I made a mental note that anytime she started to unravel, I should drag her off to St. Benedict's and let "Father O" settle her down.

After the service, there was that customary "meet and greet" business at the church door. Twink was glowing as she introduced me to "Father O," and he gave me a rather curious look. "So this is the big brother Renata speaks of so often," he said.

"I think somebody's been telling tales out of school, Father O'Donnell," I said, as we shook hands.

"Would I do that?" Twink asked with exaggerated innocence.

"I think we should talk, Mr. Austin," Father O told me. "Soon, if it's possible."

That got my attention almost immediately. "I can swing by late tomorrow, Father O'Donnell," I suggested.

"Fine," he said. "About three-thirty?"

"Right," I agreed, as the crowd moved us along toward the open door.

"What was that all about, Markie?" Twink asked, as we strolled back to my car.

"How should I know? I haven't talked with him yet. Do

you want to have brunch in that restaurant up on top of the Space Needle?"

"You're going to fly me to the moon?"

"Not right away. The man in the moon's booked solid this year."

We clowned around as I drove downtown. Twink seemed to be a lot more relaxed than she'd been for a long time now. If a quick trip to church was all it'd take to wind her down, I'd make a standing appointment with Father O and take her to St. Benedict's twice a day.

On Monday morning our silvery-haired Milton professor recited extensively from *Paradise Lost*. His voice betrayed a certain stage fright at first, but once he got into it, he shed that, and he sounded like God speaking to Moses on Mount Sinai. Milton does that to people sometimes.

Yes, I thought, *Paradise Lost* was definitely a barn burner, but my paper would be on more solid ground if I stuck to his prose works.

After class, I went back to the library to continue my investigation of Whitman's British connections. I found definite proof that Whitman *had* received a copy of the *Poetic Works of William Blake* in the early 1870s. Try mixing Milton, Blake, and Whitman all together in a single morning. It definitely stretches your head.

I grabbed a burger about twelve-thirty and hit the door of my freshman class right on the button at one-thirty. Twink was in her seat, so she obviously hadn't had another one of those bad nights. I returned the papers I'd spent hours grading, and then I assigned another one—"Why Am I Here?"—which brought the usual groans. Freshmen groan a lot, I've noticed.

"All right, fun-seekers," I began, "shall we stop feeling sorry for ourselves and go to work? Your papers revealed a certain flaw that needs correcting. Let's take a look at the lowly preposition for a while. I know that it's the 'in' thing lately to omit prepositions, despite the fact that it makes the 'in' person sound like an idiot. People 'depart Sea-Tac Airport' or 'graduate high school.' Does the simple word 'from' offend you for some reason? It's a nice little word, good to its mother, and always willing to go to work, if you'll just give it a chance. Language can be very precise *if* you use it correctly. Prepositions are the glue that keeps your sentences from flying apart. They indicate the relationships between the other words in your sentence. Use them. That's why we have them. I'm not impressed by fashionable omissions. It makes me grumpy when you leave them out. Don't do it anymore, because if you think it makes *me* unhappy, wait until you hit a full professor. He'll have you for lunch."

That got their immediate attention, and they listened intently for the rest of the period.

Twink hung around after I'd dismissed the class. "What's got you on the prod today, Markie?" she asked.

"Grading papers filled with sloppy language, Twink. That's the un-fun part of teaching."

"It's your own fault. If you wouldn't assign so many, you wouldn't have to grade them. I'm supposed to say 'thank you.' Aunt Mary was all rested when you dropped me off yesterday. She slept until almost four o'clock."

"Good. She was looking frazzled when we left for church. She really needed that sleep."

"As long as it's 'let's all thank Markie' time, I'd like to add a few of mine to the heap. I really enjoyed our little jaunt to the Space Needle yesterday. I didn't know that the restaurant up there rotated like that. It gives you a view of the whole city, doesn't it?"

"Sure, unless there's a low-lying cloudbank blotting everything out."

"Say hi to the gang at your boardinghouse for me, OK? I had lots of fun there the other night."

"I'll pass that on," I promised.

"Good," she said. "I've got to run now. See ya." And then

she was gone. It was fairly obvious that we'd done *something* right lately. Twink seemed almost normal.

Then I checked my watch and headed for the parking garage. I'd almost forgotten my appointment with Father O'Donnell.

He was just coming out of a little booth along the side of the church when I got there, and an elderly lady was near the altar working her way through her rosary beads. Father O nodded to me as I came down the center aisle, and I joined him near a small door to one side of the altar. He led the way along a narrow hallway and into a book-lined office. "Have a seat, Mr. Austin," he said.

"Just Mark, Father O'Donnell. I clutch up when people call me 'mister.' "

"All right, Mark it is. I asked you to come by today because I'm concerned about Renata Greenleaf, and it seems that you know her better than anybody else."

"I'm a longtime friend of her family, Father."

"You *are* aware that she's very troubled, aren't you?"

"If you think she's bad now, you should have seen her a couple of years ago. Twink—that is, Renata—is a recent graduate of a mental institution."

"I thought it might be something like that. She was almost incoherent when she came to confession on Saturday, and every now and then she'd say things in a language I couldn't even recognize, much less understand."

"Maybe I should fill you in. There are some fairly complicated things about Renata that you probably ought to know."

"I'd appreciate that, Mark. Right now she has me so baffled that I don't know which way to turn."

"I'm not sure this'll help very much. Twink's making a career out of baffling people." I leaned back in my chair and gave him the whole sad, sordid story—right up to the paper Twink had written, and how it made everybody sit up and take notice.

Father O'Donnell seemed shell-shocked when I finished. "I'd like to see that paper, Mark."

"I've got copies, Father. I'll drop one off for you. Did any of what I just told you help at all? Twink's a little strange sometimes, but that's because she's crazy—not too crazy, but crazy all the same. She's *trying* to get well, but she's having some trouble with it—for fairly obvious reasons. If the cops ever catch the guy who killed her sister, she might get well immediately, but I don't think that's too likely. It's been over two years now, so he probably got away clean."

"He'll answer for it, Mark. Believe me, he'll answer for it."

"That's in the next world, Father O. I'd like to get my hands on him in *this* one."

"We sort of disapprove of that, Mark. God's supposed to take care of it."

"I just want to help out, Father. God can have what's left after I'm done with him."

"We might want to talk about that someday. I think I understand Renata a little better now."

"That's assuming that Twink really *is* Renata. If she's Regina, we might have to start all over from square one."

"You *had* to bring that up, didn't you?" he said ruefully.

"Just trying to brighten up your day, Father O."

The rest of the week rolled merrily along as we all settled back into harness.

The newspapers and television kept trying hard to ride the "Seattle Slasher" story, but the saddle was starting to slip on that horse. Our local cut-up appeared to have put his knife away, and the media got slightly sulky about that.

Sylvia stayed right on top of me, demanding daily reports on Twink's behavior. I started to suspect a research paper in progress there, and I wouldn't have been surprised to discover the fine hand of Dr. Fallon somewhere in the background.

James, Charlie, and I hit the Green Lantern a couple of times that week to stay in touch with Charlie's brother. The police investigation of the "Seattle Slasher" case seemed to be at a standstill. Bob more or less admitted that the cops were marking time, waiting for another murder. "We don't have enough to work with yet," he told us Thursday evening. "The general opinion is that the killings are gang-related, but there's always the possibility that we've got a homicidal maniac roaming around out there. If the two killings are just part of a turf war, two might be the end of it. If it's a crazy, though, there's certain to be more. Crazies kill people for crazy reasons, and they usually keep on killing until they get caught."

"You're just chock-full of good news, Bob," Charlie told his brother. "Are you guys looking into the possibility of a werewolf? Or maybe a vampire?"

"We're keeping an open mind, kid."

"You had to ask, didn't you Charlie?" James rumbled. "Now we'll have to break out the garlic and the silver bullets." Then he looked at Bob. "What *is* the proper procedure when you arrest a vampire?" he asked. "Do you read him his rights before or after you drive the stake through his heart?"

"I'd have to look that up," Bob replied with a perfectly straight face. "It doesn't come up very often."

Mary called me after she and Twink had returned from the weekly visit to Dr. Fallon and invited me to dinner. While we were eating, I told her that we'd been picking Bob West's brains for information about our local celebrity.

"West's a good man," she told me. "He's solid and very thorough. He's a long way in front of Burpee, that's for sure."

"Who's Burpee?" Twink asked curiously.

"His real name is Belcher," Mary explained. "Burpee has a tendency to do things backward. A good cop follows the evidence to the suspect. Burpee picks a suspect at random—possibly by drawing straws or laying out a deck of tarot cards. Then he tries to find evidence that'll back his theory."

"He *really* wants to nail Cheetah for these killings in this part of town, doesn't he?" I asked.

"Burpee's a joke," she snorted. "Cheetah wouldn't be caught dead out of downtown Seattle. Burpee wants to be a celebrity because he wants a promotion. The cop who catches Cheetah's a shoo-in for a step up in rank, so Burpee tries to connect Cheetah to any and every crime in the greater Seattle area. Shoplifting, murder, jaywalking—you name it, and Burpee tells everybody that Cheetah's our prime suspect."

"What got him so fired up about Cheetah?" I asked.

"Burpee was working out of the downtown precinct a couple of years ago, and an informant gave him a good solid lead on where and when he could put his hands on Cheetah. Burpee blew it by running his mouth when he should have kept quiet. That's what got him transferred to the north precinct, and he's desperate to get back to the head office where he can pretend to be a big shot again."

"Police department politics get kind of murky sometimes, don't they?"

Mary grinned at me. "Fun though," she added.

Saturday morning I finished up the bookshelves in James's room by ten o'clock. Then I took a quick run to the building supply store and checked out one of their sample books. They had quite a library of those—carpeting, floor tiles, wallpaper, imitation wood paneling, and several others. The idea was to let consumers do their shopping at home, I guess.

A word in passing right here. It's not a good idea to give a group of ladies *too* many choices in the area of home improvement. Paralysis sets in almost immediately when you put twenty or thirty possibilities in front of them. I think Keats referred to it as "negative capability."

"Did you really *have* to do that, Mark?" James growled at me late that afternoon. "If I get much more of that 'What do you think of this one?' I'll go bananas."

"It was a blunder," I admitted. "I should have just picked up two of the damn things—one fairly nice and the other awful. That would have simplified things a bit."

"No day in which you learn something is a complete waste, I guess," he conceded.

I let that go by. "I'll see if I can crowd the girls a bit. I *do* have to get that sample book back by this evening."

It took a little pushing, but by suppertime the ladies had narrowed the choice down to five different samples. Then I took the book away from them, went back to the supply store, and bought one of each variety for the girls to play with. As an afterthought, I picked up a linoleum knife. I was fairly certain I had one somewhere among my tools, but I wasn't sure exactly where, and it probably wasn't in very good shape anyway.

I called Twink later to ask her if she wanted to go to church in the morning, but she didn't seem too enthusiastic about the idea. That surprised me a bit. But then I remembered how worked up she had been *before* our trip last weekend, and I decided to let it pass.

The week moved smoothly along. The students had more or less settled down, my own studies advanced nicely, and nothing very remarkable was happening in the real world. Then on Thursday morning, the newspapers and all the hyper television reporters got the break they'd been breathlessly waiting for. Magnusson Park in the Windemere district fronted on Lake Washington, and an early-morning jogger came across the scattered remains of the Seattle Slasher's third victim.

CHAPTER NINE

We gathered in the kitchen, drank Erika's coffee, and watched that small TV set as the story—what little there was—unfolded. The latest victim had been another small-timer with a fairly extensive police record. His name was Daniel Garrison, and he'd been in trouble with the law since he'd been about fifteen. He'd served one year in the state reformatory before he'd graduated to the penitentiary at Walla Walla for a couple of terms. He'd never been a master criminal by any stretch of the imagination. He'd taken falls for possession of stolen property, burglary, car theft, assault with a deadly weapon—a screwdriver?—and a couple of attempted rapes. He'd evidently been a scrawny little punk with a taste for big women. On at least one occasion, his arrest for attempted rape had been more in the nature of a rescue, since his intended victim had been more than a match for him. She'd been stomping his face into a bloody pulp when the cops arrived.

"This one's going to ruin poor Burpee's day, I'll bet," Charlie noted. "I haven't heard a word about any dope deals yet."

"Our local cut-up seems hell-bent on deleting minor criminals," James rumbled. "This one seems to be a carbon copy of the one who got himself scattered around in Woodland Park a few weeks ago."

"Maybe he's a conservative who's taking the butcher knife approach to tax cuts," Charlie suggested. "It costs a lot of money to keep these small-time punks locked up—about thirty-five thousand bucks a year per head, the last I heard. This guy with a knife has already saved us about a hundred thousand a year, and he's only getting started."

"I don't think that's likely to put him in the conservative hall of fame, Charlie," Erika disagreed. "He'll have to take out several battalions of these minor leaguers before he'll make much of a dent in the state budget."

I spent the morning in the library hammering out a tentative bibliography on Milton's prose works. Then I grabbed a quick sandwich and hurried off to teach my freshman class.

Twink missed class again. That was starting to become a habit. I decided that I should have a little talk with her about that. It didn't make much difference as long as she was just auditing, but if she moved up to taking courses for real, class-cutting was a sure road to flunk city.

That evening, Charlie, James, and I dropped in at the Green Lantern to see if we could pry some more details on the Windermere killing from Charlie's brother Bob.

"We're pretty much convinced that the Slasher's picking his victims at random," Bob told us. "There doesn't seem to be any connection between them—except that they've all got fairly extensive police records. This Garrison punk wasn't really into dope dealing. He probably *used* dope now and then, but we've never busted him for selling it. As far as we can tell, the poor bastard just happened to be in the wrong place at the wrong time."

"Serial killing stuff?" Charlie asked.

Bob shook his head. "The so-called serial killer almost always has some kind of sex hang-up, and his victims are either women or children. So far, the victims are all guys, and they seem to have been straight. There's something else involved, and we haven't been able to run it down yet. The thing that's bugging *me* about these killings is the lack of noise. These guys were carved up like Christmas turkeys, and we haven't had a single report of any yelling or screaming. Somebody *should* be hearing all the racket and calling in. These guys are taking a long time to die. The coroner tells us the whole thing takes fifteen or twenty minutes at least. The Slasher's going out of his way to prolong the business and to make it as unbearable as possible. The locations are sort of secluded, but screams carry a long way, particularly at night, and so far nobody seems to be hearing anything."

"Maybe people *have* heard the noise, but they just don't want to get involved," I suggested.

"Don't kid yourself, Mark," he told me. "If a dog barks more than twice, we start getting nine-one-one calls almost immediately."

"I thought that number was strictly for emergencies," James said.

"It is," Bob said, "but different people have different definitions of the word, 'emergency.' A boom box two blocks away after ten o'clock is an emergency in some people's minds. The neighborhood around a park is a quiet one, and screaming isn't the sort of thing people are going to shrug off. There has to be some explanation, but I'm damned if I can pin it down." He laughed then. "Old Burpee's trying to sell the notion of 'a vast, unsuspected dope cartel' engaged in open warfare with Cheetah's gang, but that won't float. An operation like that would involve some very sophisticated professionals, and with the possible exception of Muñoz, these guys were third-rate street punks who probably weren't smart enough to tie their own shoes."

"I was talking with Mary Greenleaf the other day, and she told me that poor old Burpee got himself kicked out of the downtown precinct because of a major screwup," I said.

"You know Mary?" Bob asked, sounding surprised.

"Yeah. My dad and her brother were army buddies in 'Nam. She sort of agrees that Burpee's a joke. She told me that he blew a chance to nail Cheetah by running his mouth at the wrong time."

"He did that, all right," Bob agreed, laughing. "He got a tip from one of his informants, and he had a clear shot at Cheetah. But Burpee's always been desperate to be the center of attention, and this time he started bragging *before* he went to pick Cheetah up. The only trouble there is that Cheetah's got more informants than the entire Seattle Police Department's got, and word got back to him pronto. Burpee took a whole platoon of uniforms and surrounded a third-rate hotel in downtown Seattle, but by then, Cheetah was long gone. Big-mouth Burpee damn near got himself kicked off the force for *that*—or at the very least, demoted back to wearing a uniform and driving around in a patrol car. He managed to wiggle out of it, but he got transferred to the north end, so now *we* have to listen to him and all his screwball ideas."

"That *would* explain his obsession with Cheetah, though," James suggested. "I guess he has to make amends for that blunder."

"Does he ever," Bob agreed.

"Since dear old 'cut and run' has been concentrating on butchering guys, would that suggest that the ladies in our house are probably safe?" Charlie asked his brother.

"I wouldn't take any chances," Bob told him. "I don't think we know enough about this guy yet to know what sets him off. He's been killing people in parks after midnight, and you don't see too many girls strolling in the park at that time of night. For all we know, this guy will kill anything that moves when he's out hunting. I'd suggest that you travel in packs until we nail him." He glanced at his watch. "I've gotta run," he told us.

"That pretty much takes us back to square one, doesn't it?" Charlie suggested. "The girls are carrying that pepper spray, but I still think we'd better ride shotgun on them anytime they go out after dark."

"Look on the bright side, Charlie," I told him. "Here's your chance to be chivalrous—knightly duty, and all like that there."

"Whose knight night is it tonight?" he asked me.

"Somehow I knew that was coming," James said, as we all stood up to leave.

I hit my Milton Seminar on Friday morning, then dropped by Dr. Conrad's office to fill him in on the Blake-Whitman connection. "It all fits together, boss. Whitman wasn't a painter—or engraver—the way Blake was, so his poetry wasn't quite as visual as Blake's, but even Swinburne spotted the similarities. Of course, that was before Swinburne sobered up, so his perceptions might have come swimming up out of the bottom of a bottle. Over the centuries, we've lost a lot of great poetry because of booze and dope, haven't we?"

"It tends to get overemphasized, Mr. Austin. I'm not sure that 'Kubla Khan' would have gone much further even if Coleridge hadn't been nipping at laudanum. Are you thinking about taking another ride on the derivative horse? People have been comparing Whitman to Blake for over a hundred years now."

"It *is* a possibility, boss. Whitman kept revising *Leaves of Grass* until the day before he died. If the Brits got him all fired up about Blake, isn't it possible that hints of Blake's stuff might have crept into some of those later revisions?"

"You're staring a variorum edition of *Leaves of Grass* full in the face, Mr. Austin," he told me.

"I know," I replied glumly, "though Whitman's always irritated me, for some reason. I think Blake was a better poet. He looked out at the rest of the world, but Whitman was too stuck on himself to look beyond the end of his own nose. Anyway, I'm in the right place if I want to do a variorum of *Leaves of Grass*. The main library has copies of all the first editions of the damn thing, so I wouldn't have to go roaming around in computer land looking for texts. Working with a guard standing over me wouldn't be *too* thrilling, but what the hell?"

"Those first editions are valuable, Mr. Austin. What are

you aiming for? Did you want to indict poor old Walt for plagiarism?"

"I wouldn't go *that* far, boss—I just want to find out if Blake's stuff had any influence on the later editions of *Leaves of Grass*. We get hung up on compartmentalization in the English Department. Chaucer scholars don't speak to Faulkner specialists, and everybody sneers at the Victorians. It's all the same language, and good poetry—or prose—can come from almost anyplace."

"Even from a lunatic asylum. How's that girl coming along, by the way?"

"She went to church a couple of weeks ago, and she confused hell out of the priest when she confessed in twin-speak. That's something to ponder, isn't it? Is a confession valid if the priest hasn't the faintest idea of what you're saying to him?"

"I don't do theology, Mr. Austin," he said dryly. "I don't do windows, either. Keep me posted on your protégée's progress, all right? If she happens to come up with any new variations of 'The Bughouse Blues,' I'd like to see them."

"I'll mention it to her—boost her self-confidence. Give me a little more time, and I'll have the whole campus in her cheering section. Of course, if she finally *does* get well, she'll probably stop writing the good stuff. How's that for a moral dilemma on a gloomy Friday? If Twink stays bonkers, she'll keep on writing great stuff; if she gets well, she might start writing the usual freshman junk."

"Go away, Mr. Austin," he told me wearily.

"Yes, boss," I replied obediently. I had a briefcase full of papers to grade anyway, so I went back up the hill to the boardinghouse to dig into them.

When I got there, though, Renata's bike was chained to the front porch. That seemed a little odd.

Inside I found Twink and Sylvia deep in a discussion in the

living room. "Did you get lost in the library again, Markie?" Renata asked me when I looked in on them.

"No, Twink. I was just checking in with Dr. Conrad. Aren't you supposed to go see Fallon today?"

"His secretary called this morning," she replied. "There's some emergency at the bughouse, and Dockie-poo didn't have time for me today. That made me feel all lonesome and unwanted, so I tried to call you. Sylvia answered the phone, and she told me to come on over. I love Aunt Mary dearly, but all she talks about is the cop shop. I'm not that interested, really—so I've been telling Sylvia stories about the bughouse instead."

"She's opened up a whole new world for me, Mark," Sylvia said. "There's a lot more going on in mental institutions than I'd ever imagined."

"She didn't know about the lonely part," Twink told me. "Buggies get fed and watered, and they get clean sheets on their beds, but nobody's got the time to just sit and talk with us—without taking notes. Lonely sets in when that notepad comes out." She stood up then and came across the room. "I need a hug," she told me, holding out her arms.

"Oh," I said, "right." I set my briefcase down and wrapped my arms around her.

"Markie hugs good," Twink told Sylvia. "You ought to try him sometime."

"Boy-girl stuff is sort of a no-no here, Renata," Sylvia said. "We're not supposed to get that close to each other."

"Hugging doesn't have anything to do with that," Twink replied. "Every house should have an official hugger—no questions, no comments, just hugs. A few good hugs can take away acres of lonesome. The people with the notepads don't understand that. They talk and talk and talk, and it doesn't do any good at all. What we really need is hugs." She sighed then. "Nobody in the world of normies is ever going to understand the world of buggies, but you don't have to understand. A hug lets us know that it's not really important to you that we're crazy, and that you like us all the same. That's all we want."

"You could call it 'hug therapy,' Sylvia," I suggested, "and then you could get yourself into all the textbooks on the same page with Freud and Jung."

"Quit trying to be funny, Mark," she snapped. "Oh, Renata's staying for supper, by the way—we cleared it with her Aunt Mary."

"Good. Now if you ladies will excuse me, I've got papers to grade."

Erika was in a sour humor at supper. Her computer had been misbehaving, and she was right on the verge of pitching it out the window.

"Remain tranquil, baby sister," James told her. "Charlie probably knows more about computers than Bill Gates does."

"I don't know if I'd go *that* far," Charlie said. "Old Bill can make a computer sit up and beg, roll over and play dead, and shake paws with him. But I don't think he makes house calls, so I'll take a look—it's probably something minor. Computers get all huffy if you miss a step during a standard program, and they just *love* to tell you that you've made a mistake." Then he laughed.

"What's so funny?" Erika demanded.

"There's a story that's been going around at Boeing since the dark ages when people had to use IBM cards to put information into huge computers that covered an acre or more. Anyway, there was an engineer who was having an argument with an insurance company about whether or not he'd missed a premium payment. The only trouble was that he couldn't get in touch with a human being. All he got was a long string of letters telling him that he owed them money. He finally got a bellyful of that, so he went down to the shop, cut a stainless-steel sheet down to the size and shape of an IBM card, punched a few square slots into it, and then painted it buff-colored. It looked exactly like one of those old IBM cards.

Then he magnetized it and mailed it off to the insurance company. Some clerk who was only half-awake fed it into the company's computer, and it erased the whole damn thing. There was absolutely nothing in their computer."

"That's *awful*!" Erika exclaimed, but then she laughed a wicked little laugh. "What did they do?"

"What *could* they do?" Charlie demanded. "If they made *too* big a fuss about it, word would get out, and everybody who was having a beef with any company that used computers could wipe the company out anytime he wanted to. The computer age almost got derailed right there in its infancy."

"How did it all turn out?" Twink asked.

"Well, the engineer got to talk to whole battalions of live human beings for a starter," Charlie replied, "and they were all terribly polite, for some reason. As it turned out, he got about five years of free insurance, and all he had to do to get it was to promise that he'd never do that again and never tell anybody else how to do it."

"The original computer virus," James noted.

"That it was," Charlie agreed. "A computer that's just been turned into a *tabula rasa* isn't worth very much."

"I haven't heard that term in years," James said.

"The old ones are the best," Charlie replied.

After dinner, Sylvia took Twink off to her room, and it was almost midnight before they decided to call it a day. I was camped out in the living room with Milton when they came down the hall.

"Good night, Markie," Twink said.

"What did you have planned?" I asked her.

"I thought I'd go home."

"Not by yourself, you won't," I said flatly. "I'll drive you back to Mary's place."

"And leave my bike here? Not hardly."

"You're not going out by yourself, Twinkie. There's a nut running around out there with a knife."

"Oh, poo."

"You can 'poo' all you want, Twink, but you're *not* going anyplace alone. I'll borrow Charlie's truck and deliver you and your bike to your Aunt Mary's front door."

"You're being silly, Markie."

"Humor me. I'm bigger than you are, Twink, so we'll do this my way."

"He *does* have a point, Renata," Sylvia stepped in. "It's sort of dangerous out there after dark."

"Oh, all right." Twink gave up. "I still think it's silly, though."

"Let's not take any chances. Stay put. I'll be right back." I went upstairs, borrowed Charlie's keys, and came back down. It only took a couple of minutes to load the bicycle into the back of Charlie's truck, then Twink and I got in and took off.

"What's got you all burly and protective, Markie?" she asked, as I drove us through the rainy, empty streets.

"It's my job, Twink. I'm supposed to look out for you. You might as well get used to it."

"You're as bad as Les."

"Exactly. I thought you knew that already."

"You really care, don't you?"

"Of course I do. I've been looking after you since you were in diapers, and I don't plan to change."

"That's sweet."

"Don't get gushy about it, kid. Everybody has responsibilities. You're one of mine. Sometimes you're a pain in the neck, but that doesn't make any difference. Have we got that straight?"

"Yes, Master. Yes, Master."

"Oh, quit."

Sylvia was still up when I got back. "That's the *strongest* person I've ever met, Mark," she said. "No sooner do I think I've got her pegged and identified than she comes up with something new and different. One day I think she's manic-depressive, and the next day I'm positive that I'm looking at a classic multiple personality disorder. She changes so fast that I can't keep up with her."

"That's why she's so much fun, Sylvia. You never know what she'll do next. Life's isn't boring when Twink's around."

"I've got reams of things I want to take up with Dr. Fallon."

"That's why we recruited you, Toots. Fallon knows that I'm no specialist. We need a resident expert to do interpretations for us—like, what the hell is 'multiple personality disorder'?"

"Go to a video store and rent *The Three Faces of Eve*," she suggested. "Hollywood doesn't get *too* many things right, but that one hit the nail right on the head. There are a few people out there who aren't single individuals. They're two— or three—or even a dozen—totally separate and different people, and sometimes they aren't even aware of the others. Jane doesn't know that Suzy exists, and Mabel's never heard of Barbara. They have different sets of friends, different interests, and sometimes even different apartments."

"I think you're pushing that one just a bit, babe. Twink's problem goes back to Regina's murder, and there's a good chance that she'll never really face it. I say, if she can function, let's leave her alone. As the saying goes, 'if it ain't busted, don't fix it.' "

"Don't get complacent, Mark," she told me. "You *did* know that she had another 'bad day' yesterday, didn't you?"

"She *did*? This is the first I've heard about it."

"Mary told me when I called this afternoon. She says she tried to call us, but we were all gone before she got Renata settled. Renata mentioned it too, this afternoon, but she didn't really want to talk about it, so I just let it pass."

I shrugged. "It's been quite a while since her last one," I said. "There's probably some sort of sequence involved— thirteen days normie and then one day bonkers. If things are going the way they're supposed to, the normie periods will get longer and longer, and the bonkers days will get further and further apart."

"We can always hope, I guess." Sylvia sounded dubious, though.

Right after breakfast on Saturday, James and I shooed everybody out of the kitchen and started prying off the baseboards and door moldings in preparation for putting down the new floor tiles.

"Couldn't we just butt the tiles up against the baseboards?" James asked me.

I shook my head. "You always get gaps if you do it that way, and those gaps fill up with gunk every time somebody mops the floor. It starts to get fragrant after a while, and we *do* eat in here."

"Ah," he said. "I knew there had to be a reason for it."

"That's not the *only* reason, pard. I'm not all that great with a linoleum knife, and sometimes the edges I leave are kind of ragged. When we nail the baseboards back in place, they'll cover a multitude of sins. Perfection's in the eye of the beholder. You and I may know about these little goofs, but nobody else will."

"I may ponder that all day."

"Just don't tell anybody else about it, OK?"

We started on one side and worked our way across the floor. The guy who'd come up with "peel and stick" tiles had made life a lot more pleasant for people who did floors. If you get the first row good and square, you can cover a lot of floor in a hurry. It's a piece of cake—right up until you come to the far wall. That's usually when the swearing starts. Measurements get crucial at that point, and older houses are almost never exactly plumb and square. Houses settle after a few years. The doors start to stick, and the floors sag and buckle. Gravity's nice, I suppose, but it sure makes laying tile a bear.

My new linoleum knife gave me a lot of help at that stage. You really want a good sharp point when you get down to detailed cutting.

"That's one ugly implement," James observed. "I wouldn't want to have to carve a turkey with *that* thing."

"It wasn't built for carving, James," I told him. "The point's all that matters. If you get a good clean cut on the first pass, you're home free. That's why the handle's so beefy. You've got to lean into it to get through the vinyl. Things start to go to hell if you have to make more than one pass—and you've got to be careful with the silly thing. It'll slice skin even faster than vinyl, and it cuts long, wide, and deep. One little mistake earns you a quick trip to the emergency room. It usually gives you nice straight scars, though."

"I'll leave the cutting to you, old buddy," he told me. "I don't want to go anywhere near that thing." He glanced at his watch and looked around at our floor. "We might even finish up today," he said.

"That depends on how much trouble we have with the doorframes," I corrected. "*That's* the part I dread. A guy can spend more time cutting and fitting around the doorframes than he will on all the rest of the floor. Why don't you go tell Trish that we'd better send out for pizza or something this evening. You and I might be at this until midnight. We'd *better* finish up today, though, if we can. I'm only good for about one day on my knees like this—and if we tie up the kitchen for *too* long, we'll have some very grumpy ladies to deal with."

"You're probably right," he agreed. "I'll go talk with Trish." He looked at our new floor. "It *does* look nice, Mark. The girls might complain a bit, but I think they'll be very happy with what you've done today."

"I hope so. I sure wouldn't want to have to do it again. Revision's OK when it comes to essays, but it's a real pain when you're talking about a floor."

CHAPTER TEN

Twink had been making noises about wanting to go to church on Sunday. When I finally admitted that we couldn't finish up with the floor tiles on Saturday night, Sylvia volunteered to fill in for me so that James and I could finish up in the morning. Getting that kitchen back on-line was the number one priority at the boardinghouse.

Bright and early Sunday morning, James and I fixed a couple of rough spots, and put the door moldings and baseboards back in place. Then we picked up all the scraps, put my tools away, and swabbed the new floor with a damp mop. "Looks good to me," James said, as we gave it that last look-see.

"It'll do," I agreed. "There's a couple of boo-boos, but they're not too visible. Shall we show it off?"

"Might as well," James agreed. He leaned out into the hallway and called to Trish and Erika.

"It's beautiful!" Trish exclaimed, when the two of them looked in.

"It's just a floor, Trish," I told her. "It's not exactly a work of art."

"Don't bad-mouth it, Mark," Erika told me. "It makes the whole kitchen look bigger and brighter. You guys do nice work."

"Very nice," Trish agreed. "Can we walk on it? I mean, do we have to give it time to dry or anything?"

"It's all ready to go, babe. The kitchen's yours again." I

gave it a critical inspection. "It does look better, I guess. Of course the old one was pretty grubby. Did Sylvia happen to tell you when she'll be coming back? Sunday's usually my day to keep Twink away from Mary's place to give the poor lady time to catch up on her sleep. I've worked graveyard shift a few times myself, and it starts to wear you down after a while."

"Sylvia wasn't too specific," Erika replied, "but I think she plans to spend the day with Renata. They get along pretty well, but I think Sylvia's got some ulterior motives. She's been talking about a case history sort of thing—and maybe even a subject for her master's thesis."

"Oh?"

"Renata fascinates her. She knows that the poor kid's got serious problems, and she wants to see if she can put a name to them."

"She hasn't said anything to me about it."

"She wouldn't, Mark," James told me. "You're Renata's semiofficial keeper, and Sylvia's probably trying to sneak around behind you."

"Oh, that's just dandy," I said sourly. "Now I've got something else to worry about."

"Sylvia isn't going to hurt Renata, Mark," Trish assured me. "Abnormals are her specialty, so she knows what she's doing."

"Nobody knows for sure what's keeping Twink afloat, Trish, not even Dr. Fallon. I think Sylvia and I'd better have a talk about this before she goes too much further."

Sylvia didn't get in until late, though, and the house rules sort of prohibited any conferences between the upstairs people and the downstairs folks after ten o'clock.

She was still all fired up about her "case history" notion at breakfast Monday morning.

"Most of the time an interview with a mental patient only produces grunts and mumbles," she told us, "but Renata can

think and she can talk. She can describe not only her own behavior, but the peculiarities of her fellow patients as well. She
could be an absolute gold mine of information about various
mental states, ranging through all the standard ones and on up
into ones that don't even have names yet."

I decided right then to step in before she went too much
further. "Have you got anything on the fire for tomorrow evening, Sylvia?" I asked her.

"What did you have in mind?" she asked archly.

"Behave yourself," I scolded. "I think maybe we should
bounce this off Dr. Fallon before you go much further with
this case history of yours. Twink's still pretty fragile, so you'd
probably better have a set of ground rules to go by. There are
some things you don't talk about, and certain questions you
don't ask."

"I know what I'm doing, Mark," she told me in a blunt sort
of way. "I'm not going to damage your precious Twinkie."

"We don't seem to be talking on the same wavelength here,
Toots," I said flatly. "Let me put it to you right straight out. I
can have Renata all packed up and out of Seattle in about two
hours, and I can arrange things so that you won't be able to
find her. I won't like it much, but I'll do it if I have to. We go
see Fallon so that you can get instructions, or I'll pull the plug
on your little project. We are going to do things my way, because I'm the guy with the 'on-off' switch. Do you read me?"

"Whoo," Erika said. "This one's a tiger, isn't he?"

Sylvia was glaring at me, and she seemed right on the
verge of exploding.

"Let's back away from these ultimatums and declarations
of war, shall we?" James stepped in smoothly. "Do you have
any objections about this meeting with Dr. Fallon, Sylvia?"

"Of course not," she snapped, "but I don't need to have
people who don't know what they're talking about trying to
tell me how I should handle things in my field."

"I'm not trying to tell you what to do, Sylvia," I said,
backing away a little. "All I'm saying is that Dr. Fallon is the

real expert, and he can give you a crash course in how to approach Twink without putting her into meltdown. We both lose if she goes bonkers again."

"I don't object to a meeting with Dr. Fallon, Mark," she told me in a more reasonable tone. "Hurting Renata—even by accident—is the last thing I want. Don't issue commands and ultimatums like that, though. I can be just as bad-tempered as you can."

"No kidding," I said wryly. Then I grinned at her. "Peace?" I offered.

"If you promise to behave."

"Sure."

"All right, then," she agreed with a bright smile, "peace it is." Then she laughed a bit ruefully. "We weren't really getting anywhere with all the yelling and waving our arms around anyway, were we?"

"Not so's you'd notice it."

After my Milton seminar that morning I went back to the house to call Dr. Fallon.

"Is Renata all right?" he asked as soon as he answered.

"She seems fine, Doc," I told him. "Missing her session with you on Friday didn't upset her. I'm calling because I think you should talk with abnormal Sylvia. She's the one I told you about—the girl who's majoring in weirdos. She wants to do one of those case history things on Twink, and I thought you might want to kick it around with her. Sylvia's sharp, but it might be a good idea to keep a tight rein on her until we're sure she knows what she's doing. A few rounds of 'do this, but don't do that' before we let her jump in?"

"You've got that right," he agreed.

"If you aren't going to be busy tomorrow evening, I thought I might bring her up so that you can talk it over with her. Telephones are all right, I guess, but sometimes things should be handled face-to-face."

"Good point," he agreed. "How about seven-thirty?"

"No problem, Doc. We'll see you then."

Tuesday was a light day for me. It seems to turn out that way in grad school. Tuesdays and Thursdays are usually devoted to research, and Mondays, Wednesdays, and Fridays are class days.

Sylvia was edgy while we waited for the five o'clock rush to subside, and she'd even gone so far as to put on a suit, for God's sake. I decided not to make an issue of that. She kept pacing back and forth, and I thought we ought to get started before her spring got wound too much tighter. "Let's hit the bricks, babe," I suggested about quarter to six.

"I thought you'd never ask," she replied.

We took Interstate 5 north toward Everett. It was raining, naturally. It's always raining in Puget Sound country. It's one of the few places in the country where you have to mow your lawn three times a week in the summer.

The traffic had thinned a bit when we took the Snohomish turnoff and went east across the flats.

"That's moderately depressing," Sylvia noted as we went over the soggy marshland around Ebey Slough. "How much farther is the sanitarium?"

"Five or six miles. It's sort of secluded, and there aren't any big signs pointing the way. The neighbors probably wouldn't like that very much. A bughouse isn't exactly what you'd call a tourist attraction."

We took a left at Cavalero's Corner and started up the steep hill toward Lake Stevens. It wasn't too long before we came to the turnoff. I followed the long driveway, drove in through the gate, and parked in the courtyard.

"Impressive," Sylvia said. "It's sort of spread out, isn't it?"

"Land isn't too expensive here," I told her, "and Dr. Fallon keeps the place low-key. A tall building out here in the boonies might attract attention. Let's go see the man, Sylvia."

"Oh, dear," she faltered.

"Don't get uptight, babe. Doc Fallon isn't hard to get along with. We're all on the same side here, so he probably won't bite."

Inside, the lady at the front desk knew me, and waved us through. I led the way along the hall and knocked loudly on Fallon's door. "It's only me, Doc," I called. "Don't shoot."

Sylvia gave me a startled look.

"Inside joke," I told her.

"Come in, Mark," Fallon answered.

I opened the door, and Sylvia and I went on in. Fallon looked slightly startled when he saw Sylvia for the first time. "She's small, but she's wiry, Doc," I told him. "This is Sylvia Cardinale, the lady who wants to major in Twinkie."

"Has he always been like this, Dr. Fallon?" Sylvia asked. "Or is this some recent aberration?"

"Be nice," I murmured. "This, of course, is Dr. Fallon, the resident Twinkie expert."

"I'm honored, Dr. Fallon," Sylvia said.

"Please," he replied, smiling at her. "Have a seat, Miss Cardinale. Mark tells me that you'd like to put together a case history on Renata Greenleaf, with a possible eye on expanding it into your Master's thesis."

"That might depend on how the case history turns out, Dr. Fallon," she replied. "To be honest with you, Renata has me baffled. Sometimes, I'm positive that she's manic-depressive, and other times, I suspect multiple personality disorder. She changes so fast sometimes."

"Those broad labels don't always fit the individual cases," he told her. "Over the years I've found that most patients are unique. They might lean in the direction of one category or another, but they almost always have personal idiosyncrasies. Renata's case derives from trauma, and that always complicates matters."

"I've noticed," Sylvia agreed wryly.

"I thought you might have. How much has Mark told you about the incident that brought her here in the first place?"

Sylvia recited the bare facts of Renata's case, while Fallon nodded approval. Encouraged, she started to review her own observations. "She mentions 'loneliness' fairly often, and I suspect that her sense of loneliness might be symptomatic. At the deepest level of her consciousness, she's vaguely aware that something or somebody is missing."

"Excellent," Fallon said approvingly. "A lot of people would have missed that. From a certain perspective, half of Renata isn't there anymore. Her amnesia has blocked out all memory of Regina, but there's a nagging sense of vacancy— a loneliness for something she can't even remember. I'm sure you can see the significance of that."

"Oh, yes," Sylvia agreed, "and now I see why Mark was so concerned about my 'case history.' Some of the so-called experts in the field seem to believe in the blunt object approach to therapy. If some half-wit decided to hit Renata over the head with Regina's death, all he'd succeed in doing would be to put her back into a straitjacket."

"Miss Cardinale seems to be a fortunate find, Mark," Fallon said. "Don't let her get away."

"And she's cute, too," I added.

"You aren't supposed to notice that, Mark," Sylvia scolded.

"Pretend you didn't notice my noticing," I replied.

Sylvia grinned as she turned back to Dr. Fallon. "I was talking with Renata last week," she said, "and something came up. You did know that she has a strong objection to notebooks, didn't you? She as much as admitted that as soon as she sees somebody taking notes, she starts making up wild stories to hide her real feelings."

Dr. Fallon nodded. "It's cropped up before. Renata could probably send poor Dr. Freud right up the wall. Those of us in the field reach for notebooks almost automatically, and as soon as Renata sees a notebook, she does her best to avoid the truth."

"That's not going to make my case history any easier," she complained.

"Why don't we talk with Charlie?" I mused. "I'm sure he'll be able to come up with a way to plant a bug."

"I'm sure he could," she said. "I hadn't thought of that."

"The great thing about a planted bug would be that it'll catch every word," I added, "along with inflections and other things that might reveal anything Twink's trying to hide. Notes aren't always that accurate, but a tape gets it all. What's even better, maybe, is that Sylvia can run off copies for you, Doc. You'll know exactly what's going on." Then I laughed. "This is all starting to sound like a James Bond movie, isn't it?"

"Whatever works, Mark," Fallon said. "I think this might be very useful. To be honest with you, Miss Cardinale, I had my doubts about this whole idea. The notion of taped conversations puts a whole new light on it, though. Let's try it and see what happens."

Sylvia was elated when we went out to my car. "I owe you one, Mark," she told me. "Dr. Fallon really bought into this idea when you came up with the notion of taping my conversations with Renata. Your 'let's plant a bug' suggestion brought him around."

She frowned as we drove on out of the courtyard. "There might still be a problem, though."

"Oh? What's that?"

"I'll have to make sure that Renata and I always have our little discussions in the vicinity of Charlie's microphone."

"Where have you been for the past several years, Sylvia?" I asked her. "Charlie's right on top of all the latest technology, and the FBI's been planting bugs in people's underwear for a long time."

"I hadn't thought of that," she admitted. "Hers or mine?"

I wasn't going to touch that one—either way!

It was about ten-thirty when we got back to the boarding-house, and I went upstairs to consult Charlie about making secret recordings.

"Piece of cake," he told me. "You'd better clear it with Trish, though."

"Why?"

"There's a law or six about recording conversations on the sly, Mark. Everybody knows that."

"I thought that only involved recording phone conversations."

"The laws are a little murky, but we might need a court order to stay out of trouble."

"I hadn't thought of that," I admitted. "Doc Fallon can probably persuade some judge to go along, but a Snohomish County court order might not be valid here in King County."

"It's not like we were going to take it to court, Mark," he said, "but you'd still better bounce it off Trish and see what she has to say. Bending a few laws now and then doesn't bother me too much, but if Sylvia's going to try to float an M.S. degree on this, those recordings had better be strictly legal. If they aren't, her department might throw her thesis in the garbage can. Then she'll come after you and me with a baseball bat."

"We'll clear it with Trish before we take it any further," I assured him.

I had a certain sense of accomplishment when I went to bed, and I slept very well. I was feeling all bright-eyed and bushy-tailed when I went down to the kitchen Wednesday morning. The crew was all clustered around that little TV set on the counter, though.

"Not another one?" I demanded incredulously.

"Oh, gosh yes," Charlie replied. "It's getting to be a habit in this part of town."

"Anywhere near here?" I asked.

"Gas Works Park, down on Lake Union," Erika replied. "It's about ten blocks from here."

"Gas Works?"

"Don't ask," she replied, rolling her eyes upward. "Seattle

sprouts parks almost like dandelions. I haven't checked a map lately, but there's probably a Garbage Dump Park and a Sewage Treatment Plant Park somewhere."

"Did we lose another junior hoodling?" I asked.

"Not exactly," James told me. "This one was forty-seven years old, and he evidently doesn't have a police record—at least not around here. He moved to Seattle from Kansas City about a year ago, and the local police are checking him out with the authorities there."

"It shoots Burpee's theory—and several others as well—full of holes," Charlie added. "This Kansas City guy hasn't really had enough time to hook up with any local dope dealers, and he had a regular job as a nighttime janitor in a big office complex over in Ballard."

"What was he doing in a park on Lake Union, then? Wasn't he supposed to be working?"

"I've worked nights a few times," Charlie said. "The boss doesn't come around much after midnight."

I frowned. "He doesn't have much in common with the ones who got sliced up before, does he?" I asked.

"Not even a little," Charlie agreed. "This Slasher guy seems to be spreading out. It's starting to look like we've got an ecumenical killer out there."

"There has to be some sort of connection," I protested.

"Maybe so," James said, "but the police haven't figured it out yet."

"The strange thing is that nobody ever hears anything," Erika added. "Not one of the victims died instantly. There should have been a lot of screaming, but nobody ever seems to hear it."

"That's bugging my brother, too," Charlie told her. "He mentioned it right after the Windemere killing. It's really got him baffled."

"What was this guy's name?" I asked.

"Finley," Trish replied. "Edward Finley."

"Maybe the Muñoz killing was a fluke. Andrews, Garrison, and Finley obviously weren't Chicano dope dealers. There has to be some connection, but the cops haven't spotted it yet—or if they have, they aren't talking about it."

"I'm still leaning in the direction of 'targets of opportunity,' " Charlie said. "Once our cutter gets all wired up, he'll take out the first guy he sees."

"I don't buy it," Sylvia disagreed. "Everything we've heard so far says 'psychotic,' and psychotics don't function that way. The reason may be so warped that we wouldn't understand it, but there has to be some kind of connection. Maybe all four victims used the same aftershave lotion, or maybe they were all whistling the same tune, but there's something that connects them in the Slasher's mind. The police won't solve this until somebody makes that connection."

"And as soon as he does, the media folks will all go into deep mourning," Charlie added sardonically. "Someday—someday—some TV personality's going to announce that nothing significant has happened lately, then tell everybody to turn off the TV set and read a good book—or clean up the garage."

Twink didn't make it to class the next day. That was starting to get out of hand. I'd been putting off talking with her about it, but I decided that I'd better not procrastinate anymore. I assigned another paper that day, and the groaning wasn't too loud this time. I'd pretty well thinned out the goof-offs by now, and the survivors were all fairly competent. At least they were past the "Run, Spot, run" stage, and we could get into the more complicated stuff—like subject-verb agreement and dangling participles.

After supper that evening, Charlie, James, and I made our customary "after the killing" visit to the Green Lantern to get Bob West's views on this latest crime.

"I thought you guys might show," Bob said, as we joined

him in one of the back booths. "You're starting to get predictable."

"We're still in the war zone, Bob," Charlie reminded him, "and we're sure not getting much in the way of truth from the newspapers or the TV. Did the head honcho at the cop shop clamp the lid down or something? All that's coming out of the media is name, rank, and serial number. What's the scoop on the Gas Works Park thing?"

"We don't have much in the way of scoop to work with, kid. The Gas Works Park killing torpedoed just about everything we had to go on. About the only break we got this time was an earwitness who claims he heard some noise, but he's a wino who was up to his eyebrows in Mogen David and Thunderbird. He claims he heard dogs howling at the time of the killing, but he doesn't have a watch, so he might be off by several hours. That park's in a commercial district—various little shops and whatnot—so we can't find anybody to verify his story."

"If it's not a residential area, why would there be any dogs in the vicinity?" James asked.

"There shouldn't be," Bob admitted. "We're following up on it, but it's altogether possible that the dogs came out of the same bottle our wino's pet pink elephants do."

"I think we'd better clamp down on our girls," James said. "It's starting to get dangerous out there. The Slasher seems to be killing people at random, and that throws everything up in the air."

"Way up in the air," Bob agreed, "and there are girls running around alone all over this part of town. Half the student body at the university is female, and college girls do strange things sometimes. The only real human being our wino saw last night was a girl on a bicycle riding past the park." He leaned back in the booth. "We've had four murders in the last month or so, all within five miles of the university campus. That raises the possibility that our Slasher might be a student. So far, all the victims have been guys, but if James is right about the Slasher branching out, I don't think any-body's really safe. In spite of that pepper spray, I'd say that it might be time to enforce your 'nobody goes out alone after dark' rule stringently. Lie to your ladies if you have to—tell them that you have to go pick up a book, or you need a pack of cigarettes—whatever. It's dangerous out there now, so do what you have to."

"You're just loaded with good cheer, aren't you, Bob?" Charlie said.

"You guys asked me," Bob replied. "If you don't like the answer, tough."

So we started using the buddy system for each and every after-dark excursion. Fortunately, the girls barely complained at all, and we made it to Saturday without any untoward incidents.

Early Saturday morning, I moved Operation Bookshelves into Charlie's room. That black ceiling of his really bugged me for some reason.

"Don't look at it," Charlie told me, when I started to complain.

"What's that you're reading?" I asked curiously. He seemed to be deep in a rather slender book.

"Kierkegaard," he said. "He sure comes up with snappy ti-tles, doesn't he? This one's *The Sickness Unto Death*. Great reading for a gloomy day, huh?"

"Aren't you supposed to be working on Erika's car?"

"The part I need wasn't on the shelf at the auto supply place. They had to order it."

"Convenient."

"I thought so." He set his book aside. "A little bit of that goes a long way," he noted.

"You're a hard-science guy, Charlie. What the hell are you doing reading philosophy?"

"James mentioned existentialism. The notion that only a

few people are qualified to make the choices for the rest of humanity sort of got my attention."

"It's a dirty job," I noted, "but according to the existentialists, somebody's got to do it."

"Maybe I ought to volunteer," Charlie said. "We've got all these earthshaking choices out there—which team we should root for in the World Series; which girls are prettier, blondes or brunettes; whether Fords are better than Chevys—you know, all that earthshaking crap."

I shrugged. "Your choices would probably be as good as anybody else's," I said. "Grab the other end of my tape, would you? I want to be sure I've got this measurement exact. This job would be a whole lot easier if the damn house hadn't settled so much. Nothing in the whole building is precisely plumb and square."

"Not even the people who live here," Charlie added. "We've all got our little off-center peculiarities, but that's what makes life so interesting, isn't it?"

"As long as we aren't too far off center, old buddy. If somebody's leaning thirty-seven degrees to the right or the left, he starts moving into Twinkie territory, and that's a quick ticket to the bughouse."

"How's she doing, by the way?"

"I haven't got a clue, Charlie. Some days she's just fine; other days, she seems to be heading back to the loony bin."

"Everybody has ups and downs, Mark."

"True. But if Twink flies apart again, it's a clear win for the other side."

"Then we'll all have to concentrate on keeping her bolted together, won't we?"

"All we can do is try, I guess."

Second Movement

DIES IRAE

CHAPTER ELEVEN

Sundays were always pretty laid-back at the Erdlund house. It was the one day of the week when we could sleep late if we really wanted to, and breakfast was pretty much when we got around to it.

It was about ten o'clock when I finally shambled on downstairs, drawn by the smell of Erika's coffee.

"Hey, sack-rat," Charlie said, grinning at me, "we thought you might sleep 'til noon."

"Don't pick on him," Erika scolded, pouring me a cup of coffee. "At least not until his eyes are open." She handed me the cup, and I took it gratefully and sat down in the breakfast nook.

"I feel like pancakes this morning," Charlie said hopefully to Trish.

"You don't look at all like a pancake, Charlie," Erika told him without even cracking a smile. "Corned beef hash, maybe, but hardly a pancake."

"Make her stop that, Trish," Charlie complained.

"Be nice, children," Trish told them. "Don't fight."

"It's Sunday, Mama Trish," James rumbled. "The children always play on Sunday."

Trish sighed, rolling her eyes up. "I know," she said.

"Where's Sylvia?" I asked, looking around the kitchen.

"She's getting ready for church," Erika told me. "She's going to take Renata to noon Mass."

"Sylvia's case history project's taking a lot of heat off you, isn't it, Mark?" Charlie suggested.

"You don't hear me complaining, do you?" I answered. "Did we get an OK on that bug?"

"I checked with Mr. Rankin," Trish told me. "He's a senior partner at the law firm. He didn't see any problems with it from a legal standpoint. He added one stipulation, though."

"Oh?"

"He said that if Sylvia wanted to be strictly legal, she'd have to get Renata's permission to tape their conversations."

"Ouch!"

"Rankin's one of those 'dot the i's and cross the t's' sort of lawyers," Trish said. "He wins a lot of cases, though."

"Sylvia's already taken care of the problem, Mark," James said. "She came right out and told Renata that the tape recordings would be a substitute for the notebooks that seem to cause Renata some serious problems." He smiled faintly. "There *was* a certain amount of subterfuge involved, though," he added. "The recorder was right out in plain sight when Sylvia taped Renata's permission, but our sneaky little house-mate sort of neglected to mention the hidden microphone that's going to be catching *most* of their conversations."

"Is that legal?" I asked Trish.

"It's probably close enough," she replied. "Sylvia's not going to be taking the tapes into court."

"Where did you put the bug?" I asked Charlie.

"*I* didn't," he replied. "I offered, but Sylvia told me to keep my hands to myself. I had to shield the back of the micro-phone, though. It's fairly sensitive, and it kept picking up her heartbeat."

"I don't think we need to pursue that much further," Trish told us. "Go watch television or something, gentlemen. Get out from underfoot."

James led Charlie and me through the dining room to the parlor, and we sat drinking coffee while the ladies made breakfast. "Isn't that tape recorder going to be kind of bulky and cumbersome for Sylvia to carry around, Charlie?" I asked. "If they're out roaming around in a shopping mall and Twink says something that's significant, Sylvia could miss getting it on tape."

"Haven't you ever heard of miniaturization, Mark?" he asked me with an amused expression. "They've got recorders now that're about the size of a cigarette pack, and Sylvia's microphone—the bug—is a sort of tiny radio transmitter. There are some alternatives, but she wanted it up and running in a hurry, so I kept it fairly basic."

"Whatever works for her, I guess," I said. Then I scratched my chin. "I wasn't really all that happy about Sylvia's case history scheme at first," I admitted, "but it's sure going to take a lot of chores off *my* back. She's more or less volunteered to make those weekly trips to Lake Stevens on a permanent basis, and now she's taking on the religious chores as well. Of course, if her case history thing works out and she can expand it, she'll get her master's degree out of it, so I'm not really imposing on her all *that* much, am I?"

"Just keep saying that to yourself, Mark," James suggested. "If you say it often enough, you might even start to believe it."

We were all fairly well settled in by now. A student's schedule's not at all like doing honest work: I just kept fighting with John Milton, grading freshman papers, and watching out for Twinkie.

Then on Wednesday she came apart again. She missed my class, so as soon as I dismissed the students, I made a quick run up to Mary's place in Wallingford.

"She had another one of those damn nightmares," Mary told me when I got there.

"I thought she was starting to outgrow them."

"Not so's you'd notice it," Mary said. "I hit her with a sleeping pill again, and it put her right out. You don't necessarily have to mention that to your little housemate. If she rats me off to Fallon, there'll be hell to pay."

"He *does* get a little worked up about that, doesn't he? You're looking beat, Mary. Why don't you grab some sleep? I'll keep an eye on Renata."

"I'll be all right, Mark. My schedule got juggled this week, so I've got tonight off."

"Are you sure?"

"I'll be fine. What's the deal on these tape recordings Ren told me about?"

"It came up last week," I told her, explaining about the recordings Sylvia was making—with Twink's permission. "But I don't think she realizes that Sylvia's wearing that bug, *or* that Fallon's getting copies of the tapes."

"Slick," Mary said. "We've had some cases thrown out of court because some eager beaver planted bugs without a court order."

"Yeah, we're trying to get it all nice and legal. Plus, Sylvia's making things a lot easier for you and me, taking over the Friday trips to Lake Stevens and the Sunday-go-to-church stuff."

"You noticed that," Mary said slyly. "Les called me on Saturday, and he told me that he and Inga got quite a kick out of your little friend."

"Hey, the more, the merrier." Then something sort of clicked together for me. "Oh, hell," I said.

"What?"

"I just had an idea, Mary. Maybe that bug's a way for us to get to the bottom of these damned nightmares that keep zonking Twink out of action."

"I'm all for that. Once we clear those up, I think Ren's going to be OK. What's this idea of yours?"

"The next time Twink comes unraveled, hold off on the sleeping pill. Give me a call instead, and I'll bring Sylvia over. She'll be able to get everything Twink says down on tape."

"She's not very coherent, Mark," Mary replied a bit dubiously.

"It might not make sense to you or me, but Doc Fallon should be able to figure out what it means. If Sylvia's right here with her bug, she can tape the whole thing. Then we'll pass it off to Fallon. It'll be almost like he's sitting here in person, and once he gets some details, he might be able to pinpoint what's sending our girl up the wall."

"I think you might have earned your pay today, kid," she said then. "If Fallon's got a ringside seat—on tape, anyway— maybe he can turn off these nightmares, and once those damn things are out of the way, Ren's home free."

"It's worth a try. I'll kick it around with Sylvia, and she can bounce it off Fallon and see what he thinks. Are you going to be all right, Mary? I'll stay if you want me to."

"Run along, Mark. Ren's dead to the world, so she doesn't need a baby-sitter."

I tapped on Sylvia's door when I got back to the boardinghouse.

"You rang?" she said, opening the door.

"Twink's down with nightmares again," I told her.

"Maybe I should go over to her aunt's place."

"What for? Mary put her down with a sleeping pill, so all you'd get would be snores. Mary and I came up with a plan, though, and we'd like to have you bounce it off Doc Fallon and see what he thinks."

"Whip it on me," she said with a vapid smile.

"The *next* time Twinkie takes a run through nightmare alley, Mary's going to call me instead of zapping her with a pill. Then you and I'll bag on over to Mary's place, and you can get Twink's ravings down on tape. About all we've been able to tell Doc Fallon so far is that Twink has nightmares now and then. We've never been able to give him any specifics. If you can nudge Twink for details about those dreams that wipe her out, Fallon might be able to get to the bottom of it and come up with a cure—hypnosis, maybe, or some kind of tranquilizer."

"That's a *very* good idea, Mark," Sylvia told me. "You've got a feel for this sort of thing."

"Not really, babe. It's just that I've been majoring in Twinkie for the past several years. Mary and I kicked it around, and we think that getting rid of those nightmares would probably solve most of Twink's problems."

"It might be a little more complex than that, but it'd be a big step in the right direction."

"Then it's worth a try. Keep a supply of batteries for your recorder on hand, Sylvia. These nightmares pop up without much warning, so we'll need to be ready."

Twink showed up for class on Thursday, and she seemed to be pretty much OK again. I was almost positive that if we could get her past those damned nightmares, she'd be on the road to normal.

My supply of scrap lumber was starting to run low, so on Saturday Charlie and I ran up to Everett to raid Les Greenleaf's scrap heap again. Now that I'd gotten used to them, these Saturday workdays had become almost a form of relaxation for me.

We got back to the boardinghouse, and I took my tape measure and notepad into Trish's room to get down the exact numbers I'd be working with.

"Is it going to take very long?" she asked me. "I hate having my room all torn up."

"I'll probably be able to knock them out next Saturday," I told her. "Your law books are all the same size, so I won't have to juggle the shelves around. That'll make things go faster. I've got a suggestion, though."

"Oh?"

"Take a little time when you pull your books. Stack them over against that far wall, but keep them in order. They're all the same color as well as the same size. If you jumble them all up, it'll take you a month to get them squared away. I'm *still* trying to find a couple of my books."

"I'll be careful, Mark."

Midterm examinations rolled around at the university during the week of November 3. Older heads on the teaching faculty always look forward to midterm week, since the freshman class noticeably diminishes after that one. When dear old dad finds out that junior's been goofing off for six straight weeks, he'll usually close the checkbook and tell his vagrant son to go find an honest job.

I dumped my favorite test on my freshmen on Wednesday—"Correct the grammatical errors in the following paragraph." It's a rotten thing to drop on just about anybody, but it exposes the incompetent, and it's easy to grade. If I'd had my wits about me when I first came up with the idea, I'd have copyrighted the damn thing and lived on easy street for the rest of my life.

At supper that evening, Sylvia told me that she had an appointment with her faculty advisor on Friday afternoon. "I'm going to spring the 'planted bug' idea on him," she explained. "I want to be sure that he doesn't have any objections. We tape just about every conversation in the various psycho wards we visit, but I'm going to be taping Renata out in the real world, so I want to clear it with him before I take it much further."

"That makes sense. Always cover your buns."

"I'm glad you approve. But that means I'm going to be tied up on Friday afternoon. Could you take Renata to Lake Stevens for me?"

"Sure, no problem. How many hours of tape have you recorded so far?"

"Fifteen or so. A lot of it's nothing but random conversation, though. I'm going to have to do a lot of editing to get down to the real meat."

"I don't envy you on that, babe. Trimming out the dead-wood can be moderately unfun."

"You've noticed. How clever of you."

"Be nice," I told her.

I caught Twink right before class on Thursday and told her that I'd be taking her to see Fallon Friday.

"Sylvia's not sick, is she?" she asked, clearly concerned.

"No, it's nothing like that. She has to talk with her faculty advisor, is all."

"That's a relief. I'm getting attached to her. Girls need other girls to talk with sometimes. You're nice enough, Markie, but I don't think you're ready for girl talk—not yet, anyway."

"I'll work on it."

"Don't bother, Sylvia's already got it covered." Then she giggled.

"What?" I demanded.

"Never mind," she said with a wicked little smirk.

On Friday morning I turned in my proposal for a paper on Milton's prose works and their relation to his poetry. This wasn't going to be a barn-burner paper, I realized. Milton irritated me, and I was hoping that it wouldn't show. I didn't want to offend our gentle professor, but Cromwell's Puritan theocracy during the seventeenth century had a strong odor of the assorted absolute dictatorships that have so contaminated the twentieth century. Some things never change, I guess, and that "My God's better than your God" crap keeps floating to the surface, doesn't it?

I was at loose ends after class, so I called Twink and suggested that we might as well bag it on up to Everett that morning. "We'll beat the noon rush, Twink," I told her, "and I'll buy you lunch someplace."

"Just like a real date, Markie?" she demanded in that empty-headed voice she dumped on me when she was practicing her cutesy-poo routine.

"Why not?"

"I don't have a *thing* to wear."

"Cool it, kid."

"I'll behave," she promised.

"*Sure* you will."

It was one of those cloudy, blustery autumn days, but at least it wasn't raining—yet. I parked in front of Mary's house and went around to the back door to avoid waking Renata's aunt. I tapped lightly, and Twink opened the door immediately.

"Is she asleep?" I asked quietly.

"Like a baby," Twink replied. "I left her a note."

"Good. Let's split."

"You seem sort of antsy today, Markie."

I shrugged. "Midterm fidgets, I guess. It gets to be a habit after a few years. You'd better bring a coat. It'll probably rain before the day's out."

"Rain? Here? How can you *say* such a thing?"

I let that pass, and we went out front to my car. I drove down toward the campus and then eased us into the northbound lane of Interstate 5. The traffic had slacked off, and it was easy going.

"Is it always this nervous during the midterm exams?" Twink asked me. "Everybody I run into acts like the world's coming to an end."

"It's like a dress rehearsal for finals week, Twink," I told her. "*That's* the one you've got to watch out for. The whole student body starts to come unraveled during finals week—probably because about half of them are wired up on pep pills."

"Do those things actually work all that well?"

"Not really. They *will* keep you awake, but your thinking gets pretty fuzzy after the second or third day."

She laughed. "Boy, does *that* sound familiar," she said. "Is the whole world zonked out most of the time?"

"I don't think the trees are."

"I was talking about people. There seems to be a pill for almost anything, doesn't there? There are pills to pep you up and pills to calm you down, pills to put you to sleep and pills to wake you up. You name it, and there's a pill for it. The world of normies isn't much different from the world of loonies, is it? We all live on a steady diet of pills."

"There's one slight difference, Twink. Loonies take their pills with water. Us normies wash ours down with booze."

"That could do some strange things to your head, Markie."

"Yeah, strange. Unfortunately, it sometimes leads to an overpowering urge to hop in the car and drive off to Idaho at about a hundred and fifty miles an hour."

"Loonies hardly ever do that."

"Probably because they've got better sense."

"Maybe that's why loony bins are called 'asylums.' It's a place where loonies can be protected from those awful normies."

"Take that up with Doc Fallon, Twink. It's out of my field."

Dr. Fallon seemed disappointed that Sylvia hadn't been able to make the trip that Friday. I think he *really* wanted those tapes she was cutting.

I got him off to one side where Twink couldn't hear us and filled him in on our plan to tape Twink's next nightmare.

"Now *that's* the tape I really want," he said enthusiastically.

"I *thought* that might light your fire, Doc," I told him.

After her session with Fallon, Twink and I stopped by her folks' place for supper.

Les Greenleaf and I had a little talk while Inga and Twink were busy in the kitchen. "Are you sure Renata's all right, Mark?" he asked me in a worried tone.

"Most of the time she is, boss," I told him. "She has bad days every so often, but I think we've come up with a way to get a handle on that."

"Oh?"

I told him about our scheme to tape Twink's ravings after the next siege of nightmares.

"Is she *still* having those?" He seemed surprised.

"She sure is. They don't come along very often, but they usually put her out of action for a day at least. Doc Fallon seems to think that those bad dreams are about the only thing that's stalling her complete recovery. Once we get a handle on those, I've got a hunch that we're home free."

"I certainly hope so."

"You're not alone, boss. The whole Twinkie rooting section is behind her all the way."

After dinner, Twink and I went back to Seattle. She fell asleep once we got out onto the interstate, and I drove on in silence.

It was about ten o'clock when I pulled up in front of Mary's house. "We're home, baby sister," I told her, gently pushing her shoulder.

"Did I doze off?"

"Almost immediately," I said. "You didn't snore very loud, though."

"I *never* snore!"

"You want to bet?"

I walked her to Mary's front door, and then I went back to the boardinghouse to get some sleep.

On Saturday morning I went to my little workshop in the basement and put the last coat of stain on the shelves for Trish's room. By now I had the whole procedure down pat, and I was fairly sure I could have the shelves in place before the day was out.

Trish looked in from time to time, but she generally stayed out from underfoot. By noon things were coming right along, and I guess her curiosity got the better of her, so she sat at her desk watching. "I wasn't really all that sure about this notion when you first started, Mark," she admitted, "but it's a definite improvement. When Erika and I took over here, our whole idea was to upgrade the place, then sell it. I'm not so sure now, though. Even after we graduate and move on, we could put a manager in here and hold on to the house. It'd provide Aunt Grace with a steady income."

"Only if you can keep the party boys out, Trish," I told her.

"Graduate students don't party all that much, Mark. You might not be aware of it, but the house is getting quite a reputation. Every week or so I get inquiries about vacancies. Peace and quiet are a rare commodity in student housing."

"The reputation of the place might be based on the current inmates, Trish," I suggested. "We've turned into a fairly tight group here."

"There *is* that, I suppose," she admitted. "We all sort of clicked together right from the start, didn't we? We're almost like a family, really."

"I *do* seem to be getting mommied a lot here lately."

"Mommied?"

"Sorry, Trish. I picked that up from Twinkie. She threatened to mommy all over me once when I was feeling sorry for myself."

"She's the strangest child sometimes."

"Of course she is. She got out of the nuthouse not too long ago."

"In a peculiar way, she's brought us all even closer together, hasn't she? We all want to take care of Renata."

"She's addictive, probably—she hooks just about any unsuspecting person who happens by." I squinted at the bookshelves. "Getting closer, Trish. I think I'll be able to whup this out by suppertime. If you're real extra nice to me, I might even help you reshelve all your books."

"You *had* to remind me, didn't you?" she said with a gloomy sigh.

*   *   *

I turned in my midterm grades on my freshman class on Monday, and the rest of the week marched briskly toward Thanksgiving break: Fall quarter gets chopped up by assorted holidays and special events. We had a break in the weather, though, so those crisp, clear autumn days lifted the perpetual gloom that hovers over the Puget Sound area after Labor Day every year.

I concentrated most of my attention on Milton that week, plowing my way through Milton's *Christian Doctrine*—the translation, not the Latin original. I'll admit that I choked a bit on his bland acceptance of predestination. That's been used as a justification for all kinds of misbehavior over the centuries. Once I pushed that out of the way, though, I saw most of the parallels between that work and *Paradise Lost* that scholars much better than I'll ever be had noticed. It was heavy going, and I finally gave up on Wednesday evening, put it aside, and went to bed.

I was a little punchy when Charlie woke me up on Thursday morning to tell me that I had a phone call.

I pulled on some clothes and stumbled down to the living room where the phone was. "Yeah?" I said into the mouthpiece.

"Mark?" It was Mary.

"It's me, Mary. What's up?"

"You'd better get over here, and bring the girl with the tape recorder. Ren's having problems."

"We'll be right there," I said shortly. Then I hung up. "Sylvia!" I shouted.

"What's up, Mark?" Charlie called from the kitchen.

"Twink's flipped out again. Where the hell's Sylvia?"

"She's getting dressed," Trish told me.

"Please tell her to hurry." I went back upstairs, put on my shoes and socks, grabbed a coat, and made it back down in under a minute. Sylvia looked a bit scrambled, but she was ready to go.

"Did Mary give you any details?" Sylvia asked me, as we hurried to my car.

"No, we'll have to play it by ear when we get there. I don't think I'd push her this time, Sylvia. Let's just get this one on tape."

"You're probably right," she agreed. "Dr. Fallon's the one who'll make the decisions about how to proceed."

The drive only took us about five minutes, and Mary had left her front door standing open. We could hear Twink as soon as we got out of the car. It was a lot worse than I'd expected. Mary's term "bad day" glossed over some pretty awful sounds. Twink was crying, screaming, and making animal-like noises.

I led Sylvia back to Twink's bedroom. Mary was still in uniform, and she was holding our hysterical girl in her arms and rocking back and forth. "Thank God you're here!" she said to Sylvia and me. "This is a bad one. They seem to be getting worse."

"When did you get home, Mary?" I asked.

"About a half hour ago. She was completely out of it when I came through the door."

"Markie!" Twink cried out, struggling to free herself from Mary's grasp. She held her arms out to me imploringly. "We need you!"

That "we" gave me quite a jolt. I hadn't heard *that* since before Regina had died.

"Go to her!" Sylvia gave me a push. "Quick!"

I went to the bed and gently took the sobbing girl from Mary. Then I wrapped my arms around her and held her, rocking back and forth.

"Make them stop, Markie," she pleaded. "The wolves are howling again. Please make them stop."

There was that business about wolves again. I didn't have the faintest idea what it meant.

"Blood!" she wailed in a voice filled with horror. "It's all over me! I'm covered with blood!"

Then she began to tremble violently. "Cold!" she said. "The water's so terribly cold!" Then she suddenly started whispering, her lips very close to my ear—and she wasn't whispering in any language I could understand.

CHAPTER TWELVE

"I think that's about as far as we want to let her go," Mary said bleakly, as Twink kept murmuring to me in twin. "I'd better hit her with a pill now."

"Couldn't we hold off on that for a little longer?" Sylvia asked. "She might give us a little more to work with if we just . . ." She left it up in the air.

"You're not going to get anything you'll be able to understand," Mary told her. "Once she starts babbling like that, she keeps it up for the rest of the day, and by noon they'll be able to hear her in Tacoma. I've been through this before, so I know what's coming. It's time to shut her down."

"She's right, Sylvia," I agreed. "We don't want this to get much worse."

Sylvia sighed. "You're probably right," she said regretfully. "If she'd just keep speaking English, we might be able to get to the root of the problem."

"It doesn't work that way, I'm afraid," Mary said. "I'm going to put her to sleep. You've got all you're going to get that'll make any sense." She went into the bathroom and came back a moment later with a small pill and a glass of water. "Open your mouth, Ren," she said gently.

Twink obediently opened her mouth, and Mary placed the pill on her tongue. "Drink the water now," Mary said then. I got the feeling that Twink actually welcomed the pill.

It took about ten minutes for it to start to work, and Twink murmured to me more and more slowly as the barbiturate closed down her mind. Finally, she sighed and stopped talking. After a moment or two, she started to snore.

"Let's get her undressed and under the covers," Mary said to Sylvia.

I handed Twink off to the ladies and went out to the living room. I was a bit shaken by what had just happened. Mary's term "bad days" pretty much glossed over what was really going on when Twink came unraveled. There'd been an intensity to it that I hadn't really expected.

"Was that more or less the way things have gone every time she's had these nightmares?" Sylvia asked Mary as they came out of the bedroom.

"Not always," Mary replied. "It's a little different each time. Sometimes she's already switched over to gibberish before I get home. There doesn't seem to be much pattern to it."

Sylvia frowned. "That's odd," she said. "Disturbed people almost always repeat these incidents in exactly the same way every time."

"There are some things that stay the same," Mary told her. "There's always talk about wolves and blood and cold water."

"The bit about 'blood' is fairly obvious," Sylvia said. "These nightmares are almost certainly a reliving of that night when her sister was murdered. When she's awake, her amnesia has all memory of her sister totally blotted out. At the subconscious level, though, she's aware of her sister *and* of what happened to her. Every now and then it surfaces in the form of a nightmare."

"Then she's repeating that night over and over again?" I asked.

"Probably so. She doesn't understand it, though. Dreams are filled with symbols. 'Blood' probably really means blood, but the wolves and the cold water could be symbols for something else. Dreams are filled with symbols that don't make much sense when we wake up. Dr. Fallon might recognize them. He had Renata under observation for quite a while at the sanitarium, so he might have cracked the code." She patted her purse. "I think this tape's going to be worth its weight in gold. Up until now, all we've been able give Dr. Fallon have been some rather vague descriptions of what Renata says during these incidents. The tape will give him everything she said. I think maybe you should go with us tomorrow, Mark. You probably know her better than anyone else, and I'm sure you caught a lot more of what just happened than I did."

"She's got a point, Mark," Mary agreed. "This might just be the break Fallon's been looking for. We don't want to let it slip past."

"You're probably right," I conceded, "and we might want to go up there a little earlier than usual. I've got a hunch that Fallon might need more than an hour to sort through this."

I wasn't able to get very much done the rest of that day. Mary had always glossed over what Twink went through on a "bad day." Now that I'd actually seen one, I couldn't imagine how she was able to bounce back so fast. Evidently, she was a lot tougher than she looked.

We kicked it around at the boardinghouse that evening, and Sylvia let the others hear what she'd recorded.

"That's one sick baby," Erika observed, after we'd heard the tape. "Have the other days been like this one?"

"Mary says that this one was fairly standard," Sylvia said. "We'll see if she can recover fully by tomorrow, the way she has up 'til now."

"If she can bounce back in twenty-four hours after something like that, she must be made of cast iron," Charlie noted.

"Oh, by the way, Trish," James said then, "I'll have to beg off on fix-it Saturday this week. I have to pick up a friend at Sea-Tac—family emergency."

"Something serious?"

"Well, we hope not. I've got a friend up in Everett whose wife is very sick. His son's taking a leave from law school at Harvard, and I promised to pick him up at the airport."

"He's walking away from Harvard in the middle of the autumn term?" Trish asked incredulously. "Isn't he taking an awful chance?"

"I didn't get the details," James admitted, "but I guess the dean bent a few rules for Andrew—that's the young man's name, Andrew Perry. As I understand it, though, he's doing very well there—and, of course he's a black student, so Harvard doesn't want to make waves. He'll be able to make up after he goes back."

"What's his mother's condition?" Erika asked.

"Ovarian cancer," James replied. "The doctors at the hospital in Everett *think* they've caught it in time, but you never really know with something like that."

I hit my Milton seminar on Friday morning, and Sylvia was waiting for me when I got back to the boardinghouse.

"Everything's set," she told me. "Fallon wants Mary to sit in, too. She's been through all of these bad days, so she knows more about them than either you or I could possibly know. Fallon wants you and Mary to go up early and give him the tape. He says he'll need all the details *before* I deliver Renata. I'll take her shopping or something while you two fill him in. Then you and Mary should leave before Renata's appointment, because he doesn't want Renata to know what we're doing."

"More sneaky stuff?"

"Not entirely. He just doesn't want Renata to realize that we're ganging up on her. If she catches on, she might clam up, and that'd make things difficult."

"No worse than if she starts answering all his questions in twin-speak," I added. "I've got a hunch he'd go wild if she did that to him."

"I called Mary and set everything up," Sylvia said. "I'll pick Renata up early, and we'll dawdle around in the Northgate Mall before we go on to Lake Stevens. Give me about ten minutes, then pick Mary up. That'll give you two time to fill

Fallon in on what happened yesterday and take off again. He wants everything to seem run-of-the-mill and ordinary."

Sylvia was a little sweetie, but she *did* tend to belabor the obvious sometimes. I gave her about fifteen minutes to get Twink out from underfoot, and then I picked Mary up.

"Do you think Fallon's still all torqued out about my sleeping pills?" she asked me as we drove north.

"I haven't heard any screaming from him lately. I think he finally realizes that you're not popping Twink every five minutes."

"I think I'll nail that down when we get there. People who treat me like some brainless amateur irritate me, for some reason."

"You're just oversensitive, Mary," I kidded her.

"It's a failing of mine," she replied sardonically.

Mary and I got along very well. She was one tough cookie sometimes, but that's probably what Twinkie needed.

It was about ten-thirty when we were ushered in to Dr. Fallon's office. "This is Twink's Aunt Mary, Doc," I introduced them.

"We meet at last," he said.

"It's probably overdue," she agreed. "Mark has the tape Sylvia made yesterday. Do you want to listen to it before we get down to business?"

"Maybe you should fill me in first on exactly what happened when you came home," he suggested.

Mary shrugged. "It was pretty much the way it's always been on one of Ren's bad days. It's happened often enough before that I wasn't particularly surprised. I got home from work about quarter to eight, and I could hear her raving as soon as I opened the front door. I knew what was going on, so I called Mark before I even went into her bedroom. Ordinarily, when I come home and find her like that, I just tap her out with a sleeping pill—I know you don't like the idea, Dr. Fallon, but I *do* know what I'm doing. I've seen enough hysterical people to know that if we don't do *something*, they'll go off the deep end. It usually takes a good strong sedative to get them past the crisis. Anyway, there's nothing on the tape that I haven't heard before. Ren's always hysterical when I come home on one of those days, and she's always going on about animals howling, blood, and cold water. And then she launches into that made-up language of hers. I've learned not to let that go on for too long. Once she gets wound up, it takes quite a while for the sedative I give her to take effect." Then she looked him straight in the face. "I'm a police officer, Dr. Fallon, and we've got access to some fairly heavy-duty sedatives. Every now and then we need something to deal with violent prisoners."

"Is that legal?" He seemed a bit startled.

"We don't broadcast it, so it doesn't come up in court very often. There *are* a few alternatives, but they're fairly direct and not very pleasant. People start frothing at the mouth about 'police brutality' if a few bones get broken while we're subduing a violent prisoner. A good strong sedative gets the job done without anybody getting hurt."

"We more or less follow the same procedure with violent patients," he admitted.

"I'm sure you do, since chaining people to the wall's gone out of date. Anyway, Ren usually goes through the same routine every time she has one of those nightmares. I've heard it often enough to know just about how far along she is when I get home. First she rambles on about animals howling; then she talks about having blood all over her; and she winds up whimpering about cold water. After that, she switches over to the private language she and Regina invented when they were babies."

"Is she talking to *you* in that language?"

"I don't think she is. I get the feeling that she's talking to Regina."

"Sylvia's fairly sure that the nightmares Twink keeps having are a rerun of the night when Regina was murdered," I added. "Evidently she's going to play that over and over until somebody finds a way to turn it off permanently."

"I don't think we want to do that, Mark," Fallon disagreed. "It's in the open right now. If we put a lid on it, it'll keep seething around in her subconscious, and sooner or later, it'll boil over again. If that happens ten years from now, it could be an absolute disaster. I've seen things like that happen before, and it usually turns the patient into a vegetable and a permanent resident in some custodial institution."

"That'd be a clear win for the other side, wouldn't it?"

"It sure would," he agreed, his eyes troubled. He looked at Mary. "How did Renata behave this morning?" he asked her.

"Pretty much the same as always," Mary told him. "She usually seems a little silly on the day after one of these spells— bright, bubbly, and neck deep in cute. Then she settles down and seems more or less normal for a week or two. Then another nightmare comes along, and she goes through the whole thing again. It's almost like a cycle. After the first time or two, I thought her period might have something to do with it, but the numbers don't match up at all."

"Let's run that tape," he suggested. "I'd like to hear it all the way through once. Then we'll play it over a few times, and you two can tell me exactly what Renata was doing at each stage."

Mary and I got back to Seattle about one-thirty. I dropped her off at her place, went back to the boardinghouse, and fought with Milton for the rest of the day. By now I'd pretty much resigned myself to producing a pedestrian paper at the very best. I'd come up against the same sort of thing when I'd tackled Spenser in my undergraduate years: some writers— poets for the most part—just don't click for me.

It was about four o'clock when Charlie came up the stairs. "The Slasher strikes again!" he announced in a grossly overdone tone of voice.

"Gee!" I replied. "I wonder if he's been sick or something. It's been—what?—three whole weeks since Gasworks, hasn't it?"

"Maybe he took a vacation—went to Disneyland or something."

"Where was this one?"

"Way down south—Des Moines."

"The Slasher's gone to Iowa?"

"No, *this* Des Moines is west of Kent, right on the edge of Saltwater State Park."

"I don't think I've ever heard of that park. Is it one of those rinky-dink half-acre places?"

"Not hardly. It's a big one that fronts on Puget Sound. It's just north of Federal Way, so it gets more traffic out of Pierce County than from Seattle."

"How far is that from here?"

"Eighteen, maybe twenty miles. We sure as hell ain't talking walking distance."

"Our cut-up seems to be branching out—and switching his time schedule. He's never taken anybody out on a Friday before."

"It didn't happen this morning, Mark," Charlie said. "That park's a biggie, and it doesn't get much traffic in winter. The body was stone cold before anybody found it. It's going to be a while before the medical examiner can pinpoint the time of death. The TV folks are all excited about this 'change of venue,' but I think that all it really means is that the Slasher's having trouble finding anybody to carve up in north Seattle. Everybody in this part of town's pretty well spooked about parks, so they're all staying clear of them after the sun goes down—*and*, of course, the cops have been patrolling this end of town pretty regularly. A guy can't do a truly artistic job when there's a cop hiding behind every tree."

"Have they come up with a name for the victim yet?"

"The cops haven't released it. Bob probably knows, though. I'm betting on another small-time hoodling. The TV guys interviewed a sergeant from that district, and he didn't seem very worked up about it. If it'd been a bank president, that would have been a real excited cop."

"That's out of Bob's jurisdiction, isn't it?"

"Probably, but I'm sure he'll get filled in. It's still in King County."

The girls seemed relieved by the news that our local boy was branching out and finding new hunting grounds, so supper was fairly relaxed.

After we'd eaten, Charlie and I took off for the Green Lantern. James begged off because he had to pick up the young fellow from Harvard at about three-thirty on Saturday morning.

Bob West was sitting in that back booth when we got there. "What kept you guys?" he asked, when we joined him.

"Feeding time," Charlie told him. "The girls at the boarding-house are pretty obsessed with schedules. What's the scoop on this latest killing?"

Bob shrugged. "He was another small-timer with an extensive police record of assorted low crimes and misdemeanors. His name was Phillip Cassinelli, but don't start jumping up and down and screaming 'Mafia.' He wasn't in that class. Most of his arrests were for shoplifting or breaking into cars to steal the radios."

"Hardly a master criminal," I observed.

"You've got that right," Bob agreed. "I wish the goddamn reporters would find something else to babble about. The head-shed downtown's right on the verge of cobbling to-gether one of those silly task force things, and since I've been involved in the investigation of a couple of the killings in this part of town, I don't think I've got much of a chance of squirming out. Task force *sounds* impressive, but it's mostly just a form of damage control. It's supposed to make it sound like we're right on top of things, but all it really does is keep the reporters off our backs." He made a sour face.

*   *   *

On Saturday morning I moved Operation Bookshelves to Sylvia's room, and that didn't make her just *too* happy. She was in the process of editing her Twinkie tapes, and I was getting underfoot.

"Use your earphones, Sylvia," I suggested. "That way you won't have to listen when I start swearing."

She grumbled a bit, but she eventually gave in and did it the way I'd suggested.

By now I had the procedure pretty much down pat, and I was finishing up by midafternoon.

"Have you got a minute, Mark?" she asked, as I was bolting the top shelf in place.

"Sure, I'm due for a break. Is there a problem?"

"No, it's just that I'm running into something a little peculiar, is all. Renata's voice isn't always the same. It isn't obvious on the raw tapes, but once I delete all the silly girl talk, the differences are fairly obvious."

"Are you putting several days' worth of talk on one tape?" I asked her.

"Of course. Renata and I ramble sometimes, but my editing's taking out the rambles and concentrating on the significant things she says. Her voice is usually light and clear—almost girlish. Every so often, though, it gets richer and more vibrant."

"I wouldn't make a big thing out of it, Sylvia. Nobody's voice is exactly the same every day—particularly not here in soggy city. The barometer goes up and down like a yo-yo around here, and just about everybody in town is either coming down with a cold or just getting over one. You've got a bouncing barometer and a humidity level that slides all over the scale. These voice changes might be the result of clogged-up sinuses. Why don't you check it out with Erika before you make a federal case out of it?"

"Maybe I'll do that." She laughed a bit ruefully. "I was right on the verge of saddling up the multiple personality horse again. If it's just a change in the weather, I'd have felt pretty silly. Thanks for suggesting it, Mark."

"Buddyship in action, Toots. We're morally obligated to cover each other's buns."

"I won't tell Trish if you don't."

"Are you and Twink going to church tomorrow?"

"Probably. We missed confession, but I think we'll go anyway. Renata's getting very attached to Father O'Donnell. It might have something to do with the Irish brogue of his."

"Say hi to him for me."

"Has he been trying to convert you?"

"I don't think so. We get along well, is all."

I finished driving in the screws on that top shelf. "It's all yours now, Toots," I told her.

"How am I supposed to reach anything on that top shelf?" she demanded.

"Eat lots of Wheaties. Maybe they'll make you grow."

"Up your nose!"

"You don't really have to use those top shelves, Sylvia. Put teddy bears or Barbie dolls up there and use the lower ones for your books. I just build 'em. Filling them up is your responsibility."

I woke up early on Sunday morning for some reason, and when I went downstairs, Erika was sitting in the breakfast nook communing with her coffee and the Sunday paper. She automatically got up and fixed me a cup of coffee.

"I can do that for myself, Erika. You don't really have to jump up every time I come into the room."

"Shush," she told me. Then she sat down again and pushed the front section of the Sunday paper across the table to me. "Check out the front page, Mark," she said. "Our local celebrity's been moonlighting, it seems."

"Oh. Which park did he hit this time?"

"It wasn't a park. Some workers on a highway construction area up near Woodinville just happened to uncover a body. It had all the usual cuts and slashes, but it'd been dumped in a ditch, and dirt had been kicked over it. One of the road guys had lost a tool, and he and a couple of his friends were looking for it. If they hadn't been rooting around in the dirt, the body would probably been paved over and would never have been discovered."

"Oh, that's just dandy," I said. "There could be a couple dozen bodies stashed all over King County. Now we've got 'official' murders and 'unofficial' murders. How long had the stiff been there?"

"The paper didn't say. If it's been more than a week, the autopsy won't be very precise. Decomposition rates vary a lot at this time of year. It'll depend on mean temperature and how soggy the ground is."

"Not before breakfast, Erika," I objected. "Let's hold off on rotting bodies until after I've eaten."

"Squeamish, Mark?"

"I just got up, Erika. Give me a little time before we get into the gooey descriptions, OK?"

"Whatever makes you happy."

The "unofficial" murder near Woodinville gave us something to talk about at breakfast. Actually, most of us felt a bit relieved by the discovery. The Woodinville murder and the one in Saltwater Park strongly suggested that the Slasher wasn't strictly a north Seattle butcher.

"How's your friend's wife, James?" Trish asked, smoothly changing the subject.

"The doctors at the hospital seem to think they caught her cancer in time," he replied in that deep voice of his. "Andrew's going to stick around until after Christmas, though."

"Is his dad the one who owns Perry Construction Company?" Charlie asked.

"That's him," James replied. "There's a man who started out at the bottom and worked his way up. His hand still fits a shovel handle, but he's come a long way since we were kids."

"I worked for Perry Construction one summer," Charlie said. "That's where I learned how to run a backhoe."

"Is there any kind of job you haven't tried, Charlie?" I asked him.

"Not very many," he replied. "I was going to sign on as part of the crew on a fishing boat once—one of those salmon boats that go up the inside passage between Vancouver Island and British Columbia, but I had to beg off by the time we got to Port Townsend. As it turns out, I seem to have a bad case of delly-belly."

"Delly-belly?" Erika asked him.

"Delicate tummy," he explained. "I get seasick pretty easy. I tried all the usual remedies, but they didn't seem to work. I spent the whole trip to Port Townsend leaning over the rail and trying to upchuck my toenails. I just ain't cut out to be a seafaring man. It's a shame: A guy can make a bundle on one of those salmon boats." Then he looked at James. "Did I hear you right the other day?" he asked. "Is old man Perry's kid really going to Harvard?"

"He sure is," James told him, "and from what I hear, he's tearing the Harvard Law School all to pieces. There's no affirmative action involved in Andrew's presence at Harvard. His IQ seems to go off the scale. The dean of the law school made a few arrangements, and Andrew's going to test his way through the courses he was taking before his mother got sick."

"Can they actually do that?" Sylvia asked.

"Harvard's a private university, Sylvia. They can do just about anything they want. In Andrew's case, going through the motions of taking the exams is practically a formality. I'm almost positive he could pass his bar exam right now, if he really wanted to."

Trish sighed, but she didn't say anything.

On Monday, the seventeenth, there was an apparent break-through in the Seattle Slasher case. Charlie was camped on the TV set in the kitchen when I got home after my freshman English class.

"What's up?" I asked him.

"Good news, maybe," he replied. "Some guy walked into the north precinct station about ten o'clock this morning and announced that he's the Seattle Slasher. The reporters are all peeing their pants about it, but the cops aren't letting too many details come out."

"Well, now," I said. "How 'bout that? We won't have to run around with our fingers on the button of our pepper spray anymore."

"Let's hold off on the celebration until we see what Bob has to say. Something about this doesn't smell quite right."

After supper that evening, Charlie, James, and I hit the Green Lantern to see if we could get the straight scoop on that confession. "I expected you guys," Bob said. "Let's go back to the booth, and I'll fill you in."

We retired to our traditional debriefing booth. "Does this confession you guys beat out of the suspect answer all the Slasher questions?" Charlie asked.

"Get real, kid," Bob told him. "That screwball who confessed this morning is a whacko who wants to be a celebrity. That sort of thing happens all the time, and the more fuss the reporters make, the more confessions we get. We usually manage to keep these fake confessions out of the newspapers and off TV."

"How did it get out this time, then?" James asked.

"Can you believe that this nut made his confession to Burpee, of all people?"

"You've got to be kidding," Charlie said, laughing.

"Not even a little bit. I think the desk sergeant's got a warped sense of humor. This whacko shows up wringing his hands and blubbering, and the desk sergeant hands him off to Burpee without so much as cracking a smile. Then Burpee takes the nut to an interrogation room and swallows everything the guy tells him hook, line, and sinker. Then our mighty hero of truth, justice, and Mom's apple pie calls a TV reporter and gives him an anonymous tip. The reporter flips out and puts it on the air without bothering to get verification."

"Somebody's gonna get his ass in trouble over that one, isn't he?" Charlie suggested.

"You damn betcha he is," Bob replied, chuckling wickedly. "The reporter's probably going to spend the next six months reading weather reports, and Burpee's likely to spend *his* time writing parking tickets—*if* he doesn't get kicked off the force entirely."

"The price of fame just went up, didn't it?" James suggested with a faint smile.

"You've got that right, James," Bob agreed. "We've got three guys absolutely dying to be stars, and they'll do anything to get their names up in lights. Some nut walks in off the street with a fake confession that's supposed to put him right up there with Ted Bundy. Burpee swallows his cock-and-bull story without even bothering to check it out. Then the TV reporter goes on camera with Burpee's tip almost before Burpee finishes talking because he doesn't want some other reporter to get there first. If Burpee—or the reporter— had taken a little time to check out the whacko's background, they'd have found out that he's been in and out of about a half dozen nuthouses in the last ten years. This three-way rush to fame didn't accomplish a damn thing except to embarrass the police department and the TV station. Don't relax your security measures, guys. The Slasher's still alive and well. He's out there somewhere—with knife—and he hasn't finished up yet."

CHAPTER THIRTEEN

The week of November 17th slid swiftly toward Thanksgiving, and everybody's head seemed to be turned off at dear old U.W. The word "holiday" always seems to do that to the student body, and just about anything qualifies as a holiday—Arbor Day, John Dillinger's birthday, and Groundhog Day. But I'm almost positive that a "let's break down and do some work" day wouldn't be as popular.

Then on Saturday the twenty-second, the sliced-up body of another Slasher victim was found near the shore of Lake Washington in Luther Burbank Park on Mercer Island.

James, Charlie, and I weren't able to make our usual visit to the Green Lantern to get the inside dope on the latest victim because Bob West didn't work on Saturday, and he stayed clear of the tavern on his days off. That left us nothing to go on but the usual hysteria on TV.

The dead man was identified as Anthony Purvis, a thirty-year-old Caucasian with no criminal record. All sorts of theories fell apart because of the lack of any record on Purvis. Poor old Burpee most likely went into deep mourning along about then, since Cheetah wouldn't have been interested in somebody like this latest victim.

One reporter actually got off his duff, went over to Mercer Island, and interviewed residents of the posh neighborhood near the park. A couple of them told him that they'd heard dogs making a ruckus at about the time of the murder. This had come up a few times before, and the reporter tried to make a big issue of howling dogs, but when he started babbling about the possibility that dogs have some kind of "extrasensory perception," I gave up and went back to work on my Milton paper.

Sylvia wasn't feeling well on Sunday morning, so she asked me to take Twinkie to church. I didn't have anything hot on the fire for that Sunday anyway, so I agreed and called Mary to let Twink know about the change in the game plan.

Mary answered. "Who had your phone tied up all day yesterday?" she demanded. "Ren had another one of those bad days and I wanted to get hold of Sylvia, but all I got was a busy signal."

"Damn!" I said. "Somebody must have left it off the hook. We don't use this room very much, so we wouldn't have heard it beeping at us. Did we miss anything important?"

"Probably not. This one was pretty much the same as the one Sylvia taped a couple of weeks ago."

"How's Twinkie doing today? Sylvia's feeling sort of punk, and she asked me to fill in and take Twink to church. Maybe we'd better scratch the whole idea."

"She's fine, Mark. You should know that by now. The bad days only last for that one day. When she wakes up the next morning, it's almost like it never happened. I don't think she has any coherent memory of those days."

"Maybe we should mention that to Doc Fallon the next time we see him. It might be important."

"Maybe so, but Ren's getting ready to go to church, so you'd better suit up. I'll let her know that you'll be filling in for Sylvia today. Don't make any big fuss about what happened yesterday. There's no point in getting her all worked up about something that's over and done with."

"You're probably right, Mary. Tell Twink that I'll be there in about a half an hour."

"I'll do that. Don't forget your necktie."

*   *   *

Twink was sitting at the table in Mary's kitchen when I got there, struggling with her checkbook.

"Problems?" I asked her.

"The silly thing won't balance," she said, waving her bank statement at me. "The bank's got one number, and I've got a different one."

"Put it away for now, Twink," I told her. "Father O's waiting for us."

"What's wrong with Sylvia?" she demanded.

"Nothing serious," I replied. "I think it's just that time of the month."

"Oh," she said. "Can we go up to Northgate Mall after Mass? I'd like to do some Christmas shopping."

"This early?"

"It's only a month away, Markie. That's why I was trying to balance my checkbook."

"How far off are you?"

"Six or eight hundred dollars is about all."

"Good thing you're not planning to be an accountant. When was the last time you balanced it?"

"August. Maybe September."

"Give it up, Twink," I told her. "You'll never be able to make it come out right at this stage. Just use the number the bank gave you and call it square."

"What if they're trying to cheat me?"

"Banks almost never do that, Twink. If the Feds catch them, the bank president usually winds up in jail for twenty years or so. Just write down their number in your check register and call it good. Put it away for right now, baby sister. God's waiting for you."

"I wouldn't say anything like that around Father O, Markie. He might whomp on you a few times—for your own good, of course," she assured me, folding her bank statement away.

"Oh, of course," I said sardonically.

"Be nice, Markie," she chided me.

*   *   *

We sat near the back of the church when we got there. Maybe because Twink hadn't been to confession, she didn't feel the need to be right down front this time. And I was starting to grow more familiar with Catholic customs. Many of them still didn't make much sense to me, but at least I knew they were coming.

There was the usual lineup after the service as the parish-ioners filed out of the church, pausing briefly for a word or two with Father O as they went by. We finally reached Father O, and after a few pleasantries, he asked me if I could stop by some day that week.

"Sure," I replied. "Tomorrow afternoon be OK?"

"It's fine with me," he agreed.

"What are you two up to now?" Twink demanded.

"Just some guy stuff, Twink," I told her. "You know, talking about hunting, fishing, football, cars, chasing girls—that kind of stuff."

"I pretty much avoid that last one, Renata," Father O told her. "The bishop frowns if we do that."

"Bishops just can't seem to relax, can they?" she said with a little smirk.

"Occupational hazard, probably," he agreed.

Twink and I went on to the Northgate Mall, and after Sunday brunch, I got to follow her around to every single store in the whole damned place. "Shopping" pretty much fits the defini-tion of "cruel and unusual punishment," ranking right up there with the rack and thumbscrews. A sentence of five to ten years in a shopping mall would probably be overturned out of hand by a unanimous vote of the Supreme Court. But when I said as much to Twink, she just laughed and asked what I was getting her for Christmas.

I went to St. Benedict's Church about three o'clock the next afternoon, and Father O and I retired to his office to kick a few things around.

"I'm troubled about Renata, Mark," he told me. "Her mood swings are growing more extreme. Sometimes in the confession booth, I can't be exactly sure *who's* talking to me."

"One of my housemates—Sylvia—said something like that just the other day," I told him. "She's been taping her sessions with Twink, and she noticed it when she played them back. I shrugged it off and told her it was probably changes in barometric pressure, humidity, and stuff like that. But if you're hearing different voices in the confessional during one session, there wouldn't be much change in the weather, would there?"

"Not very likely," he agreed. "There's something else, too. I believe I told you that Renata sometimes lapses into an alien language in the confessional, didn't I?"

"I think you did, yes."

"Whenever that turns up, her voice is definitely the second one. Renata's normal voice is a light soprano; her other voice is a rich contralto."

"Now *that's* something we should tell her headshrinker about. Twinkie wouldn't have any reason to start using twin-speak just for kicks. The only other person in the world who'd understand what she'd be saying would be Regina, and she doesn't remember that Regina ever existed. It sounds to me like she's flipping out right there in the confessional."

"Wouldn't that bring up an interesting possibility?" he said. "Could this voice change and that alien language be an early warning signal? If I hear them in the confessional on Friday, Renata will go to pieces on Tuesday—or something along those lines. Does that make sense?"

"It might at that, Father O. I'll drop it on Sylvia, and she can mention it to Doc Fallon—they're working together on this. If we can predict the days when Twink's going to flip out, it might be a long step toward coming up with some answers. I'd better give you the phone number at the boardinghouse. Everybody there's pretty much wired-in on Twink's problem, so they'll pass the word to me—or to Sylvia. We all assumed that Twink's nightmares were the things that were triggering the 'bad days,' but if you're right about this voice-change thing, something else is triggering the nightmares, and *that's* the thing we're *really* trying to pin down. Maybe I should grab Sylvia and bring her over this evening so we can talk it over. What time do you lock the doors here?"

"I don't, Mark. I'm an old-fashioned priest, and I don't believe in locking churches. My doors are always open. If somebody needs me, I'll always be here."

"That's real dedication, Father."

He shrugged. "It goes with the territory," he said.

I kicked the idea around with Sylvia when I got home, and she agreed that Father O'Donnell's early warning notion might be valuable, so after supper we made a quick run over to the church.

I hauled into the parking lot, and we went up the stairs, through the wide front door, and into the vestibule. Sylvia automatically dipped her fingers into the little basin of holy water, sank down on one knee, and crossed herself. I'm not certain that she was even aware that she was doing it.

The interior of the church was dimly lighted, and shadows filled the little alcoves where statues of various saints looked out over the pews and the altar.

"Hello," Father O'Donnell's voice echoed through the empty church. I looked around, then spotted him in that little doorway off to one side of the altar. There's something spooky about coming into an empty church after dark.

"It's me, Father," I called to him. "I've brought Sylvia so that we can talk over that notion we had this afternoon."

"Come on back," he told us.

Sylvia and I went down the center aisle, and she repeated that quick drop to one knee in front of the altar. They'd all told me that these little rituals were so ingrained they were automatic, but I don't think I'd realized just *how* automatic.

We followed Father O down the narrow hall to his office. "How did you know we were out there?" I asked him.

"There's a motion sensor in the vestibule," he replied with a slight smile. "I don't lock the doors, but I *do* take certain precautions."

"Modern technology? I'm shocked, Father, shocked."

"Forgive him, Father," Sylvia intoned, "for he knows not what he does."

"Are you two ganging up on me?" I said.

"You had that one coming, Mark," Sylvia told me, taking her tiny tape player out of her purse as she sat down. "The sound quality's surprisingly good, Father," she said. "I brought a couple of my edited tapes so you can compare the different voices with what you heard in the confessional."

"Aren't we bending a fairly important rule here?" I asked them. "I've heard about the sanctity of the confessional, but I'm not very clear about just how far that goes."

"We're in the clear, Mark," Father O assured me. "I won't be revealing any details about Renata's confession—just the different voices."

"You're the expert, Father, and you're the one who's going to get into trouble with your bishop if we're out of line."

"Isn't he the darlin' boy?" he said to Sylvia, exaggerating his brogue.

"He's a clown," she replied. "You'll hear my voice first on these tapes, Father. I injected dates and times when I deleted the random conversations that didn't have any bearing on Renata's problem. It was a little tricky right at first; we're trained to take notes, not sound recordings. The first time I tried this, I left out dates and times, and it didn't make much sense at all."

"Did you bring the one you recorded that morning when she was all flipped out?" I asked.

"Of course," Sylvia replied. "That's the most important one I've got so far." She looked at the labels on several of her miniature tapes. "I think this one might be the best," she said. "The differences in her voice really stand out."

She inserted the tape in the little player and turned it on. "Thursday, November sixth—Three-thirty P.M." Sylvia's voice came from the player.

"Sometimes it's awfully frustrating, Sylvia." Twink's voice was pensive. "The sorority girls talk a lot about 'the good old days' when they were in high school. I don't *have* any 'good old days.' Somehow I got cheated out of my childhood, and I don't think that's very fair at all."

"Wednesday, November twelfth. Ten-fifteen A.M." Sylvia's voice came in.

"It's something I absolutely *have* to do, Sylvia. Nobody understands it, and everybody tries to get in my way, but they can't stop me. It *has* to be done, and I *am* going to do it, no matter what it takes." It didn't even sound like the same person talking.

Sylvia stopped the tape. "Are those two entries close to the voices you've been hearing in the confessional, Father O'Donnell?" she asked.

"Absolutely identical," he replied. "That last one raises the hackles on the back of my neck. It doesn't make much sense, though. Did she ever tell you what this thing is that she feels compelled to do?"

"Not even a peep," Sylvia replied ruefully. "It drives me wild every time she does that."

"I'll check with Mary," I said, "but I believe Twink had one of her 'bad days' on Thursday of that week."

"Yes," Sylvia agreed, "she did. I've been keeping track."

"That nails it down, doesn't it?" I said. "The voice switch was on Wednesday, Twink had the usual nightmare that night, and she was climbing the walls on Thursday. There *is* a connection between the voice change, the switchover into twin-speak, and the nightmares."

"Maybe," Sylvia said. "I'd like to have a little more in the way of confirmation before I start the victory celebration, though."

"Why don't you play the tape you cut that morning when Mary called us?" I suggested. "Let Father O hear what she sounds like when she's full-bore nutso."

"Good idea," she agreed, sorting through her miniature tapes.

Father O'Donnell seemed a bit awed by the intensity of Twink's voice on the tape, and when she switched over to twin-speak, he slapped his hand down onto his desk. "That's it!" he exclaimed. "*That's* the language I've heard her speaking in the confessional. The lisping is a dead giveaway."

"They were teething when they invented the language," I explained.

"Doesn't that language suggest that Renata *is* aware that she used to have a twin sister?" Father O suggested.

"Only when she's gone bonkers," I replied. "She drops twin-speak when she goes back to being a normie."

"You might want to speak with Dr. Fallon about the possibility that this change in Renata's voice might precede—or even trigger—her nightmares and the relapses into psychosis," Father O suggested to Sylvia. "And it probably wouldn't hurt if you started bringing her to confession regularly. That other voice doesn't crop up *every* time she comes to confession, but if it *is* an advance warning, we'd better not let it slip past us."

"Good idea, Father," Sylvia agreed.

My freshman class on Wednesday afternoon had their heads pretty well turned off, so there wasn't much point to trying to teach. I took the roll, cautioned them to drive carefully, and turned them loose.

"That was quick," Twink said, after the classroom had emptied out.

"They weren't really in there anyway, baby sister," I told her. "Why waste my breath? Let's hit the bricks before the traffic starts piling up."

"Do we really have to spend Thanksgiving with Les and Inga?" She sounded a little plaintive.

"Yup," I told her.

"They get so antsy when I'm around."

"Pitch in and help Inga in the kitchen, Twink," I suggested. "Act like a normie. That might calm her down, and if Inga's calm, it might settle Les down, too."

"I don't know beans about cooking, Markie."

"Here's your chance to learn. Your mother's a good cook, so she'll clue you in on all the tricks of the trade."

"You're going to insist, aren't you?"

"Yup."

"I wish you'd get off that 'yup' stuff, Markie," she said crossly.

"Cool down, Twink. We're going home for Thanksgiving, and that's final. It's not going to hurt you to be nice to your parents, so quit trying to weasel out of this."

"Oh, all right," she gave up.

There'd been a break in the weather, and it was actually sunny and bright as Twink and I drove north that afternoon. Maybe it was a good omen—or maybe the rain god was just resting up so he could unload on us at Christmastime.

My bullying finally got through to Twinkie, and she was at least civil to Les and Inga. She even took my advice and helped Inga in the kitchen. That gave me the opportunity to fill Les in on how we hoped to use those voice changes as an early warning system, and maybe even head off the nightmares.

"There might be some hope for her after all, then," he said. "I wasn't too optimistic about that. To be perfectly honest, Mark, I was right on the verge of pulling her out of Seattle and bringing her back home."

"I don't think that'd work out too well, boss. If you did that, she'd stay semibonkers for the rest of her life, and she'd probably end up back in the bughouse. If we keep her in

Seattle where Sylvia can stay right on top of her, we'll have a lot better chance of finding a real cure and turning her into a normie. That's what we're really after, isn't it?"

"You're probably right, Mark," he admitted.

I heaved a sigh of relief. That one had been closer than I'd realized. The boss had the key right in his pocket, and he'd been ready to take it out and lock Twink away for the rest of her life.

Classes resumed on Monday, December 1, and now the holiday season was turning into a major distraction. Of course, the holiday season starts right after Labor Day, as far as the stores are concerned. Jumping the gun is a peculiarly American characteristic. Everybody wants to get there first. The Brits can elect a new government in six weeks; it takes us two years.

I coasted through Monday. I guess everybody's entitled to a goof-off day now and then. I *did* caution my freshman class about the dangers of the season, though. A semiserious student can blow some fairly good grades right out the window if the approach of Christmas shuts down his head. Of course, the ones who've been majoring in parties almost always decide at that point that they've already blown the fall quarter anyway, so they don't even bother to come to class after Thanksgiving.

At supper that evening, James told us that Mrs. Perry's doctors were certain that they'd caught her cancer in time and that her recovery would probably be total.

James, Charlie, and I were going back upstairs to boy country after supper, and Charlie suggested a quick trip to the Green Lantern to find out if his brother had anything new on the Slasher front. "None of us stayed here in town during that four-day weekend, so we might have missed a few things. If we're going to keep playing our knights in shining armor game, we'd better stay on top of developments."

"He's got a point," I told James.

"I think I'd better beg off," James replied. "I'm running a little behind right now."

"No biggie," Charlie told him. "Mark and I can fill you in when we come home. Are you up for it, Mark?"

"Sure. I'll grab a coat and we can go see what Bob's got to say."

There weren't too many people in the tavern when we got there, and Bob West was sitting on a stool at the bar.

"What's cooking, big brother?" Charlie asked as we joined Bob.

"Leftover turkey, most likely," Bob replied. "I get so damned sick of turkey after a holiday."

"Don't buy the great big ones," Charlie suggested. "Is there anything new and exciting about our local cut-up?" he asked then. "Did he maybe carve up another junior hoodling on Thanksgiving and then eat him—complete with cranberry sauce?"

"No new carcasses," Bob replied, "but we got the word on Finley from the Kansas City police department."

"The Gas Works Park guy, wasn't he?" Charlie asked.

Bob nodded. "Finley had a police record, right enough, but there weren't any dope deals or burglaries involved. He was busted several times for sexual molestation and a couple of attempted rapes. He's listed in their records as a sex offender. He was supposed to register when he came here, but evidently it slipped his mind."

"Convenient," I said.

"It happens quite a lot. That sex offender label doesn't work very well. All the guy has to do is cross a state line and keep his nose fairly clean. The Kansas City cops might have been trying to keep an eye on Finley, but once he got west of Denver, he was home free."

"That's one of the drawbacks of a democratic society, isn't it?" Charlie suggested.

"We can usually work our way around them, kid," Bob said.

"A thought for the day, huh, Bob?" Charlie said.

I concentrated on my Milton paper for the rest of that week, more to get it off my back than out of any great enthusiasm. Since John-boy and I didn't see eye to eye on much of anything, my paper was mostly a polite tip of my hat in his general direction as I moved on past him.

Sylvia got a call from Doc Fallon late Thursday afternoon, rescheduling Twinkie's Friday appointment for ten o'clock in the morning rather than the usual afternoon get-together. Sylvia was a little grumpy about that, so I offered to fill in for her.

"Thanks all the same, Mark," she replied, "but I'd better take care of it myself. There are some things I need to talk over with him, and I think they'd be better face-to-face than over the phone."

I shrugged. "You can't say I didn't offer," I told her.

"You're all heart, Mark," she said dryly.

I finished up my Milton paper about noon the next day, and my final read-through confirmed my suspicion that it wasn't going to set the world on fire. It'd have to do, though. It was too late in the quarter to go back to square one.

"Nobody's perfect," I muttered, setting the paper aside. Then I went down to cobble a couple of sandwiches together. Erika was there, though, and she intercepted me before I could get into the refrigerator.

"Sit down," she ordered. "I'll take care of it."

"Sure," I said, "and thanks. Could you clear your books out of the way this afternoon? I'll take the measurements today and build your bookshelves tomorrow. I should be out from underfoot before suppertime."

"That'll be nice," she said.

After we'd eaten, I took my tape measure into her room and started writing down the numbers.

Sylvia came home about two-thirty.

"How'd it go this morning?" I asked her.

"About the same as always," she said. "Have you got anything earthshaking on the fire for Monday?" she asked.

"Not that I know of. Why?"

"Dr. Fallon's going to be attending a conference at the university, and he wants to meet Father O. I think he might have a Renata seminar in mind—you, me, Mary, and Father O'Donnell. We're all getting bits and pieces of what Renata's been doing lately, and he'd like to put them all together and see what turns up—I think Fallon's worried about this voice-change business."

"You'd better check in with Father O," I suggested. "If we're going to set up the kind of meet Doc Fallon seems to want, the church might be the best place for it."

"I sort of thought so myself," she agreed.

CHAPTER FOURTEEN

After breakfast on Saturday morning I went down to my little workshop in the basement and sawed boards to the measurements I'd taken in Erika's room Friday afternoon.

"This might be a little noisy," I warned her when I carried the first load of boards into her room. "If you want to concentrate, maybe you'd better go to the library."

She shrugged. "I don't have anything too important to do today, Mark," she said. "It'll give me an excuse to goof off—unless having me watch is going to bug you."

"No problem," I said. "I'll try to keep the swearing to a minimum."

"I've heard people swear before. It doesn't bother me all that much."

I got the uprights in place first, and as luck had it, the settling of the house hadn't torqued the studs too far off plumb, so it went fairly fast.

"Speedy," Erika observed.

"I've done this five times before," I replied. "I've pretty much got it down pat now. I'll give you some extra room on that bottom shelf for any oversize books, and you can put paperbacks on that top shelf—assuming that you even want to use the top one. You'll need a stepladder if you do."

"I might at that," she told me. "I've got several boxes of books down in the basement. It'll be nice having them all here where I can get my hands on them."

"I take it that you're not all that hot for computerized books."

She made an indelicate sound.

"What a thing to say," I kidded her. "I'm shocked, Erika. Shocked."

"Computer nerds make me want to throw up."

"I'll float my stick with yours on that one." I banged the side of my fist on the uprights to make sure they were all firmly in place. "Good enough," I said. "I got lucky for a change. I hit a couple of problems with the uprights in Sylvia's room."

"How much further have you got to go on your doctorate, Mark?" she asked me then.

"A couple more years at least. Why?"

"Just curious. We've turned into a fairly tight little group here, haven't we?"

"The kitchen might have something to do with that. People who eat together always seem to get close."

"The feeding trough, you mean? I think it goes a little deeper than that, Mark." Her tone seemed almost wistful.

"Are we having some sort of problem, Erika?"

"I'm going to miss this place when we all move on, and I'll probably miss the group as well."

"We'll keep in touch."

"I've heard that before."

"I don't know if Trish has mentioned this, but she was telling me that she's been getting some inquiries about possible vacancies. We seem to be getting quite a reputation on campus. The party boys aren't very interested, but there *are* people on campus who aren't majoring in parties. If all six of us come out *cum laude*, you might get a long line of people waiting to sign on."

"Not until *after* we've finished. I don't want any strangers moving in to mess up what we've got going for us here."

"Sentimentality, Erika? I thought you were the ice cube in the bunch."

"That's a pose, Mark. It keeps guys who drool at arm's

length. If I pretend to be Iceberg Erika, they don't pester me. I get the same urges everybody else does, but I keep them to myself. That's one of the things I like about our arrangement here. The 'no hanky-panky' policy puts the guys here off-limits, and I don't even *have* those kind of thoughts about you or James or Charlie—well, not *too* many, anyway."

"Erika!"

She grinned at me. "Gotcha!" she said triumphantly.

"Smart aleck."

"Why, Mark, how can you say such a thing?" She gave me one of those wide-eyed vapid looks that seemed all too familiar.

"Have you been taking lessons from Twinkie?" I asked her sourly. She'd caught me off guard. I'd almost come to believe that Erika was one of those all business girls with nothing even remotely resembling a sense of humor. I'd obviously been wrong about that. There was a lot more to her than I'd even imagined.

Sylvia'd made all the arrangements for our little get-together at St. Benedict's, and we homed in on Father O'Donnell about seven-thirty on Monday evening.

Sylvia introduced Doc Fallon and Father O, and they seemed to size each other up right at first. They *did* come from opposite sides of a fairly significant fence, and I guess they both wanted to be sure that they weren't going to lock horns on certain issues.

"Sylvia mentioned the possibility that certain kinds of repetitive behavior might precede Renata's psychotic episodes," Fallon began. "I'd like to hear a few more details. This could be very important."

"Part of it has to do with cryptolalia—what I always called 'twin-speak' before Sylvia gave me the scientific term," I told him. "Since Twink has no memory of her childhood with Regina, that shouldn't be showing up at all—at least not when she's functioning as a normie. Mary tells us that there's always twin-speak involved in the ravings that come pouring out after Renata has those nightmares. If we're reading this right, the nightmares are a re-creation of the night when Regina was murdered."

"That might be a slight oversimplification," Fallon told me, "but let it go for now."

"The point is that the private language *also* crops up when Twink goes to confession. Father O'Donnell mentioned it to me quite sometime back, but I guess I spaced it out. I'd gotten so used to hearing the twins lisping at each other when they were kids that it didn't even occur to me that there was anything peculiar about its reappearance—I mean, if Twink has no memory at all about Regina, who's she talking to?"

"Then the matter of the two different voices surfaced," Father O picked it up. "There have been times when I couldn't be positive how many young ladies were in the confessional with me."

"That's been bothering me as well," Sylvia added. "It shows up very obviously when I'm editing the tapes. I was just about to resurrect my multiple personality theory, but the reappearance of cryptolalia shoots that full of holes, doesn't it?"

"Let's not dismiss anything just yet," Fallon told her.

"Anyway," I picked it up again, "Father O came up with the idea that the different voices and the reappearance of twin-speak might be something on the order of an early warning. Once those show up, the nightmares and the day of psychotic raving are almost certain to come along again. Does that make sense?"

"What if it's Ren's way to cry for help?" Mary suggested. "She might feel the bad day coming, and she's begging us to step in and stop it—but she's begging in a language nobody can understand."

"It's possible, I suppose," Fallon conceded. "Does she have any memory of these incidents on the following day?"

"She doesn't seem to. The first few times they showed up,

I'd ask her the next day if she was feeling better, and she didn't seem to know what I was talking about. Of course, she's always a little silly on the day after one of the bad ones."

"Could we possibly be dealing with a fugue here?" Sylvia asked Fallon. "At least a personal variation of the fugue state? Once she lapses into cryptolalia, she seems to blot everything out."

"Now we might be getting somewhere," Fallon said.

"Fugue?" I asked. "Isn't that a musical term?"

"It has a slightly different meaning in the field of abnormal psychology, Mark," Sylvia told me. "It's a reaction to something that's so terrible that the patient can't bear even to think about it. It usually involves a loss of personal identity. Sometimes the patient will wander off and seem to be perfectly normal. It can go on for hours—or even for days—and when the patient recovers, he has absolutely no memory of anything that happened during that period."

"It does sound like it fits what's going on when Ren flips out," Mary said.

"And it *might* just be going on for a lot longer than we'd realized," I added. "Maybe it starts when her voice keeps changing back and forth and words or phrases from that private language crop up—usually in the confessional. Then she has that nightmare again; then she wakes up talking about wolves and blood and cold until she can't stand it anymore. At that point, she shuts down and talks exclusively in twin. Then the next day comes along, and she has no memory of anything that happened." I looked at Fallon. "Does that come anywhere close to what this fugue state is all about?"

"Very close, I think," he agreed. "Basically, a fugue is a flight from reality, and the patient will even flee from her own identity to get away from a reality she can't face. In this case, Renata seems to be taking refuge in the private language—in the same way she did during the six months after her sister's death. Once she starts speaking English again, the incident is over, and everything connected to it has been erased from her memory."

"What is it about going to confession that sets her off?" Mary asked.

"It happens more often than you'd think, Mary," Father O told her. "The act of confession seems to lower certain defenses. We stress the importance of full confession, and it's not uncommon for things to come out during confession that the penitent has completely forgotten."

"What this finally boils down to is that Renata's quite probably working her way toward another breakdown and another stay in the sanitarium," Fallon told us. "It's regrettable, but it's not that uncommon."

"And then my idiot brother will use that as an excuse to take her home and never let her out of his sight again," Mary added.

Fallon smiled faintly. "Just leave that to me, Mary," he said. "I can probably stop him short if it's necessary."

Sylvia and I were feeling pretty upbeat after the Twinkie conference at St. Benedict's Church. We hadn't quite solved *all* the problems yet, but we felt we'd definitely made some progress.

Our good feeling lasted all the way through Tuesday, but then Wednesday rolled around, and Twink went bonkers again.

I was attending my Milton seminar when Mary called the boardinghouse. As luck had it, Sylvia hadn't left yet, so she grabbed her tape recorder and hustled over to Mary's place.

Twink had already gone through the business of wolves, blood, and cold water, though, so all Sylvia got on tape was an extended oration in twin-speak.

Sylvia wasn't *too* happy about that, and she was using some very colorful language when I came home around ten that morning. "If I'd *only* got there a bit earlier!" she fumed.

"You don't have to be there in person, Sylvia," I told her. "I've been thinking about that, and a tape recorder that uses standard-sized tapes only costs about twenty-five bucks. I'll pick one up and show Mary how to use it. She'll be able to get everything on tape as soon as she walks in and finds Twink climbing the walls. That way, she won't have to call you and wait around until you get there."

She glared at me for a moment, then she suddenly looked a little sheepish. "Why didn't I think of that?" she said.

"You don't really want me to answer that, do you, Toots?" I asked her. "This *does* shoot down Father O's theory about the confessional, though, doesn't it? Twink hasn't been to confession for quite some time now, and she went bonkers anyhow."

"Maybe it's been percolating in the back of her mind for a few weeks," she suggested. "I don't think there's any kind of time limit, do you?"

"It's your field, Sylvia. Half the time you and Fallon are talking to each other in a foreign language as far as I can tell. Did Mary zap Twink out with a pill again?"

She nodded. "About a half hour after I got there. Renata dozed off almost immediately."

"Whatever works, I guess," I said.

As usual, Twink bounced right back after she'd shaken off the horrors that'd wiped her out on Wednesday—she showed up bright-eyed and bushy-tailed for my class on Thursday. It seemed peculiar to me that Twink was always superhyped on the day following one of her bad ones, but it was obvious that today's ebullience fit the pattern.

It was a little noisy in the classroom when I entered that afternoon. "All right, people," I said from the front of the room, "settle down. We've got something to take care of today. Next week's the last one of the fall quarter, so I guess we'd better start thinking about a final examination. I suppose we could all compose hymns of praise to conjunctions or prepositions, but that might be a little tedious, huh? I don't know about you, but it'd probably bore my socks off. Why don't we do something a little more exciting instead?"

I paused—for effect, of course. Then I snapped my fingers. "Why don't we write another paper?" I said as if the idea had just come at me from out of the blue. "You've been college students for twelve whole weeks now, and the reason we come to college is to learn stuff, right? OK, why don't you tell me about it? This'll be your last paper, *and* it'll be your final exam at the same time. You'll whip in here next Tuesday, dump your paper on the desk, and then split—unless you'd like some kind of farewell oration from old superteacher!"

"Don't you mean next Thursday, Mr. Austin?" one of them asked me.

"I'll need a little time to grade them. Superteacher is *not* faster than a speeding bullet."

"What's the topic supposed to be?" another one asked.

"How about 'What I Have Learned This Quarter'?"

"About English, you mean?"

"Why limit it to something that pedestrian? If the biggest thing you've picked up here this quarter is how long it takes the signal light at Forty-third and University to change, write a paper about it. I *hope* that some of you've picked up a few things a bit more interesting, but that's up to you. I'm looking for thought content, gang. You're supposed to be here to learn how to think, and I'm supposed to teach you how to think on paper. Let's find out if we've all done what we're here for."

"That's awfully unspecific, Mr. Austin," a girl near the front objected.

"I know," I agreed. "I'm leaving it wide-open on purpose. That puts the ball in your court. Go for it, and give it your best shot—and about five hundred of your best words. You might want to think it over *before* ten-thirty next Monday evening. I don't want to spoil any of your plans, but you should probably know that a half hour paper's likely to get you a half hour grade—if you get my drift? Take a little time with this one. Let's bump up the old grade-point average, shall we?"

Twink lingered after class. "You're a mean person, Markie," she accused.

"I try," I said smugly. "Did you ride your bike today?"

"No, one of the sorority girls picked me up."

"Are they trying to recruit you?"

"They might be. I've kept my stay at the bughouse a deep, dark secret."

"You'll need a lift back to Mary's place, then."

"I thought you'd never ask."

"Let's split, then."

We strolled out to the parking garage and climbed into my old, trusty Dodge.

"I think I'll drop another free one on you, Markie," she told me as we headed back toward Wallingford. "I haven't written a paper for you for a long time now."

"Are we feeling creative, Twink?"

She shrugged. "I just feel like writing a paper, and this might be a good time to try another one. I like the topic, and I've learned whole bunches of stuff this quarter."

"I'm sure you have. Are you going to do another barn burner like that first one?"

"I'm not sure, Mark," she said in a throaty voice. "It's more fun to write without too much planning sometimes." She coughed then. "Frog in my throat," she said absently. "I must be coming down with something."

The little group get-together at St. Benedict's Church had made a big thing about our voice-change theory, and now it seemed that it might be collapsing around my ears. Twink's offhand "frog in my throat" shot it full of holes.

Now that I'd finished the bookshelves, I didn't have any fix-up chores scheduled for Saturday that week, and that bothered me for some reason. I found myself wandering around the house with my tape measure looking for something to do.

Finally, I rapped on the door to Trish's room. "Have you got a minute?" I asked her.

"Sure," she replied. "Is there a problem?"

"I can't find anything to do."

"Are you feeling all right, Mark?" she asked, laughing.

"It bugs me, that's all. I've gotten used to working on Saturday, and goofing off makes me feel guilty. What about those kitchen cabinets and drawers? They're pretty beat-up, and I could refinish all that exterior woodwork—spiff things up to match the new flooring."

"Whatever turns you on," she said with a shrug. "When you get right down to it, though, I think your bookshelves more than paid your dues in this place."

"I'm a creature of habit, Trish," I explained. "I'm supposed to do honest work on Saturday, and not having anything to do makes me antsy."

"Do doors and drawers then, Mark," she told me in a tone that was almost maternal.

"Yes, Mama Cat," I replied with some relief.

On Tuesday of the last week of the quarter, my freshmen turned in their final paper. Once I'd thinned out the herd with my terror tactics during the first couple of weeks, I'd actually grown almost fond of the survivors. They'd turned into a moderately competent group, and some of them even showed a few sparkles of genuine talent.

After I'd collected their papers and stowed them in my briefcase, I looked at the class. "That's pretty much it, fun-seekers," I told them. "I'm going to give you a break. Since you're all probably busy boning up for your exams, why don't we scratch tomorrow's class? How you spend the time is up to you, but my advice is not to waste it. Concentrate on whichever course is giving you the most trouble and bear down on it. Let's bump up those grades. Life is fleeting, but your academic record is permanent. A D-minus grade in some Mickey Mouse course that doesn't mean a damn thing can haunt you for the rest of your life. Pop by for the Thursday class to pick up your papers, and we'll part friends, OK? Class dismissed."

Boy, did *that* empty the classroom in a hurry. Twink and her sorority-girl chum were among the first ones out the door.

I'd never really had much use for the Greek Group—those assorted Phi Delta Whatevers and Sigma Who Gives a Damns—but Twink's little friend seemed to be a cut above the average sorority fluffhead whose main goal at the university was finding a suitable husband. It was just as well that Twink hadn't gotten around to mentioning the time she'd spent at Fallon's bughouse. It may be fashionable for sorority girls to be broad-minded, but probably not *that* broad-minded.

Back at the boardinghouse, I parked myself at my desk and pawed through the papers until I found Twink's gratuitous essay. I pushed the others aside and prepared to get my socks blown off.

WHAT I HAVE LEARNED THIS QUARTER
By Twinkie

The very first thing I learned is that normies are even more strange than bugsies are. You normies take yourselves much too seriously. Don't you know how to laugh at yourselves? That's the very first thing we bugsies pick up.

You ought to try it sometime. It makes life so much more fun.

Then I learned that clocks and calendars are terribly important to normies. Haven't you ever heard of 'close enough'? Will the world really come to an end if you're a minute and a half late?

Do you actually believe that the world cares that much?

The next thing I noticed about normies was that you all seem to believe that there's a difference between right and wrong. We bugsies all know that they're really the same thing if you look at them in the proper way. They aren't separate, you know. There's lots of right mixed in with wrong and oodles of wrong dripping off the corners of right. It all depends on how you look at things.

Lighten up, Normies.

Then I learned that normies seem to bunch up, and they're terrified that they might be just a teeny bit different from all the other normies in the world. If everybody wears a blue ribbon, you'd rather die than wear a red one.

Do you really think that anybody cares, or that it makes the slightest difference?

When Dockie-poo Fallon finally released me from his fancy nuthouse, I knew that I shouldn't tell the normies where I'd been. Normies are scared to death of us bugsies—probably because we do things normies would never think of doing. We have very good reasons to do the things we do, and just because you don't understand those reasons, it doesn't mean that they're wrong.

Does it?

The most important thing I've learned this quarter is that I have to hide what I'm thinking, because if the normies find out about it, they'll send me right back to the bughouse, and I'm not ready to go there yet.

I'm very tired now, but soon—very, very soon—I'll sleep, and when I sleep, my dreams will be all right, and nothing will ever go wrong again.

"What the hell?" I muttered. This paper started out like the first one Twink had written, but somewhere along the line, the cutesy-poo ran out and things got very strange and very serious.

The mention of ribbons *really* got my attention. It seemed merely puzzling at first glance, but it set off some bells when I read through the paper again. Twink *could* have said "green and pink," but she didn't. "Red and blue" came through loud and clear, as in the red and blue ribbons the twins had always traded off as kids. That connection back to her forgotten childhood carried some strong hints that our Twink was gearing up for a return engagement at Fallon's bughouse.

I ran several copies off on my klutzy, secondhand copy machine. I knew Sylvia would want one, another for Dr. Conrad, and Doc Fallon would scream bloody murder if he didn't get one, too.

I finished grading about half of the papers before supper, and I figured that I'd pretty much earned my pay this quarter. The surviving members of my freshman class had turned in papers that were quite a bit above average. The Dr. Conrad approach—"I won't accept crap"—seemed to be valid. Students will usually do what you expect them to do. If you don't expect much, you won't get much. If you expect the moon, you might not get it, but you'll probably get quite a few tries at it. That made me feel pretty good. I was turning a bunch of above-average students loose on the rest of the faculty, and that's what teaching is all about, isn't it?

Renata's paper was still nagging at me at supper that evening, so I must have been acting gloomy.

"What's got you down in the dumps, Mark?" Charlie asked me. "The Christmas blahs, maybe?"

"Heck, I can live with Christmas if I don't have to watch *too* many commercials on TV. No, Twinkie turned in another one of those freebee papers today, and some stuff came out that's got me worried."

"Why didn't you tell me?" Sylvia demanded.

"I just did. I made copies, so I've got one for you and another for Doc Fallon. Maybe you could fax it to him?"

"What seems to be her problem?" James asked me.

"I'm not entirely sure. Her last paper was all bright and bubbly. This one starts out that way, but then it seems to wander off. Here." I pushed one of the copies across the table to him. "You're the one with the oratorical voice. *You* read it. I'd probably start to splutter if *I* tried. Twink's definitions of right and wrong are a tad unusual."

James glanced at the copy I'd just given him. "I see that you've moved up a ways from 'How I Spent My Summer Vacation,' Mark," he observed.

"What's this one?" Charlie asked him.

" 'What I Have Learned This Quarter,' " James replied.

"Thirty pages long?" Erika asked.

"Five hundred words," I told her. "I wanted to find out if they could get to the meat."

"Let's hear it," Sylvia said to James.

He cleared his throat and read the paper to us.

"Now *that* is one strange puppy," Charlie said, when James had finished. "What the hell was she talking about there at the end?"

"I haven't got the foggiest idea," I admitted.

"Her load's shifting again, isn't it?" Erika asked Sylvia.

"It doesn't sound good," Sylvia admitted.

"The business about ribbons *really* bothered me," I said. "When the twins were about three or so, their mother used red and blue hair ribbons to tell them apart, and the girls played swapsie with the ribbons every time Inga's back was turned. Twink mentioned those colors specifically, you noticed, so maybe she's starting to catch some echoes out of the past."

"I suppose it's possible," she conceded.

"I thought that everything about those nightmares was being blotted out," Trish said thoughtfully, "but right there at the end she sounded like she knows there's something very wrong with her dreams."

"She's coming at us from about seven different directions, that's for sure," Charlie said.

"I think I'd better take a run on up to Lake Stevens tomorrow," Sylvia said then. "Things seem to be coming to a head, and we'd better wire Dr. Fallon in. Maybe *he* can come up with some way to keep Renata from crashing."

"I sure hope so," I said. "If Twink completely loses it, it'll be a clear win for the other side."

CHAPTER FIFTEEN

Sylvia took off for Lake Stevens early on Wednesday morning. Apparently Twink's paper had her more than a little worried, since her master's degree was hanging in the balance. If Twinkie happened to go completely bonkers again and got herself locked up, Sylvia's case history might go down the tubes.

I went to my Milton seminar after breakfast. I'd already finished my paper, and it was ready to go, so I was basically marking time.

I swung by Mary's place after class to see how Twink was doing. Her gratuitous essay had me pretty worried. The notion of having her audit a class had seemed like a good one last summer, but I wasn't all that sure about it now. Maybe we'd jumped the gun and thrown her into deep water before she was ready.

Mary hadn't gone to bed yet when I got there, and she answered the back door when I knocked. "Is she OK?" I asked.

"She's down with a cold," Mary replied. "She's been barking like a Great Dane ever since I came home."

"Is she running a fever?"

"That'll probably come later. She's mostly just coughing now, and she sounds like a bullfrog on a lily pad when she tries to talk."

"That shoots down the two different voices theory, doesn't it? I mean, if she's been coming down with bronchitis or something, that different-sounding voice wouldn't have anything to do with a mental condition, would it?"

"See what Sylvia has to say about it. She's the one who's supposed to be the expert."

"Is Twink awake?" I asked.

"She was a few minutes ago. Did you want to talk with her?"

"Maybe I should. I'm supposed to take her home for Christmas vacation. If she's coming down with something serious, it might be better if I held off a while. A little touch of the sniffles is one thing, but double pneumonia's a whole 'nother ball game."

"Yeah, it is. Let's check her out before she drifts off to sleep."

We went to Twink's bedroom, and I could hear her coughing before Mary even knocked on the door. "Mark's here, Ren," Mary said. "Are you up for a visitor?"

"As long as he doesn't come too close," Twink replied in a hoarse voice. "He doesn't want to catch this."

Mary and I went on in. "How are you feeling, Twink?" I asked her.

"Rotten," she told me in a raspy voice. "Stay back, Mark. You don't want any part of this one." She had a box of tissues on the bed beside her and a large paper bag on the floor near the bed about half-full of used ones.

"Why don't you scratch tomorrow's class?" I suggested. "Stay inside where it's warm and dry. All I'm going to do tomorrow is hand back the papers and say bye-bye, so you won't miss much."

"Did you like *my* paper, Mark?"

"I think you set fire to another barn, Twink."

"I'm glad you approve." She started coughing again. "What a drag," she said. "I'm going to try to sleep. I've been coughing since yesterday, and I'm pooped."

"Sleep lots," I told her. "Santa Claus is coming to town, so you'd better get back on your feet."

"Whoopee," she rasped flatly.

*   *   *

When I got back to the boardinghouse, I went up to fight my way through grading that stack of freshman papers. I hate having things like that hanging over my head.

It was about noon when James came upstairs and rapped on my door. "There's been another killing, Mark," he rumbled.

"Doesn't that guy have anything better to do?" I said. "How many does this make?"

"Eight," he replied, "if you want to count the one near Woodinville."

"Where was this one?"

"Discovery Park, over on the military reservation. Our cut-up took out a sailor this time."

"That's a switch. Are the TV guys all warped out again?"

He smiled faintly. "They all seemed a bit relieved," he said. "It's been almost a month since the Mercer Island killing, and the TV boys had pretty much exhausted the subject; they were starting to get desperate trying to find something to say that'd keep them on camera. Oh, the sailor was a black man, by the way."

"Affirmative action strikes again, huh? Doesn't that give you a warm little glow, James? Our local cut-up doesn't seem to be a bigot. He'll kill anybody who comes along. He might even have quotas."

"Get serious," James rumbled.

"Sorry. I'll come down and watch the TV guys jump up and down as soon as I finish grading these papers. First things first."

"Suit yourself," he said.

I finished the last of the papers by midafternoon, and then I went downstairs to watch the hysterics on television. Somebody had obviously clamped down a lid on details about this latest killing, and that *really* bugged the reporters. Name, rank, and serial number was about all they'd been able to get, and that made for a fairly skimpy news story. The military seemed to be holding firm on their "none of your damn business" position, and certain orders had been issued about talking to reporters.

"I'm not permitted to discuss that" drives a reporter absolutely wild. It was almost fun to watch.

The details the reporters *did* get were that the victim's name was Thomas Walton, and he'd been wearing civilian clothes when the Slasher had taken him out. He'd been a seaman second class, which seemed a bit unusual, since he'd been in his second six-year hitch. He'd evidently been in trouble a few times, but the Navy didn't want to talk about how or why or when. That didn't make the reporters too happy.

After supper, Charlie, James, and I made our customary jaunt to the Green Lantern to see if we could get the straight scoop on the Walton killing from Charlie's brother.

Bob West seemed to be moderately pissed off about the Navy's attitude. "They won't talk about Walton's record," he fumed, "and they even refused to release the body so that our medical examiner could perform an autopsy. They say that the Navy doctors are going to do it, but military doctors don't know beans about pathology."

"Can't King County just step in and take the body away from the Navy?" James asked.

Bob shook his head. "The body was found on the military reservation. That's federal land, so King County doesn't have jurisdiction. We expect a certain amount of cooperation in a murder case, but we're not getting any from the Navy on this one. I'm wondering if we'll see some kind of cover-up. Walton had obviously been in trouble quite a few times, but the Navy refuses to talk about it. They don't want any dirty laundry flapping around in the breeze, so they clam up. This is just a guess, but I'd say that Walton screwed up on a fairly regular basis, and he got off with a slap on the wrist for things he should have done hard time in the slammer for. Now the

Navy's trying to cover its own ass, so they won't give us diddly-squat on Walton's record."

"Can't you get a subpoena?" Charlie asked.

"Against the Navy? Get serious. This is touchy ground, kid. Nobody's going to stick his neck out on this one on the off chance that something useful might turn up. I'm afraid this killing's going to turn out to be a dead end."

Sylvia got me off to one side after breakfast on Thursday morning. "I think we might have a problem, Mark," she told me.

"Oh?"

"Dr. Fallon's almost positive that Renata's right on the verge of flying apart again. Her paper really upset him."

"I think he might be reading more into it than was really there," I disagreed. "Every now and then a freshman student writes himself into a corner and doesn't know how to wriggle out of it. Twink took a wrong turn in her essay and hit a dead end, that's all. That last bit about dreams was just a tack-on to give the paper a conclusion."

"I'm not sure about that, Mark. Those nightmares are the core of her problem, after all, and she fervently hopes that she can get rid of them."

"Maybe so, but I still think it was just an afterthought. Twink's at the freshman level, so 'rewrite' isn't part of her vocabulary. As far as a freshman's concerned, everything he puts down on paper's set in concrete. He's incapable of reading his own stuff critically, and he's positive that 'revision' is an obscene word."

"We don't see it that way in my field, Mark. I think that last bit about dreams was a Freudian slip. She might not have meant to say it, but it popped out anyway. I think Dr. Fallon agrees."

"We'll see what happens, but probably not until after Christmas vacation. I'm going to take her home tomorrow— if her cold doesn't get worse—and a lot of things might change during the next few weeks. I've managed to back her dad off a little, but I still might have to do some fast talking to even get permission to bring her back to Seattle. Her dad's still not very happy about Fallon's decision to turn her over to Mary last fall, and if he finds out that she's having serious problems, he might put his foot down."

"Oh, dear," Sylvia said. "I hadn't thought of that."

"You'd better, Sylvia, because it *could* happen."

I made a quick run to Mary's place to see how Twink's cold was coming along. If she was running a high fever, I sure as hell wasn't going to take her out in the weather on Friday.

"I think it's mostly sniffles, Mark," Mary told me. "She still sounds hoarse, and she's using up Kleenex by the boxful, but she doesn't have a fever. I'll pack a couple of suitcases for her, and you can run her up to Everett tomorrow."

"She has to go see Fallon tomorrow, doesn't she?"

"If you're going to be busy, Inga can take care of that."

"I don't have anything urgent on the fire, Mary," I told her. "After I get Twink settled in, though, I'll probably come back. I'm not going to blow two weeks watching Rudolph the Red-nosed Reindeer on TV. I should be able to get a lot of work done during the vacation."

"You're turning into a grind, Mark."

"I know. Depressing, huh? Get some sleep, Mary. You're starting to look a little frazzled again."

"Up your nose!" she flared.

"That's our girl," I said, grinning at her.

After lunch I drove down to Padelford to hand the papers back to my freshmen. They looked a little antsy, so I kept it fairly short. "All in all, you've done pretty well this quarter, gang," I complimented them. "Sometimes your logic's a little on the shaky side, but you'll get better at that as you go along. Some of you are still a little stiff, but that'll probably wear off with more practice. Keep those MLA style sheets handy—

particularly if you're dealing with the History Department. The history people are sticklers for the correct format when it comes to footnotes. One last thing, and then we'll split. Give some serious thought to scribbling down an outline before you jump feetfirst into a paper. If you try to wing it without knowing where you're going, you'll have about a fifty-fifty chance of falling flat on your face, and the odds of that go up the longer you wait to get started. If a paper's due on Wednesday morning, don't wait until midnight on Tuesday to start writing. Give yourself enough time to do it right. It *will* improve your overall grade-point average. Have a nice Christmas, and drive carefully. Class dismissed."

All right, I was a little pompous; so what? None of them were likely to remember anything I'd said anyway, so what the hell?

I hit my Milton seminar on Friday morning to turn in my paper. Despite my irritation with John-boy's rigidity on theology, I had to admit that he *was* a major poet. I just wish it hadn't always taken him so long to get to the point.

After our gentle professor had wound up the course by reciting the entirety of "Lycidas" to us, he let us go, and I drove to Mary's place to see how Twink was doing. The sky was fairly murky, but at least it wasn't raining yet. I decided that if she were about halfway ambulatory, I wouldn't be taking too many chances if I ran her on up to Everett. Mary had to go to work every night, but Inga didn't have to leave home for anything, so she'd be able to keep an eye on Twink and get her to a doctor if that cold got any worse.

Twink was sitting in the kitchen when I got there. She was still in her bathrobe, but at least she was up and moving around. "How are you feeling, Twink?" I asked her.

"A little better," she replied. Her voice was still sort of hoarse, but at least she wasn't coughing anymore. "I think it wasn't really a cold, Mark," she added. "It's more likely that it was some thirty-seven-and-a-half-hour bug."

"The short ones are the best, I suppose. Where's Mary?"

"She's taking a bath. She always does that after work. You should know that by now."

"Are you feeling up to the trip to Everett?"

"Do I really *have* to spend two weeks with Les and Inga?" she asked.

"Yup," I told her.

"Are we going back to that damn 'yup' routine, Mark?" she demanded.

"Yup."

"I hate you!"

"No you don't, Twink. You're just grouchy because that bug bit you and gave you the sniffles. Look on the positive side of 'yup.' It's short, to the point, and it doesn't leave room for arguments. You're going home for Christmas to stay on the good side of Les and Inga. Help Mommy in the kitchen and bring Daddy his pipe and slippers when he gets home from work. Keep a tight lid on the buggy stuff, and do your very best to act like a normie. Les can pull the plug on the 'Twinkie goes to college' game plan at any time, so keep him happy. Look upon it as an investment in the future."

"You're probably right, Mark," she agreed. Then she gave me a sort of sidelong look. "Since it's come up, what's the game plan for winter quarter? Am I going to audit your class again?"

"I suppose you can if you want. Wouldn't you rather branch out, though?"

"Do any of the rest of the gang at the boardinghouse teach classes?"

"James teaches an Introduction to Philosophy course, and every so often I think Sylvia takes a section of Basic Psychology. I'll have to find out if she's doing one next quarter."

"I'd like to stick with familiar faces, if it's possible," she told me. "They already know that I'm a little bugsie, so I won't have to explain everything to them."

"I'd suggest auditing those classes, Twink," I told her.

"You've been having quite a few 'bad days' here lately, so you don't need any pressure just yet. Take things easy, hang out with the sorority girls, and get well before you start taking courses for credit."

"We'll see," she said, clearing her throat as she stood. "I *wish* this damn frog would find someplace else to play," she growled irritably as she padded down the hall to get changed.

It was about ten-thirty when we pulled into the driveway of the Greenleaf house. I unloaded Twink's luggage and loafed around while she unpacked and got settled in. "Why don't you doze a while, Twink?" I suggested. "We've got to run up to Lake Stevens this afternoon, and you're looking a little pooped-out from all that coughing."

"Yeah, pooped," she agreed. "Do you think I could get away with calling in sick?"

"I wouldn't bet on it. Doc Fallon yearns for your company, and he'd get all pouty if you pulled a no-show on him."

"You're probably right, Mark," she agreed. "Go pester Inga for a while, and I'll try to sleep."

I found Inga in the kitchen watching a small TV set tuned to a Seattle station. Some earnest young lady was ranting about—what else?—the Seattle Slasher.

"Les and I've been very concerned about this maniac in the university district, Mark," Inga said. "Do you think Renata might be in danger?"

"No, not really," I told her. "The Slasher cuts up guys, not girls, and he works at night. We don't let Twink go out alone after dark. If she wants to go someplace, I drive her—or Sylvia does. Charlie West's brother is a cop, and he told us that it might be safer if we travel in groups until after the Slasher gets busted. Twink's as safe as we can make her."

"Yes, but how's she *really* doing, Mark? Dr. Fallon tries to put the best face on things, but I don't think he tells Les and me the whole story."

"She's still having some problems, Inga," I told her. "Every so often, she goes through a siege of nightmares. She bounces right back, everything seems fine for a couple of weeks, then the nightmares pop up again."

"Has Renata been going to church regularly?" she asked.

"It runs in spurts—two or three Sundays in a row, and it seems to do her a lot of good. Then a couple Sundays off. She really likes Father O. Of course, everybody likes him. That Irish brogue of his has a lot of charm to it. He doesn't *quite* get into 'Faith and begorrah,' but he comes pretty close sometimes."

"I've met him," she said with a faint smile.

"Then you know he's a good guy, and he's pretty sharp, too. Father O was the one who noticed that Twink's voice changes every so often. He picked up on that in the confessional."

"He's not supposed to tell anybody about that!" she exclaimed.

"He didn't talk about *what* she said, Inga. All he told us was that her voice isn't always the same. Sylvia thought that the voice change might be some sort of early warning signal, but that doesn't really float, since Twink's picked up some bug, and she sounds a lot like a foghorn right now."

"She is a little hoarse," Inga agreed. "The twins used to come down with that every so often. I think there might be some kind of allergy involved."

"I'll pass that on to Fallon this afternoon. If nothing else, he could probably write her a prescription for something that'll clear it up. If all it really amounts to is the sneezy-snifflies, a good allergy medication should take care of it, and we can stop wasting time on this 'mysterious voice-change' crap."

Twink was still a little hoarse when we went up to Lake Stevens that afternoon, so I kept the car heater turned up. I certainly didn't want her taking a chill just before Christmas.

"Aren't you feeling well, Renata?" Fallon asked her when he heard her raspy-sounding voice.

"A little snarky, that's all," she replied hoarsely. "I think it's some kind of virus. It doesn't seem to be a full-bore cold."

"Inga thinks it might be an allergy," I chipped in. "She told me that the twins used to come down with sneezing and coughing fairly often when they were kids. Aren't there some antiallergy pills that'd clear it up?"

"Several," he replied. "How are you feeling otherwise, Renata?"

"I'm sort of at loose ends, Dr. Fallon," she told him. "After the holidays, I'll have to sign up for a different class—or even two. I've gotten used to the people who were taking Mark's class, and now I'll have to meet a whole new bunch. That might be a little disturbing. Bugsies need stability, and the whole world changes at the beginning of each new quarter at U.W. I'm not ready to start taking classes for credit, not just yet. I've still got some things I need to clear away before I tackle real studenthood. A little more time as an imitation student probably wouldn't hurt."

"Would you like to talk about these problems you want to put behind you?" he asked her.

"Talking about them wouldn't do much good, Dr. Fallon," she replied. "I'm dealing with them in my own way, and I'm not even sure I could put them into words." Then she gave me one of those sly sidelong looks. "How does 'actions speak louder than words' strike you, Mark?" she asked.

"Tired, worn-out, pompous, threadbare—take your pick, Twink. Clichés are like that most of the time."

"That doesn't take away the truth, though, does it? I'm still having those 'bad days' Aunt Mary talks about, but I'm getting closer to a solution. It's trying to hide from me, but I've got its number, so it won't be able to hide much longer. As soon as I see its face, Twinkie can go back to being a normie. Isn't that neat?"

I pondered that cryptic announcement as I drove back to Seattle that evening. Twink was obviously being deliberately obscure, but I honestly feared an impending crisis. The only problem was that Twink wouldn't tell anybody just exactly what she was dealing with. She'd seemed almost inhumanly confident that she was going to come out on top, and that struck me as a one-way ticket back to the house with rubber rooms.

Back at the boardinghouse, Trish, Erika, and Sylvia were putting a Christmas tree in the living room, for God's sake!

"What's this all about?" I asked them.

" 'Tis the season to be jolly, Mark," Erika replied. "Hadn't you heard about that?"

"It just seemed like a good idea," Trish told me. "We'll all be spending Christmas Day with family, but we can have our own private little celebration here. How does Sunday grab you?"

"The day after tomorrow? Sure, I guess."

"We'll even relax the rule about no in-house booze and have a few nips of eggnog," Sylvia added, draping tinsel over the branches of the artificial tree.

"Hanky-panky's still an official no-no, though," Erika said. "We'll see how Trish feels about it after she gets half in the bag, so don't give up hope yet."

"All right, Erika," Trish told her sister, "quit clowning around."

"You're turning into a real drag, Trish," Erika replied. "You really ought to lighten up once in a while."

"Let's not get carried away on any Christmas presents," Trish told us all at the breakfast table on Saturday. "That might be sort of embarrassing."

"A ten-buck limit, maybe?" Charlie suggested.

"That sounds about right to me," Erika said. "I probably wouldn't get *too* upset if you wanted to buy me diamonds, but the neighbors might start to talk."

"Nothing over ten dollars, then?" Trish asked, looking around at us.

"Are we putting it to a vote?" James asked her.

"The chair will entertain a motion to that effect," Trish replied.

"So moved," I said, remembering the times I'd gone to union meetings.

"Seconded," Charlie chimed in.

"All in favor say aye," Trish said, falling into line.

We all sort of agreed.

"The motion is carried," Trish said then, rapping her knuckles on the tabletop.

"You left out 'opposed,' " I scolded her.

"Did you object, Mark?"

"No, but you're supposed to make the offer."

"That's silly."

"*Robert's Rules of Order* says that you're supposed to give the opposition the chance to say 'no.' Haven't you ever been to a union meeting?"

"I've never belonged to a union."

"Shocking!" Charlie said. "Let's organize the workers and lead them out on strike, Mark."

"I'd be just a little careful there, Charlie," James rumbled. "Things might start getting hungry around here if you take that *too* far. The International Sisterhood of the Ladies Who Do the Cooking might set up a picket line at the kitchen door, and we don't cross picket lines, do we?"

"He's got a point, Charlie," I agreed. "It might be best if we don't rock the boat."

"You guys sound almost like our dad," Erika told us. "He's a devout member of the carpenter's union. He thinks that *everybody* should belong to a union and go out on strike at least once a year—just to keep the boss honest."

We clowned around over breakfast for a while. We didn't have any classes hanging over our heads, so we had time to kick back and take it easy. The past three months had brought us closer together, and by now we were almost like a family. We didn't make an issue of it, but we all knew that it was

there. I think that was probably the reason behind our private
little Christmas party. The time would come when we'd all
move on, of course, but for right now we were all here, and
"right now" was a good enough reason for a celebration.

We gathered in the parlor after dinner on Sunday, and there'd
obviously been a fair amount of kidding around involved in
the last-minute Christmas shopping. You can't buy serious
presents for under ten dollars. I'd say that the grand prize for
goofy went to Erika. I'm not sure where she found it, but the
necktie she'd picked up for Charlie was absolutely hideous.
Nobody in his right mind would ever wear something like
that in public.

After we'd opened all the presents, we sat around drinking
eggnog and enjoying ourselves.

"How's our favorite nutcase, Mark?" Charlie asked me.
"She hasn't been around lately."

"She's sort of upsie-downsie," I told him. "Some days she's
all bright and bubbly, and other days she starts coming apart.
She's driving her headshrinker straight up the wall, though."

"What do you mean?" Sylvia asked in a worried kind of
voice.

"I ran her up to Lake Stevens on Friday. It seems that our
grand theory about the earthshaking importance of the
changes in her voice didn't really float. Twink's got allergies,
that's all. Her mother says the twins used to have sneezing fits
on a regular basis—depending on which weed was in bloom.
Anyway, last Friday she was all business. She told Fallon that
she's shopping around for some other introductory classes
she can audit."

"Send her around," James suggested. "I'll be teaching Introduction to Philosophy."

"Or you could hand her off to me," Sylvia stepped in. "I'm
stuck with a psychology class during winter quarter."

"Now there's a mix that'd send just about anybody off to
the bughouse," Charlie noted, "and since Twinkie likes to

write papers she's not required to write, she'll probably whip out a few that'll send a couple of department chairmen off to the funny farm. She'd have a ball with 'Existential Paranoia' wouldn't she?"

"I'd go with 'Stoic Manic Depression,' " Erika said.

" 'Schizophrenic Utilitarianism?' " Trish offered.

"I think we might be in trouble, Sylvia," James said. "If you and I try to double-team Renata this next quarter, she might very well send the both of us 'round the bend."

"At least we'd keep her in the family," Charlie said. "That girl's a treasure, so we should do our best to hang on to her for as long as we can."

Third Movement

APPASSIONATA

CHAPTER SIXTEEN

There always seems to be a lot of scurrying around during registration for winter quarter, probably because New Year's Day tends to interrupt things. Fortunately, getting Twinkie signed up to audit the classes James and Sylvia were teaching was no big chore, since there isn't much paperwork involved in auditing classes.

I'd persuaded Dr. Conrad that I'd served my time as a graduate teaching assistant, so he'd almost grudgingly agreed to let me out on parole. It wasn't as if I really needed the stipend to keep me eating regularly, and I wanted to wash the taste of Milton out of my mouth with a couple of seminars in modern American fiction. It might have been a little arrogant, but I took on Hemingway and Faulkner in the same quarter.

I stopped by Conrad's office after I'd finished registering. It's always a good idea to stay in touch with the boss.

"Did you have problems, Mr. Austin?" he asked me.

"Not really, Dr. Conrad," I replied. "I gather you put in a good word for me, because I breezed through."

"I didn't have to pull any strings, kid," he told me. "Your master's thesis is still ringing quite a few bells. How's your protégée coming along?"

"Twinkie? She's having some problems. I've got a hunch that she's just about due for a return engagement in the house with rubber rooms. We're keeping her in the family this quarter, but I'm still not sure she'll make it to spring."

"I'm sorry to hear that. Did you get any clarification from her on that last paragraph in her second paper?"

"Not so much as a peep. She sidestepped some questions from her headshrinker about it."

"You're passing those papers around? Are we contemplating a career as a literary agent?"

"Not too likely. Her paper was medium-whacky, though, so we ran a copy for Doc Fallon—along with copies of the tapes abnormal Sylvia's been recording on the sly."

"Abnormal Sylvia?"

"In-house joke, boss. Sylvia's majoring in abnormal psychology, and she's doing a case history on Twink for her master's degree. If Twink happens to burp, Sylvia's probably got it on tape."

"You live in a very strange environment, Mr. Austin."

"I know—fun, though. A regular live-in symposium of six different disciplines." I glanced at my watch. "I'd better go hit the bookstore, boss. My library's a little light on Faulkner."

"Enjoy," he said.

"Thanks a bunch," I replied sardonically.

"Aw, don't mention it."

I should know better than to try to top Dr. Conrad.

Sylvia was all tied up that Friday, so about noon I picked Twink up for her weekly visit to Doc Fallon's funny farm. She seemed edgy, for some reason. "What's bothering you, baby sister?" I asked as we pulled out onto the freeway.

"Is it always like this at the beginning of a quarter?" she responded. "I mean, everything gets scrambled, doesn't it? New courses, new teachers, different times, different classmates—it's almost like stepping into a whole new world."

"Get used to it, Twink. It happens three times a year—four, if you take summer courses. Like they say, 'variety's the spice of life.' "

"I'd rather stick to bland. We bugsies don't like change all that much."

"But you're not a bugsie anymore, Twink. Aren't you supposed to be masquerading as a normie?"

"That's just for show, Markie. Deep down where it really counts, I'm still moderately whacky."

"Fake it, Twink," I suggested. "If you act like a normie long enough, it might get to be a habit."

"Don't hold your breath," she told me.

We drove north in silence for a while.

"How does somebody go about finding the name of the registered owner of a certain car, Mark?" she asked me finally.

"If you've got a license plate number, it's no problem at all—particularly not for you. Mary's a cop, remember? Give her a number, and she can punch it into one of the computers at the cop shop and give you the owner's name, address, police record, blood type, and probably copies of his fingerprints in about thirty seconds."

"I never even thought of that," she admitted a bit sheepishly. "I must have had my head turned off."

"Is it important, Twink?" I asked her. "Are you trying to track somebody down?"

"No, I was just curious, is all. It came up in a conversation before Christmas. One of the sorority girls said that the cops can't hand out that information. She thought it was restricted—or ought to be. 'Right to privacy,' or something like that."

"Not hardly, baby sister," I told her. "That's part of the fun of living in the computer age. There's no such thing as privacy anymore."

"Charlie could probably fix that, couldn't he?"

"I hadn't thought of that," I admitted. "He probably *could* jerk somebody's name out of every computer in the world with a click of a couple of buttons. That could turn out to be a gold mine, couldn't it? A lot of people out there would pay big bucks to become nonpersons. We could set up a corporation—Anonymity Incorporated, or something. It'd send every computer nerd in the world straight up the wall, wouldn't it?"

"It couldn't happen to a nicer bunch of people," she said smugly.

For some reason our silly little conversation about computers seemed to unwind Twink's spring, and she appeared calm and rational during her session with Fallon that afternoon. There's a lot to be said for kidding around when you're talking to a nutcase, I guess. "Laughter is the best medicine" is a pretty tired old cliché, but it still seems to have a certain validity—particularly in Twink's case. Both of her papers had strongly hinted that normies take themselves too seriously and that they needed to learn how to laugh at themselves. If a few laughs would bring Twinkie back to earth, I'd go out and buy joke books by the dozen.

The session with Fallon went pretty well, and Twink was all bright and bubbly on our way back to Seattle. Maybe we'd all been a bit too uptight about her. As far as I could tell, she wasn't really ready to go back to Fallon's bughouse just yet.

On a hunch I hauled into a gas station when we got to Seattle, went to the pay phone, and called the boardinghouse. Trish answered.

"What are we having for dinner tonight, Trish?" I asked her.

"Spaghetti and meatballs. Why?"

"Would there be enough if I brought Twinkie home with me?"

"Is she all right? I mean she's not climbing the walls or anything, is she?" Trish sounded a bit dubious.

"She's fine, Trish. It's one of her cutesy-poo days. She doesn't get out very much, so I thought it'd be good for her if I invited her to dinner."

"It's fine with me, Mark. She's a lot of fun to have around when she's behaving like a normie. It's when she's bugsie that people get nervous." Trish laughed. "Now she's got me doing it," she said. "I never used those terms until I met her. Bring her along, Mark. There's plenty of spaghetti."

And so it was that Twinkie joined us for dinner that evening, and she was a smash hit again, since she had the volume on cute turned all the way up. All in all, it seemed to me that it'd been a very good day for her.

I'd pretty much exhausted the possibilities of those Saturday chores around the house, so I spent the next day puttering around my little workshop down in the basement. It seemed to me that a workbench might be useful, along with some shelves for tools, since Charlie's tools were stacked in one corner, James had his in another, and mine were scattered all over the place. Maybe if things in the shop were better organized, I wouldn't have to spend so much time looking for a particular tool when I was right in the middle of a project.

I sketched out some plans and checked my supply of scrap lumber. I don't know if I accomplished much that Saturday, but I managed to keep busy.

James had spent quite a bit of time in Everett during the holidays, and he'd told us that Mrs. Perry's doctors were fairly certain that they'd caught her cancer in time. He seemed very relieved about that. "Cancer" is a word that you don't want to hear very often.

At supper on Saturday James told us that he'd be making a run to Everett Sunday morning. "Now that Andrew's sure that his mother's going to recover, he thinks it might be time to check back in at Harvard."

"I'm sure it's still there," Charlie said. "It'd probably take quite a while to pick it up and move it. Transplanting all that ivy could be a real bear."

"What time does his plane leave?" Trish asked.

"About seven tomorrow evening," James replied. "Why?"

"Why don't you invite him to dinner here, then?" she suggested. "We'd like to get to know him."

"I'll give him a call and see what he has to say," James agreed.

*   *   *

It was about noon on Sunday when James and his young friend arrived and joined us in the kitchen. Andrew Perry was a slender young fellow who didn't seem to be overly impressed with himself the way some Ivy League students are. At least the word "Harvard" didn't crop up in every other sentence. James introduced him, Erika poured him a cup of coffee, and he seemed to blend right in.

Trish had quite a few questions for him, naturally, and she seemed a little wistful when he told her the names of some of his professors. Every discipline has its celebrities, I guess, and Harvard seems to have more than its share of the heavy hitters on its faculty.

"James was telling us that this house is picking up quite a reputation at U.W.," Andrew told us. "He said that just about everybody wants to live here."

"All except for the party boys," Charlie said. "They might lust after our ladies, but our prohibition policy turns them off. Party boys *do* like their booze."

"We were lucky," Erika said. "The right people showed up on the doorstep at the right time. And our assorted disciplines make for some interesting conversations at the supper table—especially Sylvia's case history."

"Oh?" Andrew said curiously.

"The Twinkie story," Charlie told him. "Mark introduced us to a real-live nutcase. She's a screwball, but she *is* sort of fun."

James snapped his fingers. "I almost forgot something," he said to Sylvia. "I think Andrew's got the answer to one of your problems. He knows why Renata keeps talking about wolves howling after she has those nightmares."

"Is this Twinkie person the girl whose sister was murdered in Forest Park a few years back?" Andrew asked him.

"That's the one. Mark knows her family, and he introduced her to us during the fall quarter. Go ahead and tell them about it."

"There's not really a lot to tell," Andrew said. "Our house

isn't far from Forest Park, and we all remember the night of that murder vividly. One of our neighbors has a kennel, and he's been experimenting with a crossbreed dog—part Alaskan husky and part timber wolf. It's not working out too well for him—the wolf keeps popping up, and wolves aren't good house pets. Anyway, on the night that girl was murdered in the park, those wolf-dogs went absolutely crazy. They howled all night and kept at it even after the sun came up."

"I never saw anything about that in the newspapers," I said. Andrew shrugged. "We told the police about it."

"So *that's* why Renata keeps moaning about wolves howling!" Sylvia exclaimed. "It didn't make sense until now. We were right, Mark. Renata's recurrent nightmares *are* a reliving of the night when Regina was murdered. I've got to pass this on to Dr. Fallon."

I had a few doubts about that, though. If the sound of howling wolves terrified Twink, why would she play that unmarked tape with some woman singing along with the wolves for hours at a time? If wolf howls were part of nightmare city, she shouldn't really be hooked on that tape. . . .

There were still some things that didn't quite match up.

Sylvia was all fired up about what Andrew had told us, though, so I kept my suspicions to myself. I knew one thing for certain, however. By hook or crook I *was* going to get a copy of that tape.

Classes began on Monday the fifth of January, and not having that freshman English class hanging over my head was a pure joy.

My Hemingway seminar met for the customary two hours early on Monday morning and Faulkner followed hot on Hemingway's tail. Now, that's a stylistic jolt for you. Hemingway seemed to be hell-bent on writing one-word sentences, and Faulkner's sentences wandered around to the point that it was virtually impossible to pinpoint the subject.

My schedule that quarter was a grad student's dream. My

classes were both in the morning, so my afternoons were free. I almost felt a little guilty about that—just a little.

I felt a slight sense of a vacancy, though, and it finally dawned on me that I'd miss seeing Twinkie's face in the middle of a classroom four afternoons a week. I'd made a few smart-alecky remarks about foisting her off on James and Sylvia, but she was still *my* responsibility. Having her in my freshman class had given me the chance to keep an eye on her, but that chance was gone now, and I'd have to rely on sec-ondhand reports—*or* spend most of my wonderful free time at Mary's place.

That took a lot of the shine off my day.

Sylvia's introductory class met on Monday, Wednesday, and Friday, but James only had Tuesdays and Thursdays to cram several thousand years of philosophy down the throats of assorted underclassmen. Sylvia's course, like mine, was pretty much required of all students, so she got more than her share of reluctant dum-dums. James, the lucky dog, taught an elective course, so *his* students hadn't been dragged kicking and screaming through the door.

"Did Twink seem to be OK today?" I asked Sylvia at the supper table that evening.

"A little withdrawn, maybe," Sylvia replied. "Of course, we weren't there for long. All I do on the first day is gather the enrollment cards and give out a reading assignment. No-body's head is functioning on the first day of class, so I don't waste time trying to get through to them."

"The technical term for that is 'goofing off,' isn't it?" Charlie suggested, grinning at her.

"No, it's not!" she flared.

"Watch it, Charlie," James cautioned. "Our Sylvia's got a short fuse sometimes."

"You know, I've noticed that myself," Charlie agreed.

"I thought I'd noticed you noticing," James observed.

*   *   *

After supper, James, Charlie, and I ran over to the Green Lantern to see if Bob had anything new and exciting to tell us about the Seattle Slasher.

"What's the good word, Bob?" Charlie asked his brother when we'd retired to one of the back booths.

"There aren't any, kid," Bob replied sourly. "Did you want to hear a few bad ones?"

"I already know most of those," Charlie replied. "Are you getting any closer to chasing down old 'cut and run'?"

"Not really," Bob admitted. "Do you remember that sailor who got carved up just before Christmas?"

"The black man?" James said.

"That's the one. I think I told you guys that the department was all pissed off because the Navy refused to release the body for an autopsy, didn't I?"

"Yes," James replied. "Didn't you say that the Navy doctors were going to do it themselves, then pass the results on to the Seattle police?"

"That's the way it went. Our pathologists came up with egg on their faces about *that* one," Bob said. "They were positive that the Navy doctors didn't know the first thing about conducting an autopsy, and that turned out to be *way* off base. Those Navy boys are real pros. They ran tests that never would have occurred to our guys, and they turned up something that our medical examiners had totally missed."

"Oh?" Charlie said. "What was that?"

"Have you ever heard of curare?"

"Isn't that some kind of poison?" Charlie asked.

"Sort of. It's a concoction of certain plant extracts that some Indian tribes in the Amazon jungle smear on their arrows. It paralyzes animals—or people—when it gets into the bloodstream. And there was a whole bunch of curare in that dead sailor's blood."

"So *that's* why nobody's ever heard any screaming when the Slasher starts cutting chunks off of people who ain't dead yet," Charlie said.

"You got it, kid," Bob replied, "and after they'd found the curare in the sailor's blood, those Navy doctors went over the carcass with a microscope. Guess where the needle mark was."

"In the guy's *throat*?" Charlie demanded in a half-strangled tone.

"You guessed 'er, Chester," Bob said. "Evidently, the Slasher carries a loaded hypodermic needle, and he nails the guy he wants to kill right straight in the gullet with the damn thing. After that we get these real quiet murders. The curare paralyzes the vocal cords and the lungs, so the poor bastard can't even squeak while he's getting all cut to pieces—*and*, of course, within seconds he can't run or even raise his arms to protect his face."

"Where could anybody get his hands on a supply of curare?" I asked. "That's pretty exotic stuff, isn't it?"

"Our pathologists tell us that it's available in any well-stocked pharmacy. It's a muscle relaxant, and doctors use it to bring a patient out of convulsions—usually when somebody's having an epileptic seizure, but I guess there are some other things that cause convulsions as well."

"Wouldn't that suggest that the Slasher's a doctor—or maybe a male nurse or a pharmacist?" James asked.

"Not necessarily," Bob disagreed. "It almost has to be somebody who knows what curare does, but that could just be some guy whose sister or cousin was an epileptic. I mean, it's not some great big secret. Anyway, after we found out that the Slasher was using curare, one of the guys ran a quick computer check, and the word 'curare' turned up in the burglary of a drugstore over in the Queen Anne district last October. It was unusual, because whoever broke in passed up all kinds of opiates and other feel-good products and *only* grabbed the curare."

"It sounds to me like having the Navy doctors do the autopsy was a stroke of good luck," Charlie noted.

"Come on, kid," Bob protested. "Our pathologists have

carcasses by the dozen they have to check out. Sometimes they get rushed, that's all. They're not going to start looking for poison in the body of a guy who's been gutted out like a fresh-caught fish. The cause of death is pretty obvious, so our pathologists concentrate on pinpointing the exact time of death. Those Navy doctors weren't rushed, so they could go into greater detail. They even started to get exotic. They took measurements on every single cut and scrape on that sailor's body, and they came to a very peculiar conclusion."

"Oh?" Charlie said.

"They seem to think that the Slasher's using some kind of homemade knife. It's got a blade that's only about two and a half inches long, shaped like a hook. The Navy guys think that the Slasher stabs the point in and then pulls the blade through the meat—shoulders, throat, belly—wherever. The poor bastard getting carved up can't move or make a sound—because of the curare—so the Slasher can drag it out and make it last for as long as he wants it to. If he's halfway careful, it could take at least an hour for his victim to die."

"Ouch!" Charlie said, wincing.

"Yeah, ouch," Bob agreed. "We've *got* to get that maniac off the streets. A shooting, or a stabbing with a regular knife is one thing, but this Slasher isn't satisfied with just killing somebody. He wants pain, and lots of it. I've got a hunch that in the right circumstances he'd do his very best to keep the guy he's killing fully conscious for a week or more while he was getting this, that, and various other things cut away. And to make it even worse, the poor bastard can't move a muscle or even squeal. *That's* the part that raises the hair on the back of my neck."

That first week of classes was a bit scrambled. It always takes a while to make the adjustment. I was reading Hemingway's "Torrents of Spring" on Thursday morning, having a ball with that outrageous parody of the ponderous writing of the once-famous Sherwood Anderson. If we can believe Papa, he churned that one out in ten days, and it was one of the great literary swindles of the twentieth century. Hemingway'd gotten a very interesting offer from Scribner for *The Sun Also Rises*, but he was already under contract to Boni and Liveright—who were also Anderson's publishers. In fact, Anderson was the heavy-hitter for Boni and Liveright, so when Hemmingway turned in the mocking "Torrents of Spring," B&L wouldn't touch it with a ten-foot pole. That freed Hemingway from the slave clause, and he immediately cut a deal with Scribner for much bigger bucks. Papa could be very shrewd sometimes.

It was about nine o'clock when Erika yelled up the stairs. "You've got a phone call, Mark," she shouted.

"Be right there," I called as I dashed downstairs.

It was Mary. "Ren's flipped out again, Mark," she told me.

"Damn! I thought she was getting over those."

"Not really. She was going full-bore when I came home. I got about fifteen minutes of it on tape, then I zonked her out."

"Did anything at all unusual show up this time?" I asked her.

"No, I think she's going to keep doing these same things over and over until somebody—Fallon, or Sylvia—cracks the code. And I don't think we should wait too long, because we can't be positive about how many more of these blowouts she's got left in her. The day's going to come before too much longer when she won't bounce back. At that point, it's back to the funny farm, and *this* time, I don't think she'll graduate."

"You might be right, Mary," I agreed. "We'd better kick some butt and see if we can put Fallon and Sylvia into high gear. Time could be running out on us."

"See if you can find Sylvia. Let's get copies of this tape before I lose it."

"I'll get right on it, Mary," I promised her.

CHAPTER SEVENTEEN

Sylvia was on campus that morning, and I could probably have spent the whole day looking for her. I *did* have an alternative, though. I had an old dual-deck tape player-recorder that I'd retired when I'd replaced it with a better sound system, so I dug it out of the back of my closet, stuck a couple of blank tapes in my pocket, and carried the heavy recorder downstairs.

"What's up, Mark?" Erika asked me.

"Twinkie's flipped out again," I replied. "Mary got most of it on tape, and I want to run copies. Sylvia's going to want one, and so will Doc Fallon."

"That's happening more and more frequently, isn't it?"

"Yeah, it is. Mary seems to think that if we don't get a handle on it pretty quick, Twink's going to wind up back in the bughouse, and this time she won't be coming back out again."

"Damn!" Erika swore.

"At least damn," I agreed.

Mary was waiting when I got to her place. "Where's Sylvia?" she demanded.

"She's on campus somewhere," I replied, "and I don't feel like chasing her down. I can run copies of your tape on this machine and hand them off to her when she comes home."

"Good thinking," Mary agreed. "Let's set up in the kitchen. There's room enough for that big recorder of yours there, and we won't mess up the living room."

258 David & Leigh Eddings

"Sounds good to me," I agreed.

I ran off several copies of Mary's tape, and I was just about to pack things up and go home when I had an idea. "Has Twink ever played her favorite tape for you, Mary?" I asked.

"The one where there's a woman singing along with a pack of wolves?"

"That's the one. Does she play it very often?"

"Often enough to make me pretty sick of hearing it. Why?"

"You know the way she complains about wolves howling when she goes bonkers? Doesn't it seem odd to you that she complains about it on her bad days, but listens to it when she's a normie?"

"Now that you mention it, it *does* seem peculiar."

"If she's always listening to it, it's probably in her tape player right now. If you can sneak into her room without waking her up, I'd like to run off a copy of that tape too. It might give Sylvia and Doc Fallon a few clues about what's bothering her so much."

"I won't have to sneak, Mark. Right now, an earthquake wouldn't wake her up. I'll go pull that tape out of her player."

"I'd appreciate it, Mary. I've got a hunch that it might turn out to be pretty important."

"Let's get some copies of it then."

It was about three o'clock that afternoon when Sylvia came home and read the note I'd Scotch-taped to her door. "Hey, up there," she called up the stairs.

I went out into the hallway. "I'm here," I told her. "You'd better come up. Twink had another bad one, and Mary got most of it on tape. I made some copies."

"Was there anything new this time?" she asked, climbing the stairs.

"Not that Mary and I picked up. It seems like a rerun of that one last November."

"Play the tape," she directed.

The tape started with Twink moaning about the wolves

howling. After Andrew Perry'd told us about the wolf-dogs near Forest Park, it made a lot more sense than it had back in November. The "I've got blood all over me," business *might* have been a reference to something that hadn't shown up in the police reports, or in the local newspaper. When Twink had found Regina's body, she might very well have tried to take her sister in her arms, and that would have definitely bloodied her up more than just a little. I still couldn't make any sense out of the whimpers about how cold it was. If these bad days *were* in fact the result of the recurrent nightmare during which she relived the night of her sister's murder, "cold" was *way* out of place. Regina had been murdered in late May, and it's not cold in May. I stopped the tape.

"Her voice is different," Sylvia said. "Did you notice that?"

"It seems pretty much the same to me," I disagreed.

"You probably haven't listened to the November tape as many times as I have. There's a definite difference, Mark. She's more strained and filled with horror. Back the tape up and play it again."

I rewound the tape and then punched the PLAY button. Then I listened very carefully. "Maybe you're right," I said, stopping the tape again. "I guess I was listening for 'what,' not 'how.' She *does* sound more agitated, doesn't she?"

"Run it on for the rest of the way," she said.

"All you get from here on is twin-speak, Sylvia."

"That's not important. I want to hear the *tone*, not the words."

The agitation we'd both noticed in the first part of the tape carried over into the twin-speak section, and if anything, it grew even more pronounced.

"It sounds to me like she's coming apart, Sylvia," I said glumly, after we'd heard the rest of the tape. "Oh, I've got something else for you, too. There's a tape that Twink plays all the time, and I cut some copies." I pulled the copy of Mary's tape, and stuck in the wolf tape. "You'd better brace yourself,"

I warned her. "This one's sort of spooky." I punched the PLAY button.

Sylvia's eyes grew wider and wider as the woman's voice joined in with the howling of the wolves. "Dear God!" she choked when the tape ended. "What *is* that awful thing?"

"I haven't got the faintest idea," I admitted. "Twink's tape of this doesn't have a label, and for all I know, it might be something Regina copied. The first time I ever heard it was last fall—right after Twink moved in with Mary. I gave her a call one evening, and I could hear this playing in the background. Her voice was kind of dreamy, and she told me not to pester her while her wolves were singing to her. Then she hung up on me. I'd almost forgotten about it until Twink started moaning about wolves howling. Doesn't it seem a little odd that she listens to this over and over when she's a normie, but starts carrying on about wolves howling when she's all torqued out?"

"I'll have to pass this one off to Dr. Fallon," she said. "I'm *way* out of my depth here. I *do* think this tape is important, though."

"I'm glad you liked it."

"I didn't say that I like it, Mark. It might turn out to be important, but it scares the hell out of me."

After Sylvia's class on Friday morning, she took Twink to Lake Stevens. Sylvia was trying to put the best face possible on the situation, but she was obviously very worried.

After my Friday classes, I went back to the boardinghouse for lunch, and I found Charlie camped on the kitchen TV set. "What's up?" I asked him.

"They found another stiff," he said. "It's down near Auburn, and it's been there for quite a while—long enough, anyway, that the Pierce County coroner can't come up with a precise date. The TV guys are all excited about it, but I don't think the cops are going to get anything useful out of it. It's a pretty stale body."

"Have they put a name to it yet?"

"They're still working on it—or else the cops are keeping it under wraps. Bob probably knows, but it's not really that important. Auburn's quite a ways from here. We'll see what he has to say this evening."

I fixed myself some sandwiches while Charlie ridiculed the assorted reporters and commentators trying to ride the Slasher story to celebrity. When you get right down to it, TV reporters are a pathetic bunch. Their desperate need for attention drives them down the path to absurdity, and their pious babbling about "the public's right to know" overlooks the fact that most of their viewers were probably sick and tired of the whole damn thing. I know I was.

After supper that evening, James, Charlie, and I made our customary pilgrimage to the Green Lantern to get the inside dope from Bob West. I suppose that if somebody wanted to pursue it, we were being as silly as all the other empty-heads hungrily watching the TV sets for the latest bit of dumb-show and noise.

Bob seemed a little tense when we got to the Green Lantern. "What's got you so worked up?" Charlie asked him.

"I ran my mouth when I should have clammed up," Bob said bluntly. "I want you guys to keep what I told you about curare strictly to yourselves. We don't want that to leak out. Right now, it's the only solid thing we've got to work with, and if word leaks out, the guy we're looking for might change the way he operates—or take off for Chicago."

"I gather that curare showed up during the autopsy of the fellow they found in Auburn?" James said.

"It sure did," Bob replied. "The body wasn't in very good shape, but there was enough left for the coroner to find traces of curare. Evidently, that's been going on since day one—all the way back to the Muñoz killing last September. We're guessing, obviously, but we're fairly sure that the guy we're after isn't six-foot-six and three hundred pounds. He's using curare instead of brute force to keep the victim from trying to fight him off."

"Have they come up with a name for the guy in Auburn yet?" I asked.

"Larson," Bob replied. "Samuel Larson. He was another small-timer—like a lot of the other ones the Slasher's taken out. Most of his arrests were for shoplifting or illegal possession of drug paraphernalia. He was a suspect in a rape case in Tacoma a few years back, but that was before the public realized the DNA is even better than fingerprints when it comes to identifying people. The victim took a long hot bath before she reported the rape, and she couldn't positively point the finger at Larson in the lineup, so the Tacoma cops didn't have enough on him to take it to court."

"Rape or attempted rape shows up in the record of quite a few of these victims, doesn't it?" James suggested.

"It's not particularly unusual, James," Bob told him. "We're dealing with a subculture here. Girls who hang out with petty criminals aren't too bright to begin with, and the line between rape and consensual sex can be pretty blurred among those people. If the girl doesn't scream or pull a knife, the guy—who's usually about half-drunk or doped up— thinks she's just being coy, so he doesn't wait for anything like formal permission. Just about all of these small-timers have at least one rape or attempted rape on their police records." He glanced at his watch. "I've got to run now," he said, standing up. "Don't forget what I told you guys. Keep the curare thing strictly to yourselves. It's the only solid thing we've got to work with, so don't screw it up for us."

I spent that weekend holed up with Hemingway. The writers of that period between the two world wars had some peculiar work habits. F. Scott Fitzgerald wrote a short story at a race-track once, they say. And when Papa Hemingway lived in Paris during the 1920s, he'd go to a little bistro on a cobble-stone street about six o'clock every morning and do his writing on a small table with a checkered tablecloth and wire-backed chairs. He'd keep at it for as long as the writing was going well, and he'd stop at a place in the story when he knew exactly what was coming next. He wrote several of the classics of twentieth-century short fiction there, using a small notebook that'd fit in his coat pocket and a stubby little pencil, quite probably sharpened with his knife. So much for the notion that you absolutely *must* have a computer if you want to write good fiction.

I was still coming down from the quarter I'd spent with Milton, and I had to shift gears just a bit to move into Hemingway territory. The guys who'd been through the First World War were a somber bunch. The mind shudders from the horrors they'd faced in the trenches, and it seems that they all had to keep a tight grip on their emotions to avoid flying apart. Their writing was very visual—almost clinical—and emotions were understated. You can't just skim the surface when you take on Hemingway. You have to get in there with him. I think that maybe the sixties seriously damaged American literature. That "spill your guts" approach doesn't produce very good fiction.

Since I wasn't teaching during that quarter, I couldn't keep a close eye on Twinkie the way I had during the fall quarter, so I had to rely on James and Sylvia to keep track of her for me. She was still "in the family," so to speak, but she was about one step removed from where she'd been before, and that made me a little edgy. Both Sylvia and James were sharp, that goes without saying. But no matter how hard they tried, they'd never know her as well as I did. I could spot things they'd probably miss, and Twink would tell me things she'd never mention to either of them.

"She keeps asking questions that I can't answer," James told us at the supper table on Tuesday. "Every so often we have arguments about the ethics of the criminal justice system and whether it really serves any purpose."

"Oh?" Trish asked.

"She takes the position that X number of years in jail isn't really a deterrent—*if* the criminal feels that he has a moral or ethical duty to commit the crime. Sometimes she almost sounds like a Mafioso—'if Luciano beats up on my buddy, I've got a moral obligation to blow his brains out,' for example. The rule of law flies out the window at that point, and moral justification takes over."

"That's ridiculous!" Trish exclaimed.

"Maybe so, but it does raise some interesting questions, doesn't it?"

"If you think *that* raises difficult questions, you should hear her when she gets started on psychosis," Sylvia said. "She'll even give lectures on that. Her position is that the psychotic is simply responding to the external world in his own personal way. *We* think he's crazy, but *he* knows that he's not."

"Welcome to the wonderful world of Twinkie," I told them. "Now you two can see why I had so much fun last quarter."

On Tuesday of that week there was another confession to the Slasher killings. This time, though, the reporters took the time to check out the guy's record *before* they rushed to the studio to get on camera. Evidently, this was another nutso who'd confess to just about anything. One reporter who actually had his head screwed on straight made a very interesting observation. He said that these guys who confess compulsively seem to suffer from a form of hypochondria. Instead of "you name a disease and I've got it" though, the guy making phony confessions takes credit for crimes he couldn't possibly have committed. The hypochondriac wants the doctors to pay attention to him; the guy confessing is trying to get the attention of the cops—*and* the media. A *real* whacko will sometimes even go so far as actually to kill a celebrity, just to get his name in the papers—which takes "Look at me! Look at me!" out to the far edge.

All this particular nutcase got out of his performance was a

couple of weeks in the psychiatric ward of a Seattle hospital
for observation. Sylvia told us that he probably belonged in a
bughouse, but since he wasn't really dangerous, he'd probably end up back out on the street again before very long.

I got up early on Thursday morning and spent an hour with
Faulkner's *The Sound and the Fury* before I went downstairs
in the hope that Erika's coffee would unscramble my head.

Charlie and Erika were glued to that little TV set when I
went into the kitchen. "The Slasher's coming home to roost,"
Charlie told me. "He nailed a guy in Montlake Park last
night, and that's only about two miles from here."

"Hot spit," I replied sourly. "That guy's starting to make
me tired." I actually made it to the coffeepot before Erika
could intercept me. She gave me a hard look. "Don't get
antsy, Erika," I said. "See? I really *do* know how to pour myself a cup of coffee." I filled my cup. "Notice that I didn't even
spill much on the floor."

"Smart-ass," she said.

"Sorry." I sat down. "Where the hell *is* Montlake Park?" I
asked Charlie.

"In the Montlake district, naturally. It's just across Portage
Bay from the campus—right in our own backyard."

"Another junior hoodling?" I asked.

"Pretty much, yeah. He was a crack-cocaine addict, and
he'd been busted for that and some other low crimes and misdemeanors over the past few years. Our cut-up seems to be
getting careless. The cops *are* patrolling all the parks here in
north Seattle, and a couple of them came pretty damn close to
catching our boy right in the act."

I hit the library that morning, then I stopped by Dr. Conrad's
office—just to stay in touch.

"How's that little screwball friend of yours doing, Mr.
Austin?" he asked me.

"Who can say, boss?" I replied. "She's auditing classes in

psychology and philosophy this quarter, and she's still having some serious problems that probably don't have anything to do with the courses she's sitting in on."

"You're going to fool around and let her get away from us if you don't tighten her leash," he warned me.

"Not my fault, boss—my roomies sort of appropriated her. But don't worry—she's got 'em spooked already. She's asking some questions they can't answer."

"That's our girl," he said fondly.

It was almost noon when I got back to the boardinghouse, and there was one of those yellow stick-up notes pasted to the door of my room. "I need to see you—James." I set my briefcase inside my room and went down the hall to tap on James's door. He opened it almost immediately.

"What's up?" I asked him.

"Renata was behaving peculiarly in class today, Mark," he told me.

"What else is new?"

"No, I mean *very* peculiarly. When class first started, she was talking a mile a minute, and she didn't make any sense at all. Then she stopped right in midbabble and looked around as if she suddenly didn't know where she was. Then she grabbed up her books and left the room, practically running!"

"That doesn't match anything she's done before."

"I know," he agreed. "If I've been following what's been happening correctly, this is something entirely new. I think you'd better track her down, Mark. This might be serious."

"I'll get right on it." And I did—I drove straight over to Mary's place, and tapped on the kitchen door, but nobody answered. Then I went around to look through the window of Twink's room, but the shades were drawn. "Damn!" I muttered. I didn't have any choice at that point. I went to the front door and rang the bell. Mary probably wouldn't like it, but I *had* to find out where Twink was.

I rang the doorbell again, and after a few minutes Mary opened the door in her robe, rubbing sleep out of her eyes.

"I didn't want to wake you," I apologized, "but I've got to find Renata."

"She went to class, Mark," she told me. "You know that."

"She might have gone, Mary, but she didn't stay. James told me that she was behaving very strangely, and then she just jumped up and ran out of the classroom. Could you check and see if she came home?"

"Come on in," she said, opening the door wider. Then she went back to Twink's door and rapped. There was no answer, so she opened the door. "She isn't here, Mark," she called to me.

"Damn!" I swore. "Now what the hell are we going to do? If James is right, she may have flipped out completely."

"Is there anyplace on campus where she usually hangs out?"

"The sorority house, maybe. She's not a member yet, but she spends a lot of time there."

"Why don't you give them a call while I get dressed?"

"I have to look up the number. Have you got a phonebook?"

Just then the back door opened. "What the hell are you doing, Mark?" Twink demanded from the kitchen. "You know we don't wake Aunt Mary up in the daytime."

"Where have *you* been?" I said. "James told me that you went bonkers during his class and ran out like a scalded dog."

"*When* are you people going to back off?" she said crossly. "Every time I so much as sneeze, you all come unglued. I ate something that didn't sit right, and now I've got the trots. I had to find a ladies' room in a hurry."

"Oh." I felt pretty foolish at that point. "James must have misunderstood. He said that you were talking very strangely, then you just jumped up and ran."

She rolled her eyes upward. "We're reading Plato right now, Mark," she told me with exaggerated patience. "You *have* heard of Plato, haven't you? Anyway, I think I caught the old boy off base, and I wanted to tell James about it *before* I had to make another run to the ladies' room. It was probably just a little garbled because nature was calling me in a very loud voice." She stopped abruptly. "Oops!" she said. "Here we go again." She turned and went quickly to the bathroom.

"Does that solve your problem, Mark?" Mary asked in an amused sort of way.

"It looks like I goofed, Mary," I apologized. "My panic switch seems to be a little loose here lately."

"I noticed that," she agreed with a yawn.

"Sorry I woke you up," I said. "I'll go home and hide for a while."

"Do that," she said.

It was about one-thirty when I got back to the boardinghouse, and everybody was in the kitchen locked on to the little TV set. "What's happening?" I asked.

"You'd better get a grip on something solid, old buddy," Charlie told me. "The whole city of Seattle just got turned upside down."

"Would somebody translate that for me?" I asked the rest of the crew.

"The word hit the television news about a half an hour ago, Mark," Trish told me. "Evidently, the police found a footprint at the scene of the Montlake Park murder. There was a puddle right beside the body—a puddle that was part mud and part blood. The Slasher left a footprint there, and one of the cops was sharp enough to take a plaster impression before the print dissolved into a muddy blur."

"I'm not sure that a footprint's going to be a major break-through, is it?"

"*This* one is," Erika disagreed. "It appears that our local celebrity wears a pair of those fancy athletic shoes that rather conveniently has the shoe size imprinted on the sole."

"Big deal," I scoffed.

"It is this time, Mark," Trish told me. "The shoe was a size eight."

"So?"

"It was about an inch and a half shorter than a men's size eight," Charlie said. "That footprint was made by a woman's shoe. Evidently, the Seattle Slasher is a woman."

"You're not serious!"

"The cops are, and the TV reporters are absolutely ecstatic about it." He grinned at me. "Brace yourself, Mark. Some lady reporter with a flair for the dramatic came up with an alternative to 'Seattle Slasher.' How does 'Joan the Ripper' grab you?"

CHAPTER EIGHTEEN

James, Charlie, and I took off for the Green Lantern right after supper that evening, after a brief but fairly intense argument with the ladies. They definitely wanted to come along. Charlie had to talk fast to persuade them that his brother would almost certainly clam up if three strangers joined us in the booth. There was some discontented muttering about that, and the term "male chauvinist pigs" cropped up a few times.

Bob West was seriously pissed off when we joined him in our usual back booth. "I think it's just about time to take that goddamn Burpee to a veterinary hospital and have him put to sleep," Bob growled. "If he doesn't learn to keep his goddamn mouth shut, we're *never* going to get this killer off the streets!"

"Are you saying that it was Burpee who leaked the bit about that footprint in Montlake Park?" Charlie asked.

"I can't prove it," Bob replied, "but it sure *smells* like a Burpee foul-up. Anytime a reporter gets to within a half block of Burpee, that klutz spills his guts all over the sidewalk."

"Have they come up with a name for the guy who got cut up yet?" I asked.

"Kowalski," Bob replied. "Roger Kowalski. He was pretty well loaded up on crack cocaine, but there was definitely curare in there as well."

"A mix like that could do some real strange things to a guy, couldn't it?" Charlie asked.

"Yeah, strange—particularly if some lady happens to be slicing off these, those, and thems while you're flying high."

"If the cops were that close, how did the killer manage to get away?" I asked.

"Near as they could tell, she swam away before they even found Kowalski."

"*Swam?* In *January*?"

"Getting away *is* sort of important, Mark."

"Is it possible that the footprint could be a ruse?" James asked Bob. "A small man *could* jam his feet into a pair of women's shoes, couldn't he?"

"It doesn't float, James," Bob told him. "There were a few things that Burpee didn't know about, so he couldn't—thank heaven—leak them to the reporters. I've talked with those two cops, and they told me that whoever was butchering Kowalski was *singing*, for God's sake!"

"Singing?" James asked incredulously.

"I didn't believe it right at first either, but both cops swore up and down that they heard it. They said that it wasn't exactly a song—more like some kind of moaning—but it was definitely a woman's voice."

The guys probably thought that I'd gone a little spacey after Bob unloaded *that* on us. Some things had clicked into place, and my conclusions had made me go cold all over. I didn't trust myself to say anything at all.

"Are you OK, Mark?" Charlie asked me after Bob had left. "You're acting like you're not even in there anymore."

"Sorry," I said. "This came out of left field, and I'm trying to readjust my thinking, is all."

"It puts a whole new twist on things, that's for sure," Charlie agreed. "I've got a hunch that the media folks are going to flounder around with this for a while before they get their act together. Let's hit the bricks, guys. I've got work waiting for me at home."

"That's assuming the ladies don't tie you to a chair as soon

as we get there," James said. "I doubt they're going to be satisfied with a brief summary of what your brother just told us."

James was right on *that* one. The girls wanted all the details
when we got home. I let James and Charlie do most of the
talking, though. I wanted time to think my way through some
disturbing possibilities.

We sat in the kitchen hashing things out until almost midnight. The concept of a female serial killer took some getting
used to, that much was certain. I was surprised that Sylvia
hadn't made some of the connections that were bothering me
so much. That might come later, but I was glad she'd missed it
for right now.

We finally hung it up and went to bed. I was sure I wouldn't
sleep very much.

The discovery that the Seattle Slasher was a woman had
brought me face-to-face with a distressing possibility. There
were quite a few "what-ifs" involved, and the biggest one was
"what if Renata was the Slasher?" Since most—if not all—of
the victims had a record of assorted sexual offenses and a
rapist had murdered Regina, God knows that Renata had a
motive. And the fact that Mary worked the graveyard shift at
the cop shop gave Twinkie plenty of opportunity.

Our assumption that Twinkie's nightmares were a rerun of
the night when Regina'd been raped and murdered was fairly
logical, I suppose, but there *was* a possibility that they'd been
something entirely different. What if those nightmares hadn't
been dreams, but reality instead? What if Twink *wasn't* getting wiped out by something that'd happened back in the
spring of '95, but by something that was only a couple of
hours old?

The thing that'd triggered my growing suspicion had been
Bob's almost offhand revelation that the Slasher'd made good
her escape by taking to the water and swimming away in the
dark. That might have been just a spur-of-the-moment means
of escape from a couple of cops who'd been almost on top of

her, but what if it'd just been a standard operating procedure? Cutting somebody to pieces while he's still alive is likely to be a very messy business. And since there'd been a lake, or a river, or Puget Sound right there after every slaying, a quick dunk would be the fastest way to clean off the blood—*and* it'd explain why Twink was always moaning about cold water when she went bonkers.

That, of course, would mean that those "bad days" would always follow a murder. There'd been several, of course, that'd popped up when there *hadn't* been any reports of murders, but all that probably meant was that the cops hadn't found the body yet. If I was anywhere close to right about this, when Twink had a bad day, there was a dead guy somewhere in the general vicinity.

That brought me up short. There'd been a killing last night, and Twink had been anything *but* bonkers in the morning. She'd gone to James's class just like a normie, and except for that bout of diarrhea she hadn't had anything wrong at all.

Clearly, I was going to have to do some digging here. What I *really* wanted was some clear proof that Twinkie *hadn't* committed those murders, and trying to prove a negative is damn near impossible. My best bet would be to pinpoint a murder that Twink couldn't possibly have committed. One that'd happened on a night when Mary hadn't gone to work would be the best—or maybe one that'd come along when Twink hadn't been in town.

"Oh, hell," I said then as I suddenly remembered something. Twink couldn't possibly be the Slasher; she didn't have a car. It was quite a ways to Woodinville and even farther to Des Moines. Twink had that silly bike, but twenty or thirty miles out and twenty or thirty back put *those* murders way out of range, and the notion that she might have taken a bus was absolutely ridiculous.

So Twinkie was in the clear . . . So why were my insides still roiling?

I knew that this whole idea would bug me until I'd plowed

my way through the entire series of events, matching bad days with murders—and hoping to high heaven that they wouldn't match after all. The first step—dating the killings—wouldn't be any problem. The university library had copies of the *Seattle Times* dating back to the early twentieth century, so pinpointing murder dates would be a piece of cake.

Dating those bad days when Twink had gone bonkers might be a little tougher, though. Unless Mary kept a diary, she probably couldn't be very precise. If anybody would have those dates, it'd be Sylvia. Her case history might not go all the way back to the time of that first murder, but anything since early November was almost certain to be in her notes.

My next problem would be finding some way to ask Sylvia for those dates without alerting her to what I was doing and why. *That* might turn out to be tougher than I thought. . . .

After my seminars on Friday, I managed to catch Sylvia before she left to take Twink to Lake Stevens.

"Have you got a minute, babe?" I asked her.

"Sure, Mark," she replied. "What's up?"

"Mary's got me a little worried," I lied. "This notion of hers that Twinkie's on the fast track back to Fallon's bughouse is starting to tighten up my jaws. Maybe it's just my imagination, but it seems to me that these days when Twink flips out are getting more frequent. I was wondering if you've been pinpointing them in your case history."

"Of course I have, Mark. Dates are very important in a case history."

"Then you can probably fill me in on every one of them that's popped up since early in November, can't you?"

"I can go back even further if you want me to. Renata checks in with Dr. Fallon every Friday, remember? He questioned her closely during her visits last fall when she kept lapsing into the fugue state, and he spotted the blank days almost immediately. I don't think Renata's fully aware of it, but she's had quite a few six-day weeks since she moved to

Seattle. I knew that he'd be keeping close tabs on those dates, and I wheedled them out of him. I've got the list, you've got a copy machine—so you can have a list of your very own in just a few minutes." She went across the hall to her room and came back a moment or so later with a sheet of paper. "Here you go," she said, handing the paper to me. "Don't lose it."

"I'll copy it now," I said, "and bring it right back."

"There's no real rush, Mark."

"Let's play it safe," I told her. "I've got stacks of paper on every flat surface in my room, and your list might slip off into a black hole if I don't keep my hands on it." I pounded upstairs, got my little copier running, and ran off a copy of her list. Then I hurried back downstairs and handed it to her. "I owe you, Sylvia," I panted.

"Don't worry," she replied with an impish little grin. "Someday I might need a favor from you, and I'll remind you about this one."

"I sort of expected that."

"It's an Italian tradition, Mark," she told me. "We *always* collect these debts." She glanced at her watch. "I'd better get moving. Dr. Fallon's a stickler for punctuality."

I stowed my copy of Sylvia's list in my briefcase, then headed for the library, fervently hoping that the dates wouldn't match.

The Muñoz killing had hit the front page, largely because he'd been a minor celebrity as a dope lord. The similarities between *that* murder and a couple of the later ones got *those* killings onto page one as well. That had been back when the reporters were all riding Burpee's "gang killing" horse. I was actually grateful for Burpee's obsession with Cheetah at that point. Andrews and Garrison were such small-timers that normally they would have rated only a paragraph or two on page thirty-seven. The possibility of some connections between their murders and the killing of Muñoz had elevated them to the limelight.

Once the media had come up with that "Seattle Slasher"

designation, though, the assorted nonentities who'd gotten themselves butchered became front-page news, and it didn't take long to get all the dates and places.

I had a sick feeling by the time I got into the December newspapers. I had two lists now, and they matched almost perfectly. Twinkie *had* suffered three or four bad days when there hadn't been an "official" murder, but that didn't brighten my day very much. There were several "unofficial" murders as well as the ones that'd made the headlines—Woodinville, Auburn, and so on—so I couldn't really wiggle out of it. Much as I hated the idea, my off-the-wall theory seemed to be growing increasingly valid. There appeared to be a definite connection between the killings and Twinkie's psychotic episodes.

I was muttering quite a few obscenities when I finished up and left the library.

The newspapers had latched onto that "Joan the Ripper" tag, and it was an immediate smash hit. It was grossly overdramatic, of course, but the parallels were fairly obvious, and the news media *love* to be obvious. The cloth-heads who breathlessly hang on to anything lurid and spectacular that hits the TV screen aren't too bright to begin with, so it doesn't take much to wind them up. People who rely on newspapers are a little more intelligent . . . but not very much. The public in Seattle was treated to a lurid rerun of the Jack the Ripper story every time they turned around. The attempts to compare late-nineteenth-century London with late-twentieth-century Seattle didn't come off too well, and several lady reporters were obviously taking a gender-specific approach to the story. The victims *were* sexual predators of one stripe or another, after all, and the more militant lady reporters were slanting their stories in the general direction of justifiable homicide. I'm fairly sure that wouldn't come off very well in a court of law, but it *did* sell a lot of newspapers.

Under different circumstances, I might have been amused

by this applause for vigilante justice, but I'm sure you can understand why I wasn't laughing this time.

I stewed about my growing suspicion over the weekend, and I couldn't concentrate on much of anything else. Every time I sat down to read Hemingway or Faulkner, I'd find myself staring at the wall and trying to find some kind of hole in my theory. I tried my best to keep it under wraps, but I'm fairly sure that the boardinghouse gang knew that I was having a problem of some kind.

After supper on Monday, James suggested to Charlie and me that maybe we should make a quick run to the Green Lantern. "There's something I'd like to check out with Bob," he told us.

"Oh?" Charlie said. "What's that?"

James smiled faintly. "I wouldn't want to spoil it for you," he replied.

"What do you think, Mark?" Charlie asked me. "Should we humor him?"

"We might as well," I said grimly. "I'll get my coat."

Bob was sitting at the bar when we got there, and the four of us adjourned to a back booth. "What's up?" Bob asked us.

"James has a question for you," Charlie replied.

"Oh?" Bob said, looking at our friend.

"Something occurred to me over the weekend," James told him. "We've got a workshop in the basement at the boardinghouse, and I went down there on Saturday to get my pipe wrench. I spotted one of Mark's tools, and it set me to wondering about something. Those Navy doctors who performed the autopsy on Walton said that the murder weapon might be some sort of homemade implement, but I think they might have overlooked something that's fairly common. Last fall, Mark and I resurfaced the floor in the kitchen, and when we came to fitting the linoleum around the doorframes, Mark had a special tool he used to trim the tiles to fit. I'd forgotten about it, but when I saw it again last Saturday, I started to wonder if the Slasher's weapon could be a linoleum knife?"

Bob blinked. "Oh, shit!" he said. "It *could* be, couldn't it? Boy, did we drop the ball on *that* one! It fits exactly—short, hook-pointed, and with the sharp edge on the inside of the curve. It'd leave wounds exactly like the ones we've been looking at since last September."

"And you can pick one up in any hardware store for under ten bucks," Charlie added.

"We owe you one, James," Bob said.

"I should have thought of it earlier," James replied. "It wasn't until I saw that knife of Mark's that it dawned on me that it might be the Slasher's implement of choice."

"You see, big brother?" Charlie said, grinning, "Anytime you come up with a problem you can't solve, bring it to us. We'll take care of it for you. How's Burpee handling the 'Joan the Ripper' discovery?"

"He's not a happy camper, I'll tell you that much." Bob chuckled. "Cheetah left town this past weekend."

"Aw," Charlie said, "shuckey-darn. Poor old Burpee! What sent Cheetah off in search of greener pastures?"

"From what our informants told us, it was the 'Joan the Ripper' thing. When Burpee leaked the word that the Slasher's a woman, I guess Cheetah hit the panic switch. One of our informants told us that Cheetah's positive that the lady with the knife's out looking for him—specifically. He's convinced that the other killings have just been for practice, and Joanie-girl's ultimate target is him. I guess that when the news broke on television last Thursday, Cheetah started hiding under his bed. He was shaking all over and babbling incoherently. Then he stuffed a week's supply of dope and a pair of clean socks in a paper bag, ran down to his car, and drove off at about eighty miles an hour."

"Then there might be something to all this folk heroine crap the lady reporters are babbling about," Charlie observed. "Joan managed to get rid of Cheetah without even reaching

for her knife. Did your snitch happen to tell you where Cheetah was going?"

"He was headed south the last time our informant saw
him," Bob replied. "He might be headed for Tijuana, but that
might not be far enough south to make him feel comfortable.
I'd guess maybe Mexico City—or Buenos Aires. I think he
wants to get as far away from Seattle as he possibly can."

"We'll miss him terribly," James said.

"Not as much as Burpee will." Bob chuckled. "Burpee was
hanging all of his hopes for promotion on his whacko
Cheetah theory, and Joan the Ripper just pulled the rug out
from under him."

"Aw," Charlie said, "what a shame."

"I've got to split, guys," Bob said then. "I want to hit a
hardware store on my way home. If I'm going to talk with the
coroner about the possibility that the murder weapon in all
these killings is a linoleum knife, I'd better have one handy so
that he can see what I'm talking about."

No matter how hard I tried to shrug off my theory that
Twinkie could be the Seattle Slasher, it kept nagging at me.
Too many things fit too closely. The next question, obviously,
was what the hell was I going to do about it.

I certainly wasn't going to go see Bob West and rat her
off. When I got to the bottom, I realized that I had a strong
tendency to agree with the militant feminist point of view
that the assorted killings were justifiable homicides. There
was a distinct possibility that every victim was a rapist who
richly deserved what had happened to him. That was beside
the point, though. Twink obviously had some serious mental
problems that needed medical attention—probably back in
Doc Fallon's bughouse. My best bet would be to get some
good solid proof—one way or the other—that she was or
wasn't the Slasher, and if it turned out that she *was*, to present
my findings to Fallon and persuade him to quietly recommit

her. The killings would come to a halt, and after six months or so the media would find something else to babble about.

The next question was how to go about it. How the hell was I going to prove—or disprove—my suspicions?

Does the term "stakeout" ring any bells for you? It didn't make me very happy, but I was damned if I could come up with any alternatives. To make matters worse, it'd have to be a one-man stakeout—I couldn't enlist James or Charlie or anybody else to help me. I had to keep this strictly to myself, and that meant that I'd probably have to forgo sleeping. I might be able to last four or five days that way, then I'd probably lapse into a coma. It wasn't going to work.

Obviously, I wouldn't be able to keep an eye on Twinkie for twenty-four hours a day for weeks at a time. The more I thought about it, though, the more I came to realize that it wouldn't *be* a twenty-four-hour job. These killings had all taken place after midnight, and I could skip the nights when Mary wasn't working. *If* Twink decided to go hunting on any particular night, she'd probably take off right after Mary left the house to go to work. That was about ten o'clock. I could watch the house from ten o'clock until about one or two in the morning and then hang it up. If Twink hadn't left by then, it'd be obvious that she wasn't going out that night.

That moved the whole idea into the realm of possibility. I might be a little sandy-eyed, but I wouldn't fall apart after the first week.

"What the hell?" I muttered. "Let's give it a try and see what happens."

CHAPTER NINETEEN

On Thursday of the week after the Montlake killing, I took my first try at playing the private eye game. To be honest about it, the whole thing made me feel silly: I wasn't cut out to be Sam Spade or Mike Hammer. I had a couple of cover stories I'd cobbled together to explain why I'd be taking off late in the evening, but as luck had it, all the rest of the boardinghouse gang were in their rooms when I slipped out, so I didn't have to lie to anybody.

It was about nine-thirty when I drove past Mary's place. Her car was still parked in front of the house, so she obviously hadn't taken off yet. I pulled into a space about a block away on the opposite side of the street. I could see the house from there, but I wasn't parked right across from it. I knew that Mary would recognize my old Dodge, so I didn't want be too close. After she left, I could move in closer if it seemed necessary. I wasn't entirely certain whether Twink would spot my car if she happened to be in the fugue state. For all I knew, she might not even recognize *me*. I made a mental note to check that with Sylvia.

It was about five minutes after ten when Mary came out and got into her car. I was sure she wouldn't drive past the place where I was parked, but I didn't want to take any chances, so I ducked down behind the dashboard until she'd driven off.

Then I moved my car up to the intersection and watched the house. I *hoped* that this wasn't going to go on forever. All

I really needed to put my suspicions to rest would be a nice, messy murder on some night when I was watching Mary's house. If Twink was home in bed while Joan the Ripper was busy carving out some guy's tripes, it *would* prove a negative, and logic be damned.

After Mary left, the light stayed on in the living room until about eleven-thirty. Then the living room light went out and the bathroom light came on and stayed on for a half hour or so. Twinkie was probably taking a bath. The chances that she might go out prowling now were pretty remote, I thought.

Then again, maybe not. I didn't really know enough about the fugue state to be sure of much of anything. If it was something like sleepwalking, maybe Twink would have to go to bed and drift off before her alternative identity took over.

I watched the house intently as the bathroom light went out and the kitchen light spilled out into the backyard. I made a mental note to find a better parking place: I needed to see the back of the house.

Then Twink's bedroom light came on. I could see that one OK from where I was. It stayed on for about ten minutes, and then the house went dark.

I looked at my watch. It was about ten after twelve. If Twinkie *was* Joan the Ripper and she was planning to go hunting tonight, she'd better get on with it.

The key to the whole thing, I reasoned, was that bike of hers. It wasn't likely that she'd walk. As long as her bike was chained to Mary's back porch, she was almost certainly in bed.

At twelve-thirty, I started my car, drove to the end of the block, hooked left, and then turned into the alley. I drove slowly past the back of Mary's house.

Twink's bike was still on the back porch.

I drove back to where I'd parked before and sat watching.

At quarter to two, I took another run through the alley. Twink's bike was still there at that point, so I decided to go home. There wasn't enough time left for Twinkie to go out prowling, locate a victim, butcher him, clean up, and get back here before Mary came home from work. The procedure was a bit more complicated and time-consuming than a simple drive-by shooting.

I realized that I'd made a couple of boo-boos, but it was my first time out. I was sure I'd get better at it with more practice. Hopefully, though, this wouldn't be a permanent thing. All I needed was a murder when Twink was right there in Mary's house where I could see her—or her bike. Then I wouldn't have to play Sherlock Holmes anymore.

I was a little sandy-eyed when Charlie banged on my door the next morning. "Daylight in the swamp," he announced, "and it's feeding time."

"Tell the girls I'll be right down," I replied, sitting up. "I'll only be a couple minutes." This stakeout business had already cut into my sleep time. Four or five hours a night wasn't going to cut it. I pulled on my clothes, hit the bathroom long enough to splash some cold water on my face and brush my teeth. Then I stumbled downstairs.

"Sorry," I apologized when I went into the kitchen. "I must have forgotten to flip the switch on my alarm clock."

"How late were you out last night?" Trish asked. "I heard you leave, but I must have been long asleep by the time you came home."

"It was about two or so, I think," I replied evasively. "I had something I had to take care of."

"Have we got a new girlfriend, maybe?" Charlie slyly suggested.

For some reason that didn't go over too well. The ladies didn't say anything, but there was a definite chill in the air after that. I floundered through a couple of vague denials, and that seemed to make things even worse.

I wolfed down my breakfast and took off for the campus. Hemingway and Faulkner were waiting for me.

*   *   *

It was noon when I got back to the boardinghouse, and Sylvia was in the kitchen fixing a sandwich. "You look awful, Mark," she said.

"I'm running on short sleep," I said. "I think I'll crash for a while this afternoon. Did Twinkie make it to class today?"

"She was there—physically, anyway. Her head seemed to be turned off, though. After class, I reminded her that this was 'Friday-go-to-meeting-day,' and she seemed surprised. I actually think she'd forgotten that we have to run on up to Lake Stevens today."

"She gets spacey every now and then, Sylvia—you know that. If you get to talk privately with Doc Fallon, you'd better let him know that Mary's worried. She's almost positive that Twink's close to the breaking point. If we don't come up with some answers pretty damn soon, we're liable to lose her."

"You're just filled with good cheer today, aren't you?" she replied sourly.

I dozed a little that afternoon, but I was still pretty groggy at suppertime. "I'm off to the library," I announced after we'd finished.

"I'll come with you," James volunteered.

"Don't bother," I said, grabbing up my stuff. I was out the door before the others could object to my breaking our no-going-out-alone-after-dark rule. "Don't wait up," I called over my shoulder. It was a none-too-polite way to tell them all to butt out. I was having enough trouble without any more snooping by my housemates.

I regretted it before I even got to my car, but by then it was too late.

I *did* go to the library, but I didn't accomplish very much. I was still punchy from lack of sleep and worried that Twinkie might decide it was time to go hunting again.

I got to Wallingford about nine-thirty and parked a few blocks from Mary's house. I didn't want to make a habit of parking in the same place every night.

Getting out, I locked the car and strolled toward Mary's place, putting on what was probably a grossly overdone show of nonchalance. Us private eyes do that every now and again. Overacting is actually pretty dumb, but I seemed to be coming down with a bad case of high drama.

I backed up against a conveniently high hedge about a block and a half from Mary's place and waited.

At five minutes after ten, Mary came out, in full uniform and pistol belt, and got into her car. She was predictable, that's for sure.

I hunkered down a bit to stay out of sight until she drove off. Then I went back and got my car. It was colder than hell that night, and a chilly fog was drifting in from Green Lake. That was all I needed. Even if Twink left Mary's house, there was a fair chance that I'd lose her in the fog if I tried to follow her.

I drove back to the place where I'd parked on the previous night so that I could watch the house.

The light in the living room stayed on until a quarter to twelve. Then it went out, and the bathroom light came on for a while.

By twelve-thirty, the only light that was on was the one in Twink's bedroom. When it went out, I fired up my car and made a pass down the alley behind Mary's house. Twink's bike was still on the back porch, so I went home to catch up on my sleep.

We always slept a little later than usual on Saturday mornings, and that gave me the chance to sleep in. This stakeout business was definitely cutting into my sack time.

Trish whipped up some buttermilk pancakes that morning, and we all pigged out.

"Who's the lucky girl, Mark?" Charlie asked me, as we lingered over coffee.

"What lucky girl?" I tried to evade his prying.

"Get real," he said. "When a guy doesn't come home until way past midnight, it can only mean one thing."

"Can I take the fifth amendment on that, Trish?"

"If it makes you feel better," she replied in a rather un-friendly tone.

"Let it lie, Charlie," James suggested. "It's none of our business, you know."

"Just making conversation." Charlie shrugged it off. Then he stood up. "Gotta hit the books," he said then.

There was a definite chill in the air that morning, and I couldn't figure out why. I went down to my basement work-shop, mostly to get away from the ladies. All three of them were scowling at me every time I turned around. The house rule against hanky-panky didn't involve a vow of celibacy, but the ladies were behaving as if I'd broken some rule. Charlie's "Mark's got a girlfriend" joke wasn't coming off very well. Trish, Erika, and Sylvia seemed to be offended.

Maybe it was group possessiveness. Women get strange now and then.

When I thought about it, though, I realized that the "Mark's got a girlfriend" thing might just solve a problem that was certain to come up in the very near future. I definitely didn't want my housemates to know about my suspicions or that I was camped out in front of Mary's house every night. If they were convinced that I was out chasing some girl, they might get a little grumpy about it, but they wouldn't catch on to what I was *really* doing—or why. Probably the best way to pull that off would be to spiff up before I left the house—dress the part. It was devious and probably a little dishonest, but we start moving into "the ends justify the means" terri-tory here.

The more I thought about it, the better I liked it, and I felt pretty good when I started to cobble together a rough sort of workbench.

After supper I went upstairs to change clothes. If I was going to pull off this "girlfriend" scam, I should probably look the part. This time, though, nobody offered to keep me company when I hustled out the front door.

It was already a little foggy when I fired up my car, and there was a fair chance that the weather would get worse as the night wore on. That could definitely complicate matters. If Twinkie really *was* Joan the Ripper and she decided to go hunting that night, it wouldn't be hard for her to get away after Mary went to work. Even if I saw her leave the house, she wouldn't have much trouble slipping out of sight in that damned fog.

I'd left the boardinghouse early, more to persuade my housemates that I was off to see my fictitious lady friend than out of any necessity. Rather than just sitting in my car watching the fog grow thicker, I cruised the alleys in the neighborhood of Mary's house to get the lay of the land. If Twink left the house on her bicycle, I'd be at a definite disadvantage. People *do* park cars in alleys, even though it's not exactly legal. A bike wouldn't have any trouble slipping through, but a car would never make it. A little scouting in advance seemed appropriate.

The streets in residential neighborhoods are usually fairly tidy, but you wouldn't *believe* how much stuff piles up in the alleys. There are junk cars, old refrigerators and stoves, Dumpsters, and beat-up old garbage cans. Driving a car through an alley is almost like trying to run an obstacle course. That didn't brighten my evening very much.

At about quarter to ten, I hauled into the parking place I'd used the previous night and started to consider my options. I might have to get a bike of my own—I could stow it in the trunk of my car, pull it out in no more than a minute, and stay on Twink's tail no matter where she went.

That jerked me up short. My goal was to prove a negative, and here I was scheming up ways to prove that Twink *was* in fact the Seattle Slasher. Or Joan the Ripper—or whatever else the media wanted to call her.

Mary left the house at the usual time, and after she'd gone off to work, I moved my car closer so I could watch the house.

At ten-thirty, the living room lights went out. Then the bathroom light came on. Then it went out, and the kitchen light followed. Then, even as it had on the two previous nights, the light in Twink's bedroom came on.

That light stayed on for about fifteen minutes, and then it went out and the whole house was dark.

I didn't even bother to take a pass through the alley. I just fired up my car and went home.

Mary had Sunday and Monday off, so I wasn't going to have to play the stakeout game until Tuesday. That gave me some time to think things over. So far, all I'd managed to do was waste a lot of time and lose a lot of sleep. My suspicions weren't holding water. It was fairly clear that Twinkie did *not* go out on the prowl every time Mary left the house.

I'd done enough ordinary hunting in my own time that I knew that no hunter scores every time he picks up his rifle or shotgun. And it's pretty much the same with fishing: Some days they just aren't biting. The Slasher-Ripper-whatever had managed to score eight times—officially—and probably four or five times unofficially. The killings in Woodinville and Auburn might be just the tip of the iceberg. To score that often, the Ripper would almost have to be out there nearly every night, trolling for game, and Twinkie was passing up a lot of opportunities. A dedicated hunter doesn't do that.

Actually, that should have made me feel better. I didn't *want* to pin the Ripper murders on Twinkie. What I was trying to do was prove that she *wasn't* the one who'd been carving people up since last fall. If the *real* Joan the Ripper would just cooperate and butcher some minor hoodling while I was camped on Mary's doorstep making sure that Twink hadn't left the house, I'd be off the hook.

About noon on Sunday, James rapped on my door.

"What's up?" I asked when I opened it.

"Have you got a minute, Mark?" he asked quietly.

"Sure. Come on in."

He came into the room and closed the door. "What's bothering you, Mark?" he asked me, keeping his voice very soft. "You've obviously got a problem of some kind; maybe I can help."

James was probably as close a buddy as I'd had in years, and I felt a strong temptation to lay the whole thing right out in front of him. I pulled back from that at the very last moment, though. My suspicions about Twinkie were based on a hunch that I couldn't even come close to proving, and I wasn't about to do a Burpee imitation just to pass the time. "I don't know, James," I said. "Partly it's just the weather—fog always depresses me. A big part of it, though, has to do with my Blake-Whitman theory. It's falling apart on me. I thought I could nail Whitman's hide to the barn door, but the old boy's too slick for me. I'm positive that the connection's there, but Walt's smooth enough not put it right out in plain sight. I could bust my butt trying to nail him, and it probably still wouldn't float. Now I'm going to have to scrounge around and find another topic for my dissertation, and that sure doesn't wind my watch very tight."

"Really?" he said then with a faint smile. "I thought it might be something a little more personal."

"You aren't going to get much more personal than having your dissertation collapse on you, James. Isn't that the academic version of a natural disaster?"

"It *would* come fairly close, I guess," he agreed. He sounded dubious, though. I was obviously going to have to watch my step. Evidently, I was giving too much away.

I attended my seminars on Monday morning, then spent the rest of the day reading Faulkner. Hemingway stuck to the real world, so it wasn't too hard to stay with him. Faulkner's mythical Yoknapatawpha County puts him in the world-builder class, and that takes some getting used to.

Since Mary had Monday night off, I didn't have to go out to play in the foggy darkness that night, so I managed to get quite a bit of work done.

On Tuesday, February 3, I went down to the library to dig into some of the critical works on Faulkner. The more recent opinions took him to task for his failure to be "politically correct." The N-word shows up frequently in Faulkner's writings, and that immediately starts some critics to frothing at the mouth. The fact that he was quite accurately recording the culture and speech patterns of early-twentieth-century rural Mississippi seems to have escaped those critics.

By midafternoon, the fog had thinned out, but the weather forecast wasn't too promising. Evidently we were in for at least another week of fog and below-freezing nights. If Twinkie *did* go hunting this week, trying to follow her could be a real bitch-kitty.

After supper that evening, I changed clothes again to keep the "Mark's got a girlfriend" scam afloat. I decided that my mythical honey found me handsome and mysterious in dark colors—which was fortunate, since those dark sweaters blend into the background pretty well on a dark night.

Nobody said anything to me when I left the house, but they were thinking pretty loud.

I took up my usual position about a block and a half from Mary's house to keep an eye on the place. At five after ten—right on the nose—Mary came out and got into her car. You could set your watch by Mary.

I waited until she'd had time to get out of the immediate vicinity, then I drove down the block so that I could see the house better. That damned fog was complicating things, that's for certain.

The light in the living room was still on, the same as it'd been all the other times I'd watched. This was getting to be a drag. Twink was sitting tight, and all I was doing was losing sleep. About my only entertainment came from firing up the car so that I could turn on the windshield wipers. That fog was settling down fast.

Then the light in Twink's bedroom came on. That didn't quite fit her usual routine, but there could have been a dozen reasons for it.

Just on a hunch, though, I drove to the end of the block to a place where I could keep an eye on that back porch.

Then the light in Twink's bedroom went out, and the kitchen light came on briefly. "She's probably just hitting the refrigerator for a can of pop or something," I muttered.

But then the back door opened, and Twink stepped out onto the back porch. She locked the door behind her and fumbled around unlocking the chain on her bike. I'd brought my binoculars, so I could see her clearly.

I discovered that I was holding my breath. I let it out slowly and kept watching.

She trundled her bike down the back-porch steps and pushed it back to the alley. Then she climbed on and rode off to her right.

I fired up my car, wrapped a U-turn at the end of the block, and sped to the intersection. I didn't turn on my lights, though.

By the time I got to the intersection, Twink was already down at the far end of that cross-street block. As she passed the streetlight, I got a fairly good look at her. She was wearing that glossy, black raincoat and was pumping right along.

I sped up to keep her in sight. She didn't seem to be in any big hurry, but the fog—and that damned black raincoat— made it difficult to see her. The clock on my dashboard said 11:10, and that told me that Twink had left the house at eleven on the dot—exactly when Mary was punching in to start her shift at the cop shop. This wasn't looking good. The previous nights—when I'd watched Mary's house and nothing had happened—had about half convinced me that my suspicions were totally unfounded. Now they came rushing back again, and that black raincoat Twink was wearing added another dimension.

She was riding east on Thirty-ninth Street through a residential neighborhood, and then she hooked a right at Sunnyside. I wasn't too far behind her, but I didn't have my lights on, so I don't think she knew that I was following her. When I got to the intersection of Thirty-ninth and Sunnyside, though, she was nowhere in sight.

I spent about two hours cruising around in the fog, but all I accomplished was to waste a lot of gas. By midnight, I couldn't see much more than a half a block because of the damned fog. I finally gave up and drove back to Mary's place. The living room light was still on, but a quick swing down the alley showed me an empty back porch. Twink's bike hadn't slipped back to where it belonged while I'd been out in the fog.

Now what the hell was I going to do? Confronting Twinkie—*if* indeed she'd been out in some park cutting some poor guy into dog meat—wouldn't be a good idea. I was *almost* positive that she wouldn't try it on me, but there's a lot of uncertainty in "almost," isn't there?

I parked down the block from Mary's place and opened the window on the driver's side so that I could watch the house without running the windshield wipers every five minutes. The humidity level must have been about 200 percent, because that fog was piling up on anything that wasn't moving, and there was that mournful sound of water dripping off telephone lines, tree branches, and the outsides of the rain gutters on every house in the neighborhood.

I cruised through the alley about every fifteen minutes to check the back porch, but when Twinkie rode home about two-thirty, she came right down the street instead of sneaking in the back way. She pushed her bike around to the back of the house, and a moment later the kitchen light came on. Then the living room light went out, and the one in the bathroom came on. From the outside, the house looked so ordinary that nobody driving by would give it a second glance. God only knows what kind of horror was going on inside, though.

CHAPTER TWENTY

I didn't sleep very well that night, for obvious reasons, and I even gave some thought to skipping my classes in the morning. If some late-breaking news popped up on television, I wanted to be right on top of it. I wasn't sure exactly what I'd do if there *had* been a murder during the night, but I wanted to catch the news just in case.

There was the core of my problem. If Twink really *was* Joan the Ripper, and if I happened to get lucky—or unlucky—enough to catch her in the act, what was I going to do about it? I certainly wasn't going to turn her over to the cops. I still thought that my best bet would be to lay the whole thing in front of Doc Fallon. If Twink *had* butchered some guy last night, she'd be bonkers today, and Mary would zonk her out with a sleeping pill. If I moved fast enough, I could have her back in Fallon's bughouse before the sun went down. It wouldn't be a very happy solution, but it'd sure beat some lurid murder trial. If everything went smoothly, we could quietly get Twink off the streets and into a safe environment with no one the wiser.

The Ripper murders would remain unsolved, but that wouldn't bother me.

The only problem with my brilliant solution was the lack of a murder. If Twinkie *had* been out hunting that night, she'd come up empty. Now I was staring down the bore of night after night camped on Mary's doorstep.

Erika came into the kitchen about six. "What are you doing up so early, Mark?" she asked me.

"Couldn't sleep," I told her.

"Why didn't you turn the coffeepot on?"

"Is it ready to go?"

"Of course it is. Where have you been? I set it up every night. All you have to do is punch the button, dummy."

"I didn't know that."

"Men!" she grumbled, rolling her eyes upward. "Is there anything new and exciting on television?"

"The fog probably won't let up for another week or so," I replied.

"Wow! Stop the presses! It's foggy in Seattle!"

"Smart aleck."

"Come here. Now."

"No hitting," I said.

"Do as you're told."

I slid out from behind the table.

"This is the coffeepot," she said. "Am I going too fast for you?"

"Be nice."

"This is the on-off button." She pushed it, and the light came on. "You see how it works? All you have to do to get coffee is push that button. If you're the first one up, push the button. It's a moral obligation: The first one up turns on the coffeepot. Have you got that straight?"

"Yes, ma'am."

She patted me on the head. "Good boy. Now get out of the way. It's my turn to make breakfast, and I don't need you underfoot while I'm doing it. Scoot."

"Yes, ma'am." Erika obviously needed at least one cup of coffee to get her fire going in the morning, and you didn't want to get in her way before she'd had her morning fix.

I didn't pay very close attention during my seminars that morning. I had a lot on my mind, and I *really* wanted to get back to that TV set to find out if Twinkie *had* scored the previous night.

After my Faulkner seminar, I bagged on back to the boardinghouse and camped on the living room TV set for the rest of the day. As Hemingway might have put it, I got whole bunches of *nada*. Then, to cap off a notably unproductive day, I was treated to a big helping of frosty at the supper table. My "Mark's got a girlfriend" scam was definitely mildewing the sheets at Castle Erdlund.

I spiffed up again about nine o'clock, and hit the bricks—looking sharp—at nine-thirty.

I pulled into my usual parking place and watched Mary's house. As expected, Mary came out at five after ten on the dot. I let her get out of the neighborhood, then I pulled in closer to the house to keep an eye on things.

After about a half hour, I noticed something that was almost certain to give me problems. The damn fog was freezing up on my windshield. I'd have to keep the motor running and the defroster turned up to high. If my windshield iced up, I'd be out of business.

It was a good thing I caught it when I did, because about ten minutes to eleven, the light in Twink's bedroom came on, the same way it had the previous night. Evidently Twink had travel plans.

Once again, she came out the back door at precisely eleven o'clock, unlocked her bicycle, and rode off down the alley to Thirty-ninth Street again. I trailed about a half block behind her, and *this* time I was close enough to see her turn into an alley after she'd hooked a right on Sunnyside.

I drove to the end of the next block, but I didn't see her come out of the alley. I couldn't figure out how, but she'd gotten away from me again.

I tried cruising around the general vicinity with my headlights on—but as close as I could tell, she wasn't anywhere in the neighborhood. So finally I drove back to that alley and parked at the curb. There had to be some reason Twink kept

coming back to that same place. I got out of my Dodge and
walked on into the alley. There was all the usual junk there,
and I knew I couldn't drive through—not unless I wanted to
bash in one side of my car.

There was a Dumpster about halfway down, and that was
the thing that was really blocking the alley. Sometimes the
guys on garbage trucks get a little careless when they set a
Dumpster back down. The things *do* have wheels, though—
maybe I could push it back a foot or so to give myself a little
room. It looked pretty full, but I leaned on it to see if I could
budge it.

It was as solid as a rock. It occurred to me that there might
be something behind it that had it blocked. I went around to
the back side to see if I could possibly clear it.

There, neatly concealed behind the Dumpster, was Twinkie's
bike.

This didn't make any sense at all. There weren't any parks in
the immediate vicinity, so what had possessed Twink to stash
her bike in that alley? *Something* sure as hell didn't fit.

Then it occurred to me that she might be meeting some
guy who lived nearby. I tried to dismiss that notion, but if she
did have a boyfriend on the side, it'd explain a lot of things.
Talk about brain-freeze: I'd been willing to accept the possibility that she was a murderer, but the notion of a secret
boyfriend shocked me.

We all get strange now and then, I suppose.

I tried to collect my thoughts. Whatever she was doing,
she'd obviously gotten away from me again. She might possibly have spotted me trailing along behind her and stashed
the bike to get me off her back. The combination of the fog
and that black raincoat would make her damn near invisible,
and—if she was hunting—she'd could hide out almost anyplace in the neighborhood. After I went home, she could
come back, pick up her bike again, and ride off into the night
to hunt down her next victim.

I gave up and went on back to Mary's place.

Twink rode in shortly after two in the morning, went inside, and, as closely as I could tell, went to bed.

I gave up and went home.

I didn't have any classes on Thursday, so I camped on the living room TV set to find out if Joan the Ripper had scored again. I knew that Mary would have advised us if Twink had gone bonkers again, but I wanted to be absolutely certain. After the foul-up of the Montlake Park killing, Twink might have modified a few things.

James came home about eleven. "Are we watching soap operas now, Mark?" he asked me with an amused expression.

"Just catching up on the news, old buddy," I replied. "Did Twinkie make it to your class today?"

"Oh, yes. She's taking these classes she audits more seriously than a lot of students who take them for credit."

"Did she seem to be OK?"

"As far as I could tell, she was." He looked at me speculatively. "You've got something on your mind that's troubling you, haven't you, Mark?"

I meant to just shrug it off, but I'd reached the point where I *had* to talk to somebody. "This is strictly between you and me, James," I said, "OK?"

"If that's the way you want it." He sat down in one of the easy chairs. "What's up?"

"The whole town's jumping up and down about this Joan the Ripper stuff."

"I've noticed that," he said.

"Something came to me a while back, and it's bugging the hell out of me."

"Oh?"

"After the cops found that footprint that sort of proved that the Slasher's a woman, I did some checking. As it turns out, every time the Slasher's wasted somebody, Twinkie has one of her 'bad days.' "

"Do you think there's a connection? Renata sees those lurid stories on the news and starts climbing the walls—or something along those lines?"

"I don't think the TV stories have anything to do with it, James. Twink goes bonkers even before the cops find the body."

"You're not serious!"

"Stay with me on this. I'm *hoping* that you'll spot some great big hole and shoot this theory down. Then I might be able to get some sleep. When Twinkie came out of the fog at Fallon's bughouse, she had no memory whatsoever that Regina had ever existed."

"That's what Sylvia tells us," he admitted.

"Fallon says that she *does* know, though—at the subconscious level—and that's what these nightmares she keeps having are all about."

"That's just a theory, Mark."

"I know, and I think it's way off base. I *don't* think Twink's having nightmares. I think she's reacting to something a lot more recent than Regina's murder. Every so often some sexual predator gets butchered, and if *anybody's* got a motive to take out rapists, it'd be Renata."

"Well—maybe. But I don't think she's capable of the things the Slasher's doing to these people."

"Not when her head's on straight, I'll go along with that. *But,* if she's flipped out, her head's anything *but* straight. After she comes out of it, she's got some scattered memories of the gory details, and they blow her away. I don't *want* to believe it, James, but the possibility keeps coming back and whopping me up alongside the head. Come on, show me where I'm wrong."

"Don't rush me," he rumbled, frowning. "Why didn't you drop this on Sylvia instead of me?"

"Sylvia's not equipped to handle it, you know that. Twinkie's got Sylvia wrapped around her little finger. Sylvia could catch Twink red-handed, and she *still* wouldn't believe it."

"You could be right about that . . ."

"Besides," I added, "the ladies are pissed off at me right now. They're buying into Charlie's theory that I've got a girlfriend stashed away somewhere. I don't see where it's any of their business one way or the other, but *they* seem to think it is."

"Women can be very possessive, Mark. Sometimes it doesn't make too much sense, but that's the nature of the beast."

"Beast?"

"Poor choice of words, maybe. Let me brood about this theory of yours. It might take a while for me to get used to. There *could* be a remote possibility that it's valid, but I wouldn't bet the farm on it."

I didn't quite have the nerve to admit that I was already keeping Twink under surveillance. It *was* sort of silly, after all.

I left the boardinghouse at the usual time that evening, but I didn't bother to get all gussied up. I figured I'd established my cover by now, so I didn't have to beat it into the ground anymore. James gave me an odd look, though.

The fog was *really* thick that evening, and when I got to my usual stakeout spot, I couldn't even see Mary's house. I took a chance and eased up a little closer.

Mary left for work at the usual time, and I settled in to watch. I'd noticed that Twink was as punctual as her aunt about certain things, so if she had any plans for a hunting expedition on a given night, she'd probably hit the bricks on the stroke of eleven.

Eleven came and went, and the lights in Mary's house didn't go on and off in the sequence that'd preceded Twinkie's previous outings. Evidently, she'd scratched any plans she might have had for that particular night. I think the fog might have had a lot to do with that. You've got to be able to see what you're doing when you're hunting.

I decided to hang it up at eleven-thirty. It was fairly obvious by then that Twink was going to sit tight.

I attended my seminars on Friday, and Sylvia and Twink had already left for Lake Stevens when I got back to the boardinghouse.

I spent the afternoon reading *For Whom the Bell Tolls*. Sometimes we tend to shrug Hemingway off. His interest in bullfights and big-game hunting puts him in the macho crowd, and that's generally considered politically incorrect these days. But the old boy could really write up a storm when he set his mind to it.

Mary called me about four-thirty, and she seemed a little grouchy. "You just *had* to run your mouth, didn't you, Mark?" she demanded.

"What'd I do now?"

"Ren's been hanging out with a bunch of sorority girls, and I guess one of them's developed a lech for some guy who drives a beat-up old pickup truck. She told Ren what the license plate number was, and then you pop up and tell Ren that *I* could find out who owned that junker."

"Well, you *can*, can't you?"

"Of course I can, but now every time one of those fluffheads wants that kind of information, she'll sic Ren on me to get it."

"Sorry, Mary. I didn't think of that," I admitted. "To be honest, I was surprised that Twink hadn't figured it out for herself."

"She probably would have eventually, kid," Mary conceded. "I just needed to put the blame on somebody."

"If it makes you feel better, what the hell."

Then she laughed. "Don't worry, I think the Sigma-whatever girl got the number scrambled. The name that came up when I ran it through the computer was Walter Fergusson. He's pushing forty, and he's some kind of construction worker.

I don't think he'd be the sort that'd make a college girl get all gaga."

"Maybe he bought the truck from some handsome young dude."

"No. He's owned that pickup for at least ten years. He lives over near Green Lake, so he's probably puttering around in this part of Seattle on his days off. I still think the girl misread the license plate, though."

"Maybe his kid brother borrowed the truck."

"It's possible, I suppose."

"Does this Fergusson guy have a police record? If he does, maybe Twink should warn her friend about it."

"He seems clean—hell, if he was dealing dope on the side, he could afford something fancier than an '82 Jimmy pickup. I'm sorry I jumped on you about this, kid. I've got the grumpies. The other dispatcher's down with the flu, so my work schedule's all screwed up. It looks like I won't be getting any days off for a while."

"Has Twink made it back from Lake Stevens yet?"

"No. She and Sylvia usually have dinner with Les and Inga on these Fridays. She'll probably make it back before I have to go to work. I'd better whip up some supper—I'm starving."

"Enjoy," I told her.

"Sure, kid."

I set the phone back in the cradle and sat staring at the floor for a while. The story Twink had foisted off on Mary *could* have been legitimate. Twinkie *did* buddy up to quite a few sorority girls, and one of them *might* have asked her to track down that license plate number ... But a guy who drives a fifteen-year-old pickup truck would have to look like Mr. America to get a sorority girl's attention. It just didn't ring true.

By eight-thirty that evening, the fog was thick enough to walk on. I probably could have scratched the stakeout that night, but I didn't want to take any chances. My main goal now was to prove to myself that Twinkie didn't have anything to do with all the killings, and that meant that I'd have to camp out near Mary's house pretty regularly. I was sure missing a lot of sleep, but I didn't have any real choice.

Fortunately, Twink seemed to be a creature of habit. If she *was* going out, she'd be out that back door at eleven on the dot. If she didn't leave by eleven-fifteen, I could go home and crash. God knows I needed the sleep.

Mary left at the usual time. I could barely make her out in that fog, though I wasn't parked far from her front door.

I took a chance at that point. I was fairly sure that if Twink *did* decide to go hunting, she'd stash her bike behind that Dumpster in the alley off Sunnyside Avenue, the way she had on Wednesday night. I knew where the alley was, and I could drive there faster than she could bike it, so I got out of the car and went around to the alley behind Mary's place. I couldn't see diddly from the street because of the fog, so I had to get closer.

Eleven o'clock came and went, and Twink's bike was still on Mary's back porch, so I decided to hang it up for the night.

A thought came to me on my way back to where my car was parked. If I could pick up a pair of bolt cutters, I could slip back about three in the morning, cut that chain, and steal Twinkie's bike. That'd keep her off the streets for a while at least.

I decided against it. If I started tinkering at this point, I'd probably blow my chances of proving that Twinkie couldn't possibly be Joan the Ripper.

The fog hadn't let up much on Saturday morning, and I woke up tired, dejected, and unpopular. But I was determined to make some progress, and on a hunch I looked up the name Walter Fergusson in the phone book to get an address. As it turned out, there were three of them, but one was way off at the south end of town, and another was in a fairly posh retirement home. That left the one who lived on East Green Lake Way, and it put him in the general vicinity.

The more I thought about it, the less convincing I found Twink's story about some sorority girl's burning interest in a guy in his late thirties who drove a beat-up fifteen-year-old pickup truck. I had some time, and this Fergusson guy lived not far from the boardinghouse, so I decided to drive on over and have a look.

As it turned out, Fergusson lived in an apartment house on the west side of Green Lake—and there was a beat-up grey '82 Jimmy pickup parked out front. I pulled off onto a side street and parked. I wasn't sure how far I wanted to take this—I could make up some story and actually end up knocking on Fergusson's door. Twinkie was interested in this guy, and that got my attention. I got out of my car and walked to the corner.

The fog had lifted a bit, and I looked out toward the lake. A park lined the lakeshore on the other side of the street, and the word "park" set off some bells for me. If Twink *was* the serial killer, she'd been taking out targets of opportunity up 'til now. If she was suddenly homing in on a specific guy, she must have a pretty good reason for it.

I walked on to the apartment house and went up to the front door to check the mailboxes. Fergusson's name was on the box marked 2-A; that didn't help all that much. The box marked MANAGER was 1-A, and the name was Sharon Walcott. That gave me an idea. I went back to my Dodge and drove around looking for a pay phone. I found one at a convenience store, leafed through the phonebook, and found a number for a Sharon Walcott at that Green Lake Drive address. I poked a couple of coins into the slot and punched in the number.

"Hello?" It was a woman's voice.

"I'm looking for a Walter Fergusson," I told her. "There are three of them in the phone book, and I'm not sure which one is the fellow I'm supposed to contact."

"Why didn't you just dial *his* number?"

"I've been trying, but his line's busy. It's sort of important. The one I'm trying to find is a distant cousin of mine. There's a family estate involved, and I need to get in touch with him. He'd be about thirty-five or forty, and the last we heard, he was a construction worker. If the Walter Fergusson who lives in your building is a lawyer or investment broker, I'm obviously barking up the wrong tree."

"Walt might be the one you're looking for," she told me. "He *is* in his midthirties, and he works with drywall panels. Is there an inheritance involved in this?"

"I wouldn't call it an inheritance," I told her. "Our great-aunt passed away, and there are a few legal technicalities involved in freeing up her house so that her daughter can sell it. I need to get hold of Walt so I can get his signature on some papers. Is he likely to be around for the rest of the day? I'm sorry I had to pester you, but I can't get through on *his* phone."

"He almost never gets up before noon on weekends," she replied, "and he probably mutes his telephone when he doesn't want to be pestered. He might even have left it off the hook."

"That would explain it."

"I could push a note under his door if you'd like. If you give me a phone number where he can reach you, he'll probably call you when he wakes up."

"I don't *have* a local phone number, ma'am; I'm just passing through town on business. I haven't seen Walt since we were kids, so I doubt if I'd even recognize him. Could you describe him for me?"

"Midthirties, like you said. Sort of balding on top, a little overweight, and he wears work clothes all the time. He keeps pretty much to himself, but he does go out at night fairly often. If you'll give me your name, I'll tell him that you're trying to get in touch with him."

"Marlowe." I picked another fictional private eye name.

"Phillip Marlowe. Walt probably doesn't even remember me. How many apartments are there in your building? I might have to come by and start knocking on doors."

"There are only four apartments. Walt lives in the second floor front."

"I appreciate your taking the time to fill me in," I said. "I'll get off the line now and quit pestering you." I put the phone back on the hook.

A lot of things didn't exactly fit, but if Twink was homing in on Fergusson, now I'd know where to go if she gave me the slip the next time she left Mary's place to go hunting.

The fog came back full force that evening, and Twink stayed home again. I watched until eleven-thirty, then went back home.

Mary had to work on Sunday night, so I watched the house again, but I drew another blank. The fog seemed to be settling in permanently, and until it lifted, Twinkie wasn't likely to suit up for another hunting trip.

CHAPTER TWENTY-ONE

A wind came up early on the morning of Monday, the ninth of February, and it cleared away the fog in fairly short order. I was happy to see it gone when I got up, but the more I thought about it, the more I started to worry. That dense, freezing fog had kept Twinkie more or less housebound. Now that it'd cleared off, she'd be able to go hunting again.

I didn't say much at breakfast that morning. I had a lot on my mind, and I was half-afraid that if I started talking, things might start popping out that I really should keep to myself. When you get right down to it, all I had to go on were several unconfirmed suspicions. I wasn't about to go galloping down the Burpee path. It'd be best if I kept my mouth shut until I had something concrete to work with. All right, Twinkie went out on the town at night every so often. Big deal. Lots of people go out after dark. It's not as if there was a curfew in Seattle. What's more, she'd gone out for bike rides after Mary'd left for work, and nobody had turned up dead the following morning. That didn't exactly prove a negative, but we were still well within "innocent until proven guilty" territory.

I hit my seminars that morning, but I wasn't paying very close attention. Then I holed up in the library for the afternoon, mostly to avoid my housemates. I was wound pretty tight, and I didn't feel like answering questions. This was most definitely *not* spill-your-guts time.

I got home just in time for supper. I wolfed it down without even noticing what I was eating, curtly excused myself, and got the hell out of there. I could apologize later; right now I wasn't in the mood for conversation.

I went back to the library, but that was really a waste of time. I couldn't even begin to concentrate. I gave up and went back out to where I'd parked my car.

The wind that'd cleared away the fog had died down, and the fog was starting to seep back. It wasn't as thick as over the weekend, but it still made anything more than a block away look pretty damn fuzzy.

I drove to Wallingford and parked about a block away from Mary's front door. If this went on *too* much longer, I probably *would* have to get my hands on an alternative vehicle.

After Mary left for work, I drove around to the alley behind her house. It was a bit chancy, but I had a hunch that Twink wouldn't notice me if she went out hunting.

Her bedroom light came on at quarter to eleven, and then it went out. Then the kitchen light came on briefly, and Twink came out onto the back porch.

I sat tight until she reached the end of the alley, then I drove directly to Sunnyside. I parked near that alley and waited. I'll admit that I was wound up pretty tight. After what seemed like a long, long time, Twinkie came out of the alley on foot. She was wearing that black plastic raincoat again, and I couldn't for the life of me figure out why she kept stashing her bike behind that Dumpster.

She walked down to the corner and got into a tan Honda that was parked there. Boy, did *that* explain a lot of things! Of *course* she stashed her bike every time she went out. She had an alternate means of transportation. That gave me a sick feeling in the pit of my stomach. I'd been clinging to the notion that some of the Ripper murders had been *way* out of bicycle range. Twink had a car, though—a car that none of us knew about—and that put everything within a fifty-mile radius close enough for her to reach while Mary was at work.

The car didn't move for quite a while, but the smoke coming out of the exhaust pipe told me that the motor was running. I couldn't quite figure that out, but then it dawned on me that she *had* to run the motor for a while to get warm air coming out of the defroster. It was foggy enough and cold enough to ice up her windshield.

After about five minutes, she turned on her lights and drove off. I let her get a block or so ahead of me, and then I turned on *my* lights and followed her. I was almost positive that I knew where she was going, but I didn't want to take any chances.

She drove north on Sunnyside, took a left at Fiftieth, and went on to the south end of Woodland Park. Then she turned right on Green Lake Way and drove straight to the neighborhood where Fergusson lived. If I was reading this correctly, Twink wasn't out looking for targets of opportunity—not this time. She was after one specific guy, and his name was Fergusson. I didn't know exactly why yet, but an awful lot of things were coming together. I could worry about that later, though. For right now, all I could do was stay close enough behind her that she couldn't slip off into the fog.

She drove past Fergusson's apartment house and parked about two blocks away. I took a quick left onto a side street, parked, and ran back to that main road. I could see that tan Honda, and it looked to me as if the motor was still running. I stepped back out of the light and watched.

The dome light in Twink's car came on when she opened the door and got out. She wasn't wearing that raincoat, but it looked as if she had it slung over her arm.

I'd brought my binoculars with me, and I scoped her out. I almost choked when I got her in focus. She was wearing a very short skirt and a blouse that didn't leave much to the imagination. The term "bait" pretty much covers what she had on. She was definitely displaying the merchandise.

She crossed the street and sauntered along the sidewalk in front of Fergusson's apartment house. She didn't even *look* like the Twinkie I knew. After she'd graduated from Fallon's bughouse, she'd seemed in many ways to be gender neutral.

She'd always worn nice clothes and makeup, but there'd never been any element of sexual provocation in her behavior. I guess I'd assumed that Regina's rape and murder had suppressed those instincts. Evidently the fugue state unleashed them, and now they were coming through loud and clear. If she'd been walking through the various parks and construction sites in the Seattle area in the way she was parading past Fergusson's place, she wouldn't have had much trouble getting lots of attention from exactly the kind of guys she was trying to attract. "Asking for it" comes pretty close.

I raised my binoculars up to look at Fergusson's front window. The light in the front room of his apartment wasn't on, but I could see the outline of somebody standing there. I'd say that Twinkie was definitely getting Fergusson's attention.

She strolled on down to the end of the block. She was getting pretty close to me, so I stepped back behind a tree to avoid a "fancy meeting you here" exchange. I waited a couple of minutes, then poked my head back out. Twink had turned around and was going back up the block, walking slow and sensual.

The figure in Fergusson's window was gone.

Twinkie sauntered across the street again and stood on the sidewalk. Even with my binoculars I couldn't see her very clearly. The fog was rolling in off the surface of Green Lake.

Then I caught a flicker of movement on my side of the street. I swung the binoculars around and saw a dark, almost shadowy figure moving along the side of the apartment house. I was fairly certain that it was Fergusson, and he wasn't moving very fast. He obviously didn't want to attract attention.

Twink turned and strolled into the foggy park. She didn't seem to be in any hurry.

Then that goddam fog swirled in and blotted out everything. I couldn't see more than ten feet away. Well, if I couldn't see *them*, they couldn't see me, so I crossed the street. I was the third player in this little game, and my advantage lay in the fact that the other two didn't even know I was there.

I wasn't sure what I was going to do if I suddenly encountered one—or both—of them in that fog.

City fog isn't much like the fog you'll run into out in the country. It glows because of all the streetlights and automobile headlights, where country fog is pale but dark at the same time. Trees and bushes—and other things—seem to leap out at you in city fog.

It occurred to me that I was taking some dangerous chances. Fergusson was out there in the fog, and he had some evil intentions. Twinkie was *also* out there, and maybe her intentions were even worse. If Twink happened to mistake me for Fergusson, I could wind up being Joan the Ripper's next victim. The concept of actually being afraid of one of the Twinkie Twins had never even entered my mind. But if Twink was carrying a syringe loaded with curare and she jumped me, I wouldn't have time enough to identify myself. Even if I could, there was a distinct possibility that if Twink *was* going through an episode of fugue, she wouldn't even recognize my name.

I started being very cautious along about then.

Suddenly a bright light came lancing in amongst the trees. Somebody in the street was obviously probing around with a spotlight. It wasn't hard to figure out *who* was so curious: the Seattle Police Department had been very interested in parks for quite some time now.

The playing field was getting a little crowded. My only advantage was that *I* knew who all the other players were.

The spotlight moved on, slowly sweeping back and forth through the fog, and I stepped out from behind the bushes where I'd taken cover.

Then, from down near the lakeshore, I heard a peculiar sound that made my blood run cold—the undulating sound of a woman's voice singing wordlessly in a minor key. There was no specific melody involved, but I recognized it immediately. God knows that I'd heard it often enough. The sound coming out of the fog was an almost perfect duplication of the woman's voice on that unlabeled audiotape that Twinkie could listen to by the hour. And from off in the distance, another sound joined with the woman's voice in an eerie counterpoint. My skin crawled as I realized that the wolves in the Woodland Park Zoo were howling a response to the soulless song of the woman in the fog near the lakeshore.

Then the spotlight returned, probing through the fog as that police car came back down Green Lake Way. The cops had obviously heard the same sounds that I had, but I was sure that they didn't have any idea of what they really meant.

My head sort of shut down at that point. Cops usually work in pairs, and it wouldn't be too long before two cops—with guns—would be searching the foggy darkness by the shore for the source of that strange sound Renata was making. If they found her while she was cutting Fergusson to pieces, they'd probably shoot first and ask questions later. I absolutely *had* to get to Renata before they did. I wasn't exactly sure what I'd do when I caught up with her, but I could worry about that later. Right now, I *had* to get her out of the line of fire.

I didn't exactly run as I moved through the fog, but I was going pretty fast.

Then the spotlight made another sweep, and I dove for cover. If those cops happened to get trigger-happy, I could end up being their first target.

Renata was still singing somewhere out there in the fog, and the Woodland Park wolves were still singing along, so I was fairly sure she hadn't finished with Fergusson yet.

The spotlight from Green Lake Way swept past me, and I could tell by looking at that light that the police car had stopped and wasn't moving. It'd only be a few minutes before the cops realized that they were going to have to get out of the car and come down through the park on foot.

I came up running. My original plan had been to cut Renata off before she could nail Fergusson with her curare, but that'd gone out the window once she'd disappeared in the fog. The way things stood now, about all I could hope for was to get her away before those cops caught her in the act.

The singing rose in a crescendo, and then it faded—almost regretfully, it seemed. The wolves kept singing, though.

Then I heard a faint splash out in the lake. Renata was going for a swim after she'd finished butchering her latest victim. At least she wouldn't be standing over Fergusson's bloody corpse when the cops arrived.

I glanced back over my shoulder. Sure enough, I could see a couple of flashlights moving around in the fog back near Green Lake. The cops *were* out of their car, searching that park.

Off in the distance, I could hear sirens wailing, coming this way. Those first two cops had obviously radioed for backup. Ironically, they'd probably made the call to Mary.

I was still quite a ways ahead of them, though. If I got lucky, I might be able to catch Renata when she came out of the water, and get her away from the murder scene before the cops nabbed her. If I could just get her back to my car, I'd be able to take her to Mary's place. Then *I'd* be the one who'd root around in Mary's medicine cabinet looking for sleeping pills. If I could pull *that* off, I could have Twink back in Fallon's bughouse before daylight.

The only problem was that I could see several blinking red lights back out on the street. The backup cars were arriving, and it wouldn't be long before that narrow strip of trees and grass was crawling with cops. Several other flashlights joined the first pair and they began to fan out.

I reached the shore of Green Lake and started along the edge of the water. I couldn't see more than ten feet out because of the fog, and I couldn't be sure if Renata was just wading or if she was out farther, swimming in deeper water.

Then I heard a faint splash. That answered the question:

Renata was swimming. I looked back again and saw why. There were flashlights all over the place back near Green Lake. Renata might be crazy, but she *wasn't* crazy enough to swim right into the arms of the Seattle Police Department.

I kept moving along the edge of the water, following the occasional splashes. I couldn't *see* anything, but I could *hear* enough to stay with her.

Then I saw that black plastic raincoat on the grass at the edge of the water. A few yards back from the raincoat, there was something huddled motionless near a tree trunk. I was fairly sure that it was Fergusson's body. I wasn't thinking very clearly at that point, and it occurred to me that if I dragged Fergusson away from the shore and shoved him under some bushes, the cops wouldn't find him immediately. That might give Renata time enough to get clear. I'd have to hurry, though. Those flashlights were getting closer.

I'd just reached that huddled figure when one of the spotlights on a police car came probing through the fog. I dropped to the ground near the body to stay out of sight.

When I raised my head, I found myself looking directly at Fergusson's face. That spotlight was setting the fog aglow, so I could see a lot more than I really wanted to see. The look of stark terror on the dead man's face will probably stay etched on my memory for the rest of my life. He'd obviously recognized the face of a girl he'd murdered almost three years ago.

I retched and scrambled back, almost like a crab trying to escape. Then I rolled over and came up running in a low crouch until I got to the water's edge.

Things were starting to get a little intense. I had to stay ahead of the cops, but Renata wasn't swimming very fast. She probably wasn't even thinking at this point. All she seemed to be doing was trying to stay ahead of the flashlights. I was trying to do the same thing, but it was a little more complicated for me, because I was trying to keep track of her as well.

Then I heard a shout from somewhere behind me. I looked

back and saw all the flashlights converging on the place I'd just left. One of the cops had obviously found Fergusson—or what was left of him. That *might* give me a little more time. *I'd* known from the beginning what was probably going to happen. The cops had just been investigating some strange sounds. The discovery of Fergusson's body would distract them. It'd take them a little while to realize that they were almost right on top of Joan the Ripper. The first two cops had heard Renata singing, but they hadn't realized exactly what that meant.

The splashing sounds out in the lake were growing fainter. Renata seemed to be swimming out farther away from shore. Things weren't going too well. She *could* drown out there. I was sure she'd been pretty well hyped-up while she was cutting Fergusson to pieces, and the water was probably colder than hell. Once that all caught up with her, she *might* stop swimming and sink.

The lakeshore began to curve off toward the left, and the lights from the street began to recede into the fog. The howling of the wolves in the zoo seemed closer now, and it suddenly dawned on me that I'd left the strip-park between Green Lake Way and the water, and moved into Woodland Park itself.

I looked back again. The flashlights were still clustered together in the same place. That gave me a little breathing room.

I hadn't heard any splashing out in the fog for quite some time, and *that* didn't make me feel very good.

Then I saw something that seemed to explain it. As luck had it, there was a narrow sand beach at the edge of the lake, and a line of footprints came out of the water and ran up into the grass of Woodland Park.

It had to be Renata. You won't find *too* many people swimming around in Green Lake after midnight in February.

That freezing fog that I'd been cursing all week suddenly seemed like a gift from God. Where it had settled on the grass, it'd frozen, laying a pale white veil on that well-manicured lawn. And running across that frosty grass was the track Renata had left when she'd emerged from the lake.

Tracking her was easy now, but it'd be just as easy for the cops—assuming that they didn't all stay bunched up around the body. I hurried after her, cutting back and forth across the trail she had laid down in the frozen grass, zigzagging to lay down false trails leading off in several different directions. I hoped that would slow them down, in the event that one of them was sharp enough to realize that Fergusson's murderer was probably still in the general vicinity. If they started to fan out for a general search, they'd end up obliterating even more tracks by accident than I was trying to do on purpose.

I was positive that Renata was going to have to find shelter, and soon. It was freezing, and she was soaking wet after her swim. Plus, she hadn't been wearing very much to begin with. If she didn't find someplace in out of the weather fairly soon, hypothermia would set in, and that was only about one step away from pneumonia.

The trail she'd laid down through the park ran due south. I quit zigzagging and started to run. I had to get her in sight before she reached Fiftieth Street. Once she hit cement, she wouldn't be leaving a trail anymore.

Then I saw her. Thank God she'd been forced to leave that black raincoat behind. She was hiding behind a large tree right at the edge of the park, obviously waiting for a break in the traffic on Fiftieth Street. Even if her brains were scrambled, she was still sharp enough to stay out of sight until she'd put more distance between her and what was left of Fergusson.

I hunkered down behind a large bush and watched her tensely. The fog pretty much obscured the neighborhood on the other side of the street at the edge of the park, but a sudden eddy pushed the fog aside, and I saw a familiar structure rising out of the surrounding rooftops—the spire of St. Benedict's Church on Forty-ninth Street.

I'd assumed that Renata had been trying to get back to that alley where she'd stashed her bike, and cycle from there back to Mary's place. Then she'd wait a day or so and take a bus to the neighborhood where her car was parked so she could drive it somewhere closer to home.

The proximity of St. Benedict's, though, raised an entirely different possibility. If her head was *really* turned off, wasn't it possible that the term "sanctuary" had something to do with that beeline she'd laid down in the grass? Had she been running to reach the church from the moment she'd come out of the lake?

More to the point, though, did the concept of sanctuary still have any legal validity? Could Father O just slam the church door shut and tell the cops to buzz off? I didn't *think* he could, but a lot of strange things from the Middle Ages are still kicking around in the legal system.

I tensed up when Renata stepped out from behind that tree and hurried across Fiftieth Street. There weren't any cars in sight, so she made it to the shadows on the other side before anybody came along to spot her.

"What the hell?" I muttered. Then I crossed the street as well. By the time I got to the other side, Renata was a half block down Stone Way, headed toward Forty-ninth Street. When she got to that corner, she went off to her right. That nailed it down: She *was* headed toward the church.

I hurried along and reached that corner in about two minutes. I didn't want to lose her now. She was still in plain sight, walking directly toward the church.

It was only two blocks, and it didn't take her long to get there. She started up the front stairs to the church door, and I gave a vast sigh of relief. Wonder of wonders, I'd guessed right for a change.

Father O had left the church door unlocked, as he'd told me he always did, and Renata opened it and went inside.

Now what the hell was I going to do? I definitely didn't want to go barging into that church right behind her.

Then the church door opened, and Father O'Donnell stuck his head out. "Hello?" he called, sounding baffled. I guess the motion sensor in the vestibule had told him that he had a visitor, but evidently he hadn't spotted Renata.

"It's me, Father O'Donnell," I called to him.

"Mark? Is that you?"

"Right," I replied. "Renata just went inside your church."

"I didn't see anybody."

I went up the steps and joined him. "We've got big trouble, Father," I told him.

"Come inside," he told me.

"Let's hold off a minute. I'd better fill you in. Renata definitely went inside, but she's having one of her episodes. I've been following her for the last couple of hours, and we don't want to get too close to her right now. She's dangerous."

"*Renata?* Be serious, Mark."

"I am, Father O'Donnell—dead serious. I hate to say this, but Renata's the serial killer who's been butchering guys all over the Puget Sound area since last fall."

"*Renata?*" His voice sounded incredulous.

"I choked on it myself, but she just took out another one. The cops are probably right behind me, so I'd better keep this short. Renata might *seem* to be recovering, but every so often, she goes psychotic. I don't think she realizes what's happening, but when she flips out, she goes hunting, like some avenging angel. I can't prove it, but I *think* the guy she just took out was the one she's been after since last September— the guy who murdered her sister."

"Good for her!"

"Father O'Donnell," I said in a pained voice, "she doesn't need a rooting section. We've *got* to get her off the streets. If her load shifts just a little bit more, she'll start killing anything wearing pants—you, me, the postman—anybody!"

"Maybe I *was* being a little . . ." He left it hanging. "What do you think we ought to do?"

"The best thing would probably be to take her back to Doc

Fallon's bughouse. He might have to keep her doped up, but she'll be safe. If the cops get her, they won't know what's going on, and she'll probably spend the rest of her life screaming. I'm not *about* to let that happen."

"Amen," he agreed. "Let's go back inside and see if we can find her."

"Right—but be careful. As far as I know, she's still got that knife. Maybe you'd better lock this door behind us. We don't want her slipping out again. The cops are wound up pretty tight, and they might start shooting if they happen to come across her."

"Good idea," he agreed.

We went into the vestibule, and Father O locked the heavy door behind us. "Let's go down to the altar," he whispered. "Maybe if we try talking to her, we can persuade her to come out."

"It's worth a try, I suppose," I agreed. "Wrestling her to the ground wouldn't be a very good idea."

The two of us went quietly through the dimly lighted church. I think we were both pretty well spooked. I know *I* was.

"Maybe *you* should try to talk to her," Father O suggested.

I was about to agree, when I heard a lisping sound coming from one of the alcoves off to my right. "Hold it," I whispered to Father O. "She's right over there."

We both listened intently—not that it did us any good. I recognized the sibilant hissing of the twins' private language. If Renata was talking to herself in twin-speak, she was obviously completely out of it.

I cautiously moved a little closer, trying to spot her in that shadowy alcove where the statue of Saint Benedict stood with one hand raised in blessing.

Then the headlights from a passing car briefly flickered through the stained-glass windows on the other side of the church.

I almost lost it right there. In that momentary flicker I could swear that I saw *two* figures in that alcove.

Father O'Donnell drew in a sharp breath. "Holy Mother of God!" he choked.

We moved slowly closer to the alcove, and I could see the two figures more clearly now. They were identical in every detail, except that one figure had wet hair and the other didn't. I don't think they realized that Father O'Donnell and I were there; they probably didn't even realize where they were. They were speaking urgently to each other, the lisping words tumbling out in half whispers. One voice seemed anguished, but the other was triumphant.

Then the anguished figure began to weep, and the other one embraced her as if to comfort her.

And then, even as Father O'Donnell and I stood staring in stunned disbelief, they merged, and what had been two became one, and the sibilance of twin-speak died to be replaced by the song I'd heard earlier on that particular night.

The lights from another car flickered inside the church, washing the walls with color from the stained-glass windows, and Father O'Donnell and I could clearly see Renata for a moment. She'd sunk down onto the floor in that alcove with vacant eyes and an untroubled face, and she was singing softly to herself under the watchful eyes of the statue of Saint Benedict.

Fourth Movement

AGNUS DEI

CHAPTER TWENTY-TWO

Father O'Donnell and I stood staring at Renata in stunned and speechless disbelief. "I'd better get a blanket to wrap her in," the father said quietly after several minutes. "She's soaking wet, and she just came in out of the cold."

That brought me to my senses. "What do you think, Father O?" I asked him. "Should we call an ambulance and get her to a hospital?"

"It might be best, Mark," he said seriously. "She's suffering from exposure, and it's dreadful cold out there tonight."

"Tell me about it."

"How did she get all wet like that?"

"She dunked herself in Green Lake to wash off the blood. Then she saw all the lights, so she swam down to the beach on the north end of Woodland Park—about a quarter of a mile. If she's got hypothermia, we'd better get her to a hospital. I can take her to Lake Stevens *after* she recovers."

"I'll get that blanket, and then I'll call an ambulance." He hurried back toward the rectory.

The ambulance arrived about ten minutes later from the University of Washington Medical Center, the closest hospital to St. Benedict's. The ambulance guys said I could ride along. Somebody was going to have to fill out all the paperwork, and my car was still over on Green Lake Way.

"I'll keep you posted, Father," I promised as I followed the stretcher out to the ambulance. Father O watched us go from the doorway of the church, his expression grave.

The driver hit the flashing lights and the siren, even though there wasn't very much traffic, and it didn't take long to reach the medical center down on campus. Renata was shaking violently now, and moaning that song she'd picked up from her favorite tape. I held her hand, but I don't think she was even aware of it.

After we got her inside the emergency room I was short-stopped by the lady who needed certain information to fill out a whole stack of papers. I tried to cooperate, but I wasn't in the mood to answer a lot of questions. I finally cut across them. "She's got some serious mental problems," I said by way of explanation. "She seemed to think it was a nice night for a swim."

"In *February*?" the lady said incredulously.

"Like I said, she's disturbed. Her dad's stinking rich, so don't worry about who's going to pay the bills."

"Could you give me his name, address, and phone number."

"I'll go you one better. Hand me your phone and I'll call him. He can give you all the details himself."

Les sounded groggy when he answered the phone—it *was* after two in the morning. "Renata's flipped out again, boss," I told him. "She fell in the lake in Woodland Park and wound up at St. Benedict's Church. I've got her here at the university medical center, and the lady who's filling out the admission forms needs some information. I'll keep you posted on how she's doing just as soon as I find out how serious this is." I handed the phone to the admissions lady and went back to the desk to ask for an update.

I didn't get too many specific answers, so I sat in the waiting room for about half an hour until the doctor came out. He was fairly young—probably a second-year intern—but he seemed to know what he was doing. "We're treating Miss Greenleaf for hypothermia, Mr. Austin," he told me. "We have to be careful, because if we rush things, the patient can go into shock."

"We wouldn't want to add that to her other problems," I agreed.

He hesitated for a few seconds, then he came right out with it. "Since it's come up anyway, is Miss Greenleaf suffering from some sort of mental condition? She's moaning and babbling incoherently."

"She's a psycho, Doc," I told him bluntly. "She graduated from an asylum last year, but she still flips out every so often. We all thought she was on the road to recovery, but it looks like we were wrong. Patch her up as best you can, and I'll take her home to that private sanitarium."

"It's *that* bad?" He looked startled.

"That only *begins* to describe how bad it is, Doc. Watch yourself when you're close to her. She could be dangerous."

"Maybe we should move her to the psychiatric ward after she gets out of intensive care," he suggested.

"I didn't realize that there *was* a psycho ward here," I said.

"We *are* a large hospital, Mr. Austin, not just a clinic to patch up students who get drunk and fall down stairs. We're a teaching hospital, and med students need to be exposed to just about every medical condition that comes down the pike."

"I should have realized that," I admitted. "One of my housemates is a medical student. She doesn't talk much about what goes on in med school, though—probably because we've asked her not to. A clinical description of an autopsy doesn't go down very well at the supper table."

"You're a student, then?"

I nodded. "English. We dissect poems, though, not people."

He smiled faintly. "I'll caution the staff about Miss Greenleaf," he assured me.

I called Father O to give him an update—such as it was—and he suggested that I try getting in touch with Mary. I rooted around in my wallet until I found the slip of paper with the cop-shop phone number she'd given me. It took me a while to get connected to her, but I kept waving "family emergency" around until whoever was on the other end of the line gave up and patched me through to her.

"You're not supposed to call me at work, Mark," she scolded.

"We've got a serious problem, Mary. Twinkie flipped out again. She was wandering around up near Woodland Park, and she fell in the lake. She's got a fairly serious case of hypothermia. I'm at the University of Washington Medical Center, and they're treating her right now. You'd better come by here when you get off work."

"Did you get in touch with Les?"

"Yeah, I called him as soon as we got her here."

"How did you find out about it?"

Oops—I realized I'd have to be careful here. There was a distinct possibility that this call was being monitored—and recorded. "She homed in on St. Benedict's Church, and Father O gave me a quick call," I replied. I didn't want to get *too* much more specific.

"I'll come by as soon as I get off work," she promised.

I hung up the phone and went back to the waiting room. I hadn't really blown anything so far. If I played this right, I might still be able to keep Twink in the clear. OK, Fergusson was dead, and it'd been Twink who'd taken him out. Big deal. The way I saw it, my job was to get Twink safely back to Doc Fallon *before* the cops caught up with her. It'd take some fancy footwork and a fair amount of just plain lying, but if I could keep things low-key, the cops might not make the connection, and I could still get her out of town. When she'd given me the slip and hacked Fergusson to pieces, I'd thought that everything had gone out the window, but now I began to hope that I *still* might be able to pull this off.

I dozed off in the waiting room until about seven. Then I called the boardinghouse.

"Yes?" It was Erika.

"It's me, babe—Mark. I'm at the emergency room at the University Medical Center. Renata flipped out last night, and she fell in the water somehow, and then wandered around in Woodland Park. Then she got herself to St. Benedict's, and Father O called an ambulance."

"Hypothermia?"

"That's what they tell me. As soon as I'm sure that she's going to be OK, I'll come on home."

"You don't sound very good, Mark."

"I'm running on short sleep, Erika. It's all I can do to keep my eyes open right now. I could definitely use a cup or six of your coffee."

"Try the hospital cafeteria. The coffee's sort of rancid, but it's got a pretty good kick to it."

"I'll give it a shot. Pass the word, OK?"

"Got it covered."

I hung up the phone and went down the hall to the men's room. I was washing my hands, and then I suddenly froze, staring at my reflection in the mirror. There was a blood smear on the front of my jacket. I'd obviously flopped down a little too close to Fergusson's body back there in the park, and I'd been parading around in public flaunting something I really didn't want anybody to see. I tried to wash it off, but I don't think I got all of it. I finally gave up, and I carried my coat back to the waiting room instead of wearing it.

I should have guessed that the girls at the boardinghouse wouldn't just let it lie, but I *was* a little foggy upstairs by then. It only took Erika and Sylvia about three-quarters of an hour to join me at the hospital. "You two stay here," Erika told Sylvia and me. "I'm going to find out what's *really* going on."

"You look awful, Mark," Sylvia said.

"You should see it from in here."

"What really happened last night?"

"Damned if I know. Renata showed up at St. Benedict's

dripping water and sprouting icicles. She was babbling in twin-speak and shivering hard enough to start an earthquake. Father O got hold of me, and then he called an ambulance."

"I thought you were out on the town last night. How did he know how to get in touch?"

Don't try to tell lies when you're groggy. You'll mess up every time. "I was just coming in," I replied—a little too quickly. "I heard the phone ringing, and it was Father O. The call was for me, so I didn't wake anybody."

Sylvia gave me a skeptical look. I don't think *anybody* would have bought that one.

Then Erika came back, and she looked *very* concerned. "Renata was apparently coming down with a cold," she told us. "This hypothermia seems to have kicked it across the line. She's running a high fever, and my best guess is full-bore pneumonia."

"Oh, dear!" Sylvia exclaimed. "Is it serious?"

"It's no joke, that's for certain," Erika told her, "but if you ever decide to come down with pneumonia, do it in a hospital. The staff here is right on top of it. I'll stay and keep an eye on things. Sitting around wringing your hands won't accomplish very much, so you two might as well get out of here. Take Mark back home and put him to bed, Sylvia. He looks like he's just about ready to fall apart."

Sylvia drove me back to the boardinghouse, and I went upstairs to the boys' bathroom. I scrubbed down the front of that jacket and carefully checked the rest of my clothes for any other bloodstains. I didn't see any, but I decided not to take any chances. I went to my room and stuffed all the clothes I'd been wearing into a large plastic bag. I could take a quick trip to a laundromat after things quieted down. Right now I was too groggy to think clearly, so I crashed. I doubt I've ever been that tired in my whole life.

I'd been almost sure that I'd sleep the clock around, but I woke up at one that afternoon. I was still pretty tired, but I was too worried about Renata to fall asleep again. I got up, put on clean clothes, and grabbed a different jacket.

Charlie's door was open, so I fed him the same story I'd dropped on Sylvia. I must have been getting better at it, because he didn't look *nearly* as skeptical as Sylvia had. "Can you run me back to the hospital?" I asked him. "My car's still where I left it when I rode down to the hospital in the ambulance."

"Sure," he agreed. "No problem."

Mary was in the waiting room when we got there. "I called Les," she told us. "I thought he ought to know that Ren's got pneumonia. He and Inga should be here before long."

"Is she getting any better?" I asked.

"They've got her in intensive care, Mark. Does that answer your question?"

It was about three-thirty when Bob West showed up. He glanced around the waiting room to make sure there weren't any strangers there. "What the hell's going on, Mark?" he demanded in a quiet voice that seemed pretty strained. "The hospital staff put in a call. They inventoried that purse the Greenleaf girl had strapped around her waist, and there was a hypodermic needle in the damn thing. They did a routine check for heroin or cocaine, but they found traces of curare instead, for Christ's sake!"

That's when I realized that I'd blown it. I'd been so stunned by what'd happened in the church that I'd forgotten that plastic purse. My scheme to keep my mouth shut and hustle Twink back out to Fallon's sanitarium without letting anybody know what'd *really* happened fell apart at that point.

"Curare?" Mary exclaimed. "That's impossible!"

"They tested it three times, Mary," Bob told her. "We'd put out an alert that anybody in any health-care facility who came across curare was supposed to call us immediately because of the connection of curare with the Slasher murders. What the hell was that girl doing with a hypo filled with curare?"

"What else was in the purse?" I asked him, hoping against hope that Twink had thrown her linoleum knife away.

"Lots of real interesting stuff, Mark," he replied sarcastically. "There were a couple of strings of rosary beads—one red and one blue. There was a driver's license that belonged to a girl named Regina Greenleaf—even though the picture shows that girl who's in intensive care right now, and her name's Renata, isn't it? That was about all we found—except for a linoleum knife with traces of blood on it. They're doing a DNA check, but I think we all know whose blood it is, don't we? You'd better come clean, Mark, and do it right now. It was just sheer dumb luck that *I* picked up the phone when the hospital called. If it'd been Burpee, half the Seattle Police Department would be here right now—along with three or four SWAT teams."

I knew that he'd stay right on top of me until I gave him what he wanted, but there was something I needed to know first. "How crazy does somebody have to be to pull off the insanity defense?" I asked him.

"Pretty far gone—particularly in a case that's gotten as much publicity as this one has. With that curare and the knife, the prosecutor's going to have an open-and-shut case. He'll fight an insanity plea all the way to the wall."

"What the hell is this all about?" Charlie demanded.

"Grow up, kid," Bob told him. "That Greenleaf girl is Joan the Ripper."

"But she's just a baby!" Charlie protested.

The waiting room door swung open, and a couple of worried-looking strangers came in. "We'd better find someplace a little more private," I suggested. "We've got a touchy situation here."

"Sit tight," Bob agreed. "I'll be right back."

I'm not sure what strings he pulled, but he came back after a few minutes with a hospital orderly who led us over into the main hospital and an empty office.

"All right, Mark," Bob said after the orderly had left, "let's have it. What happened last night?"

"Let's go back a little ways first. Mary can back up most of what I'm going to tell you, so I'm not just scraping this off the wall. Renata Greenleaf had a twin sister—Regina—up until the spring of '95. They were about to graduate from high school up in Everett—"

"What's that got to do with it?" Bob demanded. "Get to the point, Mark."

"This *is* the point, Bob," I told him. "This is what these Seattle Slasher murders are all about." And then I told him everything—everything except what I'd seen in the church last night. I wasn't ready to tell *anybody* about that.

"Why didn't you come to me with this, Mark?" Bob demanded.

"Because I was *hoping* that I was wrong. If I was camped right outside her front door when some other guy got cut to pieces, but she'd stayed home, that'd prove that she *wasn't* the Slasher." I sighed. "That's not the way it turned out though. I guess she finally worked up enough nerve to ask Mary to run down the name of the guy who owned that pickup truck. I'm sure she realized that Mary would make the connection just as soon as Fergusson turned up dead. That's probably why she held off on asking Mary for the information, until it reached the point that killing Fergusson was more important than getting away with it."

"You tell good stories, kid," Mary said dryly.

"That's for sure," Charlie said. "I'd say that the next thing on the agenda is coming up with some way to get Twink off the hook. Does anybody have a problem with that?"

"It's gonna take some fancy footwork, kid," Bob told him. "If Fergusson had been the only guy she'd taken out, a jury *might* go for 'justifiable homicide' or 'diminished mental capacity.' But there are all those other carcasses littering various parks around here. This is a high-profile case, so the media will go into a feeding frenzy. That means that the DA's going to have to play hardball if he wants to get reelected. If things were a little more low-key, 'insanity' might slip by, but this one's gonna be front-page all the way."

"You almost sound like you're on our side, Bob," Mary said.

"If Mark's right about what's been happening around here since last September, just about anybody with a shred of decency's going to be on the Greenleaf girl's side. That's off the record, of course. Mary, do you think your brother can afford a top-notch lawyer?"

"You bet your bippie he can, Bob," she replied with a broad smile.

I'd deliberately avoided any mention of the apparition—vision? miracle?—that Father O and I had seen in the church before we'd called the ambulance. Now that the hypo with traces of curare and the linoleum knife with Fergusson's blood all over it had come out into the open, things were obviously headed for serious legal proceedings, and whether I liked it or not, I'd probably be the star witness for the defense. If I got up on the witness stand and started telling ghost stories, things would start to fall apart—real fast.

CHAPTER TWENTY-THREE

I overslept the next morning, probably because things were unnaturally quiet around the second floor of the Erdlund house. James and Charlie must have been tiptoeing around, whispering to each other to avoid rousing me. Tired or not, though, I could only sleep for so long at a stretch. We get programmed after a while, and most students hit the deck fairly early. So it was nine or so when I finally woke up, showered, shaved, and brushed my teeth. I gave some serious consideration to hiding in my room until the gang had all left. I wasn't ready for another question-and-answer session.

I *really* needed some coffee, though, so I went downstairs. I could hear Charlie in the kitchen when I reached the foot of the stairs, filling the others in on the story I'd told his brother just a few hours before. "If Mark hadn't been so rattled, he'd probably have remembered to get that belt-on purse away from Twinkie. That's what blew the whole thing."

I went into the kitchen at that point.

"We didn't wake you, Mark, did we?" James said. "We were trying to be quiet."

"It's Erika's fault," I said with a faint smile. "The smell of her coffee would wake the dead."

"I'll fix you a cup, Mark," Erika told me.

"I know how to pour coffee, Erika."

"Shush!" she told me. She pointed at my usual place at the breakfast table. "There," she commanded. "Sit. Stay."

"Woof-woof," I replied and sat down.

"What are we going to do about this, Mark?" Sylvia asked in a worried tone.

"I don't know, babe," I answered truthfully. "I think we'll just play it by ear. The next move is up to Bob West."

"I'll talk with Mr. Rankin," Trish told me. "If any lawyer in Seattle can possibly get Renata off, it'll be Rankin. He's the absolute best."

"I'll pass that on to Renata's dad, Trish," I promised.

It was about eleven o'clock when Bob West called me. "Are you busy, Mark?" he asked. "I mean, have you got classes or appointments or anything right now?"

"No, I'm free. What's up?"

"I need to pick up the Greenleaf girl's car. You know where it's parked and what it looks like, so I thought maybe you could come along."

"No problem, Bob. I need to pick up my own car anyway— it's still parked over there. You can save me a bus ride."

"We're big on public service," he said. "I'll come by in about a half hour."

"I'll be here." This was peculiar: Theoretically, Bob and I were supposed to be on opposite sides of the Twinkie fence. But over the past several months we'd gotten to know each other fairly well, and now I found myself hoping that buddy-ship would step over the fences between us.

I went back upstairs to grab my jacket.

"What's up?" Charlie asked me when I passed his open door.

"Bob wants me to show him where Renata's car's parked," I replied. "My car's there, too, so I'll be able to pick it up."

"I'll come along," he said. "I've got an equation that's fighting me, and maybe some fresh air would help clear my head."

"And there's that crime scene, too, huh?"

"I'm big on scenery, Mark," he said, grinning.

*   *   *

Bob picked us up a little later. It was misty-moisty out, but at least it'd warmed up a little, so the windshield wasn't icing over.

"What I can't figure out is how the Greenleaf girl was able to buy a car without anybody knowing that she'd done it," Bob said while we were waiting for a traffic light to change.

"Her dad's got lots of bucks, Bob," I told him. "She had a fairly beefy checkbook." Then I remembered something. "Oh, hell," I said. "I must still be a little foggy in the head. Just before Christmas I stopped by Mary's place, and Renata was having a wrestling match with her checkbook. She couldn't get it to balance, and it was off by about six hundred bucks! That Honda she had parked on a side street was a junker—six hundred would probably have been the sticker price. This is just a guess, but evidently her other personality cropped up now and then during the daytime—at least long enough on one occasion to go out and buy that car. Renata obviously didn't know about it, so the alternate identity was keeping it a secret from her."

"I don't entirely buy this 'other personality' business, Mark," Bob said then. "It sounds like a put-up story to get this girl off the hook."

"Her headshrinker thinks it's valid, Bob," I told him. "I didn't really understand it myself right at first. Abnormal Sylvia says the scientific term is 'fugue,' which suggests something composed by Johann Sebastian Bach, if you ask me. In music, it involves counterpoint—two or more parts played at the same time. That's probably why psychiatrists used the term. Renata doesn't know what the other side of her is doing— buying cars, sneaking out at night to burglarize drugstores, cutting assorted guys all to pieces after midnight—the fun part of life." Bob gave me a stern look. "Sorry. But this split-personality stuff *does* happen, though, and it's not some put-up job. Doc Fallon might not agree with me, but I've got a gut feel that the alternate Renata is her twin sister—Regina—and Regina's the one who's been cutting guys to pieces around here since last September. Right at first, I guess she'd carve up any guy who hit on her. But once Mary told Renata who owned that pickup truck, Regina had a specific target—and Fergusson was the guy she'd been after right from the start."

"This fugue thing's a one-way street, then?" Bob suggested. "The nighttime girl knows everything the daytime girl knows, but the daytime girl doesn't know the other girl even exists."

"She gets hints once in a while," I told him, "and those hints are what trigger her crazy days."

"It's fairly obvious that Fergusson was number one on her hate parade," Bob said. "She did an extra special job on *that* poor bastard—the coroner looked sick after he finished the autopsy. Fergusson definitely went out the hard way." He looked sort of apologetically at me. "I have to take her into custody, Mark," he said. "I'm not going to yank her out of the hospital or anything, but if I don't do *something* official before Burpee gets wind of it, he'll dash on over to the hospital, slap the cuffs on her, and drag her off to jail. If she's in *my* custody, I can lay down the rules. I'll keep her in that hospital for as long as I can. We might have to wing it, but I think I can keep her out of the slammer."

"Thanks, Bob. That's all that really matters."

Bob parked near Fergusson's apartment house, and the keys he'd found in Renata's purse unlocked the tan Honda. My theory about Renata's alternate personality was pretty much confirmed by the registration slip, which listed the owner of the car as Regina Greenleaf.

Bob called for a tow truck to haul the car away, and I went around the corner and got my car. Then Charlie and I went home.

There was one of those yellow Post-it notes stuck to the door of my room when I went upstairs. "Father O wants you to call him," it said. I heaved a tired sigh and went back downstairs to use the phone in the living room.

"It's me, Father O'Donnell—Mark," I told him when he answered the phone. "What's up?"

"I think you'd better come by, Mark," he said. "Something's come up that we need to talk about in strict privacy."

"I'll be right over," I promised him. Lucky I had my wheels again, I mused.

There was actually a brief spell of sunshine as I drove to the church. It didn't last long, but it was nice to know that the sun was still out there. I was starting to get a real bellyful of fog.

Father O was puttering around near the altar when I reached the church. His face had a bleak, apologetic look. "Come on back to the office, Mark," he suggested. "This is something we *don't* want anybody to overhear."

"You're making me nervous, Father," I said, following him through the small door off to the side of the altar and down the hall to his office.

He led the way inside, then firmly closed the door behind him. "How's Renata doing?" he asked, after we'd sat down.

I brought him up to speed—the pneumonia, the plastic purse, and the police. "What it all boils down to is that the cops have an open-and-shut case against Renata. She's definitely the Seattle Slasher. Our only hope now is the insanity defense. Father, I'm not sure if what you and I saw the other night—whatever that *was*—is going to play any part in that."

"You'd better not count on it, Mark," he told me gravely. "I reported the incident to my bishop, and there are some rules about things like that. You and I both know we saw something extraordinary—but my bishop has forbidden me to talk about it."

"You said *what*?"

"Church policy, Mark. We're not permitted to discuss any supernatural incidents that occur in or near a church. In most cases these apparitions are nothing more than cases of mass hysteria, and the clergy isn't supposed to get involved in things like that. If you stop and think about it, I'm sure you'll be able to see why."

"I guess it *does* make sense, Father. But dammit, you and I *both* know what we saw."

"I wouldn't make an issue of it in court, Mark, because I won't be permitted to confirm anything you say about it. Have you mentioned it to anybody?"

"Not yet. I wasn't sure how to bring it up, to tell you the truth."

"Good. I'd keep it that way, if I were you. Are the police going to arrest Renata?"

"I don't think so, Father O'Donnell. She's completely out of it. They'll probably put her in protective custody, but if we can float mental incompetence past a judge, this won't ever go to trial. They'll just quietly lock her up in some insane asylum and throw away the key. It's not a good solution, but it's probably about the best we can hope for."

He got that shrewd, squinty-eyed look that every Irishman comes up with now and then. "I think there might be an alternative to that, Mark. Let me work on it a bit. I'll have to call in a few favors, but there's nothing new or unusual about that, don't y'know."

I went home for supper, then back to the hospital. Les and Inga were in Renata's room, and they both looked pretty haggard. I took Les off to one side. "Why don't you let me take the night shift, boss?" I suggested. "You and Inga ought to get some sleep."

"You don't look too good yourself, Mark," he replied.

"It's been a couple of pretty rough weeks, boss," I told him, "but I'm an expert at sleeping in Renata's hospital rooms, remember?"

He glanced over at Inga. "Maybe I *should* get her out of here for a while," he conceded. "She's taking it hard."

"She's not alone, boss. Lots of people are upset about it."

"Will this never end?" he demanded in a choked-up voice.

"All we can do now is hope, boss," I said. What a silly thing *that* was to say. I wanted to bite my tongue after that absurdity came rolling out. "Mary's probably awake. Why don't you give her a call, then get Inga out of here until tomorrow?"

"I'll do that. Thanks, Mark."

"It's no biggie, boss."

After Les and Inga had left, I pulled a chair over to Renata's bedside, grabbed another one to prop my feet on, and assumed a very familiar position. Renata had an IV plugged into her arm and an oxygen mask covering the lower half of her face. I could still hear her talking, though. The mask muffled the sound, but enough came through to let me know that she wasn't speaking English.

I'm not sure exactly why I did it, but I reached out and took her hand. She probably wouldn't even know I was there, but it made *me* feel a little better.

About seven o'clock the next morning, the doctor came into the room, and Bob West and a uniformed police officer were with him. "How's she doing, Mark?" Bob asked me.

"I don't see much change," I told him.

"This is Officer Rauch," he introduced the burly policeman. "He'll take the day shift guarding the door. We need to put together a list of people who'll be allowed into this room. So far I've got you, her parents, and Mary. Who else should we include?"

"Hell, Bob, I don't know—the boardinghouse gang, I suppose—Sylvia and Erika certainly, and probably James and Trish, too."

"What about Charlie?"

"Yeah, we might as well."

"Write down their names for me, OK? Anybody else?"

"I've got to talk with Les—her dad. Trish thinks he should hire a partner in the law firm where she works. His name's Rankin. From what she says, he's a heavy hitter."

Bob nodded. "I've heard of him."

"And we'd better put her psychiatrist on the list, too. His name's Wallace Fallon—oh, we'd probably better include Father O'Donnell as well. He's her priest."

Bob nodded. "Put him on the list."

The doctor had been checking the progress report hanging from the foot of Renata's bed. "Excuse me," he said. "Is she still going on in that peculiar language, Mr. Austin?"

"I haven't heard her say anything in English yet."

"That might be the result of her high fever," he said thoughtfully, "but if she doesn't switch over into English pretty soon, I'd strongly suggest that she be transferred to the psychiatric ward here. It's fairly obvious that she isn't ready to deal with reality yet."

Bob put on a perfectly straight face. "We can live with that," he replied. "What do you think, Mark?"

"Sounds OK to me," I agreed. This would put us one jump ahead of Burpee and all the reporters who were drooling over the prospect of a lurid criminal trial. If the staff of the medical center put Renata in the psychiatric ward, it'd add some weight to the insanity defense and point this whole business in the direction we wanted it to go.

Les came back to the hospital at noon, but Inga wasn't with him. "She's pretty upset, Mark," he told me. "Mary's been slipping her tranks on the sly."

"That's Mary for you. She likes to keep everybody nice and calm. Listen, boss, I'm supposed to bounce something off you. One of the girls at the boardinghouse—Trish Erdlund— is in law school here at the university and she works part-time in a downtown law firm. One of the senior partners there is John Rankin, and from what she says, I guess he's the real thing. We've got to get somebody sharp enough to float an insanity defense past a judge. Renata's obviously totally out of it, but the prosecuting attorney's likely to fight a sanity hearing tooth and nail. This is one of those big-time cases that gets lots of attention, and the district attorney's hoping for a splashy criminal case that'll get him reelected."

"Have you met this Rankin, Mark?"

"Not personally, no, but I'll take Trish's word for it. She's almost as smart as her sister is, and Erika's so smart she scares me—but never mind *that*. What do you think about talking to Rankin?"

He shrugged. "Whatever seems best to you, Mark. My head isn't working too good right now."

"I'll get one of his business cards from Trish and drop it by so that you can get in touch with him."

"Whatever you say."

That really surprised me. Les Greenleaf wasn't the kind of guy who shrugged things off this way. This mess was obviously hitting him very hard.

The TV set in the kitchen was going full blast when I got back to the boardinghouse, and the gang was camped on it.

"How's she doing, Mark?" James asked me.

"She still seems pretty much out of it," I told him. "Her fever's down a little, but she's still talking to herself in twin. Bob came by this morning with a uniformed cop who's going to pull the day shift in the chair outside her door. Her doctor wants to move her to the psychiatric ward once she recovers from this bout of pneumonia. Bob pretty much went along with him on that one. He won't come right out and admit it, but I'm fairly sure that Bob's on our side. Oh, one other thing. I talked with Les Greenleaf, and he says he'll hire Mr. Rankin as Renata's lawyer."

"That's a *big* win," Trish said enthusiastically. "If any lawyer in King County can persuade a judge to go along with a sanity hearing, it'll be Mr. Rankin. We've *got* to keep this case out of criminal court." She pursed her lips and squinted slightly. "I think Rankin's first move will be to go for a preliminary hearing so that he can point this whole case toward determining if Renata's mentally competent to aid in her own defense. If it comes out the way we want, that'll be the end of it right there. Renata will go straight from the psychiatric ward at the university medical center to a mental institution—preferably Dr. Fallon's place up at Lake Stevens. Fallon will obviously be the star witness in any competency hearing, but Mark and Sylvia will probably testify, too."

"So will the district attorney square off against Mr. Rankin?" Sylvia asked.

Trish shook her head. "The DA's too important for that. He'll hand it off to some second-stringer, and Mr. Rankin will have him for lunch." Then Trish looked at me. "Is Renata still speaking exclusively in twin?" she asked.

"That's all I've heard from her so far," I replied.

Trish frowned. "Is she raving? I mean screaming, or anything like that?"

I shook my head. "The twins never spoke their private language in anything louder than a whisper," I replied. "They didn't want anybody eavesdropping."

"Good," Trish said. "She won't interrupt the proceedings then, and I'm almost positive that Mr. Rankin will want her to be physically present. One look at her should be all that it'll take to persuade the judge to rule in our favor."

CHAPTER TWENTY-FOUR

There was obviously no way to keep what'd happened out of the newspapers or off the evening news on every TV channel in western Washington. The media geeks went ballistic, and by the end of the week, you couldn't turn around without bumping into a new—and usually distorted—"Joan the Ripper" story.

The almost universal yearning for fifteen minutes of fame produced some bizarre stories, ranging all the way from, "I think I saw her in the library once," to "I saw right off that she was very strange."

The media bloodhounds tracked down several of Renata's sorority-girl chums, and by Saturday of that week the sidewalk in front of the boardinghouse was teeming with reporters and cameramen. Trish advised us that Mr. Rankin had more or less issued a prime directive. Our only response was supposed to be "no comment."

I was spending a lot of time running back and forth between the boardinghouse and the medical center. By Sunday, it was clear that I wouldn't be able to write any decent seminar papers this quarter. I didn't care too much for the notion, but my only way out would be to take "incompletes" on my two seminars, and then try again after the storm had passed.

Erika was spending more time at the medical center than I was, but at least she had connections there. She reported to the gang on Sunday evening that Renata was pretty much out of the woods on the pneumonia front, and that she'd probably be released from intensive care and transferred to the psychiatric ward by Tuesday at the latest. Trish almost danced on the table when she heard that. "That was the one thing that had me worried," she told us. "Once she's installed in that psychiatric ward, we're home free. A sanity hearing will be almost automatic at that point."

"She's such an enthusiast," Erika murmured. "The least little thing sets her off."

"Don't pick on me, Erika," Trish told her sister. "How are you doing with Dr. Yamada?"

Erika shrugged. "He bought into it, and he'll keep his mouth shut until he's on the witness stand."

"What are you girls up to now?" James demanded.

"Oh, nothing much," Erika replied with a look of exaggerated innocence. "Dr. Yamada's a forensic pathologist in the coroner's office, and he moonlights teaching pathology in the med school. I've taken a couple of his courses, so I know him fairly well. I made a suggestion, and he agreed to follow up on it."

"What kind of suggestion?" Charlie demanded.

"It's sort of technical, Charlie," Erika replied. "Let's not get into all the gory details, OK?"

"I *hate* it when she does that," Charlie grumbled.

"Aw," Erika said, "poor baby."

On Monday, the fifteenth of February, I went to Padelford Hall and hit Dr. Conrad's office before he met with his seminar. He'd heard the news, of course, and he agreed to speak with my professors for me. "It's not uncommon, Mr. Austin," he assured me. "We're fairly flexible in graduate school. An 'incomplete' doesn't show up on your permanent record. All it means is that you're on hold until the crisis passes." Then he hesitated slightly. "How's she doing?" he asked me.

"Not good, Doc," I replied. "She's pretty much shaken off

the pneumonia, but her mind's gone bye-bye, I'm afraid. She came out of the asylum for just one reason. Now that she's taken care of it, she'll probably be going back inside again."

He sighed. "It's a shame. We're losing a great talent there."

"Shit happens, Doc," I told him bluntly. I *definitely* didn't want to start getting emotional at this point. I still had a long way to go. I could fall apart later. Right now I had to keep my act together.

After supper that evening, Charlie took James and me aside. "Let's go check in with Bob," he suggested. "He's our pipeline to the opposition, and we don't want any nasty surprises cropping up."

"Won't he get in trouble if he passes things along to us?" James demanded.

"It's not as if we're going to rat him off, James," Charlie replied. "He knows that he can trust us to keep our mouths shut. I'm not all that interested in cop-shop secrets when you get right down to it. But we need to know what Burpee's up to. Bob's cut him off at the pass on this case, and Burpee's probably eating his own liver by now. Let's face it, guys. Bob stuck his neck *way* out with that 'protective custody' scam, and Burpee's most likely trying to blindside my big brother. If we want to keep Bob on our side, we're going to have to help cover his buns."

"He's got a point, James," I said. "We *really* need Bob to be in charge at this stage. If Burpee manages to get Bob kicked off the case, we're in deep trouble."

"Good point," James agreed. "Let's go have a chat with Big Brother."

James drove us to the Green Lantern in his station wagon. For some reason, the term "SUV"—sports utility vehicle— offended the hell out of him. "It's a station wagon, dammit!" he'd thunder at us any time we slipped and used the more contemporary term. James had lots of old-fashioned words in his vocabulary—"station wagon," "truth," "ethics"—all those quaint, out-of-fashion concepts.

Bob was already sitting in that back booth when we arrived—obviously, he'd been expecting us. That suggested that this meeting was a put-up job. The brothers West made a good team.

"Hey, big guy," Charlie said. "What's happening?"

"Sit down and shut up, Charlie," Bob growled at him. "We've got problems."

That tightened up my insides just a notch.

We all slid into the booth, and Bob leaned forward and spoke very quietly. "Burpee's seriously pissed off about the way I handled the Greenleaf girl last week, and he's trying everything he can think of to get me off the case. The chief of detectives thinks I did the right thing, but Burpee's trying to sneak around behind him. He's doing his best to buddy up to the lawyers in the District Attorney's office, and he's managed to persuade some half-wit over there that he's the resident expert on serial murders. It's pure, unwashed bullshit, of course, but if he can float it past some fumble-brain prosecutor, Burpee's gonna wind up on the witness stand lying his guts out."

"Can't your chief tell him to keep his goddam mouth shut?" Charlie demanded.

"Not if the prosecutor's on Burpee's side, he can't. Burpee had that Cheetah obsession, and the 'Joan the Ripper' thing scared Cheetah out of town. The way Burpee looks at it, that torpedoed any chance he'd ever have for a promotion. He blames the Greenleaf girl, and he's out to get her—any way he can. He's got enough suck-ups in the department that if we keep having these little meetings, he'll find out about them and splash the news all over any TV channel that'll listen to him."

"Damn!" James rumbled.

"Damn only begins to describe it," Bob said. "From now on, we stay away from each other. I know Burpee well enough to figure out what he'll do. He'll push the prosecutor to take this case into open court—preferably with wall-to-wall TV cameras present. He's working behind the scenes right now, but if this goes into criminal court, he won't be able to resist giving a public performance. He pees his pants every time he sees a camera, so his head'll shut down, and he'll make a big splash on TV. That'll blow any chance for a sanity hearing, and the Greenleaf girl will be tried for first-degree murder. Burpee might get demoted or even kicked off the force, but that won't do *us* much good." He paused. "Now, you did *not* hear this from me—have we got that straight? Get to that girl's lawyer and tell him that you heard this from 'a reliable source.' If Rankin's as sharp as he's supposed to be, he'll know how to shortstop Burpee. Our main goal right now is to keep that son of a bitch off the witness stand."

The girls weren't *too* happy when we got home and broke the news to them. Sylvia unlimbered the darker side of her vocabulary, but Trish went directly to the telephone.

Sylvia was still bubbling over like a little teapot when Trish came back out to the kitchen. "Cool it, Sylvia," she told our little housemate. "I just got off the phone with Mr. Rankin. He wasn't too happy about this, but now that he knows what's happening, he knows what has to be done."

"You didn't rat Bob out, did you?" Charlie asked her.

"Of course not," Trish said promptly. "Your brother's on our side, so I'm not going to get him in trouble. Mr. Rankin probably knows who our source is, but he didn't make an issue of it."

"What can he possibly do to head Burpee off?" James asked her.

"Given the circumstances and Renata's present condition, Mr. Rankin's almost certain to request a closed hearing—along with a gag order from the presiding judge. That'll cut the ground out from under Lieutenant Belcher's planned public performance."

"What a shame," Erika said. "No Academy Award for poor Burpee this year."

"Mr. Rankin *did* have some good news, though," Trish told us. "He's had a couple of off-the-cuff discussions with the district attorney, and they've more or less agreed that a preliminary hearing's in order. The DA didn't *like* the idea, but Mr. Rankin could tie the case up for years if he refuses. The way things stand, just about everything hinges on which judge presides over that hearing. If we're lucky, we'll get the right judge. There are a couple that we really *don't* want sitting on the bench."

"It all boils down to luck of the draw then, doesn't it?" Charlie suggested.

"What a clever way to put it, Charlie," Trish replied sardonically.

"Have they come up with a date for the preliminary hearing yet?" I asked her.

"That's up to the judge," she replied. "The court dockets are pretty full right now. It could all come down to a plea bargain on some other case that'll free up one of the judges. Everything's still up in the air."

The next morning I went to Padelford and arranged to take incompletes on my two seminars. Evidently Dr. Conrad had put in a good word for me, so I didn't have any problems—at least not *administrative* problems. Now that my academic career was on hold, I didn't have anything to do—except to sit around and worry.

Trish went to work at the law office on Thursday of that week. She'd never really explained what was involved in her part-time job. I guess that a law clerk spends a lot of time wading through law books looking for precedents and such.

She was all fired up when she came home, though. "We got a break today," she announced at the supper table that evening. "I couldn't swear to it, but I think Mr. Rankin called in some favors. The presiding judge in Renata's case is going to be Alice Compson. She's tough but fair, and she absolutely *hates* having reporters cluttering up her courtroom. Almost all of her hearings are closed to the public—*and* to the news media. The reporters scream bloody murder about that, but she makes them wait until the transcripts are available— sometime a week or so after the fact."

"That's a leisurely approach to the 'late-breaking-news' business, isn't it?" James noted with a faint smile.

"Judge Compson's a throwback to a more leisurely time," Trish said. "She refuses to be hurried, and she's militantly in- different to the needs of the news media. A lot of reporters have wound up in jail for crossing her."

"I like her already," Charlie said, grinning broadly.

"It gets better," Trish told him. "Mr. Rankin told me today that the prosecutor in the early stages will be a Mr. Roger Fielding. He's a new man in the district attorney's office, and probably still wet behind the ears. I'd even bet *he's* the one who swallowed Lieutenant Belcher's cock-and-bull story." She paused then. "By the way," she continued, "don't make any plans for Saturday. Mr. Rankin would like to meet with all of us on Saturday morning. He'll probably be calling most of us as witnesses during the preliminary hearing, and he'll definitely need our testimony if this goes into a sanity hearing. Lawyers hate surprises in open court, so Mr. Rankin wants to get to know us before the hearing."

"Is there any word yet on when the hearing's going to be?" Sylvia asked.

"Not yet," Trish replied. "That's up to Judge Compson, and she's not going to let anybody push her."

It was raining on Saturday morning, but there was nothing unusual about that. If rain bothers you, stay away from Puget Sound.

Since James had the largest vehicle at the boardinghouse, he drove us on downtown in his station wagon. Since Trish worked at the law firm, she had a pass that got us into the parking garage in the basement of the towering office building in the business district. Then we took the elevator to the sixteenth floor. The whole place had an air of subdued luxury about it—deep-pile carpeting, rich hardwood paneling, and broad windows overlooking Elliott Bay.

"Classy," Charlie observed.

"Just a comfortable little place we like to call home," Trish replied. She led us through the silent main office to a large conference room on the west side of the building, where she tapped lightly on the door.

"Come," a rich voice replied, and we all followed Trish into the room.

Mr. Rankin rose to greet us. He was one of those disgustingly handsome older gentlemen with snowy white hair and a robust tan. I judged that he spent quite a few hours under a sunlamp to maintain that. He was casually dressed and seemed fairly relaxed. "Why don't you introduce me to your friends, Patricia?" he suggested. "Then we can get down to business."

Trish went down the line, giving her boss our names and our major fields of study.

"Interesting combination," Mr. Rankin observed. "Now, then, let's get down to cases. As Patricia's probably told you, our main goal during the preliminary hearing will be to steer Judge Compson in the direction of a sanity hearing. Miss Greenleaf's history lends itself to that outcome, but naturally Mr. Fielding will attempt to thwart our efforts. The media, and in all probability the public as well, would prefer a lurid criminal trial that can be simplified into headlines consisting largely of one-syllable words. We'll want to complicate it. The way things currently stand, a criminal case would be open-and-shut, and it wouldn't take much more than a day or two. I'll probably be calling all of you as witnesses, and I'd like to hear each one of you speak. Try to relax. Speak in a normal tone of voice, and don't rush, no matter how much Fielding tries to push you."

Rankin had one of those rich, oratorical voices that made him sound like a member of the U.S. Senate. He could probably have made a weather report sound like earthshaking news.

"Mr. Forester," he said then, turning to James, "When did you first meet Miss Greenleaf?"

James pondered that. "If I remember correctly, she came to dinner at the boardinghouse one evening in late September or early October last fall. Mark had mentioned her background and her mental problems, so we didn't really know what to expect. She charmed us all into a corner, though, and entertained us with stories about the private sanitarium—she called it the nuthouse—where she'd spent a fair stretch of time following her sister's murder."

Rankin was staring at James with an awed look on his face. "You have a magnificent voice, Mr. Forester," he said. "I've *got* to get you on the witness stand. You sound almost like the voice of God."

James smiled. "That might depend on your definition of God, Mr. Rankin. We could talk about that if you'd like, but I'm not sure the witness stand would be the best place for such a discussion. The limitations of 'the truth, the whole truth, and nothing but the truth' could interfere with theological speculation, don't you think?"

"I could listen to this man talk all day," Rankin told the rest of us with a broad smile.

"Keep him clear of Hegel, though," Charlie suggested. "Kant's OK, but Kierkegaard and Hegel make my teeth hurt."

"Patricia tells me that you're a scientist, Mr. West," Rankin said.

"I don't know if I'd go quite *that* far, Mr. Rankin," Charlie replied. "I'm an engineer. I make stuff. A scientist works with theories; engineers work with nuts and bolts. Science guys are usually covered with chalk dust, but we've got grease and metal filings on our clothes. We get paid better than they do, though."

"And when did *you* first meet Miss Greenleaf?"

"That same evening James did. Mark brought her to dinner. She was auditing a class he was teaching, and she did a paper—'How I Spent My Summer Vacation.' *That's* what got our gang interested in her. Mark's still got copies, so he can give you one. Keep a tight grip on something when you read it, though. Reality starts to slide away about halfway through *that* puppy."

"You have very colorful speech, Mr. West," Rankin observed.

"I'm a working slob," Charlie replied with a shrug. "I was perfectly happy with a weekly paycheck and enough spare time to mess around rebuilding cars. I do read a lot, though."

Rankin nodded. Then he looked at Erika. "Your turn, Miss Erdlund," he told her. "Patricia tells me you're in medical school."

Erika nodded. "Charlie rebuilds cars; I rebuild people—at least that's what I'll be doing when I come out at the far end of med school. I've got a few years to go yet. I met Twinkie on the same evening when the rest of the gang did."

"What's this 'Twinkie' business?" he asked her.

"It's a pet name Mark had for the twins—both of them. I think Renata actually preferred that name after her sister was murdered. Sylvia might not agree, but I think that 'Twinkie' thing kept Regina sort of present in Renata's world. When you get right down to the bottom of it, I think it was Regina's absence that drove Renata crazy. The twins were a unit, and once Regina was gone, Renata was only half there."

"Now *that's* something we might want to pursue," Rankin said. "What do *you* think, Miss Cardinale?"

"I wish Erika would quit poaching in my territory," Sylvia replied.

"What a thing to say," Erika murmured.

"Oh, quit," Sylvia told her. Then she turned back to Rankin. "As usual, Erika's raised something troubling. Her notion that Renata was permanently maimed by her sister's murder suggests that Renata's apparent recovery was a pure sham. She *pretended* to recover so that she could chase down Regina's murderer and kill him. I don't think anybody who doesn't have a twin can ever fully understand the linkage that exists between twins. They share an awareness we can't even begin to comprehend. I'm sure that Trish has told you that I've been working on a case history of Renata for my master's thesis."

Rankin nodded. "It'll probably come up during the preliminary hearing," he told her.

"I was almost sure that it would," Sylvia said. She frowned. "Renata's condition doesn't quite match any of the textbook terms. At first I looked into the possibility of multiple personality disorder, but that didn't fit. The twins were so close that they knew each other completely. Dr. Fallon, her psychiatrist, thinks that fugue might come closer, but I don't believe that matches either. We may have to come up with an entirely new term for Renata's condition—'the Twin Disorder' maybe."

"I can see that I'll be talking some more with you and Dr. Fallon," Rankin mused.

"I think it's your turn in the barrel, Mark," Charlie said.

"Thanks a bunch," I replied sourly.

"Don't mention it."

"You seem reluctant, Mr. Austin," Rankin noted. "I'll grant you that this won't be very pleasant, but your testimony will probably be the key to our whole case."

"I know, but I'm not looking forward to it."

"You *were* present in the church when Renata came in on the night of February tenth, weren't you, Mr. Austin? Your previous statement didn't exactly ring true."

"I sort of made that up," I admitted. "Actually, I followed her into the church after she killed Fergusson." Then I explained how I'd spent that whole night following Twink. "I was one step behind her the whole way," I said regretfully. And then it dawned on me that Rankin had led me to the one part of the story that I *couldn't* tell. I took a deep breath and pushed on. "Father O'Donnell and I could hear her raving on in twin-speak. She was soaking wet and delirious, so we called an ambulance. You know the rest. If I'd had my head on straight, I'd have grabbed that purse of hers before the ambulance got there. She'd be back in Doc Fallon's bughouse by now, and we wouldn't have to go through all this."

"*That* gets right down to the nitty-gritty, doesn't it?" Charlie said admiringly. "You're even sharper than I thought, Mark. Shipping Twinkie back to the nuthouse would have been a perfect solution."

"Yeah, but I dropped the ball."

"You had quite a bit on your mind, Mark," James said.

"It was still a major screwup," I replied.

"Well, I'd like to thank all of you," Rankin said then. "You've given me a lot to work with, and I think the facts in this case are definitely on our side. That covers everything for now, I guess."

We all stood up at that point.

"Could you stay for a moment, Mr. Austin?" Rankin said. "It shouldn't take long."

"We'll wait downstairs, Mark," James told me as they filed out.

"Something else happened in that church, didn't it?" he asked me shrewdly. "You glossed over something just a little too quickly, Mr. Austin."

Rankin was sharp, that's for sure.

"This won't go any further?" I asked him.

"Not if you don't want it to."

"All right. I need to tell somebody about this anyway. When I got to the church, Renata had already gone in. She was hiding in one of those niches where there was a statue. Father O'Donnell and I could hear her, but we couldn't see her. Then a car went past the church, and its headlights lit the inside of the church. Then we saw her—but she wasn't alone. There were *two* people in that alcove. They were identical,

Mr. Rankin. Renata was there, but Regina was as well. Renata was crying, and Regina put her arms around her. Then they seemed to merge, almost as if they were melting together. Then once they had . . . joined, I guess, Renata began to sing, very softly."

Mr. Rankin's eyes were wide, and his face had gone pale under that perfect tan.

"Father O'Donnell says he's reported the *incident* to his bishop, and the bishop ordered him not to talk about it, not even to confirm anything I might tell anybody else. I guess that's standard church policy. It wouldn't make any difference in court anyway, so there's no point in making an issue of it. Renata's gone, Mr. Rankin, and she won't come back. She and Regina are reunited somewhere in her mind. I know the twins pretty well, and I'm absolutely positive that the rest of us don't even exist in their merged awareness. They have each other, and they don't need anybody else. They're complete just the way they are. All of these proceedings are just formalities. The Twinkie Twins are back together, and they won't even be aware of anything that's happening here in our world. Was that what you wanted to know?"

He kept staring at me, and he didn't say anything, so I quietly left the room and took the elevator to the lobby.

CHAPTER TWENTY-FIVE

Trish had advised us that the preliminary hearing was scheduled for 10:00 A.M. on Tuesday, March 3. The media had made quite a big thing out of it, so I was fairly sure that the courtroom would be filled to the rafters with curious onlookers and TV cameras by the dozen.

We all got up early that morning to get dressed and presentable. James and I had a hell of a time persuading Charlie to wear a necktie—partly because the only one he owned was that hideous one Erika had given him for Christmas. I lent him one of mine. Then I had to tie it for him.

We were all pretty tense about the whole thing, so breakfast was a bit sketchy. We *did* drink three pots of Erika's coffee, though.

James had persuaded us that we should all ride into town in his station wagon. "Let's all stick together, children. The media folks are likely to be all over us as soon as we walk out the door."

"He's right," Trish agreed, "and we'd better stick to the standard 'no comment' response."

"Aw," Charlie said, "I was gonna be a star. Don't you think the reporters would be awfully impressed if I answered their questions in German?"

"Just cool it, Charlie," Trish told him. "If we ignore the reporters, maybe they'll give up and go away."

"Fat chance," Erika murmured.

We went out the front door at about a quarter to nine, and

James, scowling and looking ominously bulky, led our little phalanx out to the street. He wasn't carrying a club or anything, but James didn't really need a club to get his point across.

The reporters stepped back to give us room, but several of them *did* throw some shrill questions at us.

Trish fielded the questions with an icy "no comment."

That didn't make the reporters *too* happy, but you can't please everybody, I guess.

Mr. Rankin had given Trish a parking permit, so James drove straight into the parking garage at the courthouse, and we took the elevator up to the fourth floor. A bailiff checked our IDs against a list and passed us on through. That list *really* upset the reporters, and the bailiff's announcement—every four or five minutes—that "This hearing is *not* open to the public—or the press," raised a lot of protest.

The bailiff was wearing a gun, though, so the reporters didn't push him *too* hard.

Mr. Rankin was waiting for us at one of the tables down front. "I don't think I'll be calling on any of you to testify today," he told us, "but Judge Compson might step over some of the more picky procedural details and move directly into a sanity hearing. Fielding wouldn't like that very much, but I want to be ready—just in case. Take your seats in that first row, and listen very carefully. This is basically a hearing where the prosecution's obliged to present its case against Miss Greenleaf."

"She won't actually be here, will she?" I asked him.

"Oh, yes," he replied. "She has to be present to hear the case against her."

"But she won't understand a damn thing," I protested.

"I certainly hope not—and I hope it shows. If she's disturbed enough, Judge Compson *could* declare her to be incompetent to stand trial before the day's out. That'd put an end to this before it goes any further. Don't get your hopes up, though."

*   *   *

Les Greenleaf arrived a few minutes later. Inga wasn't with
him, but Mary was. She wasn't wearing her uniform, but she
still had that cop aura hanging over her. The two of them
joined us in the front row. Then, a moment or so later, a tall
young man carrying a briefcase hurriedly entered.

"That's Fielding," Trish told us quietly.

The prosecuting attorney was followed into the courtroom
by four people: a uniformed cop; Bob West; a nervous-
looking oriental gentleman; and a thick-shouldered fellow
with what appeared to be a permanent case of five o'clock
shadow and bushy black eyebrows.

"That's Burpee," Mary identified the last man.

"It wouldn't be the same without him," Charlie said.

Then a side door behind the judge's bench opened, and a
couple of hospital orderlies—one man and one woman—
quietly led Renata into the courtroom.

That really jolted me. Up until then this had seemed like a
mere charade, with assorted people dancing on strings. With
the appearance of Renata, though, it got real serious in a
hurry.

"All rise," the bailiff called from the front of the courtroom.

We stood, and a woman with iron grey hair wearing a black
judicial robe entered and sat down behind the bench. "You
may be seated," she announced. She waited a moment while
we sat down, then she rapped her gavel. "This hearing is now
in session," she said. "Now then," she continued, "just to be
certain that everyone here understands the rules, this is a
closed hearing, and these proceedings are to be kept strictly
confidential. The court will be *very* unhappy with anybody
who violates the confidentiality of these proceedings." She
looked around sternly. "Am I going too fast for anybody? To
put it in the simplest of terms, keep your mouths shut. If
somebody here tries to turn my courtroom into a three-ring
circus, I'll lean on him—hard. The press can go be free some-

where else, and the public has the right to know only as much as I *choose* to let it know. This is *my* court, and we'll play by *my* rules. Have we all got that straight?"

"Wow!" Charlie whispered.

"She's not kidding," Mary quietly told us. "She's one tough cookie, and you *definitely* don't want to cross her."

"The prosecution and the defense will approach the bench," Judge Compson said then.

Mr. Rankin and the nervous young prosecutor went up to Judge Compson's bench, and the three of them held a brief conference. Then Rankin and Fielding returned to their seats.

"Call your first witness, Mr. Fielding," the judge instructed.

"The prosecution calls Officer Paul Murray," Fielding responded.

The uniformed cop rose and went to the front of the court-room. One of the bailiffs swore him in and he sat down in the witness chair beside the judge's bench.

"You were the officer who discovered the body of a Mr. Walter Fergusson on the night of February tenth?" Fielding asked him.

"Yes, sir. It was after midnight—1:13, to be exact. Because of the series of homicides in park areas during the past six months, we've been instructed to patrol the parks regularly. My partner and I were cruising along Green Lake Way, and we heard some noise coming from down by the lakeshore. It was very foggy that night, so my partner radioed for backup. We made a cursory search, and several other officers soon joined us. Then I discovered Mr. Fergusson's body, perhaps ten feet from the water's edge. I determined that he *was*, in fact, deceased. The other officers joined me, and we secured the scene. Then my partner went back to the car and radioed for the detectives."

"Could you describe the condition of Mr. Fergusson's body for us, Officer Murray?" Fielding asked.

"There were multiple stab wounds, Mr. Fielding, but they

weren't actually stabs. They were more like long cuts. An ordinary stab wound goes straight in. The wounds on the deceased's body were long and fairly shallow. I'm no medical expert, but I'd say that Mr. Fergusson bled to death."

"Have you been involved in the investigation of any of the other murders with a similar MO in the past several months?"

"Yes, sir, a couple of them. The wounds on this most recent body were consistent with those on previous ones—except that there were more of them. The killer even went so far this time as to remove the victim's shoes and slice the soles of his feet."

Fielding winced. "Ah—no further questions, Your Honor," he said.

"Your witness, Mr. Rankin," Judge Compson announced.

Rankin rose to his feet. "Could you describe the noise you heard that prompted you and your partner to investigate, Officer Murray?"

"It was peculiar, Mr. Rankin," Murray replied. "It was hard to hear very precisely, but it sounded like a cross between moaning and singing. And something had the animals over in the Woodland Park Zoo all stirred up, and the wolves were all howling—as if they were singing along with whoever was making that noise down by the lake."

"No further questions, Your Honor," Rankin said.

"Call your next witness, Mr. Fielding," Judge Compson said after the uniformed Murray had been dismissed.

"The prosecution calls Sergeant Robert West," Fielding said.

Bob West was wearing a dark suit, and his face was pretty bleak. It was obvious to those of us who knew him that he wasn't happy about this. He was sworn in, and he sat down in the witness chair.

"You are Sergeant Robert West of the Seattle Police Department?" Fielding asked.

"Yes, sir."

"And you are a detective currently assigned to the north precinct?"

"Yes, sir."

"And how long have you been on the force, Sergeant West?"

"It's going on twelve years now, Mr. Fielding."

"And you have been involved in the investigation of the series of murders which have taken place in various parks in north Seattle—and others as well, but beyond the immediate jurisdiction of your precinct?"

"Yes, sir."

"Would you characterize these murders as ordinary, gang-related stabbings?"

"They were anything *but* ordinary, Mr. Fielding."

"Would you please elaborate, Sergeant West?"

"An ordinary stabbing is usually not very well thought out in advance," Bob told him. "In many cases, it's a spur-of-the-moment act, and its main intent is to kill the victim quickly and with a minimum of noise. The Slasher killings were obviously intended to take much, much longer than a simple stab and run. The weapon was not really very efficient."

"Pardon me a moment, Sergeant West," Fielding said. He went to a table just in front of the desk and picked up a linoleum knife. He held it up so that Bob could see it. "Was this the murder weapon you just described?"

"If the tag attached to the handle has my name on it, it is."

"If it please the court, the prosecution will designate this implement as 'Exhibit A,' " Fielding said to Judge Compson.

"So ordered," the judge replied.

"This would not seem to be a very effective weapon, Sergeant West," Fielding suggested.

"That would depend on the killer's intent, Mr. Fielding. If the killer wanted quick and quiet, that wouldn't have served his—or her—purpose. But it would seem that 'quick' was the *last* thing the killer wanted. The intent was quite obviously to make the killing last for a long time. The killer's primary objective seems to have been to inflict as much pain as possible on the victim. The killer had come up with an unusual means to ensure quiet."

"And could you elaborate on that, Sergeant West?"

"We were at a loss to explain how the Slasher could slice somebody repeatedly without so much as a squeak coming from the victim. It wasn't until the December seventeenth murder that we got the answer. That was the killing that took place on the military reservation in Discovery Park. The victim was one Thomas Walton, a sailor in the United States Navy. The Navy doctors refused to release the body to the King County coroner, and they performed the autopsy themselves. They tested Walton's body for a lot of chemicals—most of them narcotics, they told us—but one of their tests revealed the presence of something decidedly unusual in Walton's bloodstream."

"And what was that, Sergeant West?"

"Curare, Mr. Fielding."

"And what exactly *is* curare?"

"I'm no chemist, Mr. Fielding. As I understand it, though, some Indian tribes in the Amazon smear it on their arrows to paralyze game animals. It has the same effect on humans, I understand. *That* was what kept the victims quiet—the killer drove a hypodermic needle into their throats for a quick dose of curare before the cutting started."

"Wouldn't curare be quite rare in this part of the world?"

"No. Doctors use it when a patient is having a seizure—or so the coroner tells us. I understand that it's available in any well-stocked pharmacy."

Fielding went back to the exhibit table and picked up a hypodermic needle with a small yellow tag tied to it. "The tag on this syringe has your name on it, Sergeant West, and it's dated February tenth. Would you tell the court who found it, and where, and what the significance is?"

"That was found in Miss Renata Greenleaf's purse by the

staff of the University of Washington Medical Center after she'd been brought to the emergency room by ambulance. The linoleum knife was in there as well, along with a couple of sets of rosary beads."

"And the syringe was tested for any chemical residue?"

"Yes, sir."

"And what chemical, if any, was found in that residue?"

"Curare, Mr. Fielding."

"If it please the court, the prosecution will designate this syringe as 'Exhibit B,' " Fielding said to Judge Compson.

"So ordered."

Fielding turned back to Bob. "Were any further tests performed on Exhibits A and B, Sergeant West?"

"Yes, sir. They were tested for blood residue."

"And what were the findings?"

"The lab confirmed that the blood on the knife was Mr. Fergusson's. There wasn't enough blood on the hypodermic to do a DNA test, but the blood type *did* match Fergusson's."

"Does this evidence confirm the probability that Miss Renata Greenleaf should be considered the prime suspect in the murder of Mr. Walter Fergusson, and of a number of other murders as well?"

"The MO is consistent. Curare and a linoleum knife appear to have played a part in many recent murders."

"And was there in your opinion sufficient probable cause to place Miss Greenleaf under arrest?"

"There's no question about that, Mr. Fielding."

"And did you arrest her?"

"No, I did not."

Fielding lost it right there. "You *didn't*? Why not, for God's sake?"

Judge Compson rapped her gavel. "That's enough of that, Mr. Fielding," she told him firmly.

"I'm sorry, Your Honor," Fielding apologized, then turned back to the witness. "Would you please explain to the court why you chose not to place Miss Greenleaf under arrest, Sergeant West?"

Bob pointed his finger at Renata. "That's why, Mr. Fielding. Step over a little closer and listen to her. I had probable cause, right enough, but she was delirious. When we arrest somebody, we're required to read them their rights—*and* we have to be certain that they *understand* those rights. I placed her in protective custody instead of arresting her because she didn't even seem to realize that I was there. If I understand the law correctly, protective custody is as far as we can go at this point. We can't arrest her in her present condition. I checked with her doctor, and he told me that she wouldn't understand anything I said to her."

"What if this is just some clever ruse, Sergeant West?" Fielding demanded, sounding desperate.

"We aren't allowed to use 'what-if' when we make an arrest, Mr. Fielding," Bob told him. "We have to be sure."

"The witness is correct, Mr. Fielding," Judge Compson told him, "and Sergeant West stayed within the strict limits of the law in a difficult situation."

Fielding got her point. He didn't *like* it, but he was smart enough not to make an issue of it. "And is Miss Greenleaf currently being held in custody at any recognized facility?" he asked lamely.

"Yes, sir," Bob replied. "She's confined in the psychiatric ward at the University of Washington Medical Center, and there's a police officer stationed at her door at all times. She's physically present in this courtroom right now, but I don't think she's aware of it."

"No further questions, Your Honor," Fielding said, sounding somewhat deflated.

"Your witness, Mr. Rankin," the judge said then.

"No questions, Your Honor," he replied.

"Wise decision, Mr. Rankin," she said almost absently.

Renata continued to whisper to herself in twin, and Judge Compson looked troubled as she listened to those sibilant whispers. Finally, she shook her head slightly. "You may step down, Sergeant West," she said softly.

Charlie gave his brother a quick, triumphant thumbs-up gesture as Bob returned to his seat. Bob shrugged and sat down. He obviously wasn't very happy.

"Call your next witness, Mr. Fielding," Judge Compson said quietly.

"The prosecution calls Dr. Hiroshi Yamada," Fielding announced.

The nervous doctor hurried to the front of the courtroom to be sworn in.

"You are Dr. Hiroshi Yamada?" Fielding asked.

"Yes, Mr. Prosecutor," Yamada replied.

"And you have served as a forensic pathologist on the King County Coroner's staff for the past eight years?"

"Yes, Mr. Prosecutor."

"And you performed an autopsy on the body of a Mr. Walter Fergusson on the twelfth of February of this year?"

"Yes, Mr. Prosecutor."

"And what were your findings?"

"Mr. Fergusson was a male Caucasian of early middle age. The cause of death was the loss of blood caused by multiple knife wounds inflicted upon his body—mainly on the upper torso—some fifty hours prior to the autopsy. Chemical analysis revealed the presence of curare in his bloodstream, as well as traces of cocaine. His blood alcohol level was point oh-five."

"Could you tell the court how many knife wounds had been inflicted upon the body of the deceased?"

Yamada checked some papers on a clipboard he'd carried to the stand. "Ah—eighty-three, as closely as we were able to determine, Mr. Prosecutor. Many of the wounds were in the same general vicinity, and it was difficult to be precise. The groin area was particularly mutilated."

"Can you confirm that samples from the knife found in the

possession of the defendant were indeed the blood of the deceased?"

"Yes, Mr. Prosecutor. The DNA match was well over ninety percent. There was some minor contamination by other DNA. The implement carried some residue from previous uses."

"Could you estimate how long it took the deceased to die from blood loss after the initial assault."

"I couldn't be precise, Mr. Prosecutor. The ambient temperature was well below freezing that night. If the assault had taken place in the summertime, I'd estimate ten to fifteen minutes. It was the last wound inflicted that finally proved fatal. That wound was in the victim's throat, and it severed both carotid arteries."

"Then, in layman's terms, the initial wounds were located in areas highly sensitive to pain, but the killer finished the victim off by cutting his throat from ear to ear."

"Approximately, yes, Mr. Prosecutor."

"No further questions, Your Honor," Fielding said then.

"The court appreciates that, Mr. Fielding." Judge Compson had a slightly squeamish look on her face. "Your witness, Mr. Rankin."

Rankin was leaning back in his chair, listening as Erika whispered to him across the little railing that separated the defense table from the courtroom.

"Are we in there, Mr. Rankin?" Judge Compson asked.

"Sorry, Your Honor," he apologized. Then he rose and approached the witness stand. "Would you please tell the court if you happened to compare Mr. Fergusson's DNA with samples taken from other sources, Dr. Yamada?" he asked.

Yamada threw a quick glance at Erika, and she nodded.

"This goes back just a bit, Mr. Rankin," Yamada said, "but I think it might have some bearing on this case."

"We'll take all the help we can get, Dr. Yamada," Rankin said with a faint smile.

"There's been an investigation under way for the last six or eight years, Mr. Rankin. Identification by DNA matching is a fairly new procedure, but it's turned out to be extremely valuable for pathologists. Over the past several years there have been a number of rapes followed by the murder of the rape victim in the Puget Sound area, and the body fluid samples taken from the victims have been preserved. Testing has indicated that the perpetrator in all those cases was the same individual. Pathologists in every hospital in the region have been advised of this, and we've been instructed to be on the alert for any possible matches. The Snohomish County Coroner advises that the same individual committed a 1995 murder in his jurisdiction. The DNA tests have positively confirmed the fact that Mr. Fergusson was indeed the rapist in the King County incidents, as well as the 1995 murder in Snohomish County." Yamada seemed quite excited.

"Objection, Your Honor!" Fielding protested. "This is irrelevant."

"Overruled, Mr. Fielding," Judge Compson told him. "The court finds Dr. Yamada's testimony *highly* relevant. Please go on, Mr. Rankin."

"And what was the name of the Snohomish County victim, Dr. Yamada?" Rankin asked.

Yamada checked his clipboard. "Ah—Greenleaf, Mr. Rankin. Regina Greenleaf."

Judge Compson called a recess and asked the lawyers to come to her chambers.

Erika was so jubilant that I almost thought we'd have to tie her down. "It worked!" she crowed. "It actually worked! It slid right past that nincompoop prosecutor! I love it!"

"Calm down, Erika," Sylvia told her. "How did you know about all those other rape-murders?"

"Dr. Yamada made a big thing about it in a class I took from him last fall," Erika replied. "He's very excited about DNA identification. He's positive that it's going to replace fingerprints before very long. He used that series of rape-murders as an example, and he just now cracked those cases. He's probably spraining his arm patting himself on the back right now."

Rankin had a triumphant look on his face when he and Fielding returned to the courtroom. Fielding looked anything *but* triumphant.

"All rise," the bailiff said, and Judge Compson returned to the bench with a no-nonsense look on her face. She rapped her gavel and then spoke to the court reporter. "Let the record show that Miss Greenleaf is to remain in protective custody within the confines of the University of Washington Medical Center. She is to be held over for a hearing to determine her competency to stand trial." Then she looked sternly at those of us sitting on both sides of the aisle in her courtroom. "I remind everyone present that there is to be no discussion of this matter with the news media or anyone else not immediately involved in this case. And I *also* remind you that a violation of this order will be seen as contempt of court." She paused. "Do you read me, Lieutenant Belcher?" she demanded in a belligerent tone. "Zip your mouth shut!"

Then she raised her gavel—almost as if it were a club. "Court is adjourned until Tuesday, March tenth at ten A.M." And then she banged her gavel down.

I glanced over at Burpee. He was scowling at the judge like some kid who'd just been sent to his room without any supper.

CHAPTER TWENTY-SIX

The reporters were still clogging the hallway outside the courtroom, but once again James ran interference for us—James had a gift for nonviolent intimidation. The reporters uneasily gave way to let us through to the elevator. One enthusiast, however, shouted a question at Charlie as we waited for the doors to open. Charlie gave him a blank look and replied, *"Nicht verstehen. Haben sie Deutsch?"*

The reporter blinked and backed off.

"Oh, *that* was clever," Erika said admiringly at Charlie.

"If you got it, flaunt it," Charlie replied.

The elevator door opened, and we all entered briskly. James stood in the doorway—ominously—to keep any of the media geeks from joining us.

There weren't any reporters in the parking garage. Either it was a standing rule or Judge Compson had been issuing more orders. We climbed gratefully into the station wagon, and James drove us back to the boardinghouse.

There was a mob scene, complete with TV cameras, waiting for us when we got there, and we treated them to a linguistic circus when we started for the front door. Trish and Erika answered—or declined to answer—the reporters' questions in Swedish; Charlie quoted Schiller's *An die Freude* extensively; Sylvia responded in Italian, probably laced with obscure obscenities; and James delivered an oratorical announcement in Latin.

I felt obligated to uphold the honor of the English department, so I recited the opening stanza of *Beowulf*—in West Saxon. All right, I was showing off. Everybody else was doing it; why should they have all the fun?

We managed to maintain our serious expressions until we got inside and closed the door behind us. Then we all started laughing. "Did you *see* their faces?" Charlie howled. "What a blast!"

"What on earth was that language you were using, Mark?" Erika asked me.

"English," I replied innocently.

"It didn't sound much like English to me."

"It's an older variation," I told her.

"How much older?"

"Oh, thirteen hundred years—or so."

"Far out," she murmured.

"Hey," Charlie said then, "I'd say our side won today, huh? We got that sanity hearing Rankin wanted."

"Let's hold off on the victory celebration, Charlie," Trish told him. "I think we're staring right down the bore of permanent institutionalization for Renata. About the best we can hope for is a private mental institution. Fielding will probably try to hold out for a state-operated institution for the criminally insane—a penitentiary with padded cells."

That took a lot of the fun out of our day.

The media geeks were *really* up in arms about Judge Compson's closed courtroom and her gag order. Channel surfing through the length and breadth of the assorted TV stations produced whole bunches of tediously pious recitations of the first amendment.

The boardinghouse gang continued the foreign language ploy. *One* station hired translators, but the fellow who converted Sylvia's remarks into English almost got the station in trouble with the FCC—Sylvia's choice of terms turned out to be *very* colorful. After that, they finally gave up and left us alone.

I was reading Faulkner on Saturday morning, and about ten o'clock, Trish yelled up the stairs that I had a phone call. I laid my book aside and hustled down to the living room.

"Mark?" It was Father O'Donnell. "If you're not too busy, could you come by the church sometime today?"

"Sure," I said. "What's up?"

"I've got a bit of good news for you."

"God knows I could use some," I replied.

"Yes, He probably does."

"Sorry, Father—that slipped out. I'll come over right now."

Father O was waiting for me near the altar, and he led the way back to his office—as if I couldn't find it on my own by now. He closed the door and we both sat down. "As I understand it, the judge who's presiding over Renata's case is conducting a sanity hearing," he said.

"How did you find out about that?" I was a little surprised.

"I have me sources, dontcha know?" he said with a slyly exaggerated brogue. "What's going to be the probable outcome of this sanity hearing?"

"It's hard to say, Father," I replied. "Renata isn't really in there anymore, but that happened after Regina's murder too, and she came out of it that time. The judge *might* order her to be held indefinitely in some mental institution. Then if she ever manages to recover enough to be able to speak a language people can understand, she could be yanked out of the asylum and tried for murder—several murders, actually."

He frowned. "Wouldn't that just postpone the case indefinitely?"

"Trish tells us that it's happened a few times before. There's one guy in the funny farm over at Medical Lake who's been in 'temporary custody' for almost twenty years now."

"That wouldn't do at all," he said. "We need a permanent decision that'll put her beyond the reach of the courts."

"Sure, except that she could very well wind up in an institution for the criminally insane, and she doesn't really deserve something like that."

"There *is* an alternative," he told me. "I was able to persuade the bishop that he owed me a favor. I promised him that I wouldn't mention what you and I saw in the church that night, and he was kind enough to have a word with the mother superior of a cloistered order of nuns that very few people know about."

"Oh?"

"They're called The Sisters of Hope—though there's not really much hope for the women in their care. For the most part, the sisters provide shelter and care for elderly nuns who've crossed the line into senility. They also care for ladies of our faith who *aren't* nuns, but have a certain social standing."

"Money, you mean?"

"That *does* enter into the arrangements, I'm told. I'm certain that if Renata's father just happened to make a sizable contribution to the order, the mother superior would look favorably upon an application for admittance for Renata."

"Let's see if I've got this straight," I said. "You blackmailed the bishop; he bullied the mother superior; and now Les Greenleaf has to pay a bribe. Is that more or less the way it goes?"

He winced. "That's an awkward way to put it, Mark," he chided me. "Accurate, perhaps, but a trifle blunt. The advantage is that Renata will be well cared for in a safe environment. That will be far, far better for her than being committed to any secular institution."

"Anything's probably better than a state-run asylum," I agreed.

"There *is* one slight problem, though. The bishop *did* tell the mother superior that Renata is a celebrity of sorts."

"Celebrity?"

"You know what I mean. The mother superior isn't happy about that. There *are* some patients at the convent who are members of fairly prominent families. If some nosey reporter starts snooping around, names might start appearing in public."

"I get your point, Father."

"Even the existence of the order is strictly confidential, but the location of the cloister is what you might call 'top secret.' The notoriety of Renata's case truly concerns the mother superior. She does *not* want a horde of reporters and television cameras on her doorstep."

"I can understand that, Father, but we'll have to float this past Judge Compson before we get into the business of sneaking this past the reporters."

"That might not be as big a problem as all that, Mark. There happen to be some fairly influential fellows in city government who might be able to persuade the judge that the cloister's a good idea. Those particular fellows are the ones who say 'how high?' when the bishop says, 'jump.' And the bishop is going to call in some favors owed to him, because this is a special case. We don't do this sort of thing very often, but we've been doing it for a long, long time so we're pretty good at it. Trust me."

"I'll get hold of Les Greenleaf and see what he has to say, Father."

I didn't want to raise any false hopes, so I didn't mention my conversation with Father O'Donnell when I got home.

We were all tense when we got up on Tuesday morning. Judge Compson seemed to be leaning in our direction, but things could still go wrong.

The reporters had obviously given up on us, so there wasn't anybody around when we left to go back to the courthouse for Renata's sanity hearing. And when we got off the elevator on the fourth floor, the hallway was deserted.

"I didn't think she'd go *this* far," Trish said, frowning slightly.

"Who was that, Mama Trish?" Charlie asked her.

"Judge Compson," Trish replied. "Evidently, she's declared the fourth floor off-limits to the media."

"Can she do that? Legally, I mean?"

"Charlie, a judge can take any steps necessary to maintain order in the courtroom, but locking off the corridors *is* pretty unusual. Mr. Rankin can probably clear it up for us. We'll see what he has to say."

The bailiff at the courtroom door checked our names off his list and waved us in. Mr. Rankin was waiting for us at the defense table, and he had Dr. Fallon and Les Greenleaf with him. "Ah," Rankin said, "there you are. We've been waiting for you." Les Greenleaf was sitting off to one side, and he didn't even seem to be listening.

Doc Fallon had a slightly amused expression on his face. "Which one of you came up with the brilliant idea of refusing to speak English to the reporters?"

"Charlie, of course," Sylvia told him. "He's our resident clown."

"We don't have too much time, here," Rankin told us. "Judge Compson's gag order is still in force, so nothing that happens here is going to show up on the evening news. Now that we've moved into a sanity hearing, the ball's in *my* court instead of Fielding's. I'm going to call Dr. Fallon here as my first witness, and I'll be questioning him at some length, so I probably won't be calling any of the rest of you today. Hopefully, we'll finish with his testimony today, but I can't predict how long Fielding's cross-examination will take. Once *he's* finished, I'll start calling you—and Renata's aunt, of course. You should pay close attention to the questions Fielding asks Dr. Fallon, because he'll probably ask each of you similar questions." Then he gave Charlie a stern look. "I'd advise you to answer questions in English, Mr. West. Judge Compson doesn't have a very well developed sense of humor, so I wouldn't clown around in her courtroom, if I were you— *verstehen sie?*"

"Jawohl, mein Herr," Charlie replied, snapping to attention.

Rankin sighed, rolling his eyes upward.

Fielding entered the courtroom then, and he had Bob West and Burpee with him. They took their seats, and a moment later the two white-coated orderlies brought Renata into the courtroom. She was obviously still out of it.

Then the bailiff said, "All rise," and we stood up as Judge Compson entered and took her seat behind the bench.

"You may be seated," she told us.

We all sat back down.

Judge Compson pursed her lips. "The purpose of this hearing is to determine Miss Greenleaf's competence to stand trial. In order to determine this, certain formalities will be relaxed. I may from time to time question some of the witnesses myself. I'm sure that neither the prosecutor nor the defense attorney will have any serious objections if I happen to interrupt them during the proceedings." She looked at Fielding and Rankin with one raised eyebrow that spoke volumes.

"Mr. Fielding and I will be guided by Your Honor in these proceedings," Rankin said rather floridly.

"Nicely put, Mr. Rankin," she said. "You may call your first witness."

"The defense calls Dr. Wallace Fallon," Rankin said.

Doc Fallon rose and went to the witness stand. The bailiff swore him in, and he took his seat.

"If it please the court, may we dispense with an extended examination of Dr. Fallon's professional credentials?" Rankin asked.

"The prosecution has no objection, Your Honor," Fielding stated. "Dr. Fallon's professional standing is well-known."

"Excellent," the judge said. "You may proceed, Mr. Rankin."

"Dr. Fallon," Rankin said then, "are you acquainted with Miss Greenleaf?"

"Yes, Mr. Rankin. She was a patient of mine for quite some

time a few years ago. Her parents placed her in my sanitarium in the early summer of 1995."

"Then she *is*, in fact, Miss Renata Greenleaf?"

"We can't be absolutely certain of that, Mr. Rankin," Fallon replied. "She's either Renata *or* Regina Greenleaf. That much we know. *Which* one she is, isn't clear."

"Could you clarify that, Dr. Fallon?" the judge asked.

"Regina and Renata Greenleaf were identical twins, Your Honor. The footprints customarily taken of infants at the time of birth have been lost, and identical twins have identical DNA. We know that the young lady present in this courtroom is *one* of the Greenleaf twins. It's impossible to say *which* one with any degree of certainty."

"Wasn't she able to identify herself when she entered the sanitarium?" the judge asked him.

"No, Your Honor," Fallon replied. "The trauma of her sister's murder had caused her to regress to early childhood, a fact that was made quite obvious by her inability to speak or to understand English. She answered any and all questions in cryptolalia."

"In which?" Judge Compson asked.

"The term means 'secret language,' Your Honor," he explained. "Virtually every set of twins invents a private language before they learn the language of their parents. In most cases, that private language falls into disuse and fades away by the time the twins are three or four years old. The Greenleaf twins kept theirs intact, however. Their family and friends referred to their private language as 'twin' or 'twinspeak.' The Greenleaf girls were very close, and the surviving twin was evidently regressing in order to escape from the trauma of her sister's murder."

"And how long did that continue, Dr. Fallon?" Rankin asked him.

"About six months," Fallon replied. "Then one morning for no apparent reason, she started speaking English. The first thing she said, though, was 'where is this, and who am I?' She obviously couldn't face or accept what had happened, so as a means of escape, she simply erased all memory of her previous life."

"Amnesia?" Rankin suggested.

"Exactly. Her amnesia was a flight from reality, and made more complicated for those of us trying to treat her by the fact that she was almost certainly thinking in two different languages, and we could only understand one of them. It's obvious that when she lapses into that private language, she's talking with her sister. They appear to have been living in an entirely different world from the rest of us—and *that's* the world where the survivor's gone."

"But her sister's not *in* that world anymore, Dr. Fallon," the judge objected.

"Miss Greenleaf seems to believe that she *is*, Your Honor."

I almost choked on that one. There was no way that Doc Fallon could know about it, but Father O and I had *seen* Renata's sister in the church. We'd heard her speak the language of that separate world to her anguished sister. And then she'd taken Renata in her arms and merged with her, and together they had left the rest of us behind and gone their own way.

Judge Compson ordered a short recess at that point, and when we returned, Mr. Rankin picked up where he'd left off. "Are we to understand then, that Miss Greenleaf had no memory whatsoever of her life prior to her awakening in your sanitarium, Dr. Fallon?"

"*Almost* no memory, Mr. Rankin," Fallon replied. "There was one exception, though. She didn't recognize her parents, but she *did* recognize Mr. Mark Austin, a longtime friend of the Greenleaf family. Mr. Austin had been a key figure in the twins' early childhood, and his presence seemed to give her something to cling to. Her motivation isn't very clear."

"What is your current diagnosis of her condition, Dr. Fallon? Is she paranoid-schizophrenic, manic-depressive, or what?"

"My best guess at the moment is the fugue state, Mr. Rankin," Fallon replied.

"Would you clarify that for us, please?"

"The 'fugue' is an episode of altered consciousness during which the patient wanders off and may do or say things that are very uncharacteristic. When the episode concludes, the patient is frequently agitated and confused. I was not aware of these episodes during Miss Greenleaf's stay at the sanitarium. They were probably taking place, but they were so brief that we didn't realize that they were happening. In her present condition, there's no way that I could verify this, but as I suggested before the recess, I'm convinced that Miss Greenleaf's alternate persona is her twin sister, Regina."

"Objection, Your Honor," Fielding stepped in. "That's pure speculation."

"Overruled, Mr. Fielding," Judge Compson said. "This is not a trial, so we can be more flexible. Please continue, Dr. Fallon."

"Yes, Your Honor. After her recognition of Mr. Austin, Miss Greenleaf's recovery seemed quite rapid, so I began to grant her furloughs to her parents' home. By the late spring of '97, she appeared to have progressed far enough that I decided to upgrade her to outpatient status, and she soon expressed an interest in attending the University of Washington." He leaned back in the witness chair, squinting reflectively at the ceiling. "Given what's been happening recently, I can't be entirely positive which of her identities was making decisions at that point. It may have been Renata's normal persona, or it could very well have been her fugue-state identity. If it *was*, in fact, the Regina side of her, she fooled me completely. I thought that permitting her to stay with her aunt and audit classes would aid her recovery, and she and I had regular weekly sessions so I could evaluate her progress. As luck had it, Mr. Austin moved into a nearby boardinghouse, and one of the other boarders there was Miss Sylvia Cardinale, a graduate student in psychology. After Renata and

Miss Cardinale became acquainted, Miss Cardinale undertook a case history on Miss Greenleaf."

Judge Compson glanced up at the clock. "Would this be a
good place to break, Mr. Rankin?" she asked. "We're getting
close to lunchtime."

"I was about to suggest that myself, Your Honor," Rankin
replied. "Dr. Fallon and I can pick up after lunch."

"How much longer do you estimate that Dr. Fallon's testimony will take?"

"Not much longer, Your Honor. Mr. Fielding should have
most of the afternoon for cross-examination."

"Good," the judge said. "Court's adjourned until one-thirty,
then."

We grabbed a quick lunch in the cafeteria. Trish assured us
that reporters weren't permitted to pester people while they
were eating, so we waited in the cafeteria after we'd finished.
Les Greenleaf ate with us, but he didn't say very much.

"How are we doing, Trish?" Charlie asked with uncharacteristic seriousness.

"Not bad," she replied. "Mr. Rankin's managed to slip several things in that wouldn't be admissible during a criminal
trial. Judge Compson's cutting him a lot of slack."

"We're winning, then?"

"Let's wait until we hear Fielding's cross-examination before we start celebrating, Charlie," she said.

Judge Compson reconvened the hearing at one-thirty on the
dot, and Rankin picked up where he'd left off. "You mentioned Miss Cardinale's case history, Dr. Fallon. Did I understand you to say that she was tape-recording her interviews
with Miss Greenleaf?"

"Yes, Mr. Rankin. Renata knew the tape recorder was running, but it didn't bother her."

"And all during this period, murders were taking place all
over the Seattle area?"

"So I understand. Mr. Austin made certain connections that the rest of us missed, and I'm sure that he'll go into much greater detail than I can."

"Then to sum up, it's your opinion that Miss Greenleaf has crossed the line into a perpetual fugue state?"

"We can always hope that she might recover someday, but given the circumstances, I'd say that the chances of that are very slight."

"Then her alternate persona—her sister—simulated recovery for one purpose only—to track down Mr. Fergusson and take her vengeance upon him."

"So it would seem."

"And the earlier killings were little more than practice murders to hone up her skills?"

"I don't know if I'd go that far, Mr. Rankin. It's more probable that she was trying to lure potential rapists into attacking her in the hope that sooner or later, the man she was *really* looking for might turn up. The alternate persona was functioning at a very primitive level, especially at first. It was only after several killings that she realized that the license plate number she'd happened to see at the time of Regina's murder was the crucial piece of information. Once she'd made that connection, the random killings stopped, and she went after the one man she'd been seeking since last September. Her revenge is complete now, and she's retreated into a near-infantile state—that period in her life before the horrors of her sister's murder and her psychotic obsession with retribution. There's no way I could verify this—Renata is the only one in the world who understands that private language—but I'm almost positive that she sees her sister. Even as she sits here in this courtroom, she and Regina are talking to each other about things that none of us here could possibly understand."

"Thank you, Dr. Fallon," Rankin said. Then he turned to Judge Compson. "No further questions, Your Honor," he said.

"Your witness, Mr. Fielding," the judge said then.

Fielding was staring at Renata with a troubled expression on his face. "No questions, Your Honor," he replied quietly.

"Very well," the judge said. "Court's adjourned. We'll reconvene tomorrow morning at ten A.M." And she rapped her gavel down.

CHAPTER TWENTY-SEVEN

I didn't sleep very well on Tuesday night, and I don't think anybody else at the boardinghouse did either. Doc Fallon's testimony had definitely gotten Judge Compson's attention, but whether it'd been enough to persuade her that Renata didn't belong in some state-run asylum was still up in the air.

Then too, Mr. Rankin had told us that we'd each be called to testify on Wednesday. The anticipatory stage fright that followed that announcement certainly helped keep us awake. I think we were all grateful when the smell of Erika's coffee came wafting out of the kitchen.

"Mr. Rankin wants us in early this morning," Trish told us at breakfast. "He's made arrangements to use one of the conference rooms in the courthouse. He doesn't like surprises coming up in open court, so he'll go over our testimony with us."

After breakfast we caught a couple of TV news programs and the reporters were still pretty miffed about the news blackout. We got some more sermons on the first amendment and the "public's right to know." For some reason, no reporter ever gets around to mentioning "the right of privacy."

Isn't that odd?

We took off at a quarter after eight, and when we reached the courthouse, Trish led us to the conference room. Mary was already there, and she was still wearing her uniform—probably at Rankin's suggestion. I guess he thought it might not hurt to let Judge Compson know that the *whole* Seattle Police Department wasn't in the same camp with Burpee.

Les Greenleaf was also there, but I think the boss was still pretty much out of it. This whole thing seemed to be almost more than he could handle.

"Now, then," Rankin told us after we'd all filed in, "this is the way we'll proceed: I'll put Mary on the witness stand first. I'll want to establish Miss Greenleaf's periodic breakdowns fairly early. Judge Compson's probably been going over Dr. Fallon's testimony in her mind since yesterday afternoon. Mary's testimony should help to confirm most of what Dr. Fallon said, and to keep the word 'psychosis' out in plain sight. Then I'll call each of you in turn. We'll start with James. Let's use that magnificent voice to our advantage. I'll want you to give Judge Compson an overall background of your housemates, James. Let's establish the fact that this is no ordinary student group—you aren't any run-of-the-mill collection of party animals."

"I can deal with that," James rumbled.

"Good. Then I'll move on to Patricia and establish *her* connection to our law firm. From Patricia, we'll go to Erika and her medical school status—just the term 'med school' makes people sit up and take notice. After Erika, I'll call Charlie. We'll briefly touch on the periodic meetings with Sergeant West. We don't want to get Sergeant West in trouble, but I'll need to show some connection between him and the boardinghouse group. You've had certain information that wasn't available to the general public, and I need to be able to show Judge Compson how you came by it. All right?"

"Just as long as you don't get my big brother all steamed up," Charlie said. "He'll kick my butt if we push it *too* far."

"I'll be careful," Rankin promised him. "From Charlie, we'll move on to Sylvia and her case history." He looked at Sylvia then. "You *did* bring those tapes as I asked, didn't you?"

She patted her oversize purse. "They're right here, Mr. Rankin," she replied.

"Good. We may not need them today, but let's have them handy, just in case. I'll probably be asking you questions in greater detail than your friends, since your case history's fairly crucial."

She smiled faintly. "Thank you," she said.

He inclined his head in an almost courtly bow. This guy had a lot of class.

"Now, then," he continued, "I can't be sure how far Mr. Fielding will go with his cross-examinations, but I'm hoping that we finish up with Sylvia's testimony by the noon recess. That should give me the entire afternoon for Mark's testimony. We want Judge Compson to have the whole thing before she adjourns this afternoon. Loose ends are distracting, so let's give her all she needs today so she can get on with her job." He glanced at his watch. "We'd better get upstairs," he said. "Judge Compson's big on punctuality, so let's not offend her."

When we trooped into the courtroom, Fielding was already there. Bob West wasn't with him, but Burpee was still camped in his back pocket, obviously not the least bit happy about this sanity hearing—and Judge Compson's gag order was driving him right up the wall.

We went through the "all rise" routine, and the judge came in and took her place at the bench. She looked fairly tired. I'm just guessing, but I'd say that Fallon's testimony had bothered her almost as much as it'd bothered me.

"You may call your next witness, Mr. Rankin," she said.

"The defense calls Officer Mary Greenleaf," Rankin said.

Judge Compson's head came up sharply at that.

Mary came forward and took the oath, then she took her seat on the witness stand.

"You are a member of the Seattle Police Department, is that correct, Officer Greenleaf?"

"Yes, sir," Mary replied.

"And you are related to Miss Renata Greenleaf, is that correct?"

"Yes, sir. She's my niece. Her father's my brother."

"After Miss Greenleaf had been released from Dr. Fallon's sanitarium, she came to live with you, is that also correct?"

"Yes, sir. She wanted to attend classes at the university, and I live in the Wallingford district."

"Now then, previous testimony has established the fact that Miss Greenleaf periodically exhibited some peculiar behavior, is that also correct?"

"Definitely, Mr. Rankin. Whenever I mentioned those incidents, I glossed over them by calling them 'bad days,' but they usually went way past 'bad.' I didn't want to start using terms like 'whacko' or 'bonkers' or 'screwball,' so I just said 'bad days' and let it go at that."

"Could you describe these incidents for the court?"

"She'd do a lot of moaning and screaming, and she'd say things that didn't make much sense—things about wolves howling, blood, and cold water. Then she'd stop speaking English and switch over to a language that nobody else could understand."

"And what was your usual response to these incidents?"

"I'd knock her out with a sleeping pill," Mary replied bluntly. "I've been a police officer for quite a few years, Mr. Rankin, and I've had a lot of experience with people who suddenly go into hysterics. We don't let that go on for too long. We don't want the subject to hurt himself—or anybody else—so we just tap him out with a pill."

"Excuse me," Judge Compson interrupted. "Is that strictly legal, Officer Greenleaf?"

"Probably not, Your Honor," Mary admitted, "but when a subject—or a prisoner—goes into hysterics, those of us who are on the scene have to take immediate steps. We don't have time to wait for court orders or any of the other niceties of the legal system. The alternative would be to club the subject into submission, and that seems a little extreme, wouldn't you say?"

"You get right to the point, Officer," Judge Compson observed.

"It saves time, Your Honor, and in these situations we don't usually *have* much time. A pill's a lot kinder than a rap on the head with a club."

"I see your point," the judge conceded. "How long did your niece usually remain comatose after you'd sedated her?"

"Usually until the following morning, Your Honor," Mary replied, "and when she woke up the next day, she'd seem perfectly normal. I'm fairly certain that she'd sleep the clock around after I'd sedated her, but I work the graveyard shift, so I wasn't always around to keep an eye on her."

"You may proceed, Mr. Rankin," the judge said then.

"I believe you ladies have already covered everything, Your Honor. I guess I'm just taking up space here."

"It wouldn't be the same without you, Mr. Rankin," Judge Compson told him sweetly.

"No further questions, Your Honor," he said with a smile.

"Splendid. Your witness, Mr. Fielding."

"No questions, Your Honor," Fielding said. He may have been a bit green, but he knew when to keep his mouth shut.

"The defense calls Mr. James Forester," Rankin said.

James was sworn in and took the seat in the witness stand.

"Are you acquainted with Miss Greenleaf, Mr. Forester?" Rankin asked him.

"We've met, Mr. Rankin. One of the residents at the boardinghouse where I'm staying is Mr. Mark Austin, who probably knows her better than anyone in Seattle—with the exception of her Aunt Mary, of course. Miss Greenleaf was auditing a freshman English course Mr. Austin taught during the autumn quarter, and she wrote a paper for him entitled 'How I Spent My Summer Vacation.' She described life as a patient in a mental institution, and her paper was highly original and in many ways very disturbing. It gave us a thought-provoking glimpse into the world of the mentally disturbed.

"Our housemates are all graduate students in a wide range of disciplines: law school, medical school, advanced psychology, and engineering, as well as Mr. Austin's major field—English—and my home base in philosophy. We're a bit more mature than the underclassmen whose primary interest lies in parties. Miss Greenleaf's paper struck sparks in our minds, and we all agreed that we'd like to meet this strange and gifted child. We asked Mark to invite her to dinner one evening. She agreed, and we found her to be thoroughly engaging. After that, we all followed her progress—particularly when Miss Cardinale, who majors in abnormal psychology, undertook a case history of Miss Greenleaf. We followed that unfortunate young woman's ups and downs, and her recent mental disintegration struck us all as something akin to a death in the family." James paused then. "These proceedings and the evidence that prompted them have elevated our sense of loss to the level of Greek tragedy," he added. "The Renata *we* knew would not have been capable of these murders, but evidently there's another Renata, and she was obviously driven by an overpowering lust for vengeance." He made a wry face then. "That sounds pompous, doesn't it? True, perhaps, but pompous all the same."

"It doesn't bother me all that much, Mr. Forester," Rankin said. "No further questions, Your Honor."

"Your witness, Mr. Fielding," Judge Compson said.

"No questions, Your Honor," Fielding replied.

Burpee glared at him, and he appeared to be right on the verge of an explosion.

"Call your next witness, Mr. Rankin," Judge Compson said, after James had left the stand.

"The defense calls Miss Patricia Erdlund," Rankin said.

Trish took the stand, and Rankin explained her connection

to his law firm to the judge. "In point of fact, Your Honor," he said, "it was largely at Miss Erdlund's urging that I became involved in this case. As Mr. Forester has so eloquently testified, the students who live in the Erdlund boardinghouse are a tight-knit group, and they have an abiding interest in Miss Greenleaf."

"The court recognizes that, Mr. Rankin. Proceed."

Trish verified Renata's impact on our little family, and then she began citing precedents. Lawyers are big on precedents, I guess. I noticed that Judge Compson was taking lots of notes while Trish was testifying.

Fielding had a few questions for Trish, mostly involving her citations. Trish spoke fluent legalese, and she impressed the heck out of both the judge and the prosecutor. She made a lot of points for our side.

Judge Compson ordered a short recess after Trish had stepped down, and when court reconvened, Mr. Rankin called Erika to the stand. Then he pulled a quick shrewdie on her. "Would you please tell the court how many classes you've taken from Dr. Yamada, Miss Erdlund?" he asked her.

"Oops," Erika said mildly.

"Would you like to clarify 'oops,' Miss Erdlund?" he said with a faint smile.

"You caught me with my finger in the cookie jar," she replied. "I *do* know Dr. Yamada quite well, and I *did* suggest that he might want to contact the Snohomish County Coroner's Office for a DNA sample taken from the body of Renata's sister. It was only a suggestion, Mr. Rankin. It wasn't as if I'd planted any false evidence or anything."

"It wasn't an accusation, Miss Erdlund. It was just a loose end that I thought we should tie up. What prompted you to make that suggestion?"

"It seemed logical, Mr. Rankin. The business with that license plate suggested that there was additional evidence available that could prove that Fergusson was indeed the murderer of Regina Greenleaf—and of quite a few others as well. There's a certain perverse charm in the notion of one serial killer murdering another serial killer, don't you think?"

"I don't believe I'd care to comment on that, Miss Erdlund," he replied blandly. "No further questions."

"Your witness, Mr. Fielding," the judge said.

"No questions, Your Honor," he replied.

"The defense calls Mr. Charles West," Rankin said after Erika had left the stand.

Charlie was sworn in and took the stand.

"Would you please tell the court of your relationship to the prosecution witness, Sergeant Robert West?" Rankin asked.

Charlie shrugged. "He's my big brother," he replied.

"And would you describe your relationship as very close?"

"We stay in touch," Charlie said. "He yells at me when I forget to call our mother every so often. He and I get together more often now than we did when I was still living in Enumclaw."

"And why *did* you move to Seattle from Enumclaw, Mr. West?"

"I work for Boeing, and they bullied me into going to graduate school."

"And what is your specialty, Mr. West?"

"I'm not permitted to talk about that. It's classified."

"Where did you and your brother customarily meet, Mr. West?"

"At the Green Lantern Tavern in Wallingford. Bob stops there for a couple of beers after he gets off work. Back in the early days of the Seattle Slasher killings, James, Mark, and I used to meet him there to get the inside dope on those killings. We weren't drooling at the mouth or anything, but there are three ladies at the boardinghouse, and we wanted to know if they were in danger. Serial killers *usually* kill women, not guys, so we were worried. Bob told us to play it safe. We weren't supposed to let them go out alone after dark.

Then he suggested that the girls carry those little cans of pepper spray—just in case. Eventually, we all had pepper spray on our key rings."

"And did he reveal any other information about the killings, Mr. West—things that weren't appearing in the newspapers or on television?"

"I'm *not* going to rat my brother out, Mr. Rankin. Let's say he gave us a couple of warnings and let it go at that, OK?" Charlie's tone was almost belligerent.

"I'll withdraw the question, Mr. West," Rankin said.

I saw Burpee grab Fielding by the arm, and the two of them appeared to be arguing about something. Burpee seemed agitated, and Fielding was having trouble keeping him calmed down. It was fairly obvious that Burpee was ready to go off the deep end, and Fielding's frequent "no questions" response was driving him wild.

It was about eleven-thirty when Charlie left the stand, and Judge Compson, Rankin, and Fielding had a brief conference at the bench—probably about when we should recess for lunch. Rankin really wanted to get Sylvia's testimony in before the noon break, and it appeared that he'd persuaded Judge Compson that he'd cover everything before noon. I thought he might be rushing things, but he appeared to know what he was doing, so I kept my mouth shut.

He returned to the table, and then he said, "The defense calls Miss Sylvia Cardinale," he announced.

Sylvia was sworn in and took the stand, and Rankin established her identity and residence.

"You are a graduate student in psychology at the University of Washington, is that correct?"

"Yes."

"And your field of interest is abnormal psychology?"

"That's right."

"And you are acquainted with Miss Renata Greenleaf and

have undertaken a case history of her mental problems as a possible subject for your master's thesis?"

"Yes."

"Would you please tell the court what prompted you to undertake this project?"

"It was the paper she wrote for Mr. Austin's class," Sylvia told him. "Mr. Forester described that paper during his testimony. It was of particular interest to me, since it gave me a glimpse into the perceptions of a patient at a mental institution. Miss Greenleaf struck me as a highly intelligent and articulate young woman who could provide insights that could be useful for those of us in the field. Many patients have a severely limited ability to communicate with a therapist, which makes it difficult to help them. It occurred to me that Renata could open doors in ways an ordinary patient could not begin to do. Moreover, her disturbed state originated in a trauma rather than a preexistent psychosis. It occurred to me that a case history growing out of an extensive personal relationship might suggest alternatives to standard therapy." Sylvia threw a quick, sly glance in my direction. "I had a little trouble persuading Mr. Austin—he tends to be protective when it comes to Renata. Our discussions were quite lively, as I recall. Eventually, though, he came to realize that my case history was *not* some experiment on a laboratory animal, so he introduced me to Dr. Fallon. The doctor had some reservations until I advised him that my case history would be based on tape recordings."

"You recorded every conversation you had with Miss Greenleaf?" Rankin asked her.

"I missed a few of the earlier ones," Sylvia admitted. "At first I was simply taking notes, but as soon as Renata saw my notebook, she'd launch into wild stories that had no connection to the truth. Once I switched to recordings, though, Renata relaxed and talked freely."

"And you were able to record her periodic lapses into raw psychosis?" Rankin asked her.

"Oh, yes," Sylvia replied, "and those tapes still give me nightmares. Dr. Fallon has explained the fugue state in clinical terms, but those tapes are raw fugue, and they're terrifying. At first, we had no idea of what was causing them, but we do now. Mark will explain what was happening, since he was the one who ultimately tracked it down."

"Do you have any of those fugue tapes with you, Miss Cardinale?" Rankin asked then.

"Yes, Mr. Rankin, I do."

"Is it your intention to play the tapes in open court, Mr. Rankin?" Judge Compson asked.

"There are two dozen tapes, Your Honor," he replied, "and they cover something in excess of sixty hours. We can play them for Your Honor if you wish, but . . ." He left it hanging.

"I see your point, Mr. Rankin," she agreed. "I *do* want copies, but it wouldn't serve any purpose to use this courtroom as an auditorium. Have you any further questions for Miss Cardinale?"

Rankin glanced at his yellow legal pad. "Ah—no, Your Honor," he replied. "I think we've just about covered everything."

"Good. Court stands adjourned until one-thirty this afternoon."

When we hit the cafeteria for lunch, I was more than a little edgy, since it was obvious that Mr. Rankin planned to hang most of his case on my testimony. As Charlie put it, "The bases are loaded, Mark, and it's your turn at bat. Knock it out of the park."

"I don't suppose he'd settle for a foul tip?" I said sourly.

"That wouldn't hardly cut it, partner. We need a home run to win the series."

"Quit, Charlie," Trish scolded. "Mark, just relax and answer Mr. Rankin's questions. He knows the story, so let him guide you. That's what he's getting paid for."

Somehow that didn't make me feel much better.

*   *   *

We went back to the courtroom at about one-fifteen, and Judge Compson resumed her seat on the bench at one-thirty on the dot. Sylvia returned to the witness chair, but Fielding didn't have any questions for her. His continual "No questions, Your Honor," had me worried—a prosecutor who just gives up on a case like this wouldn't keep his job for very long. I was fairly certain that he had *something* up his sleeve.

"Call your next witness, Mr. Rankin," the judge said.

"The defense calls Mr. Mark Austin," Rankin announced.

"Here we go," I muttered. I went up to the front of the courtroom, and the bailiff swore me in. Then I sat down in the witness chair.

"You are Mr. Mark Austin, is that correct?"

"Yes, sir."

"And how long have you known Miss Renata Greenleaf?"

"Since she was born. Our families were very close."

"And how old were you when the Greenleaf twins were born?"

"I was seven when they came along. My folks and I spent quite a bit of our free time with the Greenleaf family, and I became a sort of surrogate big brother to the twins. They used to amuse themselves by switching personalities."

"Would you clarify that for us, Mr. Austin?"

"When people use the term 'identical twins,' they usually mean 'pretty close'—one twin may be a quarter of an inch taller than the other, or have slightly larger ears. Those minor variations make it possible to tell them apart. Regina and Renata were so identical that not even their mother could say with any certainty which was which. She tried to use different-colored hair ribbons to tell them apart, but as soon as her back was turned, the twins would swap ribbons—just for fun. Their parents—and mine—thought that their little game was funny, but I thought it was silly. Not that they cared what I thought—as far as they were concerned, I was just Mr.

Fix-it. When they broke anything, they expected me to put it back together."

"And did you find that offensive, Mr. Austin?"

"No. They were the baby sisters, and I was the big brother. Fixing things was part of my job, I guess."

"And what happened in the spring of 1995, Mr. Austin?"

"The twins had grown up to be moderately gorgeous, and the boys at their high school became very interested in them. Nobody could ever pry them apart, though, so they managed to avoid the usual improprieties. In the spring of '95, the twins were seniors in high school, and their class had a kegger party on a beach near Mukilteo. By midnight, things were getting rowdy, so the twins got into their car to drive back to Everett. They took the usual shortcut through Forest Park, but they had a flat tire near the petting zoo. At least, that's where they found the car later. The next morning, the park employees found the two girls. One of them had been raped and murdered, and the other one was babbling incoherently. Nobody was ever able to prove which twin was which—we still don't know for certain."

"And what happened to the surviving twin?" Rankin pressed.

"She was completely out of it, so her parents put her in Dr. Fallon's private sanitarium at Lake Stevens."

"Let's go back a bit, Mr. Austin," Rankin said. "Where were you living and how were you occupied at that time?"

"I was in the graduate school at the University of Washington, but I was still living at home with my parents, commuting to school. Then in August of that same year, my parents were killed in an automobile accident, so I dropped out of school for the fall quarter."

"Then you were living in Everett when Miss Greenleaf came to her senses?"

"I was there when she started speaking English again, if that's what you mean." I looked over at Renata, who was still whispering to herself. "That was in November of '95. Up until then, she'd been talking to herself in 'twin,' the same as she's doing now. When she finally came out of it, she didn't know who she was. Dr. Fallon covered all that yesterday."

"She remembered *you*, though, didn't she, Mr. Austin?"

"Yes, and nobody could be sure why. This is just a hunch, but I think she recognized me because she still thought of me as 'Mr. Fix-it.' She knew she needed help, and I got elected. Whatever the reason, Dr. Fallon latched on to it—and me—and I spent a lot of time with Renata after that. When I got off work I'd go spend the evenings with her. That went on all through 1996, and she wasn't officially released until the late spring of '97. *That's* when the notion of attending the University of Washington showed up. Fallon didn't think she was quite ready for the stress, but Renata seemed excited about it. Of course none of us knew that she'd committed Fergusson's license plate number to memory. It was a King County plate, and that means Seattle to just about everybody in western Washington. I couldn't prove this, but it's my guess that Renata jumped on the idea of moving in with her aunt so that she could get closer to Regina's killer. Fergusson was her main target right from the beginning."

"Objection, Your Honor," Fielding protested. "That's pure speculation."

"Overruled," Judge Compson replied. "This is a sanity hearing, Mr. Fielding, not a trial. We can relax a few rules if it'll help us get to the truth. Go on, Mr. Austin."

"Yes, Your Honor," I replied. "I moved into the boarding-house last fall, so I was close enough to keep a close eye on Renata. Our goal was to ease her back into the world of normies, and since I was teaching a section of freshman English, I suggested that she should audit *my* class. That'd minimize stress, put a familiar face in front of her, and let me watch her for any peculiar behavior. Since she was only auditing, all she had to do was sit there and listen, but she wrote papers when my assignments caught her interest. She could write circles around just about anybody who came along. If I'd had my head on straight, I'd have known that something was seriously wrong with her when I read her first paper—the one James described. After the boardinghouse gang heard that one, they *really* wanted to meet her. She came to dinner and charmed everybody's socks off. That's what eventually led to Sylvia's case history and all those tapes."

"Approximately when was it that you introduced Miss Greenleaf to your friends, Mr. Austin?" Rankin asked.

I looked over at Trish. "About the end of September, wasn't it?" I asked her.

She nodded.

"Please don't do that, Mr. Austin," Judge Compson scolded me.

"Sorry, Your Honor. I just wanted to be sure I had it straight, is all. Anyway, it *was* after the second Seattle Slasher killing. The killings were cropping up every couple of weeks, and whenever some guy got cut to pieces, Renata would have one of those 'bad days' Mary mentioned this morning. None of us at the boardinghouse made the connection because the whole town was convinced that the Slasher was a guy. It wasn't until after Christmas that the police realized that the Slasher was female. That's when a lot of things clicked into place for me. I started watching Mary's house after she left for work, and sure enough, Renata went out on the town fairly often. She'd finally asked Mary about that license plate she'd engraved in her memory since the night when Regina'd been murdered." I hesitated. "This is all theory, isn't it?" I asked Judge Compson. "I couldn't prove any of this."

"I realize that, Mr. Austin," she said. "Please continue."

"I'm just guessing, but I think Renata had finally decided to zero in on Fergusson himself—at least her other personality did. If I correctly understand what 'fugue' means, the daytime Renata didn't have the faintest idea of what the nighttime Renata was doing. To cut it short, I followed her several times, but she kept giving me the slip. It wasn't until the night when she killed Fergusson that I finally found out that she'd bought herself a car—using Regina's name—

sometime in the middle of October. She usually parked the car on a side street a few blocks from Mary's place. She'd ride her bike to the car, hide the bike, and then drive to Fergusson's place on Green Lake Way. She wore one of those black plastic raincoats and not a whole lot under it. She was using herself as bait, and on the night of the tenth of February, Fergusson took the hook. I was right there when he followed her into that strip park along the shore of Green Lake. I'd hoped to stop her before she started to carve him up, but it was so foggy that I lost sight of her." I paused to catch my breath and pull my thoughts together. I noticed that I had everybody's undivided attention.

"Anyway," I went on, "I wasn't able to catch up to her, so she killed Fergusson, then waded out into the lake to wash off the blood. I wasn't far behind, and I stopped briefly to take a look at Fergusson. He was obviously dead, but his face seemed to be frozen into a look of absolute terror. I obviously couldn't prove this, but at the time I got the strong impression that when he saw Renata's face, he believed that his attacker was a girl he'd raped and murdered in the spring of '95. That terror of his was the thing that made the twins' revenge complete. Fergusson knew exactly why he was being butchered.

"Anyway, that's when the cops showed up, and there were a lot of flashlights sweeping around in the fog. Renata saw them, so she kept on swimming until she got to Woodland Park. It was below freezing that night, so she left a trail through the frost on the grass. I picked up that trail and followed her. She went through the park and directly to Saint Benedict's Church. She may have had some idea that the church was a sort of sanctuary. Father O'Donnell says it doesn't work that way, but Renata's head wasn't really working anymore. She went inside the church and hid in one of the side chapels."

I realized that I was going to have to be very careful here, so I paused to take a deep breath.

"Father O'Donnell and I were near the altar," I continued, "and we could hear her whispering to herself. *I* think she was talking with Regina, and both sides of the conversation were coming out of *her* mouth. I'm positive that the alternate persona Dr. Fallon mentioned is Regina, and now she's right there in front of Renata—except that Renata's the only one who can see and hear her. The fugue is over now because Regina's finally tracked down the guy who killed her, and she's taken her revenge—and he knew who she was and why she was doing it. Now that he's dead, the twins are back together again—even closer than before, really, since the two of them are both inside Renata's body. Everyone else in the world is blocked out, but that doesn't matter. Their conversation will probably go on for as long as Renata's still alive. That's about all there is, Your Honor—except that if Regina hadn't got to him first, I might have taken a shot at Fergusson myself."

"I'll pretend I didn't hear that, Mr. Austin," Judge Compson said disapprovingly. "Do you have any other witnesses, Mr. Rankin?"

"No, Your Honor. I think I'll close my case right there. Mr. Austin's covered just about everything."

"Your witness, Mr. Fielding," Judge Compson said.

Fielding was staring at Renata, and he looked almost as if he was ready to break down and cry—either out of sympathy or because he knew for certain that he'd just lost the case. "No questions, Your Honor," he said in a barely audible voice.

"I'll need copies of Miss Greenleaf's freshman English papers and Miss Cardinale's case history—along with those tapes."

"They'll be in your hands by five o'clock, Your Honor," Rankin promised.

"There's another tape you might want to hear, Your Honor," I suggested. "Renata used to listen to it for hours on end, and that moaning sound Officer Murray and the other policemen heard on the night when Mr. Fergusson was killed was pretty much an imitation of that tape. It involves a woman singing with a pack of wolves."

"I believe I *would* like to hear that tape. Thank you for mentioning it, Mr. Austin. Oh, you may step down, by the way."

I nodded and returned to my regular seat.

Judge Compson looked troubled. "I'd like to remind everyone here that this matter is still strictly confidential. If anyone here starts talking about what has transpired here, I'll find him in contempt of court. I'll advise counsel when I reach my decision. Court's adjourned."

CHAPTER TWENTY-EIGHT

I felt drained as we followed Mr. Rankin out of the court-room. I tried not to rehash my testimony in my mind. I knew that would lead to endless "wouldas, couldas, and shouldas" that wouldn't accomplish much of anything—except to make me feel even worse than I already did.

"Excellent job, Mark," Rankin told me. "You definitely gave Judge Compson a lot to consider."

"I hope so," I said. "Do you think Renata's papers and Sylvia's tapes will be enough to persuade the judge that we weren't trying to pull off some elaborate scam? People don't like it when some rich kid gets off easy because the parents can buy off whole bunches of witnesses."

"I don't believe Judge Compson's very interested in public opinion, Mark," Rankin said. "She bases her judgments on the facts, not on the evening news."

"At least we cut the ground out from under Burpee," Mary said with a certain satisfaction.

"We did that, all right," Charlie said with a wicked smirk. "There were a couple of times there when I thought he was going to strangle Fielding. Every time Fielding said 'no questions,' Burpee's blood pressure seemed to ratchet up a little higher."

"That was something I didn't understand," Sylvia said then. "After Dr. Fallon's testimony, Fielding seemed to lie down and play dead."

"The young fellow appears to have a conscience," Rankin

replied. "I think Miss Greenleaf's behavior in the courtroom persuaded him that he was on the wrong side in this case. He shows promise. My partners and I might just poach him from the district attorney when this is over."

"What do you say we get out of here?" I said then. "This place is starting to give me the whim-whams."

"I already have copies of Miss Greenleaf's papers and Sylvia's tapes," Rankin told us. "I *will* need that tape you mentioned to the judge, though, Mark."

"I've got copies back at the boardinghouse," I told him. "When we get home, I'll grab one and bring it to you."

"Good," he said. "Let's not keep the judge waiting."

Word had evidently leaked out that the sanity hearing was over, and the front yard of the boardinghouse was swarming with reporters and TV cameras again. I'm not sure what they thought they were going to get out of us—the gag order was still in force, so we weren't allowed to say anything even if we'd wanted to.

We got out of the station wagon, and James bulked up his shoulders again as he led the way toward the front porch. The rest of us said interesting things to the reporters in assorted languages they didn't understand. Then one shrill female reporter, apparently acting on the assumption that her gender gave her certain privileges, grabbed Erika by the arm, demanding answers.

That was a *real* mistake. Erika had her key ring in her hand, and there was that cute little attachment in among the keys. The pushy reporter fell back, choking and trying to cover her face as Erika gave her a heavy dose of pepper spray at close range. Trish might have used logic; and Sylvia would probably have fallen back on emotion; but Erika relied on chemistry.

The rest of us followed her example and did a quick draw with *our* key rings.

The reporters got the message almost immediately, and they backed off.

When we reached the porch, Erika took it one step further. She smiled sweetly at nervous reporters. "This has been absolutely lovely," she told them, "and we'll have to do it again one of these days—real soon."

I went upstairs and grabbed a copy of Renata's favorite tape. Then James, Charlie, and I went back to the station wagon to ferry it downtown to Mr. Rankin's office.

The reporters had all left, for some reason.

At about five o'clock that evening, one of the TV channels ran footage of Erika's performance—but they only ran it one time. Evidently some producer woke up to the fact the pepper spray response to questions might gain some popularity if it showed up on the tube too often.

The incident out front had brightened our day a bit, but at the supper table things got gloomy again. "I'm almost certain that Judge Compson will rule in our favor," Trish told us. "Mr. Rankin presented a very good case, and Renata's behavior in the courtroom demonstrated that she wasn't even aware of what was happening. I'm positive that the prosecution will try to hold out for incarceration in an institution for the criminally insane, but it'd make more sense if the judge just returned Renata to Dr. Fallon's sanitarium. It's not a great solution, but it's probably the best we can hope for."

"Maybe not, Trish," I disagreed. I looked around at the rest of the gang. "This doesn't go any further, right?" I said.

"What are you up to now, Mark?" Sylvia demanded.

"It's not me, babe," I said. "Father O'Donnell's got an alternative, and he's already put it in motion. His bishop owes him a favor, and Father O called it in. He says there's an obscure order of cloistered nuns who are dedicated to caring for older sisters who've slid over the line into senility—or Alzheimer's, or whatever else you want to call it. They'll also accept rich, usually elderly Catholic ladies with the same problem. The nuns are gentle, and they spend a lot of time tending to their charges—and their cloister's somewhere out in the boonies here in western Washington. Father O's convinced that it's the best possible solution."

"It *would* be better than Dr. Fallon's place," Sylvia agreed.

" 'Get thee to a nunnery'?" Charlie asked.

"It beats hell out of the alternatives," I said. "Anyway, Father O's bishop pulls a lot of weight with some higher-ups in city government, and he's got them slipping around making suggestions. I'm pretty sure that word of this has reached Judge Compson by now."

"What's the name of the order?" Sylvia asked me.

"Father O would rather that I didn't mention it," I told her.

By the end of the week, it was fairly clear that Judge Compson was taking her time. The delay was making me very edgy—I really wanted to put an end to this.

"Calm down, Mark," Trish told me at the supper table on Friday. "Judge Compson has to get all her ducks in a row on this one. If she rules that Renata's mentally incompetent to stand trial, the district attorney could very well appeal that ruling. She's never had one of her rulings overturned, and she's probably digging precedents out of every law book she can get her hands on and consulting with whole platoons of psychiatrists to make sure that Renata won't suddenly 're-cover' after a year or so. There were a number of cases several years back where the defendant put on a good show and got off with a brief stay in a mental institution and then walked away after a 'miraculous' recovery. That's what clouded up the insanity defense. A lot of people were getting away with murder, and the appeals courts go over insanity rulings with a fine-toothed comb to make sure that the presiding judge hasn't been hoodwinked."

"Come on, Trish," Charlie protested. "Twinkie's at *least* as crazy as the Son of Sam killer or that guy who used President Reagan for target practice."

"I'm sure Judge Compson realizes that, Charlie," she said patiently, "but she doesn't want some hard-line appeals court to overturn her decision. We wouldn't want that either, would we?"

"Maybe you're right," he conceded. "If she *does* rule in our favor, I'd be a whole lot happier if her decision's cast in cement. Let's get Twinkie inside that convent and keep her there."

"Doesn't that raise another possibility?" James suggested. "If there's an appeal pending, wouldn't Renata have to be available? They could keep her under guard in the psych ward at the university medical center almost indefinitely while this meanders its way through the court system, couldn't they?"

"In theory, I suppose they could," Trish admitted. "*Or* they could transfer her to some other facility." She frowned. "That *might* have been Fielding's strategy right from the start. If they move her from the U.W. Medical Center to a state institution for the criminally insane, the prosecution could stall their appeal for years. That would be a *de facto* win for the prosecution."

"I'm glad I'm not a lawyer," Charlie said. "There's *way* too much ifsy-andsy in the legal system for my taste. I like things to be simpler. When I push the button on a rocket, it either takes off or explodes on the launching pad. I know immediately if I've done everything right."

" 'The mills of the gods grind slow, but exceeding fine'," James quoted. "It appears that the mills of the legal system grind even slower."

"Why are you two picking on me?" Trish complained.

"We're only teasing, Mama Trish," Charlie said with an impudent grin.

*   *   *

Now I had something *else* to worry about in addition to all the roadblocks the prosecutor could throw in our way. It wasn't a very enjoyable weekend.

Then on Monday morning Trish got a phone call from Mr. Rankin. She talked with him for a few minutes, then came into the kitchen. "Today's the day," she told us. "Judge Compson's made her decision, and she'll issue her ruling at one o'clock this afternoon."

"Did the judge give him any hints at all?" Sylvia asked. She sounded tense.

"Not Judge Compson," Trish replied. "She *never* tips her hand." Then she grinned at us. "This afternoon's session *will* be closed, the same as all the others have been, and the court record will be sealed."

"Can she get away with that?" Charlie asked.

"She can get away with almost anything," Trish assured him. "Unless an appeals court overrules her."

"Absolute dictatorship? Wow!"

"It comes close. The legal system goes all the way back to the Dark Ages. Didn't you know that?"

"I make a point of not getting tangled up in the legal system, Mama Trish," he replied.

"I wonder why," Erika murmured.

We went to the courthouse before noon that day—by eleven-thirty we were all wound pretty tight.

Mr. Rankin and Les Greenleaf joined us at a quarter to one. "We're getting some help from city hall," Rankin told us. "It's pretty low-key, but there's been a fairly attractive offer floating around for the past several days."

"The convent?" I suggested.

He blinked. "How did you find out about that, Mark?" he demanded.

"I have me sources, dontcha know," I replied with a fake Irish brogue.

"I should have guessed," he said ruefully. "Did you tell the others?"

"Not in any great detail," I replied. "I was told to keep my mouth shut about the ins and outs. Do you think Fielding will hold still for it?"

"Fielding will do what he's told to do," Rankin said, "and I wouldn't be surprised if the district attorney's been receiving phone calls from some high-ranking officials in city and county government. Frankly, I'm a little baffled by all this behind-the-scenes maneuvering. I'd give a lot to know what's set this all in motion."

"You already know," I told him. "I told you about it quite some time ago."

Rankin was sharp—I could practically see his mind whirring back to the scene I'd described—Regina and Renata together in the darkened church that night. "You mean—?" He broke off.

"Exactly. Why don't we keep it to ourselves, though? This is messy enough already. Let's not clutter it up with *that*."

"What are you keeping tucked up under your armpit, Mark?" Charlie demanded.

"I've been told—firmly—not to talk about it, old buddy. And I don't think you really want to know. You won't sleep very well if you find out."

"That bad?"

"It's even worse, Charlie. It's making everybody who knows about it *real* nervous."

"He's probably right," Rankin sided with me. "We don't want any word of this leaking out. One hint of it will trigger news stories all over the known world. Why don't we just leave it at that?"

Judge Compson entered the courtroom at one o'clock on the dot. She looked haggard, and I was fairly sure I knew why. Evidently, Father O'Donnell's bishop had a long reach, and he could put a lot of pressure on various officials to get what he wanted.

The judge rapped her gavel more firmly than usual. "It is the decision of this court that Miss Renata Greenleaf is mentally incompetent to stand trial at this time," she announced. "Moreover, the court record shall remain sealed until further notice."

Fielding came to his feet. "Exception, Your Honor," he protested.

"Exception noted," she replied.

"May the prosecution inquire as to what arrangements have been made for the defendant's confinement?" Fielding pressed.

"No, Mr. Fielding, the prosecution may not. The arrangements are still pending, and this court will *not* interfere—and neither will the prosecution. Sit down, Mr. Fielding."

"You can't just turn her loose!" Burpee exploded, coming to his feet.

"Remove that person from this courtroom!" Judge Compson sharply instructed the bailiffs. "And hold him until we adjourn."

"Yes, Your Honor," the head bailiff replied.

There were three bailiffs in the courtroom, and they homed in on Burpee with grim determination.

Judge Compson's sealing of the court record caused a near explosion in the ranks of the Seattle media, and the screams of protest were probably heard in San Francisco and British Columbia.

The Tuesday morning newspaper had two full pages of letters to the editor, most of them bitching and complaining about this "unlawful violation" of their right to drool and slobber about something that was really none of their damned business in the first place.

Then, along about noon, the regular programming on one of the major network TV channels was interrupted. We were just sitting down to lunch in the breakfast nook, and the kitchen television set happened to be tuned to that channel.

The reporter seemed to be fairly excited, and then the camera panned to—guess who?—dear old Lieutenant Burpee.

The reporter briefly introduced him, and then Burpee started to read a prepared statement in a wooden voice. He didn't read out loud very well, and after a minute or so, he crumpled the pages he was reading, threw them to the ground, and launched into a diatribe of shrill-voiced denunciation.

"This has been one of the grossest miscarriages of justice in living memory!" he declared. "Judge Compson is obviously one of those bleeding heart liberals who turn cold-blooded murderers loose on society with absolutely no regard whatsoever about public safety. Worse yet, the prosecuting attorney was obviously in on the scam. He didn't even bother to question the witnesses, for Chrissake!"

A brief shot of the reporter who was conducting the interview showed us a young fellow on the verge of collapse. His look of stunned chagrin was almost comical. Burpee had obviously caught him completely off guard.

Burpee ignored him and plowed on. "This so-called sanity hearing was nothing more than a cheap excuse to let some spoiled rich brat get off scot-free without ever taking the case to trial. That Greenleaf chippy butchered nine law-abiding citizens just for kicks. These were obviously thrill killings, and now the murderer's going to get off with nothing more than a slap on the wrist. Well, I'm not going to let them get away with it. I'm blowing the whistle on them right here and now. There's been a lot of secret manipulation by a bunch of crooked politicians to hush something up that's so rotten that it makes me want to puke. They're trying to sneak this thrill killer off to some country-club nunnery operated by a bunch of nuns who are on the take. If somebody offers those so-called Sisters of Hope a big enough bribe, they'll set a female murderer up in luxurious surroundings and wait on her hand and foot for the rest of her life. That woman belongs in a prison—or at the very least in an institution for the criminally insane. She should be locked up behind bars permanently, for God's sake, but no, she'll get coddled and pampered instead. The criminal justice system just fell apart!"

Burpee's eyes were bulging, and he was obviously totally out of it. Another quick shot of the reporter showed him making desperate gestures at the camera, but evidently the cameraman was either asleep, amused, or Burpee's diatribe had caught him completely off guard and he'd frozen up.

Finally, somebody in the control room woke up and switched to a commercial.

"I wonder if Judge Compson's schedule's all filled up," Charlie said. "I think it might be time for another sanity hearing."

"Maybe after he gets out of jail," Trish amended. "When Judge Compson hears about this, she'll cite him for contempt of court."

"Aw, gee," Charlie said. "What a shame."

"Meanwhile, you *do* realize that he just told the whole world about the Sisters of Hope, don't you?" James asked. "The mother superior's not going to be happy at all. She could very well tell the bishop to forget the whole thing."

"Can she do that?" Charlie demanded. "I thought the bishop was the headman, and everybody's supposed to take orders from him."

"It doesn't work that way, Charlie," Sylvia told him. "The various religious orders have their own hierarchies. The bishop can't just issue orders to the mother superior. He'd have to go through channels, and it could take years to get a ruling. I'm not sure, but this might even have to be settled by the Vatican."

"I think we might be in trouble," Erika said.

There was some late-breaking news that afternoon that brightened up our day: As soon as Judge Compson heard about Burpee's little performance, she'd cited him for contempt of court, and now he was cooling his heels in jail. That made us all feel a little bit better.

Charlie was grinning broadly at breakfast on Saturday morning. "Well," he said, "old Burpee's history. I called Bob last night, and he told me that old blabbermouth has been suspended, and if Judge Compson ever lets him out of jail, he'll get booted off the force. That fit of his yesterday *really* upset the higher-ups in the police department, and they're going to dump him before he embarrasses the department any more."

Aw," Erika said, "poor baby."

"Let's not start gloating yet," Trish told us. "All of Burpee's blathering on camera might have closed the door of the convent for Renata. If it turns out that way, Doctor Fallon's sanitarium might be the best we can hope for."

"You always look on the dark side of things, Trish," Erika complained. "You should really try to lighten up."

Charlie had a meeting at Boeing that evening. I was more or less marking time until the Twinkie matter was settled once and for all, but life went on for the others.

It was about eight-thirty when James rapped on my door. "Are you busy, Mark?" he asked.

I set the book I'd been reading aside. "Not really," I said. "What's up?"

He came in and sat down. "Something's been bothering me, and I thought maybe we could talk it out."

"Sure," I replied. "What's the problem?"

"As I understood your testimony, the decision to call the surviving twin 'Renata' after the murder up in Everett in '95 was pretty arbitrary, wasn't it?"

I shrugged. "It sort of fit, that's all. Nobody could tell the twins apart, so all we had to go on was the dominance of Regina. She was usually the one who made the decisions for the twins. Renata usually hung back."

"It all comes down to 'usually,' then, doesn't it?"

"Where are we going with this?" I asked him.

"It seems to me that 'usually' is pretty shaky ground to base a decision like that on. We've been operating on the notion that Renata's undergoing a personality change before she goes hunting. She somehow turns herself into Regina. But just for the sake of argument, let's look at an alternative. What if Renata was the victim, and Regina was the survivor?"

I nodded. "Okay, but it doesn't fit their personalities, James," I protested. "Regina was dominant. *She* would have been the one who'd have gone looking for a telephone."

"Aren't you assuming that the twins weren't switching dominance back and forth the same way they switched hair ribbons? Were they ever really separate enough actually to have individual identities? You told us that they almost never used the words 'you' and 'me.' All they said was 'we.' Was there ever a *real* Regina or a *real* Renata?"

"Why are you doing this to me, James?" I demanded. "What set you off on this?"

"Complication, Mark. In my field, we're supposed to look for the simplest answer. All of this 'fugue' or 'multiple personality' business steps around the possibility of a much simpler answer. If the twins didn't have separate identities, it doesn't matter *which* one was killed, does it? Stay with me here. The surviving Twinkie was shocked into a psychotic state by her sister's murder, right?"

"That much is pretty certain," I admitted.

"Then she spent six months in Fallon's sanitarium talking to herself, right?"

"You're being obvious, James."

"Simple answers usually *are* obvious. She wasn't in solitary confinement during that period, was she? That first paper she wrote for your class suggests that she was aware of her surroundings and of her fellow inmates, right?"

"Well, probably, yes."

"Wouldn't that have given the twins six months to develop their game plan?"

"There's just one of her now, James," I protested.

"I'm not so sure," he disagreed, "and if you think about it a little, I don't think you will be, either."

"Are you saying that this has all been a put-up job? You seem to think that Twinkie—whichever one she is—has been faking insanity right from the start."

"I didn't say *faking*, Mark. The surviving Twinkie *is* profoundly disturbed—incurably disturbed, probably. 'Insane' doesn't mean 'stupid,' though. Twinkie—whoever she is— has been cleverly manipulating all of us in order to get what she wants—revenge." He made a sour face. "I don't really think 'revenge' is the right word. I think 'self-defense' would come a lot closer. Fergusson attacked her, and then she struck back."

"After *three years*?" I demanded incredulously.

"Would elapsed time have any meaning for her? I think she might be living in the perpetual 'now.' "

"That's crazy," I objected.

"Interesting choice of words, Mark," he said slyly. "We've all been assuming that sometimes Twinkie's a normie, and other times she's a loon. It's simpler and more logical to believe that she's insane all the time, isn't it? Just because she's faked us all out doesn't put her into the normie column, does it? I'm almost positive that we'll never really know for sure which twin was murdered or which twin survived, because as far as they're concerned, there isn't any difference. In a certain sense, they were *both* murdered, but they *both* survived. Life's simpler for them now, though. They don't have twenty fingers any more—just ten."

"Why did she keep having those 'bad days' after she carved out some guy's tripes, then?" I demanded.

"Just how bad were they, Mark?"

"Pretty damn bad. Haven't you heard Sylvia's tapes?"

"They were dramatic, certainly," he agreed, "but didn't they seem a trifle *over*dramatic?"

"You mean that she was laying a foundation for this insanity defense right from the start?"

"I didn't say that. Isn't it possible that she was bent on establishing her helplessness, her vulnerability? In a certain sense those episodes were analogous to the pose she'd assume when she was out hunting. She tricked *us* as much as she tricked her assorted victims. She tricked *us* with imitation psychosis, and she tricked *them* with curare. The result was the same—paralysis. Her victims couldn't do anything, and neither could we." He paused. "I'm obviously playing devil's advocate here, Mark," he said apologetically, "but I think it's a possibility that we shouldn't overlook. The 'twin-game' the girls played all through their childhood would have given them lots of practice. I'm not going to mention this to anybody else, but I thought that *you*, of all people, should be aware that this is a distinct possibility. No matter which twin survived, she's been damaged beyond repair, and the cloister's ultimately the best solution."

"It's the best one for Twinkie, that's for sure. But after what you just unloaded on *me*, I might need some place to get *my* head on straight too, and I'm fairly sure the nuns wouldn't accept my application."

"You're a nice guy, Mark," he said, grinning. "Maybe they'll bend a few rules for you."

"Thanks a bunch," I said sourly.

"Aw, forget it, good buddy."

Mr. Rankin called Trish on Monday morning, and she came back into the kitchen with a troubled expression on her face. "Judge Compson's going to announce her final decision this afternoon," she told us. "I don't think we're going to like it very much, but we'd probably better be there."

Maybe it was just me, but that morning seemed to drag on

forever. It was raining and blustery outside and that seemed
to make things worse.

We didn't talk much on our way downtown to the courthouse. What was there to say?

I was surprised to see Father O'Donnell in the courtroom
with Les Greenleaf when we entered. He gave me a quick
grin, and then he winked at me.

What was *that* all about?

Then the two attendants brought Renata—assuming that
she really *was* Renata—into the courtroom. She was still
murmuring to herself and wasn't paying the slightest bit of attention to anybody else in the room.

At one o'clock—on the dot as usual—the bailiff said, "All
rise," and we stood up as Judge Compson entered. Her face
was set in a stern expression, but something seemed to be
bothering her.

"You may be seated," she told us. "This won't take us very
long." Then she paused. "This case has troubled me greatly
from the very beginning," she told us all. "I can only hope
that I've made the right decision. It's been obvious that the
defendant is not even aware of her surroundings and that
she's profoundly disturbed. This being the case, my judgment
of her incompetence was obviously the correct one. The final
disposition, however, was not quite so simple. Miss Greenleaf is beyond punishment, obviously. She must be placed
somewhere where she can receive custodial care and attention of a sort that goes somewhat beyond the capabilities of
an ordinary mental institution. It is, therefore, the judgment
of this court that Miss Renata Greenleaf shall be placed in the
care of a religious order of her faith for the balance of her
life." Then Judge Compson rapped down her gavel. "This
court stands adjourned," she declared.

That *really* jolted me. How was she going to force the sisters to take Renata in if they didn't *want* to? Something
strange was going on here, and I was fairly certain that I knew
who might be able to explain it.

As soon as the judge left the courtroom I zeroed in on Father O'Donnell. "You've been pulling some strings again, haven't you, Father?" I demanded.

"Oh, I wouldn't go quite *that* far, Mark," he said. "The mother superior of the Sisters of Hope needed just a wee bit of information, that's all, so I gave it to her."

"You *told* her?" I exclaimed. "I thought your bishop ordered you to keep your mouth shut about it."

"He was talking about outside the family, Mark. The mother superior and I are old friends, so I was almost obliged to let her know about something that significant. It helped her to make the right decision."

"You guys play by a complicated set of rules, don't you, Father?" I accused him.

"It's OK as long as it gets the job done, Mark," he said smugly. "I have it on the very highest authority that everything's fine and dandy now, dontcha know."

CHAPTER TWENTY-NINE

The press release Judge Compson issued that afternoon was very terse, and it made no mention of a religious order. That left the news media high and dry. There wasn't going to be a trial or much of anything else for them to babble about. Burpee was still in jail for contempt of court, and nobody else involved would answer any questions.

The reporters didn't think that was very nice at all.

To make things even worse for them, Renata was transferred from the university medical center to Doc Fallon's sanitarium that same evening, before the reporters even knew what was going on. She was still technically being held in custody, but Fallon was now her custodian. The idea was to give the impression that Fallon's institution was going to be her final home. Then things would have time to cool off before she was quietly transferred to the cloister.

It looked good on paper, but we started running into snags almost immediately. Some blabbermouth at the medical center told a reporter about the transfer the following morning, and a dozen or so reporters showed up at Doc Fallon's gate. The guard wouldn't let them into the courtyard, of course, but they camped outside and didn't show any signs that they planned to leave at any time in the near future.

Fallon conferred with Les Greenleaf by phone, and on Wednesday morning several burly and unfriendly security guards showed up. They informed the reporters in no uncertain terms that they were trespassing on private property, and that they'd better get the hell off the grounds. The reporters sullenly retreated back down the driveway and reestablished their camp at the side of the public road beyond the sanitarium grounds—where they tried to stop every car that was entering or leaving.

Fallon told his entire staff that he'd fire anybody who talked to a reporter about anything—even the weather.

The reporters were still clustered around the entrance to the driveway, though, so Doc Fallon took the next logical step. One of his golf buddies was a Snohomish County judge, and he got a restraining order—no loitering within a quarter mile of the entrance to the sanitarium.

There was a lot of screaming about that, and several reporters, claiming "freedom of the press," deliberately ignored the order. They ended up in jail for contempt of court.

The whole thing was starting to turn into a comedy—or even a farce.

I didn't laugh very much, though. By Friday of that week, it was obvious that waiting the reporters out was going to take longer than any of us had anticipated. Father O'Donnell advised us that the mother superior of the Sisters of Hope was having second thoughts about the whole thing.

We'd hit the quarter break at the university, and I probably should have enrolled in a couple of seminars, but as long as this other thing was still hanging fire, I knew that there'd be no way that I could concentrate, so I took a pass for now. That gave me all kinds of time to worry about the possibility James had raised. "Either/Or" suddenly became very significant for me. It probably wouldn't have made much difference in the final outcome. Twinkie—whichever one she was—would be quietly transferred to the cloister, and that'd be the end of it. Still—

Spring quarter classes were scheduled to begin on the sixth of April, and the rest of the gang was busy with registering, buying textbooks, and all the other minutiae that clutter up registration week. Oddly enough, though, we didn't see much of Charlie. Knowing him as well as we did, we were all fairly sure that he was "up to something." Charlie had almost made a career out of being "up to something."

He showed up on the Sunday before classes began, and Trish immediately climbed all over him. "Where have you been, Charlie?" she demanded, "and what have you been doing?"

"Just working, Mama Trish," he replied, faking wide-eyed innocence.

"Here we go again," Erika said. "Give up, Charlie. We're not going to let up on you until you come clean. You should know that by now."

"You guys are taking the fun out of this," he complained.

"Fun-schmun, Charlie," Erika said bluntly. "Talk."

"Well—" he said, "we seem to have this little problem with Twinkie."

"No kidding," I said dryly. "What a brilliant observation."

"All right," Charlie gave up. "Our problem has to do with logistics. Twinkie's at point A—Fallon's nuthouse—and we've got to move her to point B—the cloister."

"All right," James agreed. "That's fairly specific."

"The main problem is the pack of newshounds camped on Fallon's front door, right?"

"You're going to round them all up and put them in the dog pound?" Erika suggested.

"That's a slick idea," he said, "if we could get away with it. The pound would hold them for seven days, then put them to sleep."

"I could live with that," I said darkly.

"So could I, but we'd probably get yelled at if we tried it. I've been working on something that might just pull it off without too many fatalities." Charlie frowned slightly. "I'm not too clear on a couple of technicalities, though." He looked at Trish. "Maybe Rankin could give us an OK, but I've got a hunch that maybe we ought to clear it with Judge Compson before we jump in with both feet. My game plan has a couple things involved that might be technically illegal, so let's not rock the boat if we don't have to."

"I'll speak with Mr. Rankin," Trish told him.

"That's it? You're not going to give us anything more specific?" Sylvia objected.

"I'm still working on a couple things, sweet cakes," he said. "Give me some time to get it all down pat before I spread it out for you guys."

"Sweet cakes?" she said archly.

"It's an expression," he replied defensively. "I'm not breaking any rules—yet."

"Don't even think about it," Trish told him flatly.

It took Mr. Rankin a couple of days to set up an appointment with Judge Compson, and he finally passed the word that she wanted to see us in her office at the courthouse at seven-thirty on the evening of Tuesday, the seventh of April.

I went to the phone in the living room to check in with Les Greenleaf. "Charlie isn't talking, boss," I told him, "but he's got something cooking that *might* get those damned reporters off our tails. If I know Charlie, it's probably fairly complicated, and we might have trouble sneaking it past Judge Compson. Is the mother superior still willing to go along with this?"

"Only if we can guarantee the security of the cloister, Mark," he told me. "That's her major concern. If you and your friends show up at the gate with a dozen reporters hot on your trail, she won't open the gates."

"That's what Charlie's working on, I think. I'm sure he's got some sort of scam cooked up that'll confuse hell out of those reporters."

"I certainly hope so."

"How's Inga doing?"

"Not good, Mark," he told me sadly. "Her doctor's got her

on some heavy-duty tranquilizers. I think it's going to take her a long time to come out of this."

"She's not alone there, boss. I doubt I'll *ever* get over it."

"We've lost both of my girls, haven't we?" he said then, and there were tears in his voice.

What the hell could I say? I stepped around it. "Do you want to sit in, boss?" I asked him. "Judge Compson might want to ask you a few questions."

"You're right, Mark," he agreed. "I guess I'd better be there."

I tried to work on my Hemingway paper, to clear one of my incompletes from winter quarter, but I couldn't concentrate, so I put it aside so that I could worry full-time. Every time I turned around, "Either/Or" kept hitting me in the face.

Charlie still wasn't talking, and that irritated the hell out of me. I wasn't in the mood for fun and games.

Tuesday rolled around—eventually—and by then we were all wired up pretty tight. Even now, Twinkie was at the center of our attention. The girls were waspish with Charlie at supper, but he still refused to give us any details.

"Let's take the station wagon again," James suggested after supper. "It's sort of the official vehicle by now, and after Erika's little demonstration with pepper spray, every reporter in King County knows that we're loaded for bear."

"Thou shalt not look, neither shall ye touch—lest ye die," Erika announced.

"That'd make a great bumper sticker, wouldn't it?" Charlie said with a certain enthusiasm.

Erika shrugged. "It gets right to the point," she said.

The walls of Judge Compson's office were lined from floor to ceiling with bookshelves and law books. Lawyers and judges don't have to spend much money on wallpaper, that's for sure.

Mr. Rankin, Les Greenleaf, and Mary were already there

when we arrived, and Bob West showed up before we even got seated. "What are you up to now, kid?" he asked Charlie.

"Sit tight, Bob," Charlie replied. "I want to dump it on everybody at the same time, so I won't have to keep repeating myself."

"It better be good," Bob told him.

"Trust me."

"Oh, sure." Bob's voice dripped with sarcasm.

"Is everyone here now?" Judge Compson asked us. She wasn't wearing her black robe, and she looked almost motherly in her print dress.

Mr. Rankin looked around. "I think that's everybody, Alice," he said familiarly, "unless you think Mr. Fielding should sit in?"

"I think we can get along without him for now, John," she replied. "If there's anything you think he ought to know about, you can pass it on to him later." She looked around at the rest of us. "This is an unofficial meeting," she said. "I'm here to listen—and possibly to pass along some advice. Go ahead, John."

"Bob West's younger brother wanted to bounce an idea off you, Alice," Rankin said. "He hasn't given any of us the details, so we're as much in the dark as you are."

"It's in your court, then, Mr. West," the judge told Charlie. "Fire away."

"Yes, ma'am," he said, grinning at her colloquialism. "I've been kicking this idea around since you handed down your decision. I *think* I've plugged up all the holes, but if anybody spots something I've missed, let me know. What this all boils down to is a security problem. We need to transfer Twinkie from Doc Fallon's loony bin to that cloister, without picking up a convoy of reporters along the way. Is that pretty much the problem?"

"Yes," the judge said. "If by 'Twinkie,' you're referring to Miss Greenleaf. So what's your solution, Mr. West?"

"Right at first, I thought that maybe a helicopter might be

the best way to go," Charlie replied, "but then I remembered that a couple of the TV stations have helicopters of their own. They might not be right there on the scene, but I didn't want to take any chances. We're probably going to have to stay on the ground, and that means that we'll need decoys. An un-marked delivery truck *might* work, but that's still a little risky. We'll only have one shot at this, so we've got to get it right the first time."

"I think we all get your point, Mr. West," Rankin said.

"OK," Charlie said, "let's say that along toward evening on some rainy afternoon, five identical black limousines wheel into the courtyard of Doc Fallon's place and stop there."

"Wouldn't it be better if they came in after dark?" Bob asked.

Charlie shook his head. "No. We *want* those reporters to see those limos. That's part of the scam. A duck has to see the decoy before he'll land on the pond where you and your shotgun are waiting. OK, we've got five identical limos in the courtyard. Next we'll need five more or less identical tall blond girls to be led out through the front door of the nut-house. They can all wear sweatshirts with the hoods pulled up but with a lock or two of blonde hair showing, so that the long-range TV cameras can pick it up. Then each girl gets into the backseat of a different limo. Are we OK so far?" He looked around.

"I still think you should wait until it gets dark," Bob told him. "The reporters will just split up and follow every one of the limousines, won't they?"

"I sure hope so," Charlie said. "OK, now we've got five limos with those tinted windows that make sure that nobody can see inside. They drive out and scatter to the winds—one goes toward Snohomish, one to Everett, one heads north toward Bellingham, one goes east toward Stevens Pass, and the last one just wanders the back roads around the lake. The reporters have to split up to follow each one separately."

"I don't see where that's going to make any difference, Charlie," James said.

"I'm coming to that," Charlie replied. "OK, now we've got five limos scattered all over the place, with a gang of reporters trailing each one. The idea here is to get those reporters away from any side roads or driveways. That way, they've *got* to stay on the road we want them to be on."

"Right behind the limo that we *don't* want them to be following," Bob said. "Brilliant, kid. You've got a mind as sharp as a pile of limp spaghetti."

"I ain't done yet, big brother," Charlie told him. "OK, we're in Snohomish County, right? And Twinkie's dad pulls a lot of weight up there, right? Doesn't that mean that the sheriff and the state patrol are going to be on *our* side this time?"

"Maybe," Bob admitted. "What difference will *that* make?"

"This is where it gets interesting," Charlie said with a smug grin. "We tell the cops exactly which road each limo's going to follow—like before noon on D-day. Then the cops ease quietly on out to some lonely spot on each one of those roads. They set up five of those 'sobriety checkpoints.' Each one has a roadblock with cops at the back end, to make damn sure that some smart reporter doesn't wrap a U-turn and make a run for it. The cops wave the limo through, and then they check everybody in every single car behind the limo for blood-alcohol level. The cops don't have to hurry. I mean, they're protecting the public from drunk drivers, aren't they? A well-run cop stop with breathalyzers and making everybody get out of the car to find out if he can walk a straight line should hold the vultures in place for a least a half hour, so all five limos get away clean. The reporters won't have the foggiest idea which limo's carrying Twinkie, and they won't know where *any* of the limos have gone. The *real* Twinkie car can drop her off at the cloister and take off again. Then we have all five limos wander around western Washington until about noon on the following day—stopping for gas here,

buying a Big Mac there, getting a ticket for speeding someplace else, and all kinds of stuff to attract attention to places
that don't mean a damn thing. Then they all go back to the
limo garage, and we all go home and get some sleep. Can
anybody see any holes in that one? The way I see it is that the
news vultures are going to get so many conflicting reports
that they won't have the foggiest idea of where Twinkie
went."

"Would that actually work, Sergeant West?" Judge Compson
asked Bob.

"I hate to admit it, Your Honor, but my kid brother's
probably come up with the best solution to the problem. That
sobriety checkpoint idea of his is brilliant. Nobody goes
through one of those without stopping, and if he even tries, he
goes straight to jail."

"I like it," the judge said with a sudden smile.

"I've got another little gimmick in mind that'll add to the
confusion, Your Honor," Charlie added. "It's not some major
violation, but it does bend certain rules just a teensy-weensy
little bit. It'll definitely confuse hell out of the reporters, I can
flat-out guarantee that."

"Maybe we'll leave the logistical details to you, Mr. West,"
the judge said.

"It might be best," he agreed. "Now, we'll need five official-looking nut-keepers."

"The term is 'attendants,' Mr. West," Doc Fallon said with
a pained expression.

"Sorry, Doc," Charlie apologized. "Anyway, I think that
Miss Mary should suit up in those white clothes so that *she'll*
be the one in the *real* Twinkie-mobile. Mark's going to be the
driver, and Father O will have to go along to give directions.
Nobody, and I really mean *nobody*, will get any information
out of *those* three. We'll keep Father O out of sight, because
we don't want anybody making any church connection. The
decoy limos will each need a fake Twinkie, a driver, and

somebody wearing attendant clothes. Trish can be one of our Twinkie decoys, and if we put a blond wig on Erika, she can be another. We'll dress Sylvia in a white uniform to play attendant, and James and I can drive two of the decoy limos. All we need now are two more drivers, another two fake Twinkies, and three more attendants."

"You'll also need somebody to foot the bill," James added. "This might be expensive."

"That's my department, James," Les Greenleaf told him.

"I was hoping you'd see it that way, Mr. Greenleaf," Charlie said. "Now, I've spent quite a bit of this past week cruising around on all the roads that'll be involved, and I've pretty well pinpointed the locations for those sobriety checks. Mark's going to have to get in touch with Father O, and they'll decide where to set up checkpoint number five—the important one. I talked with the guy who owns a fleet of limos up in Everett, and his cars are all equipped with radios, so we'll all be able to stay in touch. We might want to use some code words about the crucial stuff, but that's just window dressing. I'll need a little time to take each driver out in a plain car to show him the exact route to follow on D-Day, and we'll need some pretty exact times so that the sobriety checks coincide. We'll want all the reporters stopped at exactly the same time so that nobody gets any advance warning. If we can arrange it with Snohomish County, I'd like to have my big brother running mission control. He knows the whole scoop, and he can smooth over any boo-boos that crop up along the way."

"You have a gift for this sort of thing, Mr. West," Judge Compson said. "Your scheme's fairly elaborate, but if it works the way you've laid it out, I don't think any reporter's going to be able to evade you."

"That was the whole idea, Your Honor," Charlie replied. "We'll need a few practice runs to make sure everybody knows what's going on, but one of *us* is going to be in each of those limos, and we'll be calling the shots on the radio."

Judge Compson looked at Rankin, then at Les Greenleaf. "What do you gentlemen think?" she asked them.

"Let's go for it," Les replied shortly.

"All right, Charlie," Erika said when we got back down to the parking garage, "What's this gimmick you didn't want to talk about?"

"Somehow I knew you'd be the one who'd ask, Erika," Charlie said. "OK, I spent a few hours in one of the shops at Boeing last Saturday evening, and I managed to counterfeit five sets of license plates."

"What on earth for?" she demanded.

"All five sets have the same number, babe," he said with his trademark smirk. "Those five limos are *really* going to be identical, and the reporters are going to discover that there's this magical limousine out there that can be in five different places all at the same time."

"It's a miracle!" she said with feigned awe. "Let's run and tell the bishop so that he can pass it on to the Vatican."

"You're an evil, evil person, Charlie," James said.

And then we all began to laugh.

CODA

Pavane

We spent the rest of that week and the early part of the next one getting to know the back roads in Snohomish County by their first names. Father O'Donnell had told us that Granite Falls was in the general vicinity of the cloister, but that was as much as he would spill. He and Charlie settled on the little town of Verlot as the best location for the roadblock. I guess "need to know" came up fairly often during their discussions.

Anyway, we finally got it all hammered together, and Trish advised Mr. Rankin and Judge Compson that Thursday, April 16, would be our own personal D-Day.

I drove to Saint Benedict's Church about five o'clock that afternoon. Our schedule was pretty tight—like right down to the minute—so I thought that it'd be better to get to Everett early rather than late.

"Are you certain this is going to work, Mark?" Father O'Donnell asked me as we went north on the interstate.

"It sure should, Father," I said. "We've been rehearsing for long enough to get all the details down pat. Everything *ought* to come off right on schedule."

"Well, we can always hope." He still sounded a bit dubious.

It was about a quarter to six when I parked my old Dodge near the limousine service garage. Charlie and James were inside already, along with a couple of Dr. Fallon's security guards.

We were all wearing suits—Charlie and I had to rent ours—and James handed around those caps chauffeurs put on to make them look official.

"Check out my phony license plates, Mark," Charlie said, pointing at the line of limos with a certain pride.

The counterfeit plates he'd cobbled together were neatly in place on each limo, and they covered the real plates. As nearly as I could tell, they were indistinguishable from genuine plates, and they all showed the same number.

"Nice job, Charlie," I congratulated him. "Did you get your training in the official license plate factory, maybe?"

"Not hardly," he replied. "That one's in the state prison over at Walla Walla, and I ain't been there yet."

"It's only a matter of time, Charlie," James said in that deep voice. "Just keep on bending rules, kid. You'll make it—eventually."

"Very funny," Charlie replied sarcastically.

"When are we going to take off?" I asked him.

"Bob says we should hit Fallon's bughouse at about six thirty-three," Charlie said. "We've got a little time to play with when we get there. The rush-hour traffic might delay us, but I built in a pad to cover it. We can either move right along or stall—whichever it takes for us to leave at six fifty-two. The roadblocks are set for seven forty-two. We can all either speed up or slow down to make sure we get to them right on the nose."

"Will there still be light enough for Mark and me to find the turnoff to the cloister?" Father O'Donnell asked him. "It isn't really marked."

"That part's OK," Charlie assured him, "but you might have to wait a while after you turn Twinkie over to the nuns. We don't want you coming out of that side road until after dark. Those back roads don't have very much traffic, so you'll be able to see the headlights on the reporters' car if they're that close behind you. That's the main reason for this Mickey Mouse time schedule. We don't want any reporter to see you go in or come out. Once you guys are back on the pavement, we're home free." Charlie looked at his watch. "I'd better check in with Bob and let him know that we're all in place here," he said, slipping into the front seat of one of the limos. He picked up the microphone.

"Are we sure that none of the reporters will be listening in while we're radioing back and forth?" Father O'Donnell asked me.

"There's not much chance of that, Father," I replied. "We're using an oddball frequency, and even if some reporter who's roaming up and down the dial happens to pick us up, he won't realize what's going on. We're going to use chess moves as a code. My official designation is 'king's pawn,' and when I say, 'king's pawn to king four,' it'll mean that I've made my first turnoff. Later, when we come to the roadblock at Verlot, I'll broadcast, 'king's pawn to king six—check.' If the cops manage to stop the reporters, it's 'checkmate,' and we've won the game. Trish is queen, James is castle, Erika's bishop, and Charlie's rook. If some reporter stumbles across our frequency, he'll think he's listening to a couple of people playing a long-range game of chess."

"Oh, *that's* clever," he said admiringly.

"Naturally. James and Charlie play chess quite a bit, and they worked it out between them. The boardinghouse gang's going to be manning all five radios, and we've got all the moves memorized."

"What if something goes wrong and a reporter evades that roadblock at Verlot?" the priest asked me.

I shrugged. "We all turn around and go back to Doc Fallon's sanitarium. Then we'll wait six months or so and try again—maybe with delivery trucks or ambulances. You and I'll be calling the shots, and we *won't* take the cloister turnoff unless we're absolutely sure that nobody's behind us."

We hauled out of the limousine service garage at 5:52, and we probably looked like a funeral procession—or maybe an impending Mafia convention—as we drove east through Everett on Hewitt Avenue. We went across the flats to Cavalero's Corner and then up the hill toward Lake Stevens.

We made the turnoff to Fallon's place, and Bob's voice came crackling over the radio. "Black king to castle three," he announced. Bob was monitoring the reporters' frequency.

"The reporters have spotted us," I translated for Father O'Donnell. "It was bound to happen, I guess."

We all followed Charlie into the courtyard and parked the limousines in a neat row, being careful to make sure that none of the license plates were visible.

"Stay out of sight, Father," I cautioned. "We don't want any reporter to find out that you're here."

"Right," he agreed. "This is sort of exciting, isn't it?"

"Only if it works the way it's supposed to." I slid out of the limo, and the five of us who were driving went inside to Fallon's office.

Trish and Erika were both wearing hooded sweatshirts, and Erika sported a blond wig that didn't look very good on her. Two other tall blond girls were there as well; I recognized one as a nurse who worked for Doc Fallon.

Mary and Sylvia were wearing those standard white pants and shirts that sanitarium employees always seem to wear, and the three other attendants weren't acting—they really *were* sanitarium employees. When you get right down to it, Sylvia was sort of redundant: We only needed five people to man the limo radios. We'd been smart enough not to mention it to Sylvia, though. She had a real short fuse, and we sure didn't want to light it. She'd be riding with James, who was probably best qualified to keep her calm.

"Where's Twinkie?" Charlie asked, looking around.

"She'll be along in just a few moments," Dr. Fallon replied. "Have there been any foul-ups so far? If we're going to have to scratch this, there's not much point in getting her all dressed-up and ready to go. I don't *think* she'll get agitated, but let's not take any chances if we don't have to. Is everything going the way it's supposed to so far?"

"Yup," Charlie said. "There's probably four or five long-range TV cameras zeroed in on the courtyard right now. We made sure that they won't be able to pick up the license plates, so everything's going just the way we want it to." He checked his watch. "We've got nine minutes before we have to take off."

"Did you get longer cords for the microphones, Charlie?" Trish asked him. "Erika and I *will* be in the backseats, you know."

"Got it covered," he replied. "And everybody remember to step right along when we go out the front door to the limos. We don't want to give those cameras more than thirty seconds to home in on us. We'll let Mark, Mary, and Twinkie lead off. Let's get *them* out of sight as quickly as we can. Each of the other limos will have a driver, an attendant, and a Twinkie look-alike inside. Let's keep those chess-move code sheets handy. You'll confuse the hell out of Bob if you happen to call in a wrong move. If you're talking about Snohomish and you use the chess move for Arlington by mistake, he'll think you just sprouted wings."

"Charlie," James said in a pained tone, "we've already been through this several dozen times. You're beating a dead horse."

"Well—" Charlie said defensively.

I looked at my watch. "It's getting close," I said tersely. "Let's crank it up."

Doc Fallon nodded and pressed the buzzer on his intercom.

A couple moments later one of the orderlies led Renata into the office. She was still rambling on in twin-speak, and she didn't seem to even see any of us. That's assuming that she really was Renata, of course. If, as James had suggested, she just happened to be Regina, who could possibly know what she saw or whom she recognized?

Mary took her gently by the arm, then pulled up the hood

of her grey sweatshirt to cover her face, leaving only a bit of blond hair showing. The decoy girls all rearranged their hoods to duplicate Renata as closely as they could.

"What do you think, Mark?" Charlie asked me.

"It should be close enough," I replied. "It's only about fifteen or twenty feet from the front door to my limo. I should have Renata out of sight before the cameras can zoom in, and the rest of you won't be far behind. I don't think those cameras will get much detail."

"Let's hit the bricks, then," he said.

Mary and I hustled Renata out the front door, and we had her stashed in the backseat with Mary beside her in under fifteen seconds. You'd be surprised how fast you can move if you have to. I kept my chauffeur's cap pulled down to hide my face and slid into the driver's seat while the decoys all got into their limos and closed the doors.

Father O'Donnell was scrunched over on the passenger's side of the front seat.

"You don't actually have to crouch, Father," I told him. "These are one-way windows. We can see out, but they can't see in."

"Oh," he said. "That takes a bit of getting used to, doesn't it?"

"Rook to queen three," Charlie's voice came over the radio.

"Knight's gambit acknowledged," Bob replied.

"That's our go-ahead," I told Mary and Father O'Donnell. I checked the dashboard clock. "Six fifty-two right on the nose," I said. "We aren't even a half minute off schedule."

Charlie's limo led the way out of the courtyard, naturally, and the rest of us fell in behind him down the long driveway to the public road.

"Rook to bishop five," Charlie reported to Bob, advising him that we'd left the grounds of the sanitarium.

"Where do we go from here?" Father O'Donnell asked me.

"Back to Cavalero's Corner," I replied. "There's a half

dozen highways that fan out from there. That's where we scatter."

"Black king to castle," Bob told us tersely.

"What's that supposed to mean?" Father O'Donnell asked.

"Bob's monitoring the conversations of the reporters," I explained. "Evidently, they're calling for backup. We've probably got reporters and TV camera crews homing in on us. This is where we start juggling our positions. James is going to drop back, and I'll pass him. Then Erika's car will pass both of us, and so on. One or two of those reporters out there might have been hanging around the courthouse during those hearings, so they might have recognized a couple of us when we were out in plain sight back at the sanitarium. We'll keep changing places in the line, so that they won't know which one of us is in which car."

"Shrewd," Father O'Donnell said.

"That's Charlie for you," I replied.

"Black queen to king's rook four," Trish announced from the rear of our convoy.

"We've got cars following us," I translated. "Anytime one of us identifies the color of the chess piece as black, it means that we're talking about the reporters. We're starting to get down to the nitty-gritty."

"Have there been any black knight gambits on the board yet?" Charlie called in.

"Not so far," Bob answered. "I'll keep you advised."

"We must have caught them off base," I told Mary and Father O'Donnell. "They haven't got any helicopters up yet. Once we split up and scatter at Cavalero's Corner, I think we're home free."

When we got down to the bottom of the hill, we fanned out. I was in the middle of the pack, and I held back to let Charlie and Erika get ahead of me. Then I turned right onto Sunnyside Boulevard and drove on in the general direction of Marysville. James and Trish moved up quickly to fill in the gap. During our planning sessions, we'd kicked around the possibility that I might be able to slip out of the column without being noticed, but we hadn't wanted to bet the farm on it.

"King's pawn to king four," I called in to let Bob know that I'd made the turnoff. Then I leaned back in my seat. "Check the road behind us, Mary," I said without taking my eyes off the road. "See if we've got any company coming along."

She looked out the back window. "It looks like we've still got three cars on our tail," she reported. "No, wait a minute. One of them's a beat-up old pickup truck. Reporters wouldn't be driving something like that, would they?"

"Probably not," I replied. "Keep an eye on him, though. If he's a local, he might turn off onto a side road."

"Will this road take us to Granite Falls?" Father O'Donnell asked me.

"We have to do a couple of zigzags," I told him, "but once we get on Highway 9, we'll have a straight shot at it." I checked the dashboard clock. "We're about a minute behind schedule," I said, "but I can pick that up between Granite Falls and Verlot. That's fifteen miles of backcountry road that doesn't get much traffic. Once we pass the roadblock and the cops short-stop the reporters, you'll be calling the shots."

"The pickup just turned off, Mark," Mary reported. "There are only two cars on us."

"Good. As long as we don't get a chopper on our backs, we ought to be able to get clear."

"You worry too much," she said. "This is old news by now, and it costs a lot of money to run a chopper. No station manager in his right mind would cough up that much on the off chance that he might get a thirty-second sound bite."

"I hope you're right," I said.

"Queen to bishop three," Trish reported.

"She's right on time," I said, checking the dashboard clock. "She just took the Snohomish cutoff."

The chess moves came in rapid sequence for a while as

everybody reported the various turnoffs. If somebody out there was trying to follow the game on a standard chessboard, he was probably pretty confused by now. We had a six-player chess game, and we were making moves that were *way* off the board. You almost never see "rook to queen nineteen" in a regular chess game.

We were about a minute and a half behind schedule when we reached Granite Falls, so I tromped down on the gas pedal to pick up the lost time. We passed a road sign that said VERLOT 9 MI.

"After you pass Verlot, you'll want to take the Darrington cutoff at Silverton, Mark," Father O'Donnell told me. "Then you'd better slow down. We have to be absolutely certain that nobody's following us."

"Right," I agreed. "That's pretty rough country up there."

"You're familiar with it?"

"My dad and I used to fish in the south fork of the Stillaguamish River. We pulled some pretty good-sized steelhead out of there. Is the road to the cloister marked at all?"

"No," he replied. "It looks just like any other Forest Service road. There's a gate about a quarter of a mile in. It's kept locked, but I've got the key."

"Good. After we pass the roadblock at Verlot, I'll stay off the radio. I don't *think* anybody's going to crack our code, but let's not take any chances."

Just before we reached Verlot, I saw three Highway Patrol cars parked at the side of the road. One of the patrolmen waved me on through, and then I watched in the rearview mirror as two of the patrol cars pulled out to block the road while the third one went down the road to swing in behind the reporters.

"King's pawn to king six," I reported. "Check." Behind us I saw the two press cars screech to a halt as the Highway Patrolmen flagged them down. "Checkmate!" I announced gleefully.

Four other checkmates followed in rapid succession. I'm sure that there were unhappy reporters scattered all over Snohomish County along about then.

"Where are we supposed to go after we drop Ren off at the cloister?" Mary asked from the backseat.

"We'll go on into Darrington and then hook on back toward Arlington," I told her. "Then we'll take I-Five to Mount Vernon. That's where we'll stop for gas—just on the off chance that one of the reporters has spotted us again. After that, we'll take a scenic tour of Skagit County and wind up back in Everett about two in the morning."

"That's a long night," she said.

"The pay's pretty good, though," I replied.

I drove up to Silverton, turned left, and crossed the bridge that spanned the Stillaguamish River onto the Darrington cutoff. I glanced off to the west. The clouds were all turning red as the sun went down. "How far to the turnoff, Father O'Donnell?" I asked.

"About three more miles," he replied. "You'd better slow down a bit. It's not marked, and it's a little hard to see if you're going fast."

"Right," I said, backing off to about thirty miles an hour.

We crept along the narrow, two-lane road as the sunset painted the western sky bright red.

Father O'Donnell was peering intently through the windshield. "There it is," he told me, pointing on ahead.

It was a narrow, badly rutted dirt road on the right-hand side, and it looked very much like any one of a thousand or more Forest Service roads that run off among the trees on the western slope of the Cascade Mountains.

"Checkmates cleared," Bob's voice came over the radio.

"Perfect," I said, slowing down and turning onto the dirt road. "The Highway Patrol just now turned the reporters loose. They're fifteen miles behind us, and it'll be dark before long. Charlie's going to be impossible to live with for a while, but his scam worked exactly the way it was supposed to."

"That's what really matters, Mark," Mary said from the backseat. "Let him brag about it if he wants to."

"How's Renata doing?" I asked her.

"She seems calm enough. I think she might have sensed something—not consciously, maybe, but the fact that we're all very happy about the way this has turned out might have seeped through to her."

If James had been anywhere close to being right, the surviving twin was probably much more aware of what was happening around her than she appeared to be. I devoutly wished that James had kept his theory to himself. Every time I turned around, it seemed, I kept coming face-to-face with the very disturbing possibility that it was Regina in that backseat.

"There's the gate, Mark," Father O'Donnell told me. "Stop here and I'll go open it for you."

"Right," I said. I eased to a stop, and he got out of the limo. He unlocked the gate and swung it open. I drove through and stopped to wait while he closed and locked the gate, then got back into the front seat.

"How much farther?" I asked him.

"About a half mile. Take it slow—the road's a little rough."

I crept on through the woods at no more than five miles an hour, and we finally came to what appeared to be a turnaround—one of those end-of-the-road wide places.

"Stop here, Mark," the father told me. "I'll go tell the mother superior that we're here."

"Right." I stopped the limo and turned off the engine.

Father O'Donnell got out and crossed the muddy clearing to an opening in the woods that appeared to be one of those hiking trails that wander around all over the Cascade Mountains. He quickly disappeared into the forest.

I glanced back. Mary was holding Twinkie in her arms and rocking gently back and forth, with tears running down her cheeks. This had been the best solution we'd been able to

come up with, but it still hit us all pretty hard. I tried my best
to push the possibility James had suggested out of my mind.
It didn't really matter now which twin it was that Mary was
holding. Renata or Regina—or maybe Renata *and* Regina—
was rapidly approaching the ultimate sanctuary. I still had a
long night ahead of me, and I couldn't afford to let my emotions run away with me.

Twilight was beginning to seep out of the woods, but it was
still light enough that we could see.

Father O'Donnell came back along the trail and motioned
to us.

"Could you take her, Mark?" Mary asked me. "I don't
think I'm up to it." Her voice was thick and sort of choked up.

"I'll take care of it, Mary," I said. I got out and opened the
back door. "It's only me, Twinkie," I said gently. "We're almost there now."

Twinkie reached her arms out to me, and there seemed
to be a faint flicker of recognition in her eyes—almost a
question.

I probably could have led her along the trail that obviously
led to the cloister. But that didn't quite seem appropriate, so I
picked her up and carried her instead. She wrapped her arms
around my neck as I crossed the muddy clearing, and she
murmured to me in twin, her face very close to mine. The
soft, lisping sibilance of the secret language brushed my
cheek as I carried her toward Father O'Donnell.

Together we walked slowly along that trail. It was pretty
dark back in under the trees, but after about a hundred yards
we came to another clearing, and there was the cloister.

It was a low grey building nestled in among the trees and
surrounded by a wall. It probably wasn't even visible from
the air.

"Wait here," Father O'Donnell told me. Then he crossed
the clearing, following a kind of gravel walkway toward a
narrow gate in the wall. He pulled on a slender brass chain at
one side of the gate, and I heard the faint tinkling of a small

bell inside. After a moment, the gate opened, and there was a nun wearing the traditional habit standing there.

There was that peculiar twilight clarity in the clearing— that moment that comes just before sunrise and just after sunset when everything seems to be sharply etched on the surroundings, and there aren't any shadows.

I set Renata down on the graveled walk, and then I wrapped my arms around her in a brief embrace. "It's the best we can do, Twinkie," I told her sadly. "At least you won't be alone anymore. Good-bye, then."

She touched my face with her fingertips, and then she briefly kissed my cheek. Then she said something to me in twin, and "Markie" came through very clearly. She obviously recognized me, and that meant that she was to some degree aware of what was happening.

Then she turned and followed the walk in that steel grey, shadowless twilight toward the gate and the waiting Father O'Donnell and the mother superior.

I could see very clearly, because it wasn't dark yet, so I know with absolute certainty that I *did* see what happened next. There was a kind of brief blur, and then Twinkie wasn't alone anymore. There were two of them walking toward their sanctuary. They half turned briefly to look back at me, and they were both smiling.

Father O'Donnell crossed himself and stepped out of their way.

The mother superior held her arms out to the twins and led them on inside.

And then the gate closed.

Father O'Donnell had tears in his eyes as he came back across the clearing to join me. Then he started back along the trail toward the limousine.

I was just about to join him, but something lying on the walk caught my eye. There were two ribbons, one blue and one red, lying there on the stones.

I bent over and picked them up. They felt sort of warm, and

they looked almost brand-new, with no wrinkles or smudges. I wasn't really surprised. Regina and Renata were still playing the twin-game, I guess. But it didn't matter which one was which, because, as always, they were the same. Now they'd left this final gift behind, to let me know that they were children again, and that none of what had happened had made any difference. They were back together again, and that was the only thing that really mattered. Everything was all right now.

I tucked the ribbons into my pocket where they'd be safe. Then I turned back to join Father O'Donnell and Mary in the limousine. Night was gently falling, and we still had a long way to go before we could sleep.

Millions of readers have discovered the allure of
David Eddings's *New York Times* bestselling
series The Belgariad—now, all five books in
this monumental epic are combined
in two thrilling volumes!

THE BELGARIAD
Volume One

Pawn of Prophecy
Queen of Sorcery
Magician's Gambit

THE BELGARIAD
Volume Two

Castle of Wizardry
Enchanters' End Game

Published by Del Rey Books.
Available wherever books are sold.